"Enchanting series launch from A
Cozy fans will wish upon a star f

"Likable characters . . . and an entertaining but not-too-intrusive
fairy connection make this a winner. . . . Fans of Laura Childs' work
will enjoy Gerber's new series." —*Booklist*

"Full of fun, whimsy, and a baffling whodunit. . . . After finishing
the book fans might want to try their hand at making their own
fairy garden, or test the delectable recipes in the back of the book."
—*Mystery Scene* **magazine**

"A charming murder mystery. . . . The addition of real fairies adds a
delightful twist . . . Courtney is an engaging heroine backed by a
fun, diverse cast." —*Criminal Element*

"*A Sprinkling of Murder* is an enchanting mystery that asks you to believe. Believe, not only in fairies, but in yourself and the intrinsic
goodness of people." —*Cozy Up with Kathy*

"Lively characters and plenty of action keep the pages turning. Para-
normal cozy fans will have a ball." —*Publishers Weekly*

"*A Glimmer of a Clue* is an enchanting and delightful combination of
the whimsical and the cozy mystery genre itself." —*Fresh Fiction*

"I really enjoy this author's writing voice and the way she crafts a
plot, and *A Glimmer of a Clue* is no exception." —*Reading Is My
SuperPower*

"Reading *A Glimmer of a Clue* in one sitting wasn't my plan for the
day. However, a couple of chapters in, I knew I wouldn't put it
down until the last page. It was a well-plotted mystery, within a
magical tale." —*Lisa Ks Book Reviews*

"This book is exactly what I look for in a cozy mystery. Interesting
and likable sleuths, plenty of suspects, a little humor to keep it from
being too heavy, but still a great mystery." —*The Book's the Thing*

A Flicker
of a Doubt

Daryl Wood Gerber

Kensington Publishing Corp.
www.kensingtonbooks.com

KENSINGTON BOOKS are published by

Kensington Publishing Corp.
119 West 40th Street
New York, NY 10018

ISBN: 978-1-4967-4128-8 (ebook)

ISBN: 978-1-4967-4127-1

First Kensington Trade Paperback Printing: April 2023

10 9 8 7 6 5 4 3 2 1

Printed in the United States of America

To my friends and family who have been so supportive over the years, loving me in spite of my zaniness.

Acknowledgments

It's not that I'm smart, it's just that I stay with problems longer.
—Albert Einstein

I have been truly blessed to have the support and input of so many as I pursue my creative journey. Your help and your belief in my endeavors have made it possible for me to persevere. And I do love to persevere.

Thank you to my talented author friends, Krista Davis and Hannah Dennison, for your words of wisdom. Thank you to my Plot-Hatcher pals: Janet (Ginger Bolton), Kaye George, Marilyn Levinson (Allison Brook), Peg Cochran (Margaret Loudon), and Janet Koch (Laura Alden). You are a wonderful pool of talent and a terrific group to bounce around ideas, share jokes, tell interesting stories, and just plain have fun! I adore you. Thanks to my Delicious Mystery author pals, Roberta Isleib (Lucy Burdette), and Amanda Flower. I treasure your creative enthusiasm via social media.

Thank you to Facebook fan-based groups: Delicious Mysteries, Cozy Mystery Review Crew, Save Our Cozies, and so many more. I love how willing you are to read ARCs, post reviews, and help me as well as numerous other authors promote whenever possible. We need fans like you. Thank you to all the bloggers like Dru Ann Love and Lori Caswell, who enjoy reviewing cozies and sharing these titles with your readers.

Thanks to those who have helped make this fourth book in the *Fairy Garden Mystery* series come to fruition: Kensington Books publisher Lynn Cully, editor Elizabeth Trout, production editor Carly Sommerstein, copy editor Scott Heim, and cover artist Elsa Kerls. Thank you to the marvelous PR team that includes Larissa Ackerman, Jesse Cruz, and Lauren Jernigan.

VIII Acknowledgments

Thank you to my biggest supporter, Kimberley Greene. Thanks to Madeira James for maintaining constant quality on my website. Thanks to my virtual assistant Christina Higgins for your creative ideas. Honestly, without all of you, I don't know what I would do. You keep me grounded.

Last but not least, thank you to the librarians, teachers, bookstore owners, and readers for sharing the delicious world of a fairy garden designer in Carmel-by-the-Sea with your friends. I hope you enjoy the magical world I've created.

Cast of Characters
(listed alphabetically by first name)

Humans

Adeline "Addie" Tan, arts and crafts teacher
Brady Cash, owner of Hideaway Café
Courtney Kelly, owner of Open Your Imagination
Dylan Summers, detective, Carmel Police Department
Ella Hock, Hunter Hock's daughter
Eudora Cash, romance author and Brady's mother
Finley Pitt, ex-wife of Brady
George Pitt, husband of Finley
Glinda Gill, owner of Glitz Jewelers
Gus, a security guy working for Kipling Kelly
Hattie Hopewell, Happy Diggers garden club chair
Hedda Hopewell, loan officer
Holly Hopewell, Courtney's landlord and neighbor
Hunter Hock, artist
Ivanka Voss, friend and coworker of Addie Tan
Janna Hamilton, Hunter's sister
Jeremy Batcheller, owner of Batcheller Galleries
Joss Timberlake, assistant at Open Your Imagination
Kipling "Kip" Kelly, Courtney's father, landscaper
Lissa Reade, aka "Miss Reade," librarian
Meaghan Brownie, half owner of Flair Gallery
Nicolas Buley, artist
Payton Buley, brother of Nicolas
Redcliff Reddick, police officer
Renee Rodriguez, owner of Seize the Clay
Sassy Jacobi, musician
Tish Waterman, owner of A Peaceful Solution Spa
Twyla Waterman, daughter of Tish
Ulani Kamaka, reporter for *The Carmel Pine Cone*

Violet Vickers, wealthy dowager
Wanda Brownie, art representative, Meaghan's mother
Yolanda "Yoly" Acebo, sister of Yvanna, and part-time employee
Yvanna Acebo, employee at Sweet Treats, weekend baker for teas
Ziggy Foxx, half owner of Flair Gallery, Meaghan's partner
Zinnia Walker, a Happy Digger

Fairies and Pets
Callie, aka Calliope, intuitive fairy in Meaghan's garden
Fiona, righteous fairy to Courtney
Merryweather Rose of Song, guardian fairy and library fairy
Phantom, Holly Hopewell's black cat
Pixie, Courtney's Ragdoll cat
Zephyr, nurturer fairy for Tish

Chapter 1

Down by the spring one morning
Where the shadows still lay deep,
I found in the heart of a flower
A tiny fairy asleep.
—Laura Ingalls Wilder, "The Fairy Dew Drop"

Slam! Slam-slam-slam! Slam!

My insides did a jig. I dashed down the hall to the back of Open Your Imagination, dusting my hands off on my denim overalls while wondering what in the world was going on. Fiona, the teensy righteous fairy that appeared to me the day I opened my fairy garden shop, fluttered to my shoulder. Her limbs and gossamer wings were trembling.

"What's happening, Courtney?" she managed to squeak out. She hated loud noises. Hated surprises. I didn't like them, either.

Pixie, my Ragdoll cat, trailed us. She mewed.

"Don't worry, you two," I said. "I'm sure it's nothing."

I drew to a halt outside the storage room. The door opened and slammed.

When it opened again, I pressed a hand against it. "Hey! Stop! Meaghan, c'mon."

The door opened wide, and Meaghan Brownie gawked at me. Her face was red, her eyes were ablaze with fury, and her curly hair was writhing like wild snakes.

"What the heck has you so angry?" I asked. I'd sent her to fetch a box of gemstones. I had plenty, so coming up empty wasn't what was upsetting her.

"Nicolas!" She huffed. "He texted me. And . . . And . . ." She waggled her cell phone. "Oo-oh!"

Nicolas was her ex-boyfriend, a temperamental artist. A few months back, she'd asked him to move out while her mother had needed comforting. He'd never returned.

"Oo-oh," she repeated, before grabbing one of the Tupperware boxes filled with gemstones and skirting past me. She stalked toward the main showroom.

Pixie and I followed. Fiona flew above my pal, sprinkling her with a calming silver dust. Fairies couldn't change human behavior, but they could offer potions that might help the human solve problems. In this case, to find peace.

"He's so . . . so . . ."

Meaghan was not using her inside voice, but I wasn't worried about her upsetting our customers. It was early. Nobody was in the shop yet. Not even Joss Timberlake, my right-hand helper. She'd asked for the morning off, so I'd invited Meaghan to help me prepare some items. Why did I need help? Because yesterday Violet Vickers, a wealthy widow who donated to numerous worthy causes, had ordered an additional dozen fairy gardens to be used as centerpieces for the theater foundation tea she was serving on Mother's Day. Why *additional*? Because she'd already commissioned me to make a dozen very large, elaborate fairy gardens to be installed when Kelly Landscaping, my father's company, completed the total redo of her backyard.

It was May first. I wasn't hyperventilating. Yet. But I also wasn't sleeping much.

"Let's go to the patio," I said. "I'll bring some tea."

"I don't want tea," Meaghan groused as she breezed out the French doors to the patio, the folds of her white lace skirt wafting behind her.

The shop's telephone jangled. I decided not to answer. Whoever was calling would call back. Meaghan, my best friend whom I'd met a little over ten years ago when we were sophomores in college, needed me more. I followed her, glancing at Fiona, wondering why the calming potion wasn't working. Fiona, intuiting my question, shook her head.

"Isn't it a beautiful morning, Meaghan?" I took the box from her and set it on the workstation table in the learning-the-craft area at the far end of the patio. "Gorgeous, in fact."

The fountain was burbling. Sunshine was streaming through the tempered-glass, pyramid-shaped roof. The leaves of the ficus trees were clean and shiny. I'd already wiped down the wrought-iron tables and chairs and organized all the verdigris baker's racks of fairy figurines. Plus, I'd removed dead leaves from the various decorative fairy gardens. Presentation mattered to me and to my customers.

Meaghan muttered, "Ugh."

"Start at the beginning," I said. "Nicolas texted you."

"Yes." She plopped onto a bench and rested her elbows on the table.

"What did he write?" I asked.

"He wants me back."

I opened the box of colorful gemstones and ran my hands through them: hematite, labradorite, amethyst, obsidian, and more.

"But I don't want him back," Meaghan said.

Fiona landed on the rim of the box. Her eyes widened. "Are they for the fairy doors, Courtney?"

"Mm-hmm."

"They're pretty."

Not only was I making the gardens for Violet, but I had three upcoming fairy garden door classes scheduled. Fairy doors were miniature doors, usually set at the base of a tree, behind which might be a small space where people left notes or wishes for fairies. They could also be installed into a fairy garden pot.

"I mean, I used to," Meaghan went on. "But I don't anymore. We have nothing in common." Idly, she drew circles on the table-top with her fingertip. "I did the right thing, don't you think? I did, didn't I?"

Over the course of our friendship, I'd kept my mouth shut. Nicolas and Meaghan had never made sense. She was outgoing and personable; he was quiet, to the point of being morose. Granted, he was a talented artist, and she, as a premier art gallery owner, appreci-ated his gift, but that was not enough to sustain a healthy relationship. Not in my book, anyway.

"Did he text anything else?" I asked, not answering her question.

"No . . . yes. That he loved me." She flopped forward on her arms dramatically.

Pixie pounced onto the bench and nudged Meaghan's hip with her nose.

Meaghan sat up, drew the cat into her lap, and petted her. "You should have seen Ziggy the last time Nicolas contacted me." Ziggy Foxx, an eccentric gay man in his forties, was Meaghan's business partner at Flair Gallery.

Cypress and Ivy Courtyard, where Open Your Imagination was located, boasted a high-end jewelry store, collectibles shop, pet-grooming enterprise, my favorite bakery Sweet Treats, and Flair, Meaghan's gallery.

"Ziggy was finalizing a sale of one of Hunter Hock's items, and when he heard me say Nicolas's name, he nearly threw Hunter's art across the room. Hunter was there at the time."

Hunter Hock, an in-demand artist in his thirties, was known for small pieces of art. Not as tiny as paintings on almonds or bottle caps or even the insides of lockets. More like three-inch-square petite canvases. Many featured landscapes of Carmel-by-the-Sea, my home-town and one of the most incredible places on earth.

"Oh, man, if Hunter could have leaped through the phone receiver"—Meaghan snorted out a laugh—"he would have strangled Nicolas. You know how he likes to protect me."

Every man who'd ever met Meaghan had wanted to protect her. Not that she needed it. She was a force to be reckoned with. But there was something about her femininity that brought out the he-man in men. Me? Most men wanted to be my friend. Period. I was the girl-next-door type. Short blond hair, athletic figure. Meaghan towered above me and had curves.

I said, "I'd bet Hunter also didn't like seeing Ziggy lose his temper."

"Destroy a piece of his art? Oh, the insanity!" Her laugh turned into giggles. Fits of giggles. And then tears.

I hurried to her and threw my arm around her. "Hey, c'mon. Deep breaths. You're beyond Nicolas. You have Ziggy."

She arched her eyebrow.

"Okay, you have Hunter," I joked.

She sobered. "I don't have Hunter. He's a friend."

I twirled a finger. "I've seen the way he looks at you."

"Like this?" She made a googly-eyed face.

"That's the spirit!" Fiona spiraled to the roof, did a loop the loop, and returned to Meaghan's shoulder. "No more crying. What's done is done." She caressed my friend's hair.

"Thank you, Fiona." Not everyone could see fairies, and Meaghan had struggled at first, but now, she was in tune with them.

"We move onward and upward," Fiona added. My intrepid fairy knew what she was talking about. She'd messed up in fairy school, so the queen fairy had booted her from the fairy realm and subjected her to probation. But she was making the most of it. By helping humans solve problems, she would earn her way back into the queen fairy's good graces—the queen fairy who, until a few months ago, I hadn't realized was Aurora, the first fairy I'd ever seen; the fairy who had disappeared from my memory when my mother died.

"When you're done with your pity party, Meaghan," I said, "help me sort these stones before we open up."

"And then I need to go to Flair."

I turned on soothing instrumental music that piped through speakers on the patio, and we worked in companionable silence for an hour, organizing and preparing.

When Meaghan was ready to leave, she gave me a hug. "Thank you for talking me down from the ledge."

"No thanks required. Nicolas wants you, but you don't want him. All you have to say is no."

"No." Meaghan shook her head from side to side. "No, no, no."

"See?" I grinned. "That isn't too hard."

"Until he comes near me and my knees turn to jelly."

"You won't turn to jelly. You'll be strong. Stalwart. You've been seeing the therapist. She's given you mantras. Repeat those. Over and over."

Fiona said, "And if those don't work, squeeze your eyes shut"— she demonstrated—"and picture what you want out of life." She popped her eyes open. "What do you want?"

"A man who thinks I'm wonderful," Meaghan replied. "A man who doesn't tear me down. A man who truly loves me for me."

I hugged her. "That's my girl."

She bounded to her feet. "Want me to unlatch the Dutch door on my way out?"

"I'll do it." It was time to open.

I followed her through the showroom. In addition to fairy garden items, we sold a variety of specialty pieces, including tea sets, gardening tools, books about fairies, and wind chimes; fairies enjoyed tinkling sounds. I weaved between display tables to the entrance and swung open the door. I stepped outside and drew in a deep, cleansing breath. "Remember, Meaghan, I'm here if you need me."

She jogged up the stairs of the split-level courtyard. "Don't forget I brought you double-chocolate caramel brownies," she yelled as she disappeared from view.

Given her last name, she'd been a brownie maker since she'd learned how to bake. I was lucky enough to reap the rewards.

I turned to go back inside.

"Courtney!" a woman called. Violet Vickers exited the silver Rolls-Royce coupe she'd parked on the street.

Inwardly, I moaned. I adored Violet, but what did she need now? I didn't have more hours in the day.

"I'm so glad you're here." She triggered the car alarm and strode across the sidewalk toward me while smoothing the shawl collar of her lavender jacquard suit. "I tried phoning, but you didn't answer."

"Hi, Violet." I beckoned her into the shop. "What's up?" I asked, closing the Dutch door behind us, but opening the top half to let in the fresh air. "I'm getting ready to put the fairy garden center-pieces together this morning. Your big pots are done and all set for delivery." I'd made the larger-sized pots in my backyard using items in my greenhouse.

"Lovely," she said, as she was wont to do. "Has your father seen the big ones?"

My father, a pragmatist in every sense of the word, didn't believe in fairies. Opening my fairy garden shop had been a bone of contention between us. But at least he was coming around to acknowledging that I and others did see them. And he'd accepted that Violet expected twelve custom-made pots in her garden. No ifs, ands, or buts. Somehow he, as her landscaper, would make them work with his design.

"Not yet," I said, "but he has approved of the plant selections and color of the pottery."

"Excellent. What are the themes of the gardens, if I dare ask?"

"Love, love, love," I chimed. "As ordered."

Though she was pushing seventy, Violet applauded like a jubilant schoolgirl. She'd asked that the fairy gardens reflect love in all its glory. How could I refuse? Fiona, who was turning out to be quite the reader, had advised me from the get-go to focus on the greatest love stories of all time: *Romeo and Juliet*; *Wuthering Heights*; *Doctor Zhivago*; *Casablanca*. Creating Rick's Café, with its Moroccan décor for the *Casablanca*-themed garden, had been a challenge.

Violet tapped her chin. "Now then, the reason I needed to see you—"

Tires screeched outside. A door slammed.

Fiona flew to my shoulder. "What now?" she asked, quivering with newfound fear.

The Dutch door burst open, and Nicolas Buley charged in, his dark hair askew, apparent shaving mishaps checked by tissue, and his paint-splattered shirt untucked from his jeans. "Where is she?"

Chapter 2

And if you just believe,
And always stay true,
The Fairies will be there,
To watch over you!
—Anonymous, "Believe in Fairies"

I backed up two feet, hands raised in front of me. "Hold on, Nicolas. Meaghan isn't—"

"There you are!" He made a beeline for Violet. "You told me to meet you at your place. But when I got there, they said you were here."

"You look a mess, young man," Violet said, patting her tight white curls into place.

"Sorry about that." He plucked the tissue pieces from his face and ran fingers through the sides of his hair to neaten the straggled mess. "Had the top down on my Beemer." Meaghan hated being a passenger in that car. Nicolas, although classified as a social introvert, was an erratic, speed-loving driver. "So why weren't you there?"

Violet sputtered. "We're not supposed to meet for another hour."

"Yeah, sure, but I figured it was your house. You'd be home."

"Well, I wasn't." Violet raised her chin imperiously.

"I want to talk to you about Hunter Hock," he went on. "Why are you displaying his work at the foundation thing, too? He's a nobody."

"He's not a nobody," Violet said. "He's well-known, and he's stylistic. His petite art appeals to a wide audience."

"*Petite art.* What a stupid name for it."

"I think it's catchy," Violet countered.

"He's a nobody and an ugly cur."

"Now, now." Violet patted his arm. "Don't be mean, Nicky."

He bridled, hating whenever someone shortened his name, but he didn't correct her. He was savvy enough to know she was his boss for the present moment.

"Having your work displayed at my tea will bode well for when you sell your work at the plein-art festival," she added.

Every year, Carmel-by-the-Sea took over Devendorf Park and held a festival that showcased plein-air painting as well as live sculpting exhibits and lots of live music. Artists created their exhibitions outdoors and brought them to the park on Friday afternoon for judging. On Sunday morning, the winning artists did a quick-draw competition with the results being sold in a silent auction. It had been one of my mother's favorite things to do. I remember her taking me as a girl every year. We'd dress up and pack a picnic lunch.

"Hock has a thing for Meaghan," Nicolas grumbled.

"No, he doesn't," I said.

Nicolas leveled me with a withering gaze. Meaghan had often raved about his green eyes. She'd said one look from him could swoon her into bed. Right now, he looked ready to bury me six feet under.

Violet must have noticed. "Why don't you go to Sweet Treats, Nicolas, and get a cup of coffee? I'll meet you there in a bit, and we'll sort this out. Courtney and I need to finalize a few things."

"Nah. Not thirsty." He punched the air, the muscles in his sinewy fingers snap-popping with anger. "I'll go to Flair. I've got a few things to discuss with Meaghan and Ziggy."

Fiona fluttered to my shoulder. "Uh-oh."

I didn't like the edge in his tone, either. "Meaghan isn't in yet, Nicolas," I lied. "Ziggy, either."

"Someone's there. The door is propped open."

"Cleaners," I suggested. "They dust daily. Why don't I pour you a cup of coffee, and you can drink it on our patio? Listen to the fountain burbling." *And chill out,* I thought as I worried the silver locket I wore around my neck, the one with my mother's picture inside. "The sound might inspire your next work."

"Nah. I'm gonna check." He stomped out of the shop.

"Ah, youth." Violet clucked her tongue.

"He's thirty-three," I said. "He's not a kid."

"You have to follow him," Fiona urged.

She was right. On my "Ways to Improve Myself" list for the month, I'd added: *You want a friend? Be a friend.*

I apologized to Violet and hurried after Nicolas, taking the stairs through the courtyard two at a time, grateful that I'd been keeping up with my morning run regimen. I wasn't completely out of breath when I sprinted past customers waiting to enter the gallery and sailed into Flair. Fiona cruised in after me.

The cleaning crew was, indeed, at work, polishing the white oak floor and dusting the white pedestals that held sleek, fluid metal sculptures. Meaghan was arranging free-standing works on the white geometric bookcase on the far wall. Ziggy, dressed in an abstract disco shirt, was tweaking the track lighting to better capture the wall filled with seascapes. I would normally spend an hour moving from painting to painting, drinking in the texture and style of each artist, but I couldn't right now because Nicolas was barreling toward Ziggy.

"Why is my art not in the display window, Foxx?" Nicolas demanded. "That was our agreement."

Ziggy turned, his forehead puckered with concern.

Meaghan fumbled a small, wood-framed painting—one of Hunter Hock's pieces, I was pretty sure. "What are you doing here, Nicolas?" she rasped as she rushed in front of Ziggy. Did she think she could protect him? She was taller than him, sure, but shorter than Nicolas with nowhere near his musculature. "You're supposed to be in Sedona."

"Yeah, well, I'm back," he said. "Surprise! I'm staying in a great Airbnb with a view of the ocean. You should see it."

I had to wonder if he'd returned because the dry desert heat hadn't stimulated his creative juices. He was known for painting turbulent seascapes. According to Meaghan, they sold extremely well. There was something about an angry ocean roiling with emotion that appealed to many of Flair's buyers.

"Nicolas, welcome." Ziggy edged from behind Meaghan. Slight as he might be, he could defend himself. He'd been a wrestler in high school and college, and for fun, he taught private self-defense classes. I'd been studying with him for the past two months, with an emphasis on karate. He strode toward Nicolas, hand extended. "Let's go in the office and chat this out."

Nicolas raised both arms. "Don't touch me, dude. We can talk right here. After I get some answers from Meaghan, like why she's ghosting me."

"I'm n-not," Meaghan stammered.

"Yeah, you are."

Fiona flew to Meaghan's shoulder.

"Nicolas," I said.

"Stay out of it, Courtney!" He stepped toward Meaghan, hand raised.

Meaghan mewled, her resolve floundering.

Fiona darted over Nicolas's head and sprinkled him with white dust, a new potion she'd learned a couple of months ago, designed to make the recipient open to reason. She muttered an incantation, too. "*By dee prood macaw hoerte,*" roughly translated to *May God make peace upon your heart.* But it didn't work. Nicolas wasn't backing down.

"Don't you dare hit her!" Ziggy yelled, striking an attack pose.

"If you do, jerk, you'll pay," Hunter Hock threatened as he rounded the half wall that divided the two rooms. Standing all of five feet four inches, he wasn't a big man. In fact, he often joked that he was vertically challenged. His dyed red hair, bushy black eyebrows, crooked nose, and hollow cheeks gave him an anime-type look.

Nicolas whirled around. "Why are you here, man?"

"For the same reason as you, I suppose," Hunter replied. "To insure my art is properly presented."

"Your art," Nicolas said with a sneer. "Your piddling petite crap isn't art."

"Nicolas!" Meaghan cried. "Take it back."

"I won't."

"Artists don't have to compete," she went on. "I've told you that for years. There's art enough for everyone, for every taste. Be civil, for heaven's sake. Take it back."

Hunter fanned the air. "It's okay, Meaghan. He's entitled to his opinion."

"Yeah, I am." Nicolas puffed up his chest. "And my opinion is you're a hack, Hock."

Hunter sniggered. "*Hack, Hock.* Gee, I haven't heard that before. How clever you are. *Not*," he added, stressing the last word. "Grow up, Nicky boy."

"Nicolas," he said petulantly.

Hock sniffed. "My nine-year-old acts older than you." Hunter and his wife ended their marriage three years ago—creative differences—but his little girl was the love of his life. Family, he once said to me when he'd brought his daughter to Open Your Imagination, meant everything to him. The last I'd heard, he'd moved in with his sister and her three children. His daughter and ex lived in nearby Monterey.

"C'mon, man," Hunter went on, "Meaghan's right. There're plenty of buyers for our work. We're not in competition." He fisted his hands on his hips. The pose didn't make him look bigger or stronger, but he probably thought it did. "Besides, you have plenty of years left to produce something good."

"Why you . . ."

Nicolas hurled himself at Hunter and slugged him in the jaw. Meaghan squealed. I gasped. Fiona *eek*ed.

"Stop!" Ziggy ordered.

Hunter careened backward, scrabbling for his footing. He crashed into a pedestal holding a sculpture titled *Dancing Dolphins.* I'd admired it on many occasions, but I couldn't afford to purchase it. Meaghan lunged for the statue, grabbing it by the base in the nick of time. Being metal, it wouldn't have broken, but it could have suffered a dent or two.

Hunter gained purchase with his feet, lurched at Nicolas, seized him by his right arm, and yanked hard. Nicolas whelped.

"That's it. Enough!" Ziggy bleated an air horn, the kind I'd heard him use to signal a robbery in the courtyard not too long ago. "Both of you, out!"

Nicolas punched Hunter's arm. "This is your fault."

"It's yours." Hunter retaliated by slugging Nicolas's chest.

"Enough, I said!" Ziggy blared the horn a second time. "Out! Now! Or I'm calling the cops. Settle your differences somewhere else, where you won't destroy thousands of dollars of art. When I'm composed, I'll contact each of you and figure out how to settle this. Understood? Remember, Flair Gallery doesn't need you. You need Flair." He motioned between Meaghan and himself. "Leave. Now."

Chastened, Hunter dusted himself off and, with a smug smirk, strode out of the gallery. Nicolas took a bit more time to collect himself, breathing through his nose like a bull, lips pursed as if he wanted to have the last word. In the end, he must have thought better about it because he jammed his lips closed and stomped out.

I hurried to Meaghan and clasped her by the shoulders. "Are you okay?"

"Yeah."

"Want to get a cup of coffee?"

"No." She pressed away from me and returned the statue to its pedestal. "I'm fine. Really. Nicolas . . . Hunter . . ." She smashed her lips together. "Men!" She glanced at her partner. "Thanks, Ziggy."

"We're a team, Meaghan. A team."

She smiled bravely.

When Fiona and I returned to the shop, I spied Violet sitting on the patio, nursing a cup of tea. As I traipsed through the French doors, Fiona raced ahead of me and retreated into the ficus trees to recover from the ordeal at the gallery. Pixie darted to me and rubbed her torso against my legs.

"Hello, sweet pea," I cooed, and petted her. Satisfied, she scampered back to her sunny spot by the fountain and fell fast asleep.

"Is everything okay?" Violet asked, her gaze filled with concern. "Did Nicolas do any harm?"

"No one got seriously hurt." I told her how Nicolas had slugged Hunter and Hunter had struck back. "No art was destroyed."

"That's good to hear."

I hadn't seen either artist outside Flair or on the sidewalk when I'd left. I wondered if they'd gone to a coffeehouse on Dolores Street to work out their issue. That would have been the sensible thing to do, but I got the distinct feeling Nicolas wasn't sensible at the moment. Was he on something? Meaghan had never mentioned him doing drugs, but he might've started after she'd asked him to move out.

Violet *tsk*ed. "Nicolas has such a temper. If I was a stronger person, I would boot him from the foundation event, but I love his work. It's filled with such passion. I adore Hunter's work, as well. I like his landscapes, but I'm partial to his pen-and-inks of coral. They're so delicate and really draw the eye. I guess one could say I'm conflicted as to where my loyalties lie." She sipped her tea. "If Nicolas acts up at the event, I don't know what I'll do."

"Perhaps you could ask him not to attend?" I suggested.

In addition to featuring Nicolas and Hunter at the theater foundation tea, she was displaying works by other local artists, including my landlord, Holly Hopewell.

"No, that wouldn't do." She wagged her head. "The artists must be in attendance so they can chat up their work. The guests will expect that. They're very excited about meeting each of them."

"Why?" I asked. "Doesn't the art speak for itself?"

"Oh, my, yes, but with artists and celebrities in attendance—"

"Celebrities?"

"Yes, I've invited a number of famous people. Donors will come in droves just to get an eyeful." Violet winked. "As you know, we ask our patrons to delve deep into those pockets of theirs to help a worthy cause. How else can we support the arts? Here's who I've invited . . ." She ticked off the list on her fingertips. "The prima ballerina for the San Francisco Ballet, the fabulous basso who's currently playing Iago in *Othello,* a race car driver that everyone tells me is the up-and-coming superstar, three Forty-Niner football players, three from the Giants baseball team, and three from the San Jose Sharks. That's an ice hockey team."

"I'm aware." My father loved watching ice hockey.

"There are a couple of pro golfers, as well as a number of actors who got their starts in Carmel but have now made a splash on the big screen."

I winced. Three months ago, a famous actress had come to town and had met her doom.

"I'm very excited to meet the action hero, George Pitt," Violet said. "Do you know who he is? He's married to a former local girl."

I bit back a groan. Pitt was the popular actor who had married my boyfriend Brady's ex-wife. Would she be accompanying him? If she did, would sparks fly the moment she ran into Brady? I wasn't sure they'd seen each other since their divorce was final.

"I'm he-ere, boss," Joss Timberlake warbled, striding onto the patio while removing her crossbody satchel and finger-combing her pixie haircut. "Good morning, Mrs. Vickers." She acknowledged Violet with a nod. "What a handsome suit you're wearing. The color is striking."

Violet liked wearing all shades of purple. "Thank you. I have a power luncheon to attend today."

"Well, you look quite powerful." Joss offered an impish smile that underscored her elfin appearance. "Boss, I'll open the register and put up a pot of coffee."

"I did that. I've been here for over an hour. I thought you weren't coming in until lunchtime."

"Mom wasn't doing well, so I made the visit brief." Joss's mother, who suffered from dementia, was living in a nursing home. "She did tell me about one of Dad's trips to Guatemala."

"Guatemala?"

"When he was in college, he went on a goodwill trip."

"I've been to Guatemala," Violet said. "I went to the Mayan ruins of Tikal. There are more than three thousand structures, ranging from pyramids to plazas and temples. And the jungle populated by a wide variety of birds and monkeys was a highlight."

"That's what Mom remembered, too," Joss said.

"I'm glad she has a few nice memories." I aimed a finger at her blue T-shirt. "What does today's slogan say?" She loved wearing pithy shirts. "The singing birdies are cute."

" 'Every little thing gonna be all right.' "

"The Bob Marley song," I said. "Sweet. Good sentiment."

"Good vibes." Joss waggled the *hang loose* shaka sign, with three fingers curled and her thumb and pinkie extended.

I mirrored it. "Good vibes."

"I'll leave you two to continue your chat, and I'll tweak the displays in the showroom." Joss jutted a finger toward the beveled casement windows that provided a full view of the L-shaped showroom.

"Thanks. I hadn't gotten to those yet." I was so lucky that she'd applied for the job of assistant the day I'd posted the NOW HIRING sign. On her fiftieth birthday, eager to seek a simpler life, she left her Silicon Valley accounting job and moved to Carmel. There was no one better when it came to organizing everything at Open Your Imagination. Now that she was readily seeing all the fairies that crossed her path, she was content to work here forever.

"Sit, Courtney," Violet said. "Let's get down to business. We have a short time to sort this all out. When will you make the delivery of the large fairy gardens?"

"Tomorrow."

"And the centerpieces? Can you have them completed by Monday?"

Yipes! Maybe I could if I didn't sleep and I worked every night without distractions. Tick-tock.

"Sure," I said tentatively.

"Superb."

"I hope this shape is acceptable." I fetched a thirteen-inch, low round bowl made of resin stone and set it on the table. "They're durable and resistant to chipping and cracking, yet simple and elegant."

"Perfect. By the way, your father is coming to the house tomorrow afternoon."

That surprised me. Dad always took Wednesdays off to go golfing.

"I was wondering if you could stop by and make sure he knows where I expect each of your large fairy gardens to be positioned."

"He'll want final say."

"But he won't get it." Violet preened. "It's my party. My garden."

I gulped. My father always took the lead when installing a garden. Did he know he would have to wrangle Violet Vickers for control? I didn't want to be put in the middle.

"I've made a sketch." Violet pulled a piece of paper from her tote bag. "Here we are."

I stood over her shoulder to catch a glimpse. In freehand, she'd drawn her magnificent four-tiered backyard. All of the tiers were lined with carved stone railings. All faced the ocean. I'd visited the house a couple of times since she'd contracted me for the creation of the fairy gardens. She'd never said where she planned on putting them.

"See the large Os?" She pointed to them. "Those are your lovely pots. The As are where we'll set the art pieces. They're all sorts of shapes and sizes. Large canvasses as well as small works, like Hunter's. There'll be a number of statues. It's going to be grand."

"Um, Violet, I'm pretty sure Dad will want to plant some type of hedge near the railings."

"Yes, he told me that was his proclivity, but I nixed that idea. You see, the tile people have laid terrazzo tiles on the upper three terraces so people can walk to the railing. His gardens will grace the sides of the tiers, and his *pièce de resistance* will be the lowest tier where he'll create a koi pond, a gas firepit, lots of seating, and lush beds of flowers. A virtual feast for the eyes and senses." She wagged a finger at my concerned face. "Don't worry. He's on board for all of that and more."

"What time will he be there?"

"Around three. Can you make it?"

"Of course. I'll—"

"Courtney!" Renee Rodriguez, the forty-something owner of Seize the Clay, a pottery shop located in the courtyard across the street, rushed through the French doors, her chest heaving, and her face, dark hair, and smock covered with a grayish dust. "I'm so sorry, but my new hire dropped the entire batch of pottery you ordered!"

Chapter 3

When they return, there will be mirth
And music in the air.
And fairy wings upon the earth,
And mischief everywhere.
—Thomas Haynes Bayly,
"Oh! Where Do Fairies Hide Their Heads?"

My pulse kicked into overdrive. I told myself to breathe. Everything was fine. Just because the day had started with Meaghan's door slamming—followed by Nicolas's outrage, followed by the announcement that Brady's ex might make an appearance, as well as the prospect that I might have to lock horns with my father—was no reason for me to panic. No reason at all.

Fiona zipped from the ficus and settled on my arm. "Courtney, you yelped. What's wrong?"

"How long until you can make more?" I asked Renee.

"Two days. Max."

"Phew." My pulse settled down. "It's all good. I didn't need them today." I was glad I'd had the foresight to set a few of her other works aside for the fairy door classes. "I just need them by the weekend. I have a class scheduled on Sunday and thought the eight-inch pots would be the perfect setting for what I intend to teach." Renee's pots were hand-painted and adorned with flower fairies, the color of their wings matching the flowers they held. Our customers loved them.

"Excellent. Do you need any fairy figurines?" In addition to throwing pots, Renee had taken to making polymer advanced-aged fairies. Most fairy figurines were young girls, boys, or babies, so hers were unique.

"I could use a dozen or so."

"You've got it." She was so bubbly that, if I didn't know better, I'd never have guessed she'd once served as a police detective. Quitting the force and starting her own business had definitely lightened her spirit. "Say, is your, you know . . ." She turned in a circle, clearly looking for Fiona. She was so eager to spy a fairy.

"Yes," I said.

Fiona sprang off my arm and flapped her wings hard in front of Renee. When Renee didn't blink, Fiona burst into a fit of giggles.

I brushed Renee's arm fondly. "Give it time. It'll happen."

Her cheeks blazed crimson. "See you soon." She waved goodbye and hurried off.

Still laughing, Fiona flew to Pixie and settled onto her head. Pixie batted her with a paw. I took a seat at the table.

"My, my," Violet said. "Are your days always filled with so much drama?"

"No. Life is pretty mundane around here." *Except for the occasional fairy sighting,* I mused.

For the next half hour, I finalized details with Violet.

Yes, I would meet my father at her house. Yes, I would convince him to put the fairy pots where she wanted them. Yes, I was over the moon about the prospect of meeting so many celebrities. *Not.* By the time she left, my cheeks were aching from smiling.

Around eleven-thirty, feeling slightly out of sorts, I texted Meaghan and asked if she'd care to join me for lunch in a half hour at Hideaway Café across the street. She jumped at the chance.

Like the other buildings in the Village Shops, the courtyard where Seize the Clay was located, Hideaway Café boasted a striking dark red wood-and-stone façade, but what made it distinctive was the beautiful English garden at the entrance.

"I'm so glad you said yes," I said to Meaghan when we met in front.

"Ziggy was insistent I take a breather."

I looped my hand around my friend's elbow and guided her inside. The strains of a jazz guitar playing instrumental music filtered through a speaker system and instantly filled me with calm.

"Hey, ladies, what a nice surprise." The owner, Brady Cash—my high school photography and hoops-shooting buddy and now my boyfriend—approached us. As always, he looked ruggedly handsome and yet affable in a good-friend-to-everyone kind of way. He kissed me pristinely on the cheek. The musky scent of him was intoxicating.

"Is everything okay?" he asked.

"Yes, fine. Sort of. Meaghan"—I motioned to her—"had an upsetting morning."

Now was not the time to mention his ex-wife.

"You, too," she said to me, and regarded Brady again. "You see, my ex . . . Nicolas . . . is in town, and he caused a stir. Courtney came to Flair Gallery to protect me."

I tsked. "As if I could protect you."

"You were so brave," Meaghan said. "Ziggy thinks it's because you're beginning to feel your power. He said you're getting pretty good with a single leg takedown."

"You'll have to show me some time," Brady said flirtatiously. "Let me show you to a quiet table for two, and I'll make sure we hold on to some nutty blond brownies for dessert."

"You know the way to my heart," I joked.

"I make it my duty to." He led the way and paused at the entrance to the rear patio. "So . . . what do you think?"

"Of . . ." I inclined my head. The patio looked the same, with white wrought-iron tables and the garden rife with flowers and vines.

"The new weatherproof roof." He brandished a hand at the tempered-glass, pyramid-shaped roof that was identical to the one over my shop's patio. Previously, his patio had been covered by swaths of tent-like material—not very useful in a rainstorm.

"Copycat," I said.

He splayed his hands. "When an idea is brilliant, it's brilliant."

"I'm glad you kept the strands of twinkling lights."

"Some things never go out of style." He bowed his head and lowered his voice. "Is your fairy with you?"

"Not on this trip."

"Are there any fairies around?" He wasn't teasing. Like Renee, he wanted to see one someday.

I spun right and left. "I don't see any."

Brady led Meaghan and me to a table and pulled out a chair for me. Close to my ear, he whispered, "Have we got a date this coming Monday?"

For the past few months, we'd been making it a steady habit to take the same day off and do something fun—hiking, photography, historic walks, wine tasting. Our trip to Garland Ranch had opened his eyes to the wonderment of fairy portals. Fairy portals, for the uninitiated, were magical doors that would lead into the fairy world. Mere mortals were not encouraged to pass through them, because if they did, they might not make it back to this world. I'd seen fairies pass through that day. Brady hadn't witnessed what I had.

"Yes," I said. "And remember it's your turn to surprise me with an adventure."

"I know just the thing." He waggled his eyebrows. He handed us our menus and moved on to greet new diners.

Meaghan leaned into me. "You've got to tell him about George Pitt coming to Violet's soirée." When I'd texted her earlier, I'd added it as an aside.

"I need to find the right time. While he's at work isn't a good idea."

"Do it sooner rather than later. If he discovers you knew and didn't warn him—"

I swatted her arm. "Stop. You're the focus of this lunch. Well, you and Nicolas."

A willowy, dark-haired waitress set two glasses of water on the table and asked if we wanted something else to drink. We both declined.

"Do you know what happened between Nicolas and Hunter after they left Flair?" I asked Meaghan.

"He texted that they'd worked it out."

So they had hooked up. Yay. That was good news.

Meaghan peered over her menu at me. "FYI, it's your job to ensure Violet Vickers keeps them eons apart at the foundation tea."

"Ha! Like I can make Violet do anything. Did Ziggy contact Nicolas yet?"

"Nope. He told me he's going to make Nicolas sweat a bit." She set her menu aside.

"What about you?" I asked, and sipped my water. "Do you think he'll continue to pester you?"

"He's nothing if not resolute. When he makes up his mind . . ." She hailed our waitress and said, "I'd like a glass of chardonnay after all." The waitress nodded and departed. "Ziggy told me to take the rest of the day off. He asked our part-timer to sub for me. You know who I mean." She rotated a finger at the back of her head, meaning the part-timer who always wore her flaxen hair in a French twist.

"I'm concerned about your safety," I said.

"Nicolas has never assaulted anyone before this morning."

"Are you sure about that?"

"He told me *never*."

"Ahem, have you forgotten that he twisted your elbow a few months ago? That's one of the other reasons why you asked him to leave."

Reflexively, she rubbed her arm. "It was once."

"But who knows what impulses he's trying to keep in check? How well do you know him?"

"How well do you know anybody?" she retorted.

Our waitress returned with Meaghan's wine and asked if we'd like to order. I decided on the zesty lime shrimp and avocado salad. Meaghan chose a decadent Monte Cristo sandwich, extra cheese.

When the waitress left, I said, "Meaghan, what if this set-to with Hunter whetted Nicolas's appetite for more violence?"

"C'mon. He's not like that." She ran her finger along the stem of her wineglass. "He's not a fighter. The elbow thing was because I'd made fun of him for even attempting to paint with watercolor. He's an oil guy."

"You made fun of him. Oh, boo-hoo." I pulled a poor-me face. She huffed and took a sip of her wine.

"What about today with Hunter?" I stabbed the table with my fingertip. "Nicolas slugged Hunter. In the face."

"He was jealous."

"And that's okay?"

"No. Of course not." She pushed the wineglass aside and leaned forward, arms folded. "But there's nothing for him to be jealous about. There's nothing between Hunter and me, and there never will be."

"And what about you and Nicolas?"

She hesitated. "There's nothing going on with the two of us, either, but he's still in love with me, and that's clouding his judgment."

I studied her face. The pinched expression. The pursed lips. Testing the water carefully, I said, "Um . . . you don't want to start up with him again, do you?"

"No. I told you earlier. No. N-O." She sat back in her chair and rotated her head on her neck to loosen the knots. "We're done. I'll tell him. I'll make sure he knows."

"In a group of people, please."

"Yes, Mo-om," she said sarcastically.

"As for other men who might be interested in you . . ."

She snorted.

"I think Redcliff Reddick has the hots for you."

"Officer Red? Get out of here."

"Have you seen the way he looks at you? He's smitten."

She guffawed.

"Red's a good guy," I said. "A decent law-abiding man with a sense of humor."

"Does he understand art?"

"Gee, I don't know. Why don't you ask him on a date and find out?"

She playfully punched my arm.

Getting serious again, I said, "Maybe you need a restraining order against Nicolas."

"No. Uh-uh. That will infuriate him."

"But it'll keep him a safe distance away. He's on edge, Meaghan. You heard him. He told Hunter to watch his back."

"He told *Hunter*," she stressed. "Not me."

The afternoon sped by. When it was time to close the shop, I was yawning and ready to take a nap, but I couldn't afford the luxury. I'd had the deliveryman, my regular guy whom I trusted with precious cargo, transport all the items for Violet's centerpieces to the greenhouse in my backyard. If I was going to finish them by Monday, I needed to get started. Organizing figurines and such only went so far. I gathered Pixie and Fiona, and we walked home.

I loved strolling through Carmel. The air was always fresh and clean, even on foggy days. As I drew near to Dream-by-the-Sea, the home I rented from my neighbor—many homes in Carmel had names ascribed to them—I could hear the roar of the surf two blocks away, and the knots in my shoulders started to relax. An evening creating gardens for Violet would help the tension melt away.

Inhaling the bouquet from the lavender and catmint, I strode along the flagstone walkway to the front door and pulled my keys from my pocket. "We're home." I opened the door and set Pixie on the floor of the foyer. She scampered to her pillow in the living room and turned three quick times before settling down for a snooze. "Lazybones," I teased.

Fiona giggled and wafted to the kitchen. "What's for dinner?"

"Do pomegranate seeds and lemon teacake sound good?" Fairies enjoyed all sorts of treats, like mallow fruits and hibiscus flowers and milk with honey.

She nodded and said, "You didn't text Brady about George Pitt."

I cringed. "You're right. I should." I pulled my cell phone from my tote and tapped a message to Brady to call me. "That should do it," I said. "Bad news is better heard than read."

I wasn't very hungry after the delicious lunch I'd eaten, although given the chance, I could down another nutty blond brownie. It had been scrumptious. I prepared Fiona and Pixie's meals and said, "I'm going to slice up some cheese and fruit and eat in the greenhouse."

Typically, I would snack at the wicker table in the backyard, but the night had grown chilly.

"I'll join you."

I put our meals on china plates and set the plates, along with a small glass of sauvignon blanc, on a blue lacquer tray with gold handles. Then I threw on my peacoat, switched on the fairy lights in the backyard, and went outside.

"The fountain is so pretty," Fiona said as she fluttered past it.

"*Tà*," I said, thanking her in her native tongue.

A few months ago, I'd splurged on the copper fountain, which featured a fairy pouring water into a shell. I'd decided to forgo any new clothes for six months so I could afford it. After all, how many clothes did a woman who dug in the dirt all day truly need?

I stepped into the polycarbonate greenhouse and inhaled the aroma of the herbs. Natural scents of all kinds soothed my soul. I placed the tray of food on a wood shelf, sipped my wine, and eyed the pots for the centerpieces. They were sitting one on top of the other. Unfilled. Unplanted. Lacking inspiration.

I caught sight of an army of ants trying to find its way from the floor of the greenhouse to the first shelf. "Uh-uh, no, you don't."

I didn't mind ladybugs. They ate eggs and took aphids back to their hives to feast on the sugar that aphids produced. But ants were pests. Okay, they weren't inherently bad. They aerated the soil, and by marching from one plant to the next, they became natural pollinators, and they could be food for other garden helpers like lizards, frogs, and birds. But I didn't want them in my greenhouse. No way, no how. I opened a canister containing a mixture of cayenne and cinnamon that I kept expressly for the purpose of shooing ants away and started sprinkling it on the floor and around some of the plants on the lower shelf. The ants did a hasty retreat. They hated tangy spices.

Task completed, I bit back a yawn and turned toward the shelving stocked with fairy figurines. Although each of the pots was a basic resin stone, I'd landed on the idea to use multiple color schemes for the individual stories. One would feature red figurines with red environmental pieces. Another would feature pink pieces, and so on. I wasn't sure I had a dozen selections to choose from, but I could always paint the figurines. Weather affected figurines the same way it impacted the paint on a house or door. After a period of time, they needed sprucing up. There was no fairy garden law saying I couldn't spiffy them up before inserting them into a garden. I would continue to use love as a theme for the centerpiece gardens. Not only would I use boy and girl fairies, but I would extend the theme to include the platonic love between humans and their pets.

For the first creation, I chose a purple-winged fairy in a pink skirt and green tunic. She was cradling a bluebird in her lap. Praying the creator of the delicate beauty wouldn't hate me, I opened a bottle of pink acrylic paint, squirted a dollop on a stay-wet palette, and using a fine-tipped paintbrush, made the green tunic pink. I found a small pink toadstool that would serve as a seat, and placed the fairy on top of it to dry.

Fiona hummed her approval of my changes. She sounded so content that I decided to broach a sensitive subject.

"You know, Fiona, we haven't talked much about this because you always cut me off, but when we went to the fairy portal in February, there was a frollick of you." Fairy clusters were either known as herds or frollicks. "And you were all greeting Aurora, and—"

"Stop!" Fiona blurted.

"C'mon. Talk to me about her. Please." I set my paintbrush down. "Aurora was the first fairy I ever saw. I thought she was my mother's fairy, but she's the queen fairy. The *queen*." I gestured with an open palm. "She's the one who booted you out of the kingdom, and yet she invited the lot of you into the portal. What did she—"

"She's my mother."

"Wh-hat?" I sputtered.

In a teensy voice, she said, "Aurora is my mother."

My mouth wouldn't shut. I was *gobsmacked*, as I'd heard Fiona say once. It meant stunned.

Fiona spiraled upward and soared dizzyingly around the perimeter of the room for a matter of minutes. After a long flight, she returned to me and hovered in front of my eyes.

"She's your mother," I said softly.

"Yes."

"You're the princess of the fairy world."

"One of them."

"You have sisters?" Oh, my. I had no idea. She had been so circumspect about her history. "Older, younger?"

"Younger. I'm the oldest."

"How do I address you? Princess Fiona?"

"No. Just Fiona." She huffed and folded her arms, her wings working overtime. "I was supposed to set an example. I messed up. My mother kicked me out to show the youngers how to behave."

The youngers, not the sisters or other princesses. Interesting.

"And now?" I asked. "You've been behaving quite well in the human world. You help me solve all sorts of problems. Did she welcome you back?"

"Not yet." She stamped the air with one foot and made a raspberry sound. "First, I have to earn all of my adult wings; plus, I need at least three more years training with my mentor."

"Do you mean Merryweather of Song?" She was the guardian fairy who spent most of her time at the library.

I had to admit that I was surprised when I'd learned there were classifications of fairies. Four, to be exact—intuitive, guardian, nurturer, and righteous. I'd always thought fairies were merely types, like air fairies, water fairies, and woodland fairies, Fiona being the latter.

"Yes, and by the way, Merryweather is my aunt."

I started to giggle. Fitfully. "Heavens. Your aunt?"

"I wasn't allowed to tell you until now."

"What more do I have to learn?"

"A lot." Fiona finally gave way and giggled, too. "And in case you were wondering, I am the sole righteous fairy you will ever meet."

"Your sisters aren't righteous fairies, too?" I asked.

"No."

"Why is that?"

"Because I will become the queen fairy when the time is right. There is one supreme leader and one righteous fairy at a time."

"Y-you—" I pressed my lips together. "You'll become the queen?" My heart wrenched. That meant she would leave me at some time in the future.

She twirled in a circle. "Way, way, way down the line," she said. "Who knows how many moons away?" She landed on my shoulder and began stroking the nape of my neck. "Don't worry. I will always be your fairy."

"You're reading my mind," I cautioned.

"In this case, it's allowed. A fairy can calm a human who is in distress. I cannot fix the problem, but I can encourage serenity."

So why wasn't I feeling serene?

Chapter 4

If you want to see the fairies,
You must visit them at night,
When the silvery stars are gleaming
And the moon is shining bright.
—Sybil Morford, "Fairies"

I'd barely finished six gardens before realizing I was desperately in need of sleep. Throughout the night, I tossed and turned, and I awoke in the morning feeling harried.

"Drat," I muttered as I swung my feet out of bed and scrubbed my hair with both hands. To calm myself, I slogged to the window. A flurry of birds was roaming my garden for treats.

With whirlwind speed, the golden-crowned sparrows, easily identified by their yellow-striped heads, went from feeder to bush to feeder. I appreciated that they were natural predators making my garden that much prettier, ridding it of worms, grubs, insects, and more. They wouldn't be around much longer; soon they would migrate north. I noted a pair of Townsend's warblers in the cypress, too.

Fiona sailed to my side and stared in the direction I was looking. "I'm faster than them," she said.

"Don't boast," I warned her. Fairies were not supposed to be proud.

"I wasn't boasting. When stating a fact, it's not boasting." She winked at me and eyed my cell phone. "Did Brady text you back?"

"He did, but he didn't have a break in the night's activities to call me, so he'll reach out today."

"Mm-hmm," she hummed knowingly. "You'd better be prepared to tell him the truth."

"I am. I will. Oh, look at the time." I'd spent much longer watching birds than I ought to have.

Quickly, I threw on my jogging clothes to run on Carmel Beach, a spectacular arc of pale sand that stretched for close to a mile in length. The famous Pebble Beach Golf Links bordered the northern arc of the bay. I headed south toward the Clinton Walker House, an historical landmark built by Frank Lloyd Wright and open one day a month to benefit the heritage society. I loved gazing at the house, which reminded me of the prow of a ship jutting from the rocky shoreline as if it were one with the land. As a girl, I'd often dreamed I would sail away on it.

When I returned home, the deliverymen were waiting for me to pick up the twelve large pots I needed taken to Violet's house. Once that task was done, I showered and dressed in my favorite denim overalls and a lacy moss-green T-shirt. With my pale complexion, I could wear moss and loden green, but not lime or kelly green. Then I hurried to the kitchen, fed Pixie and Fiona, drank a protein shake, slipped into a pair of clogs, and raced to the shop.

By the time Pixie, Fiona, and I arrived, Joss was there and dusting the antique white oak hutch that displayed a host of china cups and saucers. The Cape Cod exterior of the building and courtyard had set the standard for the interior décor of Open Your Imagination—white display tables, white shelving, and a stylish splash of blue and slate gray for color.

"Morning, boss," Joss said. "I made a pot of coffee."

"I can smell it." The aroma tickled my senses. I was craving a cup.

"I set some new jewelry on the counter for you to peruse," she added. A few months ago, she'd decided to fill her empty evening hours with jewelry design. She'd sketched earrings and charms and had hired a jeweler to make them. They were selling well. We split the proceeds seventy-thirty—thirty for me because she was doing all the heavy lifting. The items didn't compete with jewelry sold at Glitz, the upscale jeweler in the courtyard. Joss's designs were all fairy-related and made of silver.

"Have you finished reading the book for the book club this Saturday?" Joss asked as she moseyed to the book carousel, swishing the feather duster up and down. We'd added a number of books to our sales racks, including fiction about fairies or instructionals that helped the novice learn to make fairy gardens.

"I'm halfway through." The book club selection was *A Spell for Trouble: An Enchanted Bay Mystery* by Esme Addison. I should have read some pages last night, but I was too tired after working on the centerpieces. From what I'd read so far, it was a delightful tale. I was learning so much about mermaids, otherwise known as water witches.

"Oh"—Joss snapped her fingers—"that reminds me. I put out all the mermaid figurines and related items we ordered on the shelves on the patio."

"You're always on top of things." I squeezed her shoulder. "What would I do without you?"

"Also, before I forget, Twyla asked to play a duet with Meaghan at the tea. I told her that was a superb idea. By the way, she's working out well at Sweet Treats, I hear."

Twyla Waterman, a gifted flutist, had been dissatisfied working for her mother at A Peaceful Solution Spa. Now she worked at Sweet Treats, and during our Saturday teas, she helped at the shop and occasionally provided musical entertainment.

"I'm thrilled to hear that." I set my purse under the counter by the cash register and poured myself a cup of coffee. I was taking my first sip when an Asian-American woman with silky black hair swept in through the front door.

Her black rimless eyeglasses with a minimalist nose bridge gave her a serious, don't-mess-with-me look. Her navy blue–striped, button-down shirt over skinny jeans added to that façade. But the image faded when she smiled and her eyes crinkled with well-earned wrinkles. "I'm so glad you're open. I'm Adeline Tan," she stated, as if we should know who she was. "Everyone calls me Addie."

I met her halfway across the showroom. "Adeline. What an interesting name."

"I was named after Adeline Yen Mah, a well-known physician and author. She wrote *Falling Leaves,* an autobiography."

I hadn't heard of the book.

"My parents wanted me and my siblings to have heroes to look up to."

"Are you a doctor?" Joss asked.

Addie laughed. "Not remotely close. I'm the arts and crafts teacher at the Monterey Bay Aquarium Wednesday to Friday, and I teach crafts at various parks every other weekend." The aquarium was known for its regional focus on marine habitats around the area.

"What fun," I said.

"I won't complain." She winked.

"What kinds of crafts do you teach?"

"I'm particularly good with *zhezhi*."

"*Zhezhi*?" I raised an eyebrow. "I'm not familiar with that."

"The art of paper folding that originated in medieval China."

"You mean origami?"

"Ha! My great-grandmother would string me up by my toenails if I uttered the Japanese word." She winked. "Listen, I saw your poster about the book you're reading for your book club, and I thought you might have some mermaid-themed fairy garden items I could purchase to share with my students. They're fascinated with mermaids, even though they're not real."

Joss exchanged a look with me. "They're not?"

"About as real as fairies." Addie's laughter sparkled with good humor.

At that instant, Fiona whizzed into the showroom and hovered over Addie's head. "She'll learn," she said.

I had yet to see a mermaid, but Fiona was adamant that they existed, and I believed her.

"Hello-o-o," Fiona crooned while waving furiously.

Addie made no indication that she was aware of her, not even from the breeze caused by Fiona's wings.

"As a matter of fact, Addie," I said, wishing I could shoo my impish fairy away, "we recently got in a shipment of mermaid figurines and environmental pieces." I handed her a basket to hold her selections. "Follow me." I led her to the patio and gestured to the verdigris baker's racks.

We had bags of blue stones, silver glitter, sand, dozens of sparkly turquoise mermaids, a couple of red-and-white lighthouses, quirky flamingos, and a number of clamshells. I'd also ordered a shipwreck centerpiece, a sandcastle, a fairy beach house on stilts, a couple of fairies holding baby seals, a choice of rowboats with oars, and for a bit of whimsy, an assortment of mermaid tails—just the tails—poking from water. Joss had smartly stacked wide- and narrow-mouthed pots at the far end of the racks to make the choice easier for customers. Most of the pots were in sea colors, like navy blue, royal blue, and turquoise.

"I've never walked through the Cypress and Ivy Courtyard before," Addie said as she collected items. "I came from Dolores Street, past Flair Gallery. Are you familiar with it?"

"My best friend is one of the owners."

"Nicolas Buley was inside."

I winced but tried not to show it. Had Ziggy given Nicolas the okay to return, or had Nicolas muscled his way in? Was Meaghan okay?

"I love Nicolas's work," Addie said.

"Many do."

"He's been out of town for a while."

"I think he's back to stay."

"That's nice to hear." Addie tucked a loose hair behind one ear. "I wonder why he hasn't reached out. He used to be our guest art teacher at the aquarium. He did the classes for free."

I couldn't imagine Nicolas having a generous bone in his body.

"He looked upset a moment ago when I peeked inside the gallery," Addie went on.

"Upset how?"

"He was wielding a small block of wood like he wanted to hit somebody with it."

Uh-oh. Was he threatening to destroy one of Hock's art pieces if Ziggy didn't fall in line?

"That's why I didn't go in." Addie inspected her basket of items. "Okay. I think I have enough to get me started."

I returned to the showroom, rang her up, and wrapped each of the figurines in tissue before inserting them into one of our shop's gift bags.

"Nicolas isn't a temperamental person," Addie said offhandedly.

I begged to differ. She hadn't seen him attacking Hunter Hock yesterday.

"He's so sweet with children." Her eyes glistened with positivity. "He jokes with them and knuckles their heads. Someday he'll make a wonderful father."

I studied her harder. Was she in love with him? She wasn't deceiving herself into believing Nicolas would marry her and start a family with her, was she? I didn't usually categorize people by their age, but she was well past the childbearing stage. On the other hand, I supposed adoption was always possible. How did Nicolas feel about her?

"I do hope everything's okay between him and the gallery owners," Addie went on.

I handed her the gift bag and said, "I'm sure it will be."

She pursed her lips. "Rainy days always bring an undercurrent of foreboding, don't you think?"

"Is it going to rain?" I hadn't paid attention to the weather earlier. I peered out the windows and noticed the sky had clouded over.

"Not right away," she said, "but later. Don't go out without an umbrella."

Prior to 17-Mile Drive becoming a destination, it was purely the picturesque scenic loop circling Pacific Grove, Pebble Beach, and Carmel. Now it was populated with some of the highest-priced homes in California. Violet Vickers's estate was a stunning home with a one-acre view of the Pacific Ocean, its rocky coastline peppered with a wealth of giant cypress trees. The home had at least six bedrooms and as many bathrooms, and was considered a warm contemporary, combining a vast amount of wood, stone, and glass. I would imagine whale watching from any of her terraces was a sight to behold.

I parked my MINI Cooper in the driveway beside my father's landscaping truck and climbed out. Fiona had gone to the library to meet with Merryweather and a few other fairies.

Violet met me at the front door, arms extended. "Oh, good, you're finally here."

"You told me three o'clock."

"I did. But your father arrived early, and—"

"Is he giving you a hard time?" I asked sotto voce.

"He's been the perfect gentleman. He's simply eager to see you." She beckoned me to follow her through the cavernous living room and out the French doors to the terrace.

"The terrazzo tile is gorgeous," I said.

"Don't you love it? It won't chip or crack, and the brown tones go perfectly with all the furniture." She shimmied her delight and wiggled her fingers. "There are all your gorgeous fairy gardens, delivered intact."

The dozen blue pots stood in a cluster by the staircase leading down to the next tier.

"We'll position them next week. I don't want any of your father's people disturbing them while they're moving hither and yon. My favorite garden is the *Casablanca*-themed one, though I'm also partial to *Bridget Jones's Diary*. You were so clever to have the fairy and the bunny figurines conversing."

In the movie *Bridget Jones's Diary*—I wasn't sure about in the book; I hadn't read it—Bridget attended a costume party dressed as a Playboy bunny and was rudely teased, as only a few others had dressed in costume. I'd felt her mortification down to my toes because my ex-fiancé had done something similar to me. Everything else Bridget did in the story hinged on her finding her sense of self. So in my garden, I made the pink fairy converse with the bunny, as if talking reflectively with one's alter ego. She had to love herself, just as she was, before anyone else could love her. The sign I'd crafted for the garden sealed the sentiment: LOOK DEEP WITHIN AND YOU WILL FIND TRUE LOVE.

"Sassy," Violet said, signaling to a young woman who was standing across the patio at a microphone. "I'm ready to listen. You may begin."

The young woman started strumming a beautiful rosewood guitar that hung from a custom-tooled leather strap looped around her neck.

"Her name is Sassy Jacobi," Violet said out of the side of her mouth, her gaze fixed on the young woman. "She's one of Nicolas's friends. She's going to be singing at our event."

Eyes closed, Sassy launched into "I'll Love You Till the Day I Die," the soulful lyrics spilling out of her with ease.

"What do you think?" Violet asked.

"Her voice is haunting. In a good way."

"Like Linda Ronstadt, don't you think?"

"Very similar."

Sassy had a sweetheart-shaped face and shapely figure. In jeans tucked into boots, lacy white peasant blouse, and fringed leather vest, she reminded me of a woman I'd met at the Renaissance Fair. Her blue ombre hair was tied into a dramatic waterfall ponytail, the tip of which reached her waist.

Violet elbowed me. "We have a string quartet for the first hour of the tea, but then I thought it would be nice to feature vocalists as guests tour the art. I've hired one gentleman who is as beautiful as Harry Belafonte and sings calypso." She clapped a hand to her chest. "Be still my heart." She nodded toward the young woman. "Sassy makes guitars, too."

"That's a real art."

"She's becoming the toast of the town. She has some very high-end clients from all corners of the globe, including a Saudi prince."

"Wow. So why is she performing at your party?"

"For the love of it." Violet lowered her voice. "Between you and me, I think Nicolas Buley and Sassy have a thing."

"A thing?" I loved when people used idioms that weren't typical for their age.

"You know, a *relationship*."

My eyes widened. Had Violet gotten the notion about the two of them having a relationship because Sassy had said it was so, or had Nicolas told her?

"Sassy's sister was involved with him at one time," Violet said, "but she moved away. Sassy implied that was when she and he started up, but then he relocated to Arizona, and she's been holding her breath waiting for him to come back."

Oh, my. Did Meaghan have any idea how many women were eager to win Nicolas's affections? Would she care?

"Look. There's your father." Violet waved a hand. "Uh-oh. He doesn't look pleased."

Chapter 5

They, on their mirth and dance Intent,
with jocund music charm his ear;
At once with joy and fear his heart rebounds.
—John Milton, *Paradise Lost*

My father strode toward us. As he drew nearer, his frown turned into a smile, and I breathed easier. He wasn't upset with me. In all probability, he'd been mulling over his project. He raised his arm in greeting. In his short-sleeved blue shirt and cargo shorts, his skin the tan of someone who spent hours outside, his muscles well-formed from heavy labor, he looked years younger than mid-fifties. Whenever we went for coffee to catch up, I noticed women of all ages admiring him. Despite their ten-plus years age difference, Violet seemed to be drinking him in, as well.

"You look great, Daughter," he said.

"Thanks, Father," I said playfully. We usually referred to each other as Dad and Courtney. Sometimes he'd call me *sweetie* or *kitten*. I pecked his cheek.

"Help me understand something," he began.

Uh-oh. I knew by his flinty gaze that he was serious. My knees didn't knock. He couldn't cow me. But I was on the alert.

"I get no say on where your danged fairy gardens go?" my father asked. "None whatsoever?"

I swallowed hard. "Dad, Mrs. Vickers has it all planned out." Hadn't Violet said he was *on board for all of that?*

"But she hired me for my vision. What did you say to her to make her disregard it?"

I placed a hand on my chest. "Me? Say? Dad, I didn't."

"Well, my reputation for impeccable design precedes me. Why would she take away the one thing that makes me a standout?"

"Because she's, um . . ." I weighed my words carefully. I wouldn't say she was controlling. That could come back to bite me. "She has a vision, Dad. It's nothing against you. But, you know, she has to live with it, day in and day out. Bend a little this one time."

"Bend." He grumbled. "Yeah, okay, I'll bend. Kiss my . . ." He made a courtly bow.

I laughed; crisis averted.

Though my father and I had always been close—we owed it to my mother's memory to cherish one another—over the last year, we had grown closer. I was pretty sure Meaghan's mother, Wanda, had something to do with that. Dad had allowed himself to fall in love again, and being loved in return had helped him relax a bit. His criticism of me and my chosen profession—he'd taken it hard when I'd told him I no longer wanted to work for his landscaping company—was more constructive than caustic. He still didn't believe in fairies, but I couldn't help that. Fiona said a closed mind couldn't be opened without the owner of the mind wishing it to be so.

"Come with me." He clasped my hand.

I always felt so teeny next to him. He had broad shoulders and stood over six feet tall; I was petite and had my mother's small frame. "Where are we going?"

"You'll see."

Violet said, "Hold on, Kipling."

My father bridled. "The name's Kip, Violet. *Kip.*" He hated his formal name, chosen because my nana had loved reading the classics.

"Silly me. How could I forget? Kip, Kip, Kip," she repeated, goading him with a twinkle in her eye. "'There is no sin so great as ignorance.' Who wrote that?"

My father glowered at her. "You know who."

"Rudyard Kipling, I think," she chimed.

I bit back a laugh. The woman was shameless and enjoying every moment of toying with him.

"'Being ignorant is not so much a shame, as being unwilling to learn,'" my father intoned, then waited.

Violet tapped her chin with her fingertip. "Hm. Good one. Benjamin Franklin?"

Dad aimed a finger at her and laughed. "Right."

When Violet chortled, her whole chest heaved. "Give us a few minutes, Kip. I want to introduce Courtney to Sassy."

My father glanced at his watch. "Five. I'm on a schedule."

"Aren't we all?" Violet clasped my other hand and drew me toward the young woman, who had finished the song and was setting her guitar in its case. "Sassy, dear, I'd like you to meet Courtney Kelly. She owns the fairy garden shop I was telling you about."

"Ooh, I'm so impressed by your gardens," Sassy said while tightening her ponytail. "How long does it take to learn how to make them?"

"It depends on the size and scope of what you want to achieve. Come in sometime, and I'll show you." I nodded to her instrument. "I heard you make guitars."

"Yeah."

"That's a real skill. Have you been doing it long?"

"Since I was a girl. My father taught me. He made furniture for a living, but he loved working on instruments in his spare time." Her eyes misted over. "He's passed away, but I feel him"—she patted her heart—"in here. Nicolas says he's always watching over me."

"You and Nicolas are close?" I asked.

"He's my best friend."

"You must have missed him when he went to Sedona," I said, fishing for more information.

"Nah. I mean yes." She shrugged one shoulder. "We talked every day. I'm the one who knocked some sense into him and convinced him to return."

"You?" That gave me pause. He'd certainly been adamant yesterday about inviting Meaghan back into his life, and again I wondered if this young woman, like Adeline Tan, was imagining a relationship with him.

"I can be quite persuasive." She banged her knuckles on her head. "Knock-knock, wake up, dumbbell! Smell the pines. A hauntingly beautiful woman wants to win your heart and treasure you forever." She laughed the way she sang, soulfully. For some reason, the sound sent a shiver down my spine.

"Out of my way!" a man bellowed as he stomped onto the terrace.

Trailing the angry man was a humorless woman clad in a double-breasted gray uniform with white collar and cuffs—Violet's housekeeper, I presumed.

"Where is he?" the man demanded.

"Missus," the housekeeper said. "I told him Mr. Buley is not here, but he doesn't believe me."

"Who is that?" I whispered to Violet.

"I haven't a clue," she said out of the side of her mouth.

"That's Nicolas's brother Payton." Sassy huffed. "He's a real charmer. *Not.*"

Like his brother, I thought.

Balding with fleshy cheeks and a paunch, Payton looked nothing like his trim and fit brother. He tried to button his blue blazer but failed.

"He's comptroller for a town north of here," Sassy went on. "I forget the name of it. What do comptrollers do?"

I said, "I think they supervise all the financial stuff under the direction of the town board."

"Yeah, that sounds pompous enough for him. He's always lauding it over Nicolas about what a big and important man he is." Sassy sniffed. "They're not friendly in the least. Nicolas told me, after their dad died—Nicolas was only twelve—his brother started using him as a punching bag."

"Oh, my, that's horrid," Violet said. Stepping forward and using a booming voice, she shouted, "Mr. Buley, I'm Violet Vickers. You are on my property uninvited. Leave!"

"Sorry, ma'am, but my brother owes me money, and I learned he's back in town. I'm here to collect."

"He's not on the premises."

Payton marched to the railing. "Who's that down there?"

"Landscapers," Violet said with a bite.

Sassy whispered to me, "I don't know why Payton is hounding Nicolas. He's, like, rolling in dough."

Payton spun around and aimed a finger at Sassy. "You know better than anyone that my brother is a flake."

"Me?" She threw her arms wide. "Get real."

"Stop, Mr. Buley," Violet ordered.

But Payton didn't. He stepped toward Sassy, his gaze menacing. "He's never going to amount to anything. His art is dreck. In fact, I'm shocked he's actually sold anything."

How do you really feel? I wanted to say, but kept mute, knowing this guy wasn't going to shut up until he'd said his piece.

"Being an artist is a ridiculous and self-centered avocation," Payton Buley continued. "The only real thing that matters is money." He smacked his chest. "And holding down a steady job. And putting food on the table for your family. Nicolas has never done that. He does as he pleases. He flies off to who knows where on a whim. Tell him for me that I think he's a poser, Miss Jacobi. And tell him to return my calls."

Sassy snorted. "Like he'll listen to me."

Wouldn't he listen if they were a thing? I wondered.

"Also tell him I expect him to pay up, or else."

"Or else what?" Sassy countered.

Payton Buley shot her a savage look before tramping across the terrace and disappearing into Violet's house. The housekeeper pursued him.

"Well, I never," Violet grumbled. "How utterly rude. I don't like confrontations. My husband, rest his soul, knew not to rile me. Ever. If Nicolas is going to bring this kind of grief, I must consider dropping him from the exhibit."

"Don't, please, ma'am," Sassy said. "He'll be crushed if you do."

Violet clucked her tongue. "Don't worry. I won't. I like his art far too much." She winked at Sassy. "By the by, I'll send you the details and a contract to sign by end of day. But please, when you speak to Nicolas, tell him I don't want to see his brother at my house ever again."

"Yes, ma'am." Sassy nearly curtsied as she gathered her guitar case.

Violet's jaw ticked with tension. A bull facing a toreador couldn't have appeared more riled. She harrumphed and harrumphed again.

"I'd better see to my father," I said.

Violet flipped her hand. "Yes, do. Let's not have any more upsets, all right?"

"Yes—" I almost said *ma'am* and stopped myself. "Yes, Violet. The rest will be smooth sailing."

And it was. My father's miff was a thing of the past.

When I returned to Open Your Imagination close to four p.m., I caught sight of Nicolas entering Sweet Treats in the courtyard. He was alone, talking on his cell phone, and despite the drizzle, he looked unruffled, leaving me to conclude that he had yet to run into his enraged brother. *Good luck with that*, I thought as I pushed through the Dutch door.

Later, as I was laying out items for the fairy door class for a bevy of tweens, the predicted storm hit. Rain pelted the patio's roof with a fierceness I hadn't heard since January. Most often I enjoyed the sound, but for some reason the *splat-splat* was unnerving me. I supposed it was because I was on edge after my father had given me an earful about Violet dictating limits as to his garden design. Or because Payton Buley's angry tirade kept replaying in my head. Or because Brady had yet to call, and I was getting nervous about being the bearer of bad tidings.

I'd been trying out a number of ways to tell him. I considered the direct approach: *Hi, your ex-wife and her husband are coming to town.* And the indirect approach: *Guess who's coming to town?* Of course, there was the super-indirect approach: *Violet Vickers's party will be filled with celebrities, including . . .* and letting the rest hang.

Deciding he would appreciate the direct approach—he was that kind of guy—I pushed the imaginary conversations from my mind.

"More popsicle sticks," Joss said, setting a packet on the work-station table along with hot glue sticks and containers of sparkly beads and sequins. "Do we have enough moss?"

I'd arranged five mounds of it in the center of the table. "Absolutely." I eyed the rest of the goodies: acrylic paint, paintbrushes, cups of water to wash the brushes, tiny seashells, sparkling stones, and tubes of glitter. "This will be a messy class, but the students should have fun."

When my cell phone jangled, I said, "I've got to answer this." I pulled it from my pocket and scanned the readout. Not Brady. Ziggy Foxx was on the line. I answered. "What's up?"

"I've been trying to reach Meaghan." He wheezed. "Where is she?"

"I don't know. I'm not her keeper," I joked. She was supposed to be at work, but she often met with clients at their homes or places of business. "Can I help you?"

"I . . ." His voice cracked with a sob.

My levity instantly turned to concern. "Ziggy, what's wrong?"

"Nicolas . . . he's dead."

"What?" my voice skyrocketed.

Joss raced to the patio, a hand pressed to her chest. "Are you all right?"

Fiona, who'd returned from her visit with Merryweather about the same time I'd returned from Violet's, flew to me. Her eyes went wide with fretfulness.

"Nicolas Buley is dead," I rasped. No customers were on the patio, so I stabbed Speaker on my cell phone and said to Ziggy, "What happened? Did he have a heart attack or something?"

"You have to come here," he said, not answering my question.

"To Flair?"

"No. To Meaghan's house. Courtney, someone hit him. Someone murdered him."

I gulped. "Not Meaghan."

"No, of course not. I saw someone. Running away."

"Who?"

"Don't know." The words popped out of him.

"Why are you at Meaghan's place?" I asked.

"Because I was worried. After the scene Nicolas caused yesterday at Flair. And after the set-to this morning, when he came into the shop and accused Meaghan of favoritism for Hunter Hock's work." His words leaked out between sniffles. "She let him have it then, guns blazing. No . . . I didn't mean . . ." He hiccupped. "That didn't come out right. There weren't any guns. She . . . she called him a narcissist and a good-for-nothing."

Addie Tan hadn't mentioned seeing Meaghan at Flair earlier. She'd said Nicolas was ranting at Ziggy. But I didn't think Ziggy was making it up.

"When I couldn't reach her," Ziggy went on, "I thought she might have gone home. To rest. But then I worried that Nicolas might have followed her to have it out with her. I thought she might need protection, so I hurried over and . . ." He choked back a sob. "Please come."

"Have you phoned nine-one-one?" I asked.

But he didn't answer. He'd ended the call.

"I've got to go," I said to Joss.

"I'll call the police."

"Wait. Don't. Let me see what happened first."

She gawked at me. "Because you think Meaghan might have killed him?"

"What? No. Uh-uh." I swallowed hard. She couldn't have. Meaghan didn't have a brutal bone in her body.

"Do you think Ziggy's lying?" she asked. "Do you think he killed Nicolas?"

"I don't know what to think. I have to see. In person."

"I'm going with you," Fiona cried.

"Stop. Hold on." Joss gripped my shoulders. "What if the killer is still there? Hiding?"

She was right. I couldn't rush headlong into this. No matter what had happened, the authorities needed to be involved. I sighed and dialed 911. When the dispatch officer answered, I told her the problem and the address. Then I threw on my rain slicker and, cell phone in hand and at the ready, hightailed it to my pal's house.

Meaghan lived a few blocks from the Cypress and Ivy Courtyard in a charming Craftsman that was decorated in Laguna stacked stone and fenced with scrolled ironwork. The garden, which she'd planted with a variety of daylilies, was particularly beautiful in May. In Carmel's mild climate, daylilies bloomed from early spring until late fall. In the past few months, Meaghan had been adding all sorts of garden ornaments to the mix, including wind chimes, metalwork flowers, and fairy gardens. She'd even placed a silver gazing ball designed to bring hope and prosperity into one's life on a wrought-iron, four-legged pedestal near the front door.

When Fiona and I arrived, the rain had lessened to an icky drizzle. Ziggy was standing halfway up the path, his *Starry Night* Van Gogh umbrella opened, his shoulders hunched, his textural-print T-shirt and gray trousers soaked. Why wasn't he wearing a rain jacket?

Fiona flitted off my shoulder. "I'm going to find Callie and see what's what."

Callie, aka Calliope, was the intuitive fairy that lived in Meaghan's garden. With her green hair, green wings, and shimmering green frock, nonbelievers might mistake her for a firefly or a cricket. On occasion, she blended in with the foliage.

I joined Ziggy, and he pointed to Nicolas's body on the path near the front door. My insides wrenched at the sight of him. His head had been bashed in with something round. The rain had washed away most of the blood.

"Are you going to be sick?" Ziggy gripped my elbow.

"No. It's . . ." I swallowed hard. Seeing someone alive one day and dead the next was daunting. Humbling. I noticed a wet footprint as well as smeared footprints beside Nicolas. "Did you touch the body?"

"Yes." He licked his lips. "To see if he had a pulse."

"And did he?"

"No. He was gone."

Ziggy might have left trace evidence in the crime scene. Had Meaghan? Had she seen Nicolas's body and run? Were hers the prints beneath Ziggy's?

No, she didn't do this, I told myself. *She couldn't have.*

I assessed the immediate area. "Where's the murder weapon?"

"I don't have a clue." Ziggy spun left and right, peering at the garden.

"What do you think it was?"

"Not a hammer or mallet."

"You're right. Neither of those would make a dent that large. And not a baseball bat. That would have resulted in a more cylindrical injury. That impression . . ." I paused. Was there another word for it? Was it a depression? *Ugh.* "It's round." I spied the wrought-iron pedestal near the door. It was empty on top. "Where's the gazing ball?"

"The what?"

"Gazing ball." I gestured to the stand. "Meaghan received it as a gift about a month ago. She'd perched it on that wrought-iron pedestal. The ball is stainless steel. About twelve inches." I mimed the size. "I'd say eight to ten pounds."

"I haven't seen it. Do you think . . ."

"It's a big possibility."

Fiona wafted to my shoulder. "Calliope's gone."

"Gone where?"

"I don't know. She's allowed to socialize."

Or she could be with Meaghan, consoling her because—

The bleat of a siren startled me. A patrol car stopped with a screech in front of Meaghan's house. On its heels came a second car and more screeching.

Detective Dylan Summers, dressed in a tan safari hat and a rustic, water-resistant Mac jacket over chinos and white shirt, clambered out of the first vehicle. Officer Redcliff Reddick, a lanky redhead who was a good six inches taller than Summers, emerged from the second.

Summers approached us, one eyebrow arched. "You again?" he snarled.

Chapter 6

And scattering o'er its darkened green,
Bands of the fairies may be seen,
Chattering like grasshoppers, their feet
Dancing a thistledown dance round it.
—Walter de la Mare, "The Ruin"

"Yes, me." I grimaced, hating that I was getting a reputation for stumbling upon dead bodies. "I didn't find him. Ziggy did. He said he has no pulse. It's Nicolas Buley. A local artist."

"I've met him." Like my father, Summers was ruggedly handsome, weathered, and mid-fifties. A widower, he was now engaged to Renee Rodriguez. He stepped to the body, crouched, and felt Nicolas's wrist. After a long moment, he stood up.

A Monterey County Regional Fire District vehicle parked parallel to the police cars. Two emergency medical team members bolted from the truck, engine running. "Sir," the brawniest of the two men said to Summers and bypassed him to the body. Like Summers, the EMT checked Nicolas for a pulse.

"He's dead," Summers said.

"Confirmed, yes, sir."

"Thank you. Stand by."

Officer Reddick, who I believed had a crush on Meaghan, ended a call on his cell phone. "Detective Summers, techs are on their way, a couple minutes out."

"Good. Check out the exterior of the house and report back."

"Yes, sir." Reddick jogged away, snapping photos as he went.

Summers regarded me. "What was Mr. Buley doing here?"

"Good question. He and Meaghan used to date, but they'd broken up." I was not going to go into detail about how he'd been hounding my pal. "Ziggy"—I continued, and revised—"Mr. Foxx, Meaghan's business partner, saw someone running from the scene."

"I don't know if it was a man or woman," Ziggy blurted. "I'd guess a man. He was wearing a dark green raincoat. And a rainhat. Only saw him for a split second. Didn't see the shoes." Ziggy seemed out of breath, his words clipped and husky. "He was heading around the far side of the house. He might have run off with the weapon."

"The weapon?" Summers asked.

"Courtney thinks it was the gazing ball," Ziggy said.

"It's not here," Fiona said as if everyone could hear her.

I explained what a gazing ball was.

"I'm going to check it out," she added, and flitted toward the house.

Summers frowned at Ziggy. Did he think he'd killed Nicolas? Did he see blood on Ziggy's wet clothes? Was he wondering, as I had, why Ziggy wasn't wearing a raincoat? It was obvious he hadn't stashed a twelve-inch orb on his body. Had he wrapped his jacket around the murder weapon and hidden it on Meaghan's property? Or in his Lexus SUV? I looked around for the SUV but didn't see it.

No, Courtney. Don't think like that. Ziggy didn't do this.

"Detective, you should check out Nicolas's brother Payton Buley," I said. "He came to Violet Vickers's house today, and he was extremely angry."

"Okay, that's enough theorizing," Summers snapped.

"If it helps," I continued, "around four, I saw Nicolas Buley going into Sweet Treats."

"Well, that limits the time frame. Thank you." Summer turned to Ziggy. "Why are you here, Mr. Foxx?"

In spurts, Ziggy told him about Nicolas's outburst at Flair yesterday and yet again this morning, and about Meaghan having had enough of Nicolas's bullying, which made Ziggy feel the need to protect Meaghan in case Nicolas decided to get physical.

"Did Mr. Buley have a history of lashing out?" Summers asked.

"No. I don't think so. But he could be moody," Ziggy replied. "And he could be short-tempered. He is . . . *was* . . . asocial, if you catch my drift. A maladroit."

"Big word."

"If the shoe fits." Ziggy shrugged.

"When did you last see Mr. Buley?" Summers asked.

"This morning. At Flair Gallery."

"So you don't know how long he's been dead."

"No, sir. But that person who ran away . . ." Ziggy glanced in the direction the culprit must have gone.

"The person who fled could be someone like you, sir, who saw a dead body and freaked out, except he or she didn't stick around."

"True." Ziggy bobbed his head in agreement.

Summers said, "Where is Miss Brownie?"

"Not home." Ziggy waggled his cell phone. "I've been calling her, but she isn't answering. I know that doesn't mean she's *not* home. Is she? Could she be hurt inside? Should you break down the door?"

"Deep breath, Mr. Foxx."

Reddick returned. "The house looks intact, sir. The door isn't ajar. I didn't see anyone inside."

Summers eyed me. "Do you know where she might be, Miss Kelly?"

"No, sir." I bit my tongue so I wouldn't blurt my less-than-appropriate comeback to Ziggy earlier that I wasn't her keeper. "She has clients. Perhaps she's on an appointment."

"Call her, please." He jutted his chin toward my cell phone.

"If she's not answering Ziggy's calls—"

"Just do it!" Summer snapped.

"Yes, sir. On it." If I saluted, I was sure to earn his wrath. I opened Meaghan's contact on my cell phone and tapped the phone icon.

"Am I free to go?" Ziggy asked.

"No, Mr. Foxx. I have a number of questions for you."

Meaghan answered after the first ring. Gently, I told her what had happened.

"What? You're kidding. No, no, no." She grew hysterical, repeating the words over and over.

Mercifully, her mother Wanda took control of her phone, and I filled her in. Calmly, Wanda informed me that they were at her house and asked me to come console Meaghan. Summers insisted Officer Reddick escort me. Why? I wondered. Was he worried that I'd talk my friend into hightailing it out of town?

Wordlessly, I slipped into Reddick's vehicle, and if I was honest, I was happy to have him behind the wheel, seeing as I was shaking from head to toe. Fiona joined me, nestled on my shoulder, and whispered, "I didn't see the gazing ball anywhere."

Wanda Brownie lived in a blue-and-white, gingerbread-style house. It wasn't one of the fairy tale cottages by Hugh Comstock, but its design had been influenced by the famous architect's work. A number of years after Carmel was incorporated in 1916, Comstock arrived in town and swiftly became famous for creating a series of houses with flared eaves and irregular chimneys. They were like nothing the town had seen in its history, as steeped in Spanish-Mediterranean architecture as it had been, and gave the town its storybook feel.

I knocked, and Wanda yelled, "Come in."

I entered, with Fiona fluttering in front of me.

Reddick followed and paused in the foyer, whistling softly.

"It's impressive, isn't it?" I said.

"I had no idea."

Though Wanda hadn't given up her work as an artist's representative, she was spending much more time on her own art. Her primary works were seascapes, but she'd recently started painting whimsical gardens and hollows like one might see along the region's many wondrous trails. A month ago, Meaghan had confided that her mother wanted to spy a fairy and thought opening her eyes to the wonders of nature might help her in her quest. The painting in the foyer of a fairy tale–style hollow made me smile. A few months ago, I'd written a blog about that specific area. Within the hollow was a fairy portal that not all could detect.

"In here," Wanda called from the kitchen.

I went in first. The space was homey with its farmhouse-style, dark granite counters, white cabinets, single-basin sink, copper fixtures, and rough-hewn beams. A cheery KITCHENS ARE FILLED WITH LOVE sign hung over the arch leading to the dining room. A variety of vases teemed with fresh blooms.

Meaghan was sitting at the round kitchen table, a tissue wadded in her hands, eyes swollen from crying, her face streaked with tears. Her fairy, Calliope, was perched on Meaghan's shoulder, legs crossed, nearly blending in with the lacy green sweater Meaghan was wearing. I glimpsed a dark green raincoat hanging over the back of Meaghan's chair and jolted. No way. She was not the person Ziggy had seen running from the crime scene.

"Officer," Wanda said. "Welcome. Please sit." She wiped her hands on a tea towel. Vibrant in a shimmering, sea-blue scarf-style serape over a tank top and leggings, Wanda looked way younger than her fifty-something years. Possibly the she-wolf way she was guarding her adult daughter had something to do with her animated energy. "Coffee? Tea?"

Reddick signaled he'd pass. He sat in the chair closest to Meaghan, his gaze focused intently on her. She didn't, or *wouldn't,* make eye contact with him. I wasn't sure which.

"Water," I said, and took a chair opposite Meaghan.

"Tell me what happened," Meaghan said. "Every last detail."

Reddick nodded for me to proceed.

I relayed what I could. Ziggy finding Nicolas's body. Seeing someone running away, though he couldn't describe the person. Calling me.

"Why was Ziggy there?" she asked.

"He was concerned for your safety."

Meaghan's brow puckered, not comprehending.

"Because of, you know, the interaction between you and Nicolas at Flair."

"The interaction? You mean the . . ." She paused. "Yes, I suppose we did have an *interaction*. That's a nice way of putting it. Nicolas was in attack mode. I was in defense mode. How dare he talk to my partner that way. How dare he threaten to destroy another artist's work. He could be so monstrous sometimes. He . . ." She covered her mouth. "Oh. Oh. I don't mean to trash his memory. He's dead. He shouldn't be dead."

Calliope leaped into the air and orbited Meaghan's head once before resuming her position on her shoulder. She hadn't doused her with a potion. Intuitive fairies didn't need magic to help their humans. Perhaps she'd circled Meaghan to mentally send her positive vibes.

"I suppose that would explain why Nicolas was at my place," Meaghan said. "He'd come to apologize. How did he die? Was he shot?"

"The killer hit him with a heavy object," Reddick said.

"Oof!" Meaghan exclaimed as if she'd been struck. "I wish . . . I wish I'd been there. At home." She sucked back a sob. "Maybe I could've—"

"Don't do that to yourself," I cut in. "If you'd been there, whoever did this to him might have killed you, too."

I thought about the murder weapon. If the killer had used the gazing ball, then that suggested the murder hadn't been premeditated. Grabbing the ball would have been like grabbing a rock or a brick—the first thing at hand—which suggested an act of passion. I flashed on Payton Buley storming into Violet's house earlier. He'd been furious with his brother. Beyond furious. Had he tracked Nicolas down at Meaghan's and demanded repayment of the loan? When Nicolas refused, did he attack?

"Why were you at your mother's house and not at work?" Reddick asked, his voice non-accusative.

"Around four o'clock, I just couldn't stay at the gallery any longer. I was stewing and needed time to clear my head and figure out what my future was." Meaghan twirled her hand in the air. "So I left."

"Did something or somebody make you feel that way?" Reddick asked.

"No."

Four o'clock was around the time I'd spied Nicolas entering Sweet Treats. Had he seen Meaghan leave the gallery and followed her? No; if he had, he would have ended up at Wanda's, not Meaghan's. I cleared my throat to get my pal's attention. She peeked at me and turned away, her focus fixed on the shredded tissue she was holding.

Wanda set a glass of water in front of me, then removed the tissue from Meaghan's hand and fetched her a new one. Meaghan didn't use it. She stuffed it into her fist.

"You said you needed to figure out what your future was," Reddick continued. "With Nicolas Buley?"

"With him. With the gallery. There's so much stress working with artists. They're prickly." She glanced at her mother. "You're the exception."

"That's because I'm exceptional," Wanda teased, and blew her a kiss. "She came here instead of going home because I'd made a batch of bonbons to soothe her aching heart."

"Bonbons," Reddick repeated.

"Bonbons solve all sorts of problems," Wanda said.

"We were binge-watching *Bridgerton* reruns," Meaghan added. "From the moment I arrived until Courtney contacted me."

I breathed easier. Meaghan had a full-fledged alibi and witness. I didn't need to worry about her owning a dark green raincoat. Besides, there had to be dozens of similar raincoats in Carmel-by-the-Sea.

"Would either of you like a bonbon?" Wanda asked.

"I won't say no," I replied.

"Thank you, ma'am, but first I'd like to get a few facts on the page." Like Detective Summers, Reddick preferred the old-school way of taking notes. He pulled a notebook and pen, both secured with a rubber band, from his pocket.

Wanda set a white china plate, rimmed and stacked with a tower of bonbons, on the table.

I took the topmost one and bit into it. Mouth full, I said, "Oh, wow, Wanda, wow." I swallowed. "I need the recipe."

She fetched it from her recipe box and handed it to me. I took a picture with my cell phone and gave it back.

"Are you ready for my questions, Meaghan?" Reddick asked. He wasn't as formal as his superior. He didn't feel the need to use *miss* and *mister* if he knew the person, though sometimes he did.

"Sure. Ask me anything." Her shoulders sagged. Fiona flew to her hand and kissed her fingertips. Meaghan acknowledged her with a nod.

"What time did you arrive here?" Reddick asked.

Half an hour later, he finished questioning Meaghan as well as her mother and was satisfied that their alibis would exonerate Meaghan of any wrongdoing.

Which made us all wonder who had killed Nicolas and why.

Chapter 7

There is a fountain in the forest call'd
The Fountain of the Fairies;
When a child with a delightful wonder I have heard
Tales of the elfin tribe who in its banks
Hold midnight revelry.
—Robert Southey, "The Fountain of the Fairies"

At seven, I arrived home with Pixie and Fiona and slogged to the kitchen. After fixing their meals, I poured myself a well-deserved glass of chardonnay.

"You need to investigate this," Fiona said as she hopped from herb plant to herb plant on the windowsill, posing atop each in a perfect arabesque. "For Meaghan and Ziggy's sakes."

"Not I, thank you. Uh-uh." I wagged my head. "The police have this well in hand. They'll canvass the neighborhood."

"But they might not ask the right questions."

"And what makes you think I will?" I asked. "I'm not a detective."

"You're gentler. Friendlier. People will talk to you." She coasted to the countertop and struck a pixielike stance, one foot on heel, the toe up.

"No." I was adamant. "The police will find the person Ziggy

saw running away, and that person will know who the killer is. Case closed."

Fiona stuck her tongue between her lips and blew derisively before winging to the table to sup.

The matter settled for now, I lifted my glass to take a sip of wine. At the same time, my cell phone chimed. Brady was calling. I set the wine aside and answered. Now was the moment of truth. I had to tell him about Violet's intended guest list.

"How are you?" he asked. "I heard the news. Ziggy came in and told everyone what happened to Nicolas Buley."

I blew out the breath I'd been holding. Brady wasn't calling about his ex-wife. We'd get to that. For now, we'd stick with the current, more pressing news. "The police released Ziggy?" I asked. "That's a relief."

"On his own recognizance. He said you were there when the police arrived, and you went with Officer Reddick to her mother's house to get Meaghan's witness statement."

"I went to comfort her. Reddick got her statement. She's in the clear."

"Want some company? I can bring dinner. The staff will cover the rest of my shift."

"I'd love some."

Within fifteen minutes, he arrived with his famous meat loaf pie, a dish his mother adored, so he always kept it on hand at the café. It was my father's favorite dish, too. If I brought him a whole pie, would he forgive me for not having any control over Violet's willful personality?

"Smells divine," I said, pecking him on the cheek and leading him into the kitchen. "Red or white wine . . . or beer?"

"I'll take a beer. That'd be great."

I offered him the IPA he preferred and handed him a bottle opener. He popped the top and took a sip. As I prepared two plates for dinner, I said, "Want to eat in the garden?"

"Absolutely."

I loved where I'd placed the wicker table in the backyard, at the center of the four rays of paths leading to the corners of the yard. While we dined, I replayed everything I'd noticed at the crime scene. Then I told him about the upset at Violet's with Nicolas's brother.

"Have you informed the police?" Brady asked.

"I started to, but Summers cut me off. He doesn't want me theorizing."

"Uh, gee, that hasn't held you back before." He smirked.

I threw him the stink eye.

Brady coughed out a laugh. "All I'm saying is your brain works that way. You like to figure out puzzles. I guess it's like putting together a garden. For me, it's like making up recipes."

Fiona fluttered in front of me and said, "Told you so."

"Okay, you're right. I'll call Detective Summers in the morning." I'd have to let Violet know about Nicolas, too, if the police hadn't. Perhaps she'd heard about the murder by now and had elaborated to Summers about Payton's dramatic entrance and exit. I wondered how the murder might affect her event. Would a death of one of the artists put a pall over it? Most likely not. It was over a week away. Would she continue to show Nicolas's work? A notion came to me that made me shudder. Had a rival artist, like Hunter Hock, killed Nicolas to weaken his sales?

"Ziggy seemed to think one of his artists might be the culprit," Brady said, as if reading my mind.

"Hunter Hock?"

"Yes. Apparently, he and Nicolas locked horns and came to blows."

"That was because Nicolas was jealous, and he has . . . he *had* a temper. I've never seen Hunter lose his cool. He's like serenity itself. But Nicolas struck first, and Hunter defended himself."

"Hock is the guy who paints those small things." Brady mimed the shape with his hands.

"That's right. They're very popular. They fit in any home or office. They're easy to ship and make great gifts."

"How can he make a living? I mean, you can't charge as much for something small, can you?"

"Sure you can. They're exclusive. He only does a dozen or so a year. Think of Fabergé eggs. They're one of a kind. So are Hock's petite art works. No two are alike." I took a sip of wine. "By the way, I think he has a thing for Meaghan."

"Who, Hock?"

"Honestly, every man that meets her falls for her, but yes, Hunter Hock seems enthralled by her. After Nicolas relocated to Sedona, Hunter started to come around the gallery more. He'd hang out and comment on other artists' work. One day, trinkets started appearing on Meaghan's doorstep."

"Trinkets?" Brady said. "What kinds of trinkets?"

"Garden ornaments, like a metal cat silhouette and a trio of fairies dancing on a metalwork dandelion."

Brady smiled, amused. "Those sound larger than trinkets."

Come to think of it, Hunter had also given her the gazing ball. Did the police know that?

"Courtney," Brady said, tapping my arm.

"Huh?" I asked, startled.

"Where'd you go for a second?"

"Nowhere. I'm here."

"How do you know it was Hunter Hock who left the trinkets for her?"

"Tish Waterman saw him one time." Tish was the woman who owned A Peaceful Solution day spa. "Her daughter Twyla, on another occasion." Those two were quite the walkers. Twyla had a set route. Tish let her two shih tzus steer her wherever they wanted. Tish loved to go into Flair and look around. She was the one who'd told Meaghan about her and her daughter seeing Hunter.

"So Hock is smitten with Meaghan." Brady took a swig of his beer and polished off his dinner.

"Like you were with me," I ribbed.

"Were? You mean *am*. I *am* smitten with you."

"Remember how you made fairy doors and set them all around Carmel to catch my attention back in February?"

He chuckled. He'd made over a dozen, each with a theme that I should have been able to decipher had I been savvier, but I hadn't until I'd caught him in the act of setting one by my house. They were the reason I'd been inspired to teach fairy-door-making classes.

"Has Meaghan questioned Hunter about the gifts?" Brady asked.

"She's not interested in him and doesn't want to press the point, but she doesn't want to give them back and hurt his feelings, either. She's in a quandary."

"Do you think Nicolas figured it out? Maybe he ordered Hock to stop, and Hock didn't like to be bossed around, so he lashed out."

"It's a possibility, I suppose, although that seems like a flimsy reason for murder." My theory of an artist getting rid of another artist had more heft.

Brady set his napkin on the plate and leaned back in his chair. "It's nice back here. So serene."

The chittering of nocturnal animals was the dominant sound now. The birds had gone to roost. Pixie had joined us and was nestled at Brady's feet.

"Is your fairy nearby?" he asked.

"She is. She's doing air gymnastics."

In fact, Fiona was having a gay old time flitting from one fairy garden to the next. Occasionally, glitter drifted from her wings, as if she were gracing the gardens with her magical touch. I often wondered if her magic was the reason the plants in the garden had nearly doubled in size over the past year.

"I still can't see her," he said, peering into the dark.

"She's not like a firefly. She doesn't have a tail that glows. Give it time." I pushed my plate away and, wineglass in hand, swiveled in my chair, tucking my legs and heels under my rump. "So Brady, there's something I need to tell you."

He met my gaze, his mouth slightly parted.

I pitched forward, kissed him tenderly, and returned to my tucked position.

"Was that it?" He grinned in a cocksure way.

"No . . ." I took a fortifying sip of wine. "At Violet's theater foundation event, she's not only inviting artists from all over Northern California to participate, but she's inviting celebrities. The more celebrities she has, the more she feels the donations will pour in. She wants this to be a huge success. So she's invited some people who grew up here and became famous."

"Like Clint Eastwood?" he asked, tilting his head.

Besides being known for his stint as mayor and for starring in the iconic *Play Misty for Me,* Eastwood loved Carmel, so he'd purchased the historic Mission Ranch farmhouse when it was declared unfit to preserve and had turned it into a ranch with rooms for rent as well as a restaurant and bar.

"I'm sure he'll be there. But there are some others. A few authors and playwrights and some actors like . . ." I licked my lips, reluctant to continue. "Like George Pitt."

Brady's gaze grew steely. "Pitt's invited? He didn't live here."

"But his wife did."

He huffed. "Swell."

I brushed a hair off my face. "You haven't told me much about Finley. All you've said is she left you for him because she missed Los Angeles." She'd grown up around the movie business but had been forced to move to Carmel when her grandmother got sick. "How did she and George meet?"

"He came up here for a shoot and swept her off her feet." His lips drew thin. His jaw started ticking. "There are thirty years between them, but that didn't bother her. He had money. He was suave. I was anything but."

"I think you're suave," I teased and ran a finger along his muscular forearm.

He gripped my hand and kissed my fingertip. "Don't you

worry about a thing. I will be the perfect gentlemen while they are in town. We won't have a replay of what your ex-fiancé did a few months ago."

Talk about fiascos. That interaction still made me fume.

"One more question," I said.

"Nosey."

"Always. Um, when we reconnected last year, you said secrets were overrated and to ask your ex-wife what you meant. I assumed she'd shared something about you that made it into the tabloids. What was it? Did you hit a car and forget to leave your number? Did you cheat on her? Did you—"

"I sleep with a night-light on."

I had no clue. We hadn't spent the night together. In fact, we hadn't gone past serious kissing. I was pretty sure we were both ready, but neither of us had pressed. "That's it?" I asked, biting back a smile.

"Yes. When I was a kid, I was scared of the dark. Mom would read me Roald Dahl stories and R.L. Stine books, some of her favorites because of their clever plotlines and characters." His mother was a famous novelist who'd made a name for herself writing romantic historical fiction. "She had no idea I internalized every last one of them. They came alive after she turned out the light. I'm what's known as a visceral reader. To this day, she's sorry that she hadn't been more sensitive to my needs."

"And so you still sleep with the light on?"

His cheeks blazed pink. "Yep. My ex mentioned that tasty tidbit in a *People* magazine interview. For a good year, I heard about it from customers. I was the butt of every joke."

I rose from my chair and moved to him, placing my hands on his face. "I will never tell a soul. It is now our secret."

Fiona hovered by Brady's ear and whispered something. I saw him blink. Had he heard her this time?

Before going to bed, I pressed Fiona for what she'd said to Brady. She giggled and said it was hers to know, claiming she didn't need to reveal every one of her tricks. I made her swear she hadn't done something that might hurt him. She promised she hadn't.

I slept well and awoke raring to go. An hour later, after completing my morning routine, I entered the shop. I set Pixie on the floor, and she scampered to the patio. Fiona flitted to a set of wind chimes I'd recently ordered, ten inches of silver and wood with a fairy perched atop a crescent moon, and poked the fairy's wand. The tinkling that emanated from the chimes was delicate and soothing. I found myself breathing deeply and said, "Tà!"

"You're welcome," she said, and flew off to play with Pixie.

"Morning, Joss!" I cried.

"Oh, you're here," she said as she crossed the threshold from the patio and headed to the sales counter. "I heard what happened. Another murder? I can't believe it. How are you doing? How is Ziggy? Is everything okay? I mean, of course it isn't. Nicolas Buley is dead." She was talking at such breakneck speed that words were colliding into one another. "Tell me what happened. Ziggy found him at Meaghan's?"

I braced her by the shoulders. "Breathe."

"There's nothing in the papers. Only gossip on the street."

"Breathe," I repeated.

"I canceled the fairy door class after you left. All the parents understood. The tweens were a bit miffed, but a discount coupon softened the blow. I've rescheduled it for this afternoon," she went on, her pace still at a clip. "I covered the items with a tarp. You can use them for this morning's class."

"Let me fix a cup of peppermint tea," I said, cutting her off, "and I'll tell you everything I know, which isn't much." I retreated down the hall to the office where I stowed my purse and hung my slicker on a hook. Minutes later, I returned to the beverage station.

"Love the getup," she said, indicating my outfit. "It goes nicely with your skin tone."

After my wet morning run—it hadn't been raining, but it had been damp with heavy drizzle—I'd donned a pink, long-sleeved, boat-neck T-shirt over jeans. Simple and comfy. "Thank you." I dunked a teabag into the mug of hot water I'd poured, let it steep for thirty seconds, and headed to the patio. I didn't like strong tea.

Joss made herself a cup of tea, as well, and followed me. We sat at one of the tables. Rain pattered the tempered-glass roof. The sound didn't irritate me as it had yesterday. Looking back, I wondered why it had? Had I sensed something bad was about to happen? I shooed the notion away. I did not have ESP.

"Okay, spill," she said. "I'm all ears."

I recapped what I'd told Brady last night.

Joss whistled. "A crime of passion. Do you think a woman might have done it?"

I stared at her, realizing that until Brady had shared his take on the murder, I'd focused on one and only one person—Payton Buley. Neither of us had suspected a woman. It certainly was not Meaghan, but now a number of women came to mind, in particular Sassy Jacobi and Addie Tan, both of whom had clearly adored Nicolas. Were there others? Had he broken someone's else's heart in Arizona? Had that woman followed him to Carmel? Had she believed he would throw her over if Meaghan took him back and murdered him before he could? No, that made no sense. She would've killed Meaghan first.

"I see your brain working double-time," Joss said.

I rose to my feet and crossed to the learning-the-craft area. I removed the tarp from the items for the fairy door class and examined what we'd laid out. One of my regular customers, Hattie Hopewell, headed up a garden club named the Happy Diggers. The group would be arriving shortly. They were a chatty but intent bunch, and I wanted to be thoroughly prepared to keep them entertained.

Joss sidled to me. "We don't have enough supplies," she observed, fingering the popsicle sticks. "Not for the Diggers plus guests. They love to dress up their art."

"You're right."

Today, Hattie's two sisters would also be joining in.

"So, c'mon, talk. Who came to mind?" Joss asked as she fetched more glue guns and glue sticks from a box she'd stowed beneath the table.

"No. I'm not going to theorize," I said, doing my best to tamp down my curiosity. "It doesn't involve me. Meaghan is cleared."

"What about Ziggy? He's your karate teacher and your friend."

"Ziggy didn't do it." Although I had to admit I was still wondering why he'd felt the need to go to Meaghan's house to protect her. Had Nicolas gone into Flair after I'd seen him lingering outside Sweet Treats and threatened Meaghan?

"Come on, enlighten me," Joss said.

"Okay, there was a woman at Violet's house yesterday, a guitar maker who's also a singer. She made it seem like she and Nicolas were an item. In fact, she told Violet they had a *thing*."

"A *thing*. What a ridiculous term." Joss sniffed.

I moved to the cabinet that held bags of soil and tools and fetched a box of charms and rocks. I scooped some into the dishes on the workstation table. "We need more natural sticks."

"On it." Joss headed to the stockroom beyond the office and returned in a minute with a box of each. "So what's the guitar player's name?"

"Sassy Jacobi."

"Ooh, I've heard her sing. Waterfall ponytail." Joss mimed the hairstyle. "Pretty face."

"That's her."

"I've seen her at fairs selling her guitars. They're beautiful. All heart-shaped and made with exotic wood. She has a steady gig at a wine bar north of town every Thursday and Saturday night, too. Buddy and I were there just a few weeks ago. And I believe she plays at Take Flight, the coffee and wine bar on Ocean Avenue, on Tuesdays and Wednesdays during the day."

"Who's Buddy?" I asked, my voice lilting upward.

Joss's cheeks tinged pink. "My new beau."

"But you were dating—"

"Stop. Do not utter his name." She held up a hand. "He was not the man I thought he was. I will never speed date again. Buddy is a true gentleman and a vintner."

"When do I get to meet him?"

"The next time you and I go wine tasting at his vineyard."

I threw her a dirty look. We had never gone wine tasting. In fact, we'd never done any socializing outside of the shop. I decided then and there to change that. "Two weeks from Monday, we've got a date. Does he work Mondays?"

"He will. Now, who else do you suspect besides Sassy Jacobi?"

"I was wondering about Addie Tan, the woman who came in yesterday. She was surprised that Nicolas was back in town and hadn't touched base with her."

"She's a lot older than him." Joss arranged the moss and sticks.

"Older women are allowed to have crushes on younger men."

"True."

"And what if that love was not returned?" I proposed.

Fiona sailed into view. "Bitter roots take hold," she opined. "That's a favorite fairy saying."

Joss said, "'Bitter are the roots of study, yet how sweet their fruit.'"

Fiona tilted her head. "Who said that?"

"Cato the Younger," Joss said. "A conservative Roman senator."

Fiona made a raspberry sound. "That doesn't count. He wasn't a poet or author. No fair. Okay, here's one. 'No one is angrier than a woman who has been rejected in love,'" she intoned. "William Congreve, from 'The Mourning Bride.'"

"You're supposed to let me guess," Joss chided. She was the person who'd enticed Fiona to read all of the Sherlock Holmes stories, and now Fiona was better read than I could ever hope to be.

"Sorry," Fiona said with a smirk.

My mouth dropped open. "You're learning poetry?"

"Yep." She tapped her hand against Joss's for a high five. "I finished memorizing Shakespeare's sonnets."

"All of them?" I gasped.

"Mm-hmm. I had to start something new."

"Hello-o!" Meaghan yelled. "Where are you?" Through the windows of the showroom, I spied her weaving through display tables.

"Out here," I responded.

Meaghan passed through the French doors looking under the weather, her eyes still puffy from crying, the muted brown of her lacy, long-sleeved dress doing nothing to enhance her color.

"Tea," I whispered to Joss.

"Will do."

Meaghan slumped onto a bench by the workstation and propped her elbows on the table. "Ziggy doesn't want me at the gallery."

"And rightly so. You look a mess. Did you forget to comb your hair?"

"I combed it. With my fingers. I didn't have any of my things at Mom's." She'd texted that she hadn't felt comfortable going back to her house. She didn't think the murderer was after her, but the idea of walking along the path where Nicolas was killed had freaked her out. I'd offered her the opportunity to stay with me, but she'd declined. "This is an old dress from high school, if you can believe it." She fingered the hem of the sleeve. "Back in my drab colors period. Yuck."

Fiona fluttered above Meaghan and dusted her with a purple potion. "To help with sadness," she murmured, and chanted a spell. When she was done, she kissed Meaghan's cheek. "You'll feel better soon." Seconds later, she cruised into the ficus, as if the act of enchantment had exhausted her.

Meaghan picked up one of the sticks. "This is ugly."

"It'll be pretty when it's painted."

Joss returned with a mug of tea for Meaghan. "I added honey, just the way you like it."

"Thanks."

Seconds later, the door to the shop, Glitz, opened and slammed shut. "Courtney! Joss!" Glinda Gill, owner of the jewelry store in the courtyard, hustled through the shop to the patio, the hood of her silver raincoat flopping up and down. She clapped a hand to her chest. Breathlessly, she said, "Ziggy has been arrested."

Chapter 8

I am off down the road
Where the fairy lanterns glowed
And the little pretty flittermice are flying.
—J.R.R. Tolkien, "Goblin Feet"

"Arrested?" I yelped.

"Oh, no!" Meaghan cried, and shot to her feet.

Fiona emerged from the ficus, panic pinching her face.

"Tell us everything," I said, rounding the table to clutch Glinda's hands.

It might sound silly, but the owners and staff that worked in the Cypress and Ivy Courtyard were a tight-knit family. We cared what happened to one another. We encouraged our shoppers to patronize the other shops.

"Go on," I said.

Glinda was shivering. Her eyes were brimming with tears. "The police showed up. The vehicle's siren whooped once. I raced out of the shop just in time to see Ziggy getting into the back seat of the cruiser. Detective Summers was in charge."

"What do they have on him?" Meaghan asked.

"One of the other policemen"—Glinda released my hands and swooped her blond bob with both hands, clearing any hair that might have gotten trapped by the raincoat—"the one who was told to lock up the shop since you weren't there, said Ziggy had been harboring some of Nicolas's art pieces at his house."

"Harboring?" Meaghan repeated.

"Concealing, hiding," Glinda said.

Meaghan rolled her eyes, knowing perfectly well what *harboring* meant. "He wouldn't do that," she protested. "Ziggy is as honest as the day is long."

"As honest," Fiona echoed as she orbited Glinda.

"Supposedly, he'd taken them home to view them in the proper light and intended to return them to the gallery," Glinda went on, "but he never did. And Nicolas found out and told a friend about it."

"Which friend?" I asked.

"A musician."

Sassy Jacobi, I'd bet.

"The police are accusing him of planning to sell them posthumously," Glinda said. "You both know as well as I do that the value of an artist's work goes up markedly after a death." A jeweler who supplied some of Glitz's highest-end pieces had died a year ago, and Glinda had reaped a fortune for the ones she'd still had in stock. "Especially after such a young death," she added, "when the artist would never be able to create all the work he was destined to create."

"No," Meaghan wailed. "It's not true. I'm telling you Ziggy is honorable. He'd never do that."

Fiona whizzed to Meaghan and caressed her shoulder. "There, there," she murmured.

"The police went with a warrant to Ziggy's house," Glinda said. "His housekeeper was there. She got spooked and let them in."

"Is that legal?" Meaghan asked.

"Legal enough. They found some of Nicolas's art in a closet." Glinda paused for effect. "Not hanging on a wall in the *proper light*."

Meaghan's shoulders slumped. "What was Ziggy's explanation?"

"I have no idea," Glinda said.

"I'm going to the precinct." Meaghan headed for the French doors. "I'll spring him."

"Wait! Contact Victoria Judge," I said. She was the one who had helped me, as well as Wanda Brownie, out of a legal mess. "If Ziggy needs to arrange for bail, Victoria will . . ."

Before I could complete the sentence, Meaghan was halfway through the showroom, cell phone pressed to her ear.

Glinda frowned. "Poor thing. To lose her lover and then have her partner arrested."

"Nicolas was no longer her lover. They'd broken up."

"Yes, but at one time—"

I shook a finger. "Meaghan will rally. She'll be fine."

"Yes, she will," Fiona agreed.

"What we need to do is make sure Ziggy is cleared. He saw someone running away from the crime scene. If it wasn't the killer, maybe that person could provide testimony as to when Ziggy appeared at Meaghan's house."

"Great idea. I'll ask around." Glinda left as speedily as she'd entered.

At the same time, I spotted the Happy Diggers trooping into the shop through the showroom windows. Many had their dogs in tow. Like most of Carmel, we were a pet-friendly establishment. We allowed customers to bring them in, but we expected them to be obedient. Either the group was early, or I'd made an error on the calendar. I shook out the tension in my shoulders, raised my chin, and met them as they filed through the French doors. "Welcome, ladies. Welcome, pups."

All of the women were dressed in Happy Digger floral T-shirts.

"Good morning, everyone," Hattie Hopewell trilled in her throaty voice. A flamboyant redhead in her sixties, she was accompanied by her brindled Scottie, who was wearing a collar studded with gems. "Hello, hello-o-o-o," she trilled while hoisting a finger. "Middle *G*." Hattie, a former professional singer, had perfect pitch and enjoyed showing it off.

"Nice collar on your dog," I said, pulling my cell phone from my pocket and taking a few photographs of the attendees to add to our website.

Fiona greeted each of the pups as they paraded past.

"A spiritualist made it for him," Hattie said. "It's supposed to bring him good health and well-being. He has been suffering from a bit of arthritis, but ever since I slapped this sucker on him, he's been as happy as a lark." She hailed her friend. "Zinnia, this way."

"I'm coming. I'm coming." Zinnia Walker, a trim sixty-five-year-old with a spiky silver hairdo, traipsed behind Hattie, two teacup Boston terriers peeking from her oversized tote. Their flat, scrunchy faces made me smile. "Here we go, my beauties." She set her tote on the bench by the workstation table. "Good morning, Courtney. Thank you, as always, for hosting us. I can't wait for Violet's soirée." Zinnia and Violet traveled in the same social circle. Like Violet, Zinnia was wealthy beyond belief.

"We can't wait to get started," Hattie said as she set her purse down. "I've so wanted to add a fairy door to my garden."

The oldest Digger, a ninety-two-year-old marvel with ultra-white hair, who never seemed to grow tired and rarely, if ever, pulled punches, followed Zinnia. Next came the Digger with the most incredible ocean-blue eyes—I had yet to learn her name, though I'd asked numerous times. She was rifling through her avant-garde tote for something and didn't look up as she passed me.

"Morning," I said.

"Morning," she mumbled.

"We're here, too." Holly Hopewell sauntered in with her two cream-colored Pomeranians. "This way, my sweet things," she cooed. How I adored the woman. She had the energy of a teenager and treasured her family. I was sure she was the favorite grandma with her grandchildren. She knew how to text and play video games. "Courtney, when you have a moment, I'd appreciate it if you'd tour my garden. Things are sort of so-so, and they should be thriving in May, don't you think?"

"I'll be glad to take a look."

"She's being ridiculous, Courtney," said Hedda Hopewell, the third of the Hopewell sisters. "The garden looks fab." Hedda was younger than Holly by a dozen years and a delightful woman. We often met for coffee. Though she was more conservative than her sisters when it came to her attire, she was a philosopher by nature, and occasionally emailed me messages to ponder, like *Every time I find the meaning of life, they change it.* I'd liked that one so much, I'd had a T-shirt made with the quip to give Joss for her birthday. Following the loss of her boyfriend a few years ago, Hedda believed in living each day to its fullest. "Where am I sitting?"

"In the learning-the-craft area with the others. I'll be right there."

As Hedda swept past me, I caught the musky-earthy scent of patchouli. Fiona must have detected the aroma, too, because she raced after Hedda, coaxing the fragrance toward her with her hands. Fairies tried to absorb all the healing power they could, and patchouli was packed with it.

A mother with two children under five also stepped onto the patio. She released the children, and they darted to the baker's racks. "Careful, you two," she commanded. "No touching."

A pair of middle-aged female customers traipsed behind the mother. One was a good foot taller than the other, and I instantly dubbed them Laverne and Shirley.

"Hi, I'm Courtney," I said to the newcomers. "Feel free to browse. I'm starting a class, but once I get them settled, I can answer any questions you might have."

"Let's get going," I told the Diggers as I joined them at the workstation table. "You'll see on the table a variety of nature's treasures, including stones and gems. There is no right or wrong to a fairy door other than it must be a door."

Hattie said, "Duh."

They all laughed.

"I've placed a few completed doors on the table to serve as inspiration." I motioned to one I'd made using a broad twig for the base, a thinner twig as a crossbar at the top, and supporting twigs for the door jambs. The door was made of popsicle sticks that I'd painted green. Shells, twine, moss, and stones, all in blue and green shades, adorned the rustic door.

"FYI, your doors don't need to open and close, and they don't need hinges, but you may use them if you like." I'd laid out a collection of teensy hinges, my favorites being the antique brass ones with tooled details. "To make it easy for any of you who might feel artistically challenged, I've set out a few premade door shapes. All you have to do is paint and prettify them. However, please note that they are for indoor use. They'll warp the moment they're hit with outdoor moisture. Now I'll let you get started." I patted Hattie's shoulder. "As you all know, Hattie is our resident expert with the glue gun, so ask her if you need guidance. And be careful. Leave the hot glue guns on their silicone mats so the glue doesn't drip onto your projects."

I left them and roamed to Laverne and Shirley. "Do you need my help for anything?"

The taller woman, *Laverne*, said, "My niece is going to adore this." She was holding a DIY kit tied with pink ribbon. "She's a ballerina and loves all things ballet."

I'd assembled a number of do-it-yourself kits in wicker baskets and had set them on the bottom shelf of the baker's racks. Each included a clay pot, a package of dirt, two figurines, and a nice selection of environmental pieces like benches, stumps, and toadstools, as well as a signpost, which was how I'd labeled each package. In the one she'd selected, I added a girl fairy in a tutu and a pig fairy, also in a tutu, and the sign FAIRIES DANCE HERE.

Fiona joined us, doing pirouettes around the woman, who tittered, her gaze following Fiona's every move.

"Your fairy is adorable, by the way," the woman confided. "What's her name?"

"Fiona."

"Nice to meet you, Fiona."

Fiona curtsied midair.

Her friend, *Shirley,* swatted her. "Stop it. You're a tease."

"If you don't believe, you'll never see one," the woman said, and crooked a finger to wave goodbye to Fiona.

"Did you know that woman could see you?" I asked Fiona as the twosome headed into the showroom.

"She's been watching me since she walked in."

I was always curious why one person could see a fairy and another couldn't. Holly Hopewell was eager to do so.

As if reading my mind, Fiona did a loop the loop and sped to Holly. She danced atop Holly's head, after which she landed on Holly's project—three popsicle sticks glued to a crossbar stick—and did a jig.

Holly faltered. She lost hold of the unfinished door. "Was that—"

I nodded.

Holly blinked and searched for Fiona again. The imp was hiding behind a box of gems. She poked an arm and wing out. Holly laughed nervously and wagged a hand, as if dismissing what she'd seen. Sobering ever so slightly, she said, "Courtney, dear, we were just discussing the murder."

Hattie nodded. "We sure were."

I groaned. Yes, everyone in town would be talking about it—it was to be expected—but I hadn't wanted that kind of energy to swirl around the shop, especially not while teaching a class. Bad news might stifle a student's creativity or a customer's sense of whimsy.

"Tell her what you told me, Zinnia," Hattie prodded.

Zinnia glowered at her friend. "I was planning to. Don't rush me. So, Courtney, you know I'm a big patron of the arts, and Flair is my go-to gallery."

"I didn't know," I said. There were so many galleries in town.

Meaghan and Ziggy worked hard to compete with the others, always creating new exhibits with new artists.

"Yes, I am. Ziggy Foxx and I are well acquainted."

"Go on," Hattie coaxed. "Tell her the rest."

"I saw him at Meaghan's house yesterday."

"You did?" I exclaimed. "When?"

"Right as he arrived. I was walking by."

"Walking?" Hattie snorted. "You mean running."

Zinnia threw her an exasperated look. "When I took the pups out for their walk, it was drizzling."

"Like those pups need walking," Hattie said. "What do they weigh, a pound each?"

Holly said, "Dear sister, please stop interrupting. Zinnia, you have the floor."

"Thank you, Holly." Zinnia fiddled with her hair. "Anyway, we got caught in the downpour—who knew it was going to rain like that?—and my babies hate getting soaked, so I tucked them into my coat, and we ran all the way home."

"You saw Ziggy Foxx," I repeated.

She nodded.

"Was he getting out of his car?"

"There weren't any cars around. I suspected he walked there."

Right. I forgot. I hadn't seen his Lexus parked on the street.

"He was opening the gate," Zinnia said.

"Did you see anyone else?" I asked. "Ziggy said he glimpsed someone in a green raincoat."

"My slicker is green. Perhaps he was referring to me."

I palm-slapped my forehead. "You! He saw *you* running away. Not the killer." I clasped her hand and shook it. "Your account confirms that Nicolas was dead when Ziggy got there."

"Does it?" Hattie asked and regarded her friend. "Did you see Nicolas Buley's body?"

Zinnia shook her head.

"That's okay," I said. "This should be enough to help Ziggy, I think. Thank you." I pumped Zinnia's hand again. "I can't wait to tell the police."

"Courtney," Hedda said, "I spied Detective Summers and his fiancée entering Sweet Treats as I was coming in."

"Terrific." I put Joss in charge of finishing up the fairy door class and hurried through the courtyard to Sweet Treats. I scanned the area, hoping Fiona would join me, but she'd vanished.

There was a line of customers peering into the glass display case filled with pastries, cakes, and cookies. All three of the retro pink stools were occupied at the pink counter. Yvanna Acebo, dressed in the shop's pink uniform, her dark hair tied back with a scrunchie, was packing orders into Sweet Treats bags. She acknowledged me with a nod.

To the left, I spotted Summers sitting at a table with Renee. Beyond him, I glimpsed Addie Tan with a blond woman about Addie's age. The two were holding hands across the table, but I didn't think there was anything romantic between the two. The other woman seemed to be consoling Addie, whose face was tearstained. Considering her feelings for Nicolas Buley, I imagined that Addie was heartbroken because she'd heard the news of his death. Unless, as I'd theorized, she'd killed him because he didn't return her affections. *Bitter roots take hold*, Fiona had said.

Twyla Waterman set two steaming mugs in front of Summers and Renee and opened a pad to take their orders. Though she'd been a broken woman due to her harrowing experience in a cult, now Twyla exuded confidence. Like Yvanna, her dark hair was secured at the nape of her neck. Her skin radiated health, and her gaze was direct.

I weaved through other diners and addressed Summers just as Twyla moved on to tend to more customers. "Detective, I have some information."

He narrowed his gaze. "Of course you do."

"Don't be snide, Dylan," Renee chided.

Both of them were dressed in white shirts and jeans. Their raincoats were slung over the backs of their chairs.

"Sit." Renee motioned to an empty chair. "We're having coffee and apple tarts. Want something?"

"No, don't sit, don't order," Summers said, his glower inhospitable. "Tell me what you have to say and be on your way."

Hurriedly, I filled him in on Zinnia Walker's account.

"Why hasn't she come to the precinct?" he asked.

"I suppose she didn't think much about it, not realizing the timing of everything. But if she saw Ziggy . . . Mr. Foxx . . ." I hoped being formal might win me brownie points with Summers. "If she saw him opening Meaghan's gate, and minutes later he phoned me—"

"Stop." Summers explained the flaws of my argument on his fingertips. "One, Mrs. Walker didn't give you a specific time. Two, Mr. Foxx could have mentioned seeing her as an alibi, but it wasn't until after she fled that Mr. Buley showed up, and Mr. Foxx did the deed."

I winced. What he suggested sounded reasonable. *Shoot.*

"And we have motive," Summers said.

"Which is . . ." Renee prompted and sipped her coffee.

Twyla brought the apple tarts, which had been set on doilies atop white plates, and asked if there would be anything else.

Summers shook his head and addressed his fiancée. "Mr. Foxx—"

"Call him Ziggy, Dylan," Renee said. "You've played golf with him, for heaven's sake."

"Ziggy has a few pieces of Mr. Buley's art in his house," he stated.

"Big deal," Renee said. "I have one of his works. Am I a killer?"

"Unaccounted for pieces of art," Summers said. "*Unaccounted* meaning there is no paperwork at the gallery showing he removed the items."

I said, "I'm sure he told Nicolas he was taking them home to view them in the proper light."

"Did he? Says who? Not Nicolas Buley, seeing as he's deceased."

I shifted feet.

"And for your information, the art was in a closet," Summers said, "not hanging on a wall."

Renee exchanged a worried look with me.

"For all we know," Summers continued, "Ziggy might have been planning to put in a claim to an insurance company for theft at the gallery, after which he could sell the items on the black market."

"Oh, come on," I chided. "You're making Ziggy out to be some kind of master thief. I'm sure it was an oversight."

"Oversight or not, it's enough to keep him in jail until we sort out the particulars. He did have Mr. Buley's blood on his trousers and hands."

"Because he checked his pulse," I said.

"So he claims." Summers folded his muscular arms across his chest. To say he came across as forbidding didn't even capture it.

But I didn't cower. I said, "Did you find the murder weapon? Was it the gazing ball from Meaghan's yard?"

Summers let out a long stream of air. "It was not."

"What was it?"

"Not the gazing ball," he stated. "We found that beneath the front steps of Miss Brownie's home. It must have tumbled off its stand."

Which was why Fiona had missed seeing it, I mused. "Or . . ." I held up a finger. "Or the killer—not Ziggy—used it to hit Nicolas and then hid it."

"Courtney," Renee said softly, "don't push it."

"I was sure by the indentation on Nicolas's head that the weapon was round and about the size of—"

"The gazing ball was free of any blood," Summers stated.

"As well as fingerprints?" I asked. "Or did the killer wipe it clean?"

"It had fingerprints. Meaghan Brownie's fingerprints."

"She didn't—"

"I'm not saying she did. Now, listen up," Summers said testily. "You are not a coroner. You are not a DNA expert. You are not a pro in any sense of the word. Go back to your fairy shop. Do what you're good at, and let me do what I'm good at."

"But what was the murder weapon if not the ball?"

"Go." He rose to his feet, fuming.

I lifted my chin to meet his gaze. "You don't know, do you? And if you don't know, then it means it wasn't at the crime scene, which means Ziggy isn't guilty." I pivoted and strode out the door. I didn't dare look back and give the detective the satisfaction of disagreeing.

Chapter 9

And often while I'm dreaming so,
Across the sky the moon will go;
It is a lady, sweet and fair,
Who comes to gather daisies there.
—Frank Dempster Sherman, "Daisies"

As I strode out of Sweet Treats, I was quivering. If Fiona had been with me, I would have thought she'd goaded me into confronting Summers, but she hadn't, meaning I'd found the gumption on my own. Hooray. Not that the man cowed me. He simply reminded me of my father, and any face-off that I won with him was a triumph.

Upon further contemplation, however, I wondered why I'd pressed so hard. Okay, he was correct. I wasn't a crime scene expert, but I was certain the weapon was a round object. The depression on Nicolas's skull had seemed too small to have been made by a bowling ball. A billiard ball wouldn't have been the right size, either. A Magic 8 Ball or a fortune-teller's crystal ball might have been.

I turned left, wondering if Meaghan had returned to Flair, and spied her mother entering the gallery. She was carrying something that was square and thin and covered by a tarp. I followed her inside.

Wanda set her package next to the sales counter and made a beeline for Meaghan, who was conversing with one of her staff. "Hello, sweetheart."

"Hi, Mom," Meaghan said. "What are you—" She paused when she caught sight of me and frowned. "What are you both doing here?"

"We didn't come together," her mother said. "This is not an intervention."

"I wanted to check in on you," I added. "Um, did it go well at the precinct?'

"I didn't go. I contacted Miss Judge like you suggested, and she said she would handle it." Her shoulders rose and fell. "She's not sure she can get Ziggy out on bail. The police said they have evidence against him."

I drew closer, loath to tell her that they did have evidence. Damning evidence. Was Ziggy in dire straits? Why had he taken Nicolas's art home? He must have told Nicolas he had because Sassy or some other musician knew. The other thing that plagued me was how Ziggy could have killed Nicolas if the murder weapon wasn't found at the scene of the crime?

Wanda enveloped Meaghan in her arms. "It's going to be okay."

Meaghan wriggled free. "Is it, Mom? Is it really?"

Wanda turned to me for help.

"Yes, it is," I lied, not remotely sure of Ziggy's future. How I wished Fiona was with me so she could sprinkle a cheery potion on my pal to lift her spirits.

Meaghan directed her clerk, the forty-something part-timer with the French twist, to see to the customer viewing the array of Hunter Hock's works and turned back to me. "You know something. What are you holding back?"

"I don't think the police have found the weapon the killer used."

"It wasn't the gazing ball?" She looked hopeful.

"Nope. They came across yours beneath your front steps with only your fingerprints on it."

"I didn't—"

"Don't worry. They don't think you killed him," I said to assuage her. "They ruled out the gazing ball as the murder weapon because it didn't have any trace evidence on it."

"Trace evidence." She wrinkled her nose as if she'd smelled something horrid.

"In fact, I don't think whatever was used was found at the crime scene."

"Then Ziggy can't be guilty!" she exclaimed. "I've got to call—"

"Hold on," Wanda said. "Why don't you think they've found the murder weapon, Courtney?"

"Because Detective Summers wouldn't reveal what it was, meaning he might not know."

"You've spoken to him?" Meaghan asked.

"He's—" I faltered. "Yes. He's right next door. With Renee. He was cagey when I asked about the weapon. If they don't have it, then I agree, Ziggy can't be guilty," I went on, throwing my friend a lifeline, not adding that he might have found a way to ditch the murder weapon—whatever it turned out to be—prior to my arrival on the scene.

Meaghan swooped me into a hug. "Thank you for being your nosey self."

"I'm not nosey."

"Okay, you're a curious citizen, and I mean that in the nicest way." She hugged me again and released me.

"Detective Summers would like me to butt out."

"I'll bet he would." She snickered. "I'm going to call Miss Judge, and I'll think positively and not dwell on the *What ifs*. Ziggy is strong. Resilient. He's fought so many battles in his life, this will be a blip on the map."

"That's my girl," Wanda said.

Meaghan eyed her mother's package. "What have you brought, Mom? I thought we'd discussed all your clients' works last week. I have no need of another artist right now. We have too much in the shop as it is." She flourished a hand at the other artwork.

"This is something new I've been working on," Wanda said. She unfurled the tarp.

Meaghan said, "Ooh, I love it."

I gasped. It was an acrylic painting of yet another fairy portal, but it wasn't merely any portal. It was the place I'd seen the frollick of fairies awaiting the arrival of the queen fairy. "Um, Wanda, where did you . . . how did you . . ." I pressed my lips together. Just because she'd painted the portal didn't mean she'd seen that particular one. There were plenty of places at Garland Ranch that were similar. "It's beautiful."

Wanda thanked me. "I keep having this vision in my head."

Oho. Was some fairy working overtime to help her break-through? Not Fiona. That would have been against the rules for her. Maybe Callie, Meaghan's intuitive fairy, was taking on the challenge. Or Merryweather of Song. Wanda was often at the library. She loved attending events there.

"As for my career as an artist's representative . . ." Wanda ran her lips between her teeth. "I'm thinking about giving it up and devoting all my time to painting."

"No, Mom, you can't," Meaghan said. "You're not earning enough yet. It could take a long time to build up your street cred as an artist."

"Sweetheart, I've been saving money for years." She motioned to her work. "If I don't take a risk now, then when will I? You said yourself that my work is excellent. It's heartfelt."

"Yes, but—"

"And Violet Vickers has asked me to put one of my pieces on display at her soirée," Wanda gushed. "How wonderful is that!"

"Wanda, that's terrific," I said. "Congratulations."

"Yes, Mom," Meaghan said, "it's great, but—"

"Meaghan!" Hunter Hock strode into the gallery, his face pinched with concern. "How are you? I heard the news. What a shock. I mean, I know Nicolas could ruffle feathers, but drive someone to murder him?" He glimpsed me and said, "Sorry to interrupt." His gaze returned to my pal. "But, honestly, Meaghan, how are you?"

"I'm okay," she said.

"Do the police know who did it?"

"No."

"They have a suspect," Wanda inserted.

"Who is the wrong suspect," Meaghan said adamantly.

"Who?" Hunter asked.

"Ziggy," Wanda replied.

"Ziggy." Hunter snorted. "Not a chance. I mean, sure, Ziggy can be hot-tempered, but murder? Nah."

"That's what I think, too," Meaghan said.

Hunter scrubbed his jaw. "I heard Nicolas was at your house to beg you to take him back."

"Who told you that?" Meaghan asked.

"I overheard someone talking at the coffee shop around the corner."

"That's idle gossip. Don't go spreading rumors." She held up a palm to silence him. "No one is sure why Nicolas was there."

"Why else would he have gone to your place? Do you still have some of his stuff at your house?"

"Hunter, please."

"Okay. That's private. I get it." He raised both arms. "We won't discuss this right now."

"You're right. We won't. Now or ever." Meaghan eyed the telephone on the sales counter as if she were itching to get rid of Hunter, her mother, and me so she could call Miss Judge. "If that's all you came for."

"It's not, actually." Hunter shoved his hands into his pockets. "I'm here to talk to you about Flair's cut. It's too big a margin."

"It's what we charge all our artists."

"But I'm your best seller. I'm a draw."

Meaghan frowned. "When Ziggy gets back, we'll set an appointment to chat."

"Where is he?"

"In jail," Wanda said.

"Whoa!" Hunter bit back a gasp. "Have they got something on him? Did he have a motive?"

"Yes, to both questions," Wanda answered.

"Mother!"

"But the police couldn't find the murder weapon," Wanda added.

"Mom, that's not . . ." She huffed. "Leave. You and I will talk." She aimed a hand at the door.

"But—"

"Go. Please." Meaghan rubbed the back of her neck, as if trying to ward off an oncoming headache. "You, too, Hunter."

"I'm not sorry about Nicolas being dead," Hunter said. "He was a louse."

Meaghan gawked at him. So did I.

In fact, his loathing was so visceral, I said, "Where were you when it happened?"

"Huh?" He whirled on me.

"Yesterday, around five in the afternoon."

"Are you accusing me of something, Courtney? If so, come right out and say it." His face flushed the color of his hair. "I didn't kill the jerk, although I've certainly dreamed about it once or twice. The way he treated Meaghan and all the other . . ." He let the sentence hang. "Fine. If you insist on knowing my whereabouts—because the police will get to me eventually—for your edification, I was home painting. In my studio. All night. Alas, nobody saw me. Not even fairies, pixies, or brownies."

"Hunter, cut it out," Meaghan said.

"When I paint, I'm in total solitude," he continued, his voice taut.

"Doesn't your studio have windows to let in the light?" I asked.

"One."

"You live in the cottage behind your sister's house, don't you?"

"Yes."

"Maybe she or someone in her family saw you. One of your nieces, perhaps?"

"No, no, and no!" His nose flared with exasperation. "They were off to the City for an adventure." The City was a local's nickname for San Francisco. "I don't have a verifiable alibi. That's what they call it, don't they? Verifiable? But I don't need one because I didn't do it." He dentalized all the *D*s and *T*s to make his point. "Look, you don't believe me, so be it. I don't have to explain myself to any of you."

"You hated Nicolas," Meaghan said. "Why?"

"Because he treated you like dirt." He grumbled. "You deserve better. Someone like—" He blew out a quick breath.

"Like you?" I asked gently. "Is that why you've left Meaghan all those garden ornaments? To win her heart?"

"Courtney, don't," Meaghan said.

Hunter gazed haplessly at Meaghan. "You know it was me?"

"I figured it out," she said. "A couple of friends have seen you slip through the gate. And Callie—" She stopped herself, doubtlessly realizing that if Hunter didn't believe in fairies and pixies, he wouldn't want her fairy brought into the conversation. "The gazing ball is beautiful. And the trio of fairies dancing on a dandelion . . ."

"I know you like to believe in fairies."

"It's very pretty."

"I . . ." He cleared his throat. "I left them to inspire you."

"To inspire me?"

"You're an artist, but you don't pursue it. If you don't do so now, when will you?"

Wanda snuffled. "I've been telling her that for years."

"I have a business to run," Meaghan said. "I can't spend my precious time painting. There's no guarantee."

"That's always her excuse," Wanda said.

Hunter smiled warmly at Meaghan, his miff about being accused of murder vanished. He drew closer to her and lowered his voice. "You've got to try. Art will never blossom if you deny it."

When I returned to the shop, Joss had cleaned up the morning's fairy door class items and had set out the necessary pieces for the afternoon's class—the one that we'd canceled yesterday. The four mothers and their tween daughters were due any moment, she advised me. Fiona glided to me and asked where I'd gone.

"I should ask you the same thing."

"I went to visit Merryweather," she said. "Alone. With no other fairies around."

"Why?"

"I'd like to visit my sisters, but I can't, so I asked if they might be able to visit me."

I held out my hand so she could light on it. "Didn't you see them when you went through the portal in February?"

She plopped onto my palm. "No. I only saw my mother."

"And what did your aunt tell you?"

"I have to hone my sixth sense first."

Many fairies could tap into the universal source, but young fairies, like Fiona, needed more maturity to use it wisely.

"It's okay." Her beautiful eyes pooled with tears. She swiped them away. "Merryweather said they understand why I'm gone, and I understand, too. As Winnie-the-Pooh would say, 'Life is but a journey, not a problem to be solved.'"

My eyes widened. "Now you're reading A.A. Milne?"

"They're classics. I'm also memorizing Dr. Seuss books."

"Why?" I asked, astounded.

"Because memorization improves the mind."

"No, I meant, why Dr. Seuss?"

"Because his stories make me laugh, and who doesn't need to laugh?"

Her answer brought a smile to my face. I extended a finger, and she rested on it. "You amaze me," I said.

She curtsied. "Does that mean I'm amazing?"

I chuckled. "Don't let it go to your head." I lifted my hand and blew on her. She soared away, giggling riotously.

Half an hour later, I began the fairy door class with the tweens and mothers in the same way I started many of my classes, by inviting my students to sit at the workstation table, after which I shifted to my taller but smaller instructional table to demonstrate. First, I gave them the same instructions I'd given the Happy Diggers about glue gun safety. All of the students assured me they were old pros with crafts. They knew that acrylic paint didn't take too long to dry, and they knew to brace the backs of doors with other sticks.

I lifted a tiny acorn from a bowl. "If you want to add a doorknob, think about using something this size as a knob or use a pebble or even a button. Whatever your heart desires. The beauty of making fairy gardens, and in this case, fairy doors, is there is no right or wrong. It's up to you and your vision."

For the next while, I rounded the table, advising and giving tips. The happy chatter between parents and their children always thrilled me. There was almost nothing that could bond people more than sharing a craft.

"Courtney." Violet Vickers strode onto the patio, hailing me with a hand. Her face was drawn. The jacket of her linen suit was buttoned improperly and out of alignment. "It's tragic."

I apologized to my students and strode to Violet. I told her to take a seat at one of the wrought-iron tables.

"I can't believe Nicolas is dead." She dabbed her face with a pretty handkerchief.

Fiona alit on the table. "Lilies of the valley," she said, studying the embroidery on Violet's handkerchief. "Popular for brides because the flowers represent chastity, motherhood, and purity. Is she getting married? She looks so sad."

I wanted to shush her but couldn't. Violet might want to believe in fairies, but she had yet to see one. I didn't want to spook her in her time of need.

"That brother of his," Violet said. "Do you think he killed Nicolas?"

"The police are focusing on Ziggy Foxx. They have him in custody."

"Nonsense. Ziggy couldn't kill anyone. But that brother. He has a mean streak. He's a tyrant. I was on my way to tell the police about the row yesterday, but then I saw your shop and thought I could take a moment to calm myself first. The police won't listen to an hysterical woman. Plus, I could use some advice."

"Advice?"

Violet heaved a sigh. "And am I wrong to want to show Nicolas's work at the foundation event? Will that be too macabre?"

I shuddered. It might be, but who was I to judge? "I think he would be honored, and I think your guests will understand."

Joss brought a tray set with two cups of tea and two small plates of lemon butter cookies to the table.

"Who made these?" I asked.

"I did. It's my aunt's recipe. Enjoy. I'll check out the customers and ring up the students," she whispered to me. "You take your time."

I nodded, my focus returning to Violet.

"Does Nicolas have family other than his brother?" Violet asked. "Are his parents alive?"

"I don't know."

"Neither do I. What does that say about me? I never asked him personal questions, which shows a complete lack of interest." She nibbled the edges of a cookie and set it back down. "He hasn't ever married, has he? He and Meaghan . . ."

"They considered it but never got engaged."

"He had no children?"

"None." As far as I knew.

"Who will inherit his estate?"

Good question.

"Did he have other wealth? A home?"

"He was staying in an Airbnb."

"Possessions? Did he own that Beemer?" She gently drummed the edge of the table. "There is so much to consider after death. My husband always said . . ." She let the sentiment hang. "He handled all of these things in the past. I may be a businesswoman, but he was extraordinary in this regard."

She'd loved her husband very much. They'd met in college and had traveled the world.

"Of course, Nicolas's art might fetch a pretty penny posthumously," she went on. "Especially those that had not yet been seen, like the three for the event." She sipped her tea and pushed it aside. "Although so much of being an artist is about telling a personal story, isn't it? What was he thinking when he painted this or that? One will never know."

Fiona perched on Violet's shoulder and crossed her ankles daintily. "It's sweet how much she loved him."

Like a patron would, I figured. Not in a lustful way. She appreciated art and talent far beyond anyone I knew.

"What will his fans think if I buy all of his work? Will they consider me a monster? Would they consider me selfish?" Her eyes pooled with fresh tears. "As you can see, I'm adrift, Courtney. Truly adrift."

"I understand." I patted her hand.

She rose to her feet. "I suppose it's time to visit the police. What Payton Buley said yesterday—that he would make Nicolas pay or else—those are threatening words."

Chapter 10

Believe in Fairies
Who make dreams come true.
Believe in the wonder,
The stars and the moon.
—Anonymous

By the time I got home, I was drained, but I knew I had work to do. The centerpiece gardens I'd promised Violet were not going to make themselves. I fed Pixie and Fiona—she had her heart set on mallow—and then I prepared a snack of cheese and crackers for myself and set it and a glass of sparkling water on a tray. When my two companions were done eating, I took the tray to the backyard, and they trailed me.

"Courtney! Hello!" Holly was stringing party lights through the arc-shaped heads of poles along the fence abutting our properties. Her Pomeranians, out of view, were barking their heads off. Her sister Hedda was helping her string. "*Shh,*" Holly ordered the dogs. "Hush."

"Do you want me to look at your garden now?" I asked.

"Heavens, no. Hedda and I are getting ready for a date with our beaus."

"Stop!" Hedda said. "They're not our beaus."

"They are, and that's the last you'll disagree with me, young lady."

Hedda huffed and smoothed the sleeves of her white sheath. Holly laughed. I loved how she spoke to her sister with such fondness. The words *young lady* were a total tease.

"Jeremy adores you," Holly said. "He's your beau, pure and simple."

"Well, your *beau* is smitten with you, too."

"Yes, he is." Holly fussed with the collar of her Monet-inspired top. She loved donning bold, statement-making clothing. "And well he should be. I'm a catch."

Her boyfriend, a local sculptor who worked as a part-time carpenter, was the man who had installed Holly's art studio last year. His work with driftwood was interesting. I wasn't sure it sold well; it wasn't to my liking, but then, I didn't invest in a lot of art. I loved my mother's work and Meaghan's and her mother's. The remainder of my decorating budget went to fairy gardens and garden décor.

"Courtney, did I tell you my beau is going to speak to Meaghan this week to see if she'll sell his pieces at Flair?" Holly asked.

"I wish him luck."

I didn't think Holly cared whether or not he sold anything. She simply appreciated that he had an artist's sensibility. He was a skilled carpenter. Her studio had turned out beautifully, allowing for light at all times of the day.

"I'm so sorry about how our sister acted earlier," Holly went on as she looped off the strand of lights she was stringing. "Hattie can be so pushy. Poor Zinnia barely got a word in edgewise."

"Do you know if Zinnia followed up with the police?" I asked.

Hedda said, "I believe she did. You know Zinnia. She's all about following rules."

Holly arched an eyebrow. "Like you're not?"

Holly's black cat Phantom bounded to the top of the fence.

Fiona inspected the cat from above. Phantom swung a paw in Fiona's direction, but she eluded him by doing a backflip, which made him hiss.

"How is dear Meaghan doing?" Holly asked.

"She's okay," I said.

"It must be difficult losing someone you love to murder."

I replied as I had to Glinda, saying that Meaghan wasn't in love with Nicolas anymore.

"No, of course not," Holly said. "I meant *used to love*. How could she love him after he took off for Arizona without a backward glance?"

"Well, she was the one who'd ended it."

"Yes, of course, which begs the question, why did he return? Do you think he wanted to woo her again? He was on her property, after all, when he met his fateful end."

"Yes, why was he there?" Hedda asked.

"No one knows." I thought of Hunter Hock and the rumor that he'd overheard. Was it possible the killer had lured Nicolas to Meaghan's under the pretense of being Meaghan and open to reconciliation? No, a phone call wouldn't have convinced him. He would've recognized her voice. The killer would have needed to text him to pull it off. Had the police recovered Nicolas's cell phone?

Hedda said, "You know, his brother Payton has accounts at Carmel Bank." That was where Hedda worked as a loan officer. "And I probably shouldn't be telling anyone this—"

"Then don't," Holly said.

Hedda glowered at her. "I'm not usually vindictive, but I don't like the guy. He's a bully to the officer whose cubicle abuts mine, so he deserves to be outed."

"She's not vindictive," Holly said in her sister's defense. "That's true. Our mother always said Hedda got the best of the Hopewell genes."

Fiona wafted around Hedda. She must have felt something because she shook her head before refocusing on me. On the other hand, Holly seemed oblivious to Fiona's antics, confirming my suspicion that she hadn't actually seen her yesterday.

"Anyway, Courtney," Hedda went on, "I heard Payton Buley was forced to take out a second mortgage on his house because, apparently, his brother hadn't paid him back for something."

I said, "That might explain why Payton stormed into Violet Vickers's house yesterday looking for Nicolas. Do you know how much Nicolas owed him?"

Hedda shook her head. "You should have heard Payton bemoaning his fate to my coworker. Apparently, he neglected to get Nicolas to sign any kind of document stating he'd borrowed from him. Not even something written on a cocktail napkin."

Holly clucked her tongue. "Now, that's a bad business practice."

"Especially for someone who's a town comptroller," I said. "Payton should have been more fiscally responsible."

"Yes, it sounds easy to do on paper, but . . ." Hedda spread her arms. "I can't tell you how many times I've seen families get into trouble like this, trusting one another to do the right thing until there's a rift. Two weeks ago, my colleague begged Payton to fly to Arizona and get Nicolas's signature on the dotted line."

"Did he go there?" I asked.

Hedda shrugged.

"Do you know if Payton is Nicolas's heir?" I asked.

Hedda pursed her lips. "Well, that's a valid question, isn't it? Follow the money."

Fiona echoed the sentiment. "Follow the money."

With thoughts of Payton and Nicolas cycling through my mind, I retreated with Fiona and Pixie to my greenhouse. I placed my snack tray on a shelf and set about finalizing the centerpieces, nibbling a slice of cheese and a cracker as I finished each one. For the lime-green one, I used an enchanting duo of a boy and girl in green tunics with acorn hats. For the lemon-yellow one, I chose a grouping of dancing girl fairies with extraordinarily long limbs. For the ice-blue garden, I settled on a Disney figurine of Tinkerbell. Typically, I was loath to use anything Disney in my gardens; however, when I first visited Violet at her house, she let me in on a secret that, as a girl, her lifelong dream had been to graduate college and work at Disneyland as Tinkerbell.

I put together three more and stifled a yawn. "Half done. That's good enough. It's quitting time." I headed to the house to prepare for bed.

Fiona trailed me. "Tell me about Tinkerbell."

Pixie padded behind me, warbling loudly as if she, too, were eager to hear the story.

As I did my ablutions, I told Fiona all about Peter Pan and the lost boy's adventures with Tinkerbell.

"Humans think fairies are like her?" Fiona asked. "Impetuous and temperamental?"

I chuckled. "I suppose so."

I crawled into bed and turned out the light. Fiona nestled on the pillow beside my head, and Pixie turned in circles on my comforter near my feet until she settled down.

"Humans should know the truth about fairies," Fiona said. "They need to know how much we nurture nature. How we like to inspire. How we treasure order and peace. That we are not impetuous."

"Oh, no?" I teased.

"Only sometimes."

I stroked her wing with my fingertip. "Don't worry. What did you tell me a year ago? We will win humans over one heart at a time."

"One heart at a time," she said sleepily.

Joss was at the shop when Pixie, Fiona, and I arrived Friday morning.

"You're here early," I said, setting Pixie on the floor. I retreated to the office to stow my purse and returned to the sales counter to pour myself a cup of coffee. I hadn't felt like having a cup after my morning run. Now? I needed stimulation.

"I went to see my mom," she explained as she cleaned the shelves with a bright orange feather duster. "The nursing home allows me to come at six a.m. because that's when Mom is fresh and alert. Not all family members are granted entry, but they like me."

"How is she doing?" I asked.

"Not so good, but she knew me. That's always a plus."

"Maybe Fiona could go with you one time and help boost her spirits."

Joss shook her head. "My mother will never see a fairy."

"How do you know?"

"She says it's ridiculous. Her heart is hardened."

Ah, yes, a hardened heart did have trouble processing magic.

"Perhaps I could sprinkle her with a mind-freeing potion," Fiona offered.

"Perhaps."

Fiona kissed Joss's cheek and flew to the patio. Pixie sprinted after her.

"About tomorrow's tea," Joss said. "We've put aside extra copies of *A Spell for Trouble* in case customers want to purchase one for a friend. Also, I didn't think Meaghan . . ." She paused. "You know . . . because, um . . . Nicolas died . . . would want to play her harp, so I asked Twyla to perform solo. It'll work out great, seeing as mermaids love flute music."

"Got it," I said. "You're right. Meaghan wouldn't have wanted to play."

"Twyla is learning a beautiful rendition of 'Variations on the Mermaid' for the occasion."

I knuckled her arm. "You're so clever. Whatever you want to do, you're in charge."

Close to noon, as I was passing by the sales counter, my cell phone rang. Meaghan was calling. I answered. "Good morning. What's up?"

"Do you have time to take a walk with me?" She sounded stuffed up, like she'd been crying for a long, long time.

Joss, who was ringing up a customer, must have heard Meaghan's request. She made a shooing motion for me to go.

I said, "Yes. Meet me in front."

Seconds later, Meaghan stopped by the Dutch door and rapped on it. "Hello-o-o."

I hurried outside and noticed she was wearing a lacy sweater that didn't look warm enough. Me? Though it was sunny when I'd awakened, it had been nippy, so I'd donned a thick Irish sweater and jeans. "Do you want a jacket?" I hooked a thumb toward the shop. I always kept a few on hand.

She wagged her head. "I'll be fine. Can we stop by Percolate? I need caffeine."

Fiona must have sensed the urgency. Like a soldier on alert, she appeared in a flash and fluttered beside me.

Together, we rounded the corner to our second favorite coffee shop.

The aroma of baked goods tickled my senses as I entered. So did the rich scent of arabica coffee. "Two Americanos," I said to the barista, who was dressed in a turquoise uniform to match the décor.

Tulip-shaped pendant lights illuminated the wares. On the whitewashed brick wall hung a huge chalkboard with the day's specials. A number of free-floating shelves behind the counter held plants, loaves of bread, tins of tea, and gift boxes.

I paid for the coffees, and Meaghan, Fiona, and I returned outside, turning left toward the center of town.

"I need to walk," Meaghan said.

"And talk."

"Yes. Did you know . . ." She pulled to a stop and sighed. "Did you know there are rumors that Nicolas was seeing a lot of different women, not only here but in other cities?"

"Oh, my," Fiona whispered.

"When we were together, he told me he was faithful to me. To *me,*" she stressed. "Am I the densest woman on the planet? Shouldn't I have known?" She couldn't keep the pitiful whine out of her voice. "Shouldn't I have suspected?"

"Do you know any of the women?"

"A woman named Winona Jacobi who's a nanny for some fancy schmancy San Francisco elite."

That had to be Sassy's sister, the one Violet had mentioned.

"And there was a travel agent in Albuquerque. A museum curator in San Diego. A spa owner in Palm Springs. And one more, a woman who teaches arts and crafts at the Monterey Bay Aquarium."

"Addie Tan?"

"Yes, that's the name."

"They were friends. That was all. She came into the shop the other day. Between you and me, I think she wanted him to fall for her, but he wouldn't pursue it."

"But the others." Meaghan used her coffee-holding hand for emphasis.

"Who told you about them?"

"A pointillist who wants us to sell some of her work. Her art isn't exactly what we hawk, but I kept her talking to get the skinny."

"And she revealed everything?"

"I think she felt relieved to finally be able to tell the truth now that he's dead. She was friends with the museum curator." Meaghan heaved a sigh. Fiona settled on Meaghan's right shoulder and toyed with her hair. "Do you think he actually slept with them all or simply led them on? I mean, ugh." She clutched her throat with one hand. "Can you imagine if I'd married him?"

I brushed her arm fondly. "Do you remember why you booted him to the curb?"

"Because Mom needed to stay with me."

"No-o-o," I said carefully.

She exhaled. Her chin began to quiver. "Because he twisted my elbow."

"It wasn't just that. For months, you told me you weren't sure you could trust him. You didn't know why, but you'd sensed it."

She wrapped one arm protectively around her core.

"He hid things from you. He wanted to keep separate bank accounts. That's not a good basis for a loving, equal relationship."

"True. But now that he's dead, I won't be able to find out why I wasn't good enough—"

"Stop!" I petted her shoulder. "Don't do that to yourself. You were good enough. You *are* good enough. He was the jerk. He was the one who was lacking."

She released her hold on herself and drew in a deep, cleansing breath. "I can't go home. I don't want to picture him lying there . . . in my yard . . . dead."

I understood. I certainly couldn't erase the image from my mind.

"But I do imagine it," she said, "and it's horrible."

A fairy hurried to us. Not a random fairy. It was Callie, her green wings shimmering in the filtered sunlight, her face pinched with concern.

Fiona zipped to her. "What's wrong?"

"I had a meeting with the queen fairy. She's concerned about the disruption in Meaghan's garden."

"The disruption?" I said. "You mean the murder?"

Callie wagged her head. "No. The digging. The delving. The police won't stop." She beat a fist against a palm.

Meaghan said, "It's okay. Detective Summers asked permission. The police are determined to find the murder weapon, and they think Ziggy buried it there."

"All the plants are suffering," Callie said.

"Won't you be able to repair any damage with your magical potions?" I asked.

"Yes. Sometimes. Not always. The queen fairy said we'll have to try that after they leave, but you should have seen her face. I've never seen her look so agitated."

"There, there," Fiona cooed as she gripped her pal's hands.

"Daylilies are hardy plants," I said. "But if the garden declines, Meaghan can replant."

"What about Ziggy?" Callie asked, her voice brittle.

"He's not guilty," I said.

"'The truth will out,'" Fiona crooned.

"You mean the truth will *come* out," Callie corrected.

"No, I meant what I said. It's a line from *The Merchant of Venice*. It's an idiom." Fiona was beaming, but not in a smug way. It was as if she'd surprised herself with her wealth of knowledge. "Let's go to the garden and see what we can divine," she suggested.

Callie agreed, and the two whooshed away.

Meaghan said to me, "Want to go to Devendorf Park and sit for a while? The sun's finally breaking through the clouds."

"Sure." As we walked, the question that had been gnawing at me surfaced. "Do you know whether Nicolas had family other than his brother?"

"He didn't. His mother died over twenty years ago."

"I had no idea. What happened to her? Cancer?" Because of my mother's illness, I often jumped to the conclusion that everyone who died had suffered from the dreaded disease.

"No. She fell down the stairs in their home. His father was beside himself with grief and said bad luck followed him everywhere he went. He vowed he would never marry again. I think Nicolas was eight at the time."

"Was foul play ever suspected?"

"Nicolas seemed to think it was karma. He admitted his father wasn't a very nice guy, but when his father died, the point was moot."

"Have you met Nicolas's brother Payton?"

"A few times. He and Nicolas never got along. Payton blamed Nicolas for everything bad that ever happened to him. His mother falling. His father dying."

"And yet Payton loaned Nicolas money."

Meaghan gasped. "He did? How much?"

"I don't know. He came to Violet Vickers's house demanding repayment on the day Nicolas . . ." I swallowed hard. "On the day he died."

Meaghan looped a hand around my free arm. "Can we stop talking about this for now? I just want to sip my coffee and drink in the fresh air."

"Sure."

Locals and tourists were out in droves because the weather was spectacular. Most were wearing hats or visors to block the sun. Many were carrying gift bags from various shops. Of course, I was wondering how I could gently steer them toward Open Your Imagination for a shopping spree. My mind was always working on growing the business.

"Look." Meaghan pointed.

Devendorf Park, located between Junipero and Mission Street at Ocean Avenue, was packed with artists of all stripes—painters, sculptors, weavers. One woman explained to us as we approached that it was an impromptu plein-air session. The mayor had put out a notice to drum up enthusiasm for the event that was coming in a couple of weeks.

Beneath the gigantic oak at the westernmost corner of the park, I noticed Addie Tan addressing a group of five children under the age of ten. The kids were sitting on a throw blanket and making origami—*zhezhi*—using neon-colored paper. At first glance, I thought the children were making balls, but they weren't exactly round. They were more like geodesic orbs. One of the children propelled his orb above the heads of the others, and the children began to bat it like a beach ball.

"Children, stop," Addie said, her voice cracking.

Of course, they didn't obey. They were having too good a time.

"Please, enough!" Addie shouted. Like yesterday, her eyes were puffy. She removed the handkerchief jutting from beneath the sleeve of her black blouse and dabbed her nose and eyes. "All right, now, let's focus. We don't have long before your parents return. Collect the b-balls." The word caught in her throat. "Collect them and put them in the basket." A wicker basket sat at the center of the throw blanket. The children obeyed. "Okay, now do as I do." She settled onto the blanket and held up a piece of neon-green paper. "We're going to make trees."

The children squealed with glee.

As Meaghan and I headed toward a bench at the far side of the park, out of the corner of my eye, I spied Payton Buley striding purposefully toward Addie. His blue blazer was unbuttoned, and the tails of his loosely knotted tie were flapping up and down.

Out of nowhere, Fiona winged to me. "Uh-oh," she said. "He looks mad."

"What are you doing back so soon?" I asked. "You went with Callie to Meaghan's house."

"I saw. I assessed. Now I'm on my way to discuss the matter with Merryweather of Song." The library was a few blocks from the park. "Be careful," she warned, and off she went.

Payton pulled up beside the students, aimed a finger at Addie, and said something I couldn't make out. In a flash, she was on her feet and gesticulating at him. His face blazed with indignation. He inhaled sharply and held his breath, making him look like a chipmunk with cheeks full of acorns.

Addie said loudly, "I want it back. Nicolas promised."

"Don't contact me again," Payton snarled, and stomped away.

Addie's shoulders caved in as she sank to the blanket.

"What do you think that was about?" Meaghan asked.

"Nicolas must have had something personal of Addie's."

"Ick," Meaghan muttered.

"Don't go there," I cautioned her. "Undergarments wouldn't have warranted that kind of anger." My guess was Nicolas had something else of Addie's, something she didn't want anyone to see. Was it a stolen item she'd asked Nicolas to hold onto for safekeeping? An illegal substance that her employer would frown upon? Would she have killed Nicolas to get it back?

"Why did she think Payton had it?" Meaghan asked.

"If he will inherit Nicolas's estate, it's possible an attorney has given him access to Nicolas's personal effects."

We disposed of our coffee cups and decided to take the long route back to the courtyard. On our way, I was surprised to see Detective Summers and Officer Reddick entering Batcheller Galleries. We slowed as we were passing, and I peeked inside. The gallery, unlike Flair, was a single room and packed with an eclectic collection of art—everything from canvases to sculptures to antiques. Jeremy Batcheller, a handsome bleached-blond man in his sixties who loved keeping fit by playing catch with his dog, beckoned Summers and Reddick toward the sales counter. Nearby, his Dalmatian, which was lying on a dog bed, lifted its head for a nanosecond before going back to sleep.

Summers mimed something round, and I surmised he was asking Jeremy whether he either sold or had in stock a piece of round art, similar in shape to what I believed the murder weapon might look like. Jeremy shook his head.

"What's going on?" Meaghan whispered.

I shuttled her ahead, out of Summers's eyesight. "Considering all the excavation in your garden, I'm guessing the police have come up empty. The killer didn't dispose of the murder weapon at the crime scene."

"Then Ziggy couldn't have killed Nicolas!"

Chapter 11

Fairies are elusive, wondrous little things
We saw them best as children,
Tried to touch their fairy wings.
—Felicia Dorothea Browne-Hemans, "I Believe"

I didn't argue, but added, "Knowing what a stickler Detective Summers can be for details, he won't rule Ziggy out until he rules someone else in."

"Which means we have to find the real killer."

When we reached the courtyard, Meaghan was on her cell phone yet again, touching base with Miss Judge, Ziggy's attorney, this time to tell her about the lack of evidence. She blew me a kiss goodbye and entered Flair Gallery. I made a beeline for Sweet Treats. I was craving something sugary. I purchased a dozen snickerdoodles and returned to the shop.

After downing a couple of cookies, I spent the next two hours on the patio advising customers and arranging items for tomorrow's tea. Throughout the bustle, I couldn't stop thinking about who had killed Nicolas Buley. His brother clearly had a beef with him. Why had he lent him money? Had Nicolas refused to pay, thus sparking enough anger to bash in his head? Aside from the fact that Payton had taken out a second mortgage, killing a brother over a measly debt seemed unreasonable. Hunter Hock had no fond feelings for Nicolas, either, but was he a murderer? He struck me as a mild-mannered guy. Except he hadn't kept his anger in check the other day, had he? And his comments at Flair had been blistering. Had he met up with Nicolas outside Meaghan's and lost control? And what had Nicolas kept of Addie Tan's? Had she followed him to Meaghan's and pressed him for its return, only to have him laugh in her face?

Fiona zoomed to me, her gossamer hair tangled from the wind. Using her fingertips to smooth it, she said, "What's up? You look lost in thought."

I fetched the acrylic podium from the storage cabinet beyond the learning-the-craft area, wheeled it into place by my teaching table, and locked the foot in preparation for tomorrow's tea. "I was wondering . . ."

"About the murder."

"Yes. I shouldn't be thinking about it. I have no reason to worry. Ziggy shouldn't be a suspect for too much longer."

"Yet he is now."

"Yes," I said somberly.

"And you want answers. You want justice."

I nodded. "Also, I'm worried about Meaghan. I think she'll sleep easier once the police solve the case. It happened on her property, after all."

"'There is nothing more deceptive than the obvious fact,' Sherlock Holmes said." Fiona circled my head.

"Meaning?" I raised an eyebrow.

"It happened on her property."

I frowned. "That's what I said."

"Exactly. Why?"

"Why what?" I shook my head, plainly confused.

"Why was Nicolas there?"

"He wanted her back. That was obvious."

"Perhaps he wanted to share something, like a secret."

I tapped my chin with a fingertip, taking her theory one step further. "Or he was harboring a secret that someone else wanted kept confidential." I ruled out Addie Tan. I'd bet whatever Nicolas had of hers was physical.

Fiona hummed and flew away to play with Pixie, her job of stirring my imagination complete.

"I've been meaning to tell you . . ." Joss said as she crossed the patio with a tray of cups and saucers. "Glinda was in earlier." She started setting them on the tables, cups facedown. "She told me the police are canvassing every house in Meaghan's neighborhood. After hearing Zinnia Walker's account, they think it's possible others were out with their animals and racing helter-skelter when the rain started. Many might have mistaken or forgotten that they saw anything."

"It's a worthy beginning," I said.

Merryweather of Song soared into view. The mature fairy had iridescent gossamer hair and wings sporting matching polka dots. Whenever I saw her, I adored the gaiety in her eyes. No matter how dreadful a situation, she always managed a sparkle of hope. "We're here."

"We?" I tilted my head.

Callie and Zephyr, a nurturer fairy with expressive lavender eyes, lavender wings, and wispy silver hair, came into view.

"I love coming here," Zephyr said in her high-pitched voice. "I always feel inspired to play." Invariably prepared to encourage others, she never went anywhere without her flute. She pulled it from its bow-and-arrow style pouch and tootled a song that sounded similar to "Greensleeves."

Fiona whooshed to her friends and said to me, "We're having a *comhairle*, and I'm serving tea."

"A *comhairle*?" I repeated.

"A gathering. A council. A meeting. To discuss the situation at Meaghan's yard."

"Who's pouring?" I asked.

"I pour," she said matter-of-factly. "It's my duty."

With that, they flew *en masse* into the ficus.

"Who cooks for them?" Joss asked.

"Their teas consist of fruits and honey," I said. "They don't need cookies like we do."

Joss snaked a finger in front of my face. "There's something you're not telling me."

I widened my eyes innocently. "Nope."

"Mm-hmm. It has to do with Fiona. I'll figure it out. You know I will."

Before heading to bed last night, Fiona had reminded me that I was the sole human who could know she would become the next queen fairy. She'd given the queen fairy her word. If I was honest, it was taking all my resolve not to blurt it out to my clever assistant. I'd never been good with secrets.

"Will the fairy foursome be trying to crack the case while having tea?" Joss asked. "Can Callie intuit the truth?"

"I'm not sure in this instance she can, because Meaghan or someone Meaghan knows is involved."

"But that would seem the logical thing she could do to help her human." Joss shook her head. "Fairies have so many rules."

"It's how the fairy kingdom is able to remain in balance with ours."

She harrumphed and returned inside the shop to ring up a customer.

"Courtney!" Renee Rodriguez sauntered through the French doors, her long hair braided loosely, stray wisps wafting in her wake. She was carrying a gigantic clear box. "I've got goodies." She hefted the box onto a wrought-iron table, opened the latches, and removed the lid. "Here's half of what I owe you. I'll bring the rest tomorrow. Again, I'm so sorry about the others."

I lifted out an eight-inch pot adorned with a green fairy holding a single green flower, and I *ooh*ed. Renee truly had a deft touch with pottery. "I love this one." The fairy reminded me of Calliope.

She unloaded the rest. "I made this batch all pastels. Pink, green, yellow." She reached into the box and removed a smaller latched box. "I brought some of the figurines, too. The others are waiting for the glaze to dry before I fire them. I swaddled them in cotton so they wouldn't break. Want me to unwrap them?"

"Sure."

The first fairy had the lined face of an older woman, and if I didn't know better, I'd have sworn Merryweather of Song had posed for it. The figurine had the same twinkle in her eyes and the same rosy cheeks. The next reminded me of a troll doll with a broad nose, winsome smile, and a shock of pink hair.

"These are fabulous," I said.

Renee made a brief curtsey.

"Hey," I said, "about my pressing Dylan at Sweet Treats . . ."

"Don't worry. He doesn't hold it against you. In fact, he likes you and the way you think."

"*Pfft*. He does not."

"He does, too. I was telling him about the argument I heard between Nicolas and Sassy Jacobi, and he said, 'Not you, too. I don't need more Courtney Kellys offering their brilliant two cents.'" She chuckled. "FYI, *brilliant* is a rare compliment coming from him."

"Hold on," I said. "Did you just share confidential police information with me?"

She reddened. "No, I did not, and you're bulldozing right past the compliment I paid you. He said you were brilliant."

I sidled closer and lowered my voice. "You said you overheard Nicolas and Sassy arguing. Is that privileged information?"

"No, it's not, because I heard them. Me." She patted her chest. "And there were plenty of others who witnessed the spat, too. It wasn't private. They went at it right outside the café, in plain view of all."

"When?"

"Monday. Nicolas had recently come back to town. Sassy was upset that he hadn't contacted her. Hadn't written. Yada-yada. Then she started yelling 'How dare you' and 'Who do you think you are?' She swore the debt would be paid."

"What debt? To whom? To Nicolas's brother?"

"I don't know. I barely caught a word here and there. Dylan is following up." An impish smile spread across Renee's face. "Don't say I never gave you anything."

Around four p.m., I headed to the office to collect my purse, passing by Joss at the sales counter. "I'm off to Violet's house to check on my dad's progress. Can you handle the crowd?" Three customers were standing in line. The first's basket was overflowing with items from the shop.

Joss flicked a finger. "In my sleep. Have fun."

When I arrived at Violet's, there was nowhere to park, so I pulled in behind a VW Rabbit. I wouldn't be there long. I doubted I would hold anyone up. Walking into the foyer—the door was wide open—I saw Detective Summers questioning Sassy Jacobi. Renee had said he'd be following up. Was he asking about the public argument she'd had with Nicolas? Did he think she'd killed him?

"I'm here on business," I said in passing when Summers gave me a look. "My father." I hooked my thumb. "He's installing the garden."

Summers said, "Tell him hello for me."

My father and Summers had become friends. Not while my father was on the force. After his knee injury had sidelined him and he'd started the landscaping company. They occasionally played golf together, and he and Wanda had double-dated with Summers and Renee.

"I blocked a VW Rabbit in front," I said. "Do you know who owns—"

"That's mine," Sassy said, rearranging the hem of her peasant blouse over her jeans. "It's okay. I'll be around for a bit. Violet wants to go over the playlist."

As I headed away, I noticed Sassy lowering her gaze, like she didn't want to make eye contact with the detective. Oh, to be a fly on the wall. Was he asking her about her relationship to the deceased? Was he pressing to know more about the argument Renee had witnessed?

I crossed the terrace and descended the stairs leading to the lowest tier of Violet's backyard. The scent of the salty ocean was heavenly. Matching my breathing to the rhythm of the surf, I strode to my father, who was bent over the koi pond, arranging submerged aquatic plants. A dozen of his workers—men and women—were finalizing the planting of blue hydrangeas against the retaining wall.

"Looks beautiful, Dad," I said. The blue-tone flagstone border around the pond was exceptional, as were the scouring rush reeds inside the edge. "I love the water hyacinths."

"All of the plants help increase the oxygen in the water," he said, unable to take a compliment without also offering an educational tidbit. It was a lifelong habit. "They also provide shade for the koi, and they'll keep the string algae from cropping up."

"I know. Don't you remember when we planted the pond . . ." I halted. The year after my mother died.

"You did a superb job on that," he said without skipping a beat.

"That's what made me want to follow in your footsteps and learn how to landscape."

"Your fairy gardens are pretty." He rose to a stand. "I'm partial to the *Romeo and Juliet*-themed pot."

Heart be still!

"Your mother loved that story," he went on.

"It was ill-fated love."

"Yes, but they were so madly in love that it stirred the romantic in her."

I felt tears pressing the corners of my eyes and willed them away. How I missed my mother. I completely understood Fiona's desire to see her sisters and mother again. Aiming a finger at the koi pond, I said, "You know what would look great beside the pond? A mermaid."

He frowned. "Very funny."

"I'm not kidding. There's this two-piece statue I've seen. The center part of the mermaid is buried beneath the soil so only her upper torso and tail appear. Violet would love it. She adores a bit of whimsy."

"Ha-ha. Not happening." He removed his rubber gloves and slung an arm around me. "I could use a bottle of water. You?"

"Sure."

We grabbed two bottles from an ice chest and settled onto the cypress roll rocker. As we leaned back, a dolphin crested the ocean and dove back into the water.

"Did you see that?" I exclaimed.

"It's not a mermaid."

I elbowed him. "By the way, Detective Summers is here. He told me to say hello."

"What does he want with Violet?"

"He's not here for her. He's questioning a woman named Sassy Jacobi who might have been involved with Nicolas Buley."

"The singer."

"You know her?"

"Wanda and I heard her sing at the Lush Grape."

"That's the wine bar north of town, right?"

He nodded. "Somehow I can't see her with Nicolas." He paused. "That didn't come out right. Of course, I can't see her with him. He's dead. What I meant was they don't seem like a good fit. Not that Meaghan was a good fit, either. She wasn't. If I'm honest, I never trusted that kid . . . that young man." He used his water bottle to gesture. "Neither did Wanda. She said there was something sneaky about him. She couldn't put her finger on it. Like he was lying about something."

Sneaky. Lying. Interesting adjectives. I'd felt the same. Nicolas was never good enough, in my humble opinion, but then, I was overly protective of my friends, as was Ziggy.

Thinking of him made my breath snag. How was he faring?

Would the police release him soon? Without a weapon and other physical evidence, could they continue to incarcerate him? If I put my money on who the killer was, I'd still say Payton Buley, hands down.

"What're you mulling over?" my father asked.

"Nicolas's brother had it in for him because Nicolas owed him money."

"Killing him isn't the way to get him to pony up."

"True, but Payton has a temper. What if Nicolas pushed him too far?"

"Why would they have argued in Meaghan's yard?"

"I haven't figured that out. Nicolas did want to get back together with her. He'd sent her text messages. Perhaps he'd gone there hoping to talk with her." I drank half of my water. "The police didn't find the weapon at the crime scene."

"Dylan told you that?"

"Not in so many words."

My father swiveled on the rocker. "Look, I know how your curiosity about murder gets piqued, especially when a friend is involved, but this isn't your problem."

"Ziggy is in jail. Meaghan is worried."

"Dylan is a good cop."

"Yes, he is, but if he's not asking the right questions . . ." I polished off the water and capped the bottle.

"You don't know that he isn't. Miss Jacobi might have information about Nicolas's brother. Or the loan. She might be the key that unlocks the truth." He got to his feet, took my empty bottle, and tossed his and mine into a recycle trash can. After inhaling long and slow and exhaling, he said, "Is your fairy here?"

"No. Why? Did you think you saw her?" I smirked.

He chortled. "I was poking fun. Go tend to your gardens. I've got this covered. And don't worry. I'll keep Violet happy. You didn't need to come here to rein me in."

"Understood. If you need any help . . ."

"I've got plenty of willing hands on deck. What do you think of the hydrangeas?"

"I think they're gorgeous. Hey, that's where the mermaid could lie. Beneath them."

He knuckled my arm. "Go. No more talk about mermaids or . . ." His voice trailed off.

Or murder, I finished silently. *Got it.*

Sometimes my father could be like the see-no-evil monkey. If only he'd realize that my curiosity was a good thing. And my fairy was a blessing.

Chapter 12

Have you ever heard the tapping
Of the fairy cobbler men,
When the moon is shining brightly
Thro' the branches in the glen?
—Sybil Morford, "Fairies"

At the top of the stairs, I ran into Violet, who was giving a pro golfer I recognized a tour of the property. "Everything good, Courtney?" she asked.

"Yep. Dad is following your instructions to the letter."

"Excellent."

On my way out of the house, I caught sight of Sassy standing beside the VW Rabbit, typing something on her cell phone at record speed. I'd never learned how to use my thumbs to text. I hated making mistakes, and if I used my thumbs, that was all I did, one error after another. It took more time for me to erase and rewrite than to go slowly with one fingertip.

"I'm sorry for blocking you in," I said.

She stopped what she was doing. "Oh, it's you."

"It's me."

"Cute car," she said of my MINI Cooper.

"Thanks. It does the trick. Sorry I blocked you. I hope the detective was nice to you."

"Very nice. He asked me about Payton Buley coming here the
other day. I confirmed what Violet had told him, that he'd stormed
in looking for Nicolas. Did he ask you about that?"

If I recalled, he'd dismissed me, but I didn't care. "I'm sure yours
and Violet's accounts were enough corroboration."

"He also asked about my sister."

"Winona Jacobi."

"That's right. How did you know her name?"

"I heard she and Nicolas dated before you hooked up with him."

Sassy glanced at the entrance to the house and back at me. "Violet mentioned that to you, did she? *Hmmph.*" She snuffled. "She's a
bit of a gossip, that one. Nah, him and I hadn't hooked up in the romantic way. We were sort of friends with benefits."

Why had she intimated to Violet that they'd had a *thing*? "Does
the detective want to question your sister?" I asked, pulling my key
fob from my pocket.

"Nah. I mean, yeah. He'd heard they had a tumultuous relationship, but I told him she couldn't have had anything to do with Nicolas's death. She's in Europe. She landed a gig as a nanny for an
ambassador's family."

"I heard she was working in San Francisco."

"She relocated to Paris two months ago."

"Wow. Paris. That's a big change."

"Yeah, she had a good life here, but she loves to travel. She's
gotten that in spades."

I opened the MINI and tossed in my purse. "When did she and
Nicolas date?"

"It was off and on. Before he started seeing Meaghan Brownie, if
that's what you're wondering. I know she's your friend."

I breathed a tad easier. Maybe the pointillist who'd told Meaghan
about the other women had her timelines mixed up. "I'm sorry your
sister and Nicolas broke up." I rotated my hand.

"Yeah, he wasn't the easiest guy to get along with."

"But you did?"

A hesitant smile made her lips twitch. "I didn't press him. I knew when to back off."

"What do you know about his relationship with his brother?"

"They were always at it. Payton was domineering, you know, the timeworn older brother syndrome, I suppose. He raised Nicolas after their father died, and it wasn't pretty. Nicolas told me Payton hit him more times than he could count."

I winced. "I had no idea."

"Nicolas was too proud to tell many people."

Not even Meaghan, I realized. "Hey, someone said they saw you and Nicolas arguing last Monday. Something about a debt you owed."

Sassy blinked. "Detective Summers asked me about that." Her voice grew thin. "But I told him the eyewitness got it wrong. We weren't arguing about me or my debt. We were discussing what Nicolas owed Payton. He told me to keep my nose out of his business"—her voice caught, and tears misted her eyes—"like I would insert myself." She made a hacking sound. "I wouldn't do that, but he could be melodramatic. He had an artist's temperament."

"Did he tell you why he owed Payton money?"

She shook her head. "Nah. He was private about things like that." She heaved a sigh, pocketed her cell phone, and opened her car door. "I'm going to miss him."

On my way back to the shop, I phoned Meaghan and asked her to meet me at Hideaway Café for dinner. I figured she could use a little bolstering. She leapt at the chance.

After finalizing receipts at the shop, I took Pixie home, fed her, changed into a simple black on black ensemble and ballet flats, and walked back to the café. The night air was warmer than it had been earlier in the day, giving me a spring to my step.

Fiona met up as I neared the courtyard. "There you are."

"Where have you been? Was your tea nice?"

"Yes. Merryweather of Song wants to teach Callie, Zephyr, and me plant psychology."

"Plant psychology? That's a thing? C'mon."

"Don't make fun. Plants have several different forms of memory, like fairies and people do. They even have transgenerational memory. How cool is that?" She spiraled in the air.

"So Zephyr and Callie are no better than you at this stuff?"

"We'll see. We all come to the world with different levels of expertise. Merryweather enlisted Cedrick Winterbottom to help. He's a wizard with plants! He uses photokinesis to engage them."

Cedrick was a mature nurturer fairy we'd met when I'd put together an adult fairy garden party for a client. He lived in her cypress tree and had been her fairy for years, staying steadfast even when, as a girl, she'd lost her ability to see him.

I said, "Okay, now you're pulling my leg."

"No I'm not. On my honor." She crisscrossed her heart. "You should have seen what happened when he projected light at our first lesson," Fiona said. "It turned into this ball and went flash-bam!" She made a series of exploding sounds, then threw her arms wide, her fingers pulsing with energy. "It was amazing."

"Did anyone in the shop notice Cedric's fireworks?" I asked. How could a frollick of fairies interact with nature on such a grand scale and not draw attention to themselves?

"Silly. We didn't stay there. When he showed up, we went to a private glen for the class." She cocked her head. "Where are you off to?"

"Dinner with Meaghan. Want to come?"

"I'm exhausted." She yawned. "I'll stay at the shop tonight."

I wagged a finger. "Don't do anything you'll regret."

"I won't. I really am tired. Plant psychology doesn't come naturally to a righteous fairy."

"Not even the queen fairy to be?" I teased.

She clucked her tongue. "G'night."

"If you change your mind, you know where I am."

She saluted and blazed left, and I veered right toward the café.

As I was entering, something niggled the back of my brain about the conversation I'd had with Sassy about her argument with Nicolas. It dawned on me that her tone had changed with her answer. It hadn't merely gone up a tad. It had risen to an almost childish pitch. When I was a little girl and I lied to my father, my voice would skate upward, too.

Brady met me at the hostess's station. "Hi, beauty. Meaghan is already at your table." He beckoned me to follow him. "Care to stay late and have a nightcap with me? I'm off by nine."

"I would love that."

"And then we can chat about"—he hitched his chin—"that."

I followed his gaze, and my mouth fell open. George Pitt, with his swoop of salt-and-pepper hair, rugged jawline, and broad shoulders, was sitting at a table for two in the far corner. He was even more stunning in person than he was on screen, if that was possible. Customers were craning their necks to get a peek at him. Opposite him was a woman I'd only seen in the tabloids—Brady's ex-wife, Finley, known for her yoga parties and do-gooder deeds. She was girl-next-door pretty with a swan-like neck, cheekbones for days, and round eyes that gave her a look of complete innocence. The banged auburn bob and soft blue poplin blouse with French bow that she was wearing enhanced her virtuosity. If I didn't know she'd had an affair with Pitt while married to Brady, I'd have bought into her façade.

"Did you know they'd made a reservation?" I whispered.

"Nope," he said. "I'm glad you gave me a heads-up about them coming to town. Finley hates Carmel, but she's patently enjoying flaunting her husband to people that knew her from way back when."

"*Hmmph*," I muttered. "It takes nerve to walk in here like nothing went down between you two."

"Here we are." He pulled out my chair and traced a finger up the back of my neck as I sat.

The zing I felt settled me. So what if his ex was in town. Big deal. He didn't love her anymore and never would.

Meaghan had ordered chardonnay for each of us, and for the next hour, over a dinner of perfectly prepared rotisserie chicken, roasted root vegetables, and garlic mashed potatoes, I filled her in about my thoughts about Nicolas's murder.

"Nicolas owed his brother money. If he balked at paying—"

"I still can't fathom that," she cut in. "Why would he have borrowed from Payton? He had money. Plenty of money. His art is selling at a premium. I forwarded all sorts of hefty checks to Arizona."

"Hedda Hopewell told me Payton was extremely upset. He'd had to take out a second mortgage on his house. FYI, Violet Vickers and Sassy Jacobi have both told Detective Summers about Payton making a scene on Wednesday."

"Do you think the police have questioned him?"

"By now? I'd bet yes."

"Does he have an alibi?"

"For all we know, he went back to work and has dozens of people who will corroborate his whereabouts. City comptrollers work nine to five, I'm pretty sure. He—"

"Courtney," a woman with a dulcet voice said.

I twisted in my chair, expecting to see our waitress.

"I'm sorry to intrude," Finley Pitt said, moving closer. She had a dimple in her chin that I hadn't noticed from afar, and her skin was so creamy I doubted she'd ever—and I mean ever—sat in the sun. "I'm Finley Pitt. George Pitt's wife." She acknowledged George by blowing him a kiss. He caught it in one hand.

My stomach lurched with something close to nausea.

"I asked Brady if he'd like to have a nightcap with us," Finley continued, "but he said he'd promised to have a drink with you. Would you mind if we joined?"

Oh, man. A double date? No, no, no. Brady and I did that months ago with my ex-fiancé and his wife, and it wasn't fun.

"She wouldn't mind at all," Meaghan answered for me. "In fact,

I was going to join, too, if that's all right. I'd love to find out what George is working on next."

I cut a sharp glance at her. She was biting back a wicked smile. She didn't go to the movies. She certainly didn't read the tabloids.

"Sure. The more the merrier." Finley pressed her hands together in prayer. "Thank you."

I half-expected her to say *Namaste* and then burst into a cleansing soul hum. But she didn't, thank heavens.

Without dallying, or giving me time to renege, she spun on her heel and sashayed back to George. "We're on!" she said gleefully for all to hear.

A woman at the next table snapped a photograph of Finley and George. Grinning mischievously, Finley planted a smackeroo on George's cheek and stayed put so the woman could get another shot. *Ugh.*

I caught sight of Brady watching the exchange. He shrugged a shoulder, as if saying his ex had a strong, untamable personality.

I turned my attention back to my conniving pal. "Why did you say yes?"

"Because I need a diversion." She blew me a kiss.

I caught it in one hand . . . and crushed it.

An hour later, when most of the customers had left for the night, Brady sauntered to the patio carrying a bottle of Courvoisier and five crystal brandy snifters. He set them on our table and hailed Finley and George.

After Brady made introductions, they sat and accepted a modest pour.

"Cheers," George said. "Great making your acquaintance. I can't tell you how hard it is to find true friends in this day and age. Everyone expects something from me. From *us.*" He motioned to include Finley. "It's exhausting."

True friends, I mused. *Is that what we're becoming? As if.*

"Brady, darling," Finley said, "I love what you've done with the café. The décor is fab, and the food is faber."

George said, "Yes, the dinner was delicious."

"Courtney"—Finley eyed me—"Brady tells me that you're dabbling in the fairy world."

"I didn't say dabbling," Brady countered.

"Actually, I have a fairy garden store across the street in the Cypress and Ivy Courtyard."

"Yes, he said that, too. You help people make fairy gardens so they can invite magic into their lives. Isn't that quaint, George?" Finley said.

He nodded. "Quaint."

"And Meaghan," Finley went on, "I hear you own Flair Gallery. We should buy some art, don't you think, George? Of course, we'll need to keep our checkbook open for Violet Vickers's foundation event. She'll want us to be generous. That's what life is about, isn't it? Being generous?"

"It is," I concurred.

Meaghan kicked me under the table, knowing I was being a smart aleck.

A waiter and busboy started clearing empty tables. The clatter was subtle. They talked among themselves, occasionally stealing a glance at George.

"We met Violet earlier today," Finley said. "She's lovely."

Meaghan and I tamped down giggles.

"What's so funny?" Finley frowned.

"Violet often says something is *lovely*," I said. "It's her favorite word. Go on. Sorry." I rotated a hand for her to continue.

"She was telling us about all the celebrities that she's invited to her soirée. I can't wait to meet the fabulous basso." Finley brushed George's arm with her fingertips. "I adore good opera."

"Do you now?" Brady said sarcastically. "Way back when, all you listened to was bubblegum pop. 'Sugar, Sugar.' 'Shake Your Love.' 'Yummy, Yummy, Yummy.'"

Finley let loose with a riotous laugh. "You're making fun." She squeezed George's arm. "He's making fun. I've always had an educated palate. Mother took me to San Francisco often to see the opera."

George said, "I honestly don't care for opera, but the wife makes me go."

"Stop!" Finley flicked his arm, which made her laugh even harder. "Oh, Georgie, you do make me smile."

Brady exchanged an indulgent glance with me. I sipped my brandy. Meaghan was literally vibrating with suppressed glee.

"Personally," George said, "I'm looking forward to meeting the race car driver. I hear he's the next Mario Andretti."

"Don't get any ideas about taking up racing, darling," Finley warned. "You're too o—" She nearly bit her lip to stop from saying *old.* "You're too smart for that," she revised.

Brady shared a smirk with me.

"So, George"—Meaghan leaned forward on both elbows and propped her chin on her folded hands—"I hear you're doing the next Stefan Samaras film."

"You heard correctly." George waved a hand. "We're two weeks into production, and Stefan and I don't get along, but a man's gotta do what a man's gotta do . . . when the studio demands it."

"Good one, George," Brady said. "That's a quote from *Stage-coach,* isn't it? John Wayne."

George shot a finger at Brady. "Nailed it."

"That's George for you," Finley said, ignoring the men. "He's such a nice guy. Loyal to the core. He will put on a brave smile and do what he's best at—act."

According to critics, George had some proving to do. His last film had tanked.

"Did he tell you that the movie, which is based on true life, is going to be shot in Africa?" Finley asked.

When exactly would he have mentioned that?

"He's playing a guy who's tracking down an elephant poacher who sold illegal ivory for millions."

"One of the buyers made the tusks into a dagger," George said. "It's cutting-edge stuff."

"Oh, George, bad joke," Finley said, and mock-slugged him. "The role is perfect for George. What he does on screen is magic."

"Babe, you're coming on a little thick," George teased.

A little? I mused. *Was she playing to an audience of one, mainly Brady, to make him jealous?*

Brady said, "Well, George, I hope the magic—"

Something went *crash.* People on the patio gasped. I turned to spy what had happened. A glass had fallen. The waiter turned pale. The busboy hurried away for cleaning supplies, I presumed.

Brady scrambled to his feet, but so did George.

He put a hand on Brady's shoulder. "Speaking of magic, Brady, let me handle this and take the onus off your server. Accidents happen, right?" He strode to the waiter. "Young man, let me show you a quicker way to clear the table. Heh-heh." He spread his arms, as if commanding the remaining diners to keep an eye on him.

"Ooh," Finley said, nearly swooning. "Watch this." She rose to her feet. "Show them, baby. Show them how you do it." Over her shoulder, she said to us, "George is an amateur magician."

Before Brady could stop him, George clutched the tablecloth by the hem and yanked. The tablecloth didn't slide off smoothly, as he'd planned. In fact, it snagged and bunched, and all the water glasses and remaining coffee cups went flying.

Meaghan gripped my forearm. I held my breath.

And Finley—poor Finley—turned beet red.

"I d-don't know what happened," George sputtered. "It worked the last time I did it."

The diners broke into a round of applause.

With goofy grace, George took a resplendent bow and said to Brady, "Of course, I'll pay for everything. In fact, drinks for the entire restaurant."

More applause.

Fiona suddenly appeared on my shoulder. She was shivering with giggles.

I cupped my hand over my mouth so nobody would see me talking. "Did you do that?" I whispered.

"No. Uh-uh. Not me. I mean, not I." She thumbed her chest. "But there is a fairy here. See her in the vines by the left corner?"

I caught sight of a fairy in a pink tutu with pink and yellow hair doing a kind of jig on thick branch. "Who is she?"

Fiona said, "I don't know, but I'd like to."

"Did you intuit her?" I asked. "Is that why you showed up?"

"I couldn't sleep and sensed you might need me."

Brady sidled to me. "What are you staring at?"

I kissed his cheek. "Oh, nothing."

Chapter 13

Pray, where are the little bluebells gone,
That lately blossomed in the wood?
Why, the fairies have each taken one,
And put it on for a hood.
—Jean Ingelow, "About the Fairies"

Once things settled down, Meaghan announced that she was heading home.

"Have the police released your property?" I asked.

"They have, and I want to sleep in my own bed."

I was surprised. I'd thought she was going to stay at her mother's, and I didn't feel comfortable letting her enter her house without both of us doing a walk-through. Brady offered to escort us.

When we approached the Craftsman, the exterior lights were off. Meaghan mumbled that they should have been on. Something was probably wrong with the timer. Brady offered to fix it before he left and turned on his cell phone flashlight to illuminate the path to the front door.

Meaghan climbed the steps first and drew to a halt. She groaned.

I raced around her and stared at the fairy solar globe on her doormat. It wasn't entirely round, and it was larger than a bowling ball;

therefore, not the murder weapon. It was made of durable resin that resembled crushed stone, and it had a bronze fairy sitting atop it. I'd seen one like it online and had considered ordering a few to sell at the shop.

"It must be from Hunter," she said.

"Okay, that's brazen," Brady said. "Coming here after a murder occurred and leaving something that might freak you out? Not cool."

"I'm sure he didn't mean anything by it," Meaghan said, crouching to inspect the gift. "I think he hopes by honoring a fairy, he might see mine."

"So he can't see them, either?" Brady asked.

"No. That's why he jokes about them being real." Meaghan lifted the globe, unlocked the door of her house, and pushed it open, but she didn't step inside.

"Want me to enter first?" I asked.

Brady said, "No. Let me." He skirted Meaghan and turned on the foyer chandelier as well as the lights in the adjoining living room and dining room. "All clear."

Meaghan and I traipsed after him. I held her hand for support.

Brady made a quick search of the kitchen and two bedrooms, switching on lights wherever he went.

"I'm not scared," Meaghan said.

"Okay," I replied, and released her hand.

Her home boasted Old World charm, with blue walls, white trim, hand-laid walnut floors, and intricate Italian tiles. Many pieces of art decorated the walls and built-in shelves. The canvas in the dining room was one of Nicolas's angry seascapes of Point Lobos, all dark blue and gray and green.

Meaghan balked at the sight of it and gripped my arm for balance. "I lied."

"You're scared?"

"No, I'm unnerved seeing his work. It makes me so sad. I still can't believe . . ." Her voice cracked. Tears pressed at the corners of her eyes. "I'll take it back to the gallery."

"You'll still see it there."

"When I'm in professional mode. I'll be able to handle it with all the other pieces of his we have on display."

Fiona, who had met up with Callie in the garden, fluttered to me. "I have an idea. Let's ask neighbors if they saw Hunter in Meaghan's yard."

"No, it's too late. And it doesn't matter. It's a gift, not a dead body."

Brady returned. "I think you're good to go, Meaghan. All the windows are closed and locked. Where's the box for the exterior lights?"

"In the detached garage," she said. "Go through the kitchen."

A half hour later, exterior lights restored, she shooed us out. Callie was looking over her, and her mother had checked in. She would be fine.

Brady then walked me home, the two of us holding hands. Fiona rode on his shoulder. He didn't suspect, which tickled her.

"Tonight was interesting," he said.

Moonlight graced his handsome face and made his eyes sparkle, and I thanked my lucky stars that Finley had left him. "Yes, it was."

"Finley was always dramatic, but tonight she topped herself." He chuckled.

"It didn't bother you that she lorded her life over you?"

"I didn't care a whit. I've never been into material things, art or otherwise. Travel the world? Nah. I mean, sure I'd like to do some traveling. With you." He glimpsed me out of the corner of his eye. "We could go to Acapulco or Hawaii or see the wonders of Alaska."

"You don't have any desire to go to Europe?"

"Well, sure. I'd like to go to Ireland, have a pint of warm ale, kiss the Blarney Stone, and meet a fairy or two."

Fiona tittered. "He can meet fairies right here." She tickled his ear with a finger. He must have felt it because he rubbed the exact spot.

"George seemed nice enough," I said.

"Heh-heh." Brady grinned. "He was pretty cool. The tablecloth thing was stupid."

"It did take the heat off the waiter. You won't fire him, will you?"

"Not a chance. He's one of my best. I think he was distracted. I'd better hope the famous race car driver doesn't show up. The kid loves sports cars of all kinds."

"What kid doesn't?" I asked.

We strolled in companionable silence the rest of the way. When we arrived at the front door of my cottage, he encircled me with his arms. I rested my head against his chest, and I could hear his heart beating, strong and steady. After a long moment, he lifted my chin with a fingertip and kissed me. I didn't think I would ever tire of feeling his lips against mine.

"Need me to do a walk-through?" he asked.

"I'm fine." I broke free, opened the door, and switched on the lights.

"Sleep tight then," he said. "Don't forget our date on Monday."

"Never."

As I was closing the door, Fiona whisked to me, wings flapping anxiously. "I saw someone."

"What? Where?"

"Standing on the other side of the street, staring at our house."

I tweaked her wing. "Don't tease me like that."

"I'm not teasing."

A shiver shimmied down my spine. I opened the door abruptly, hoping the action would scare whoever was out there. I peered into the dark but didn't see anyone. Brady was gone. I supposed he might've frightened off whoever it was. Or maybe Fiona had imagined seeing someone. Maybe.

Talking myself down from the fear that gripped me, I closed the door and bolted it. Needless to say, I slept fitfully.

I awoke Saturday morning at dawn, eager to get moving. I had so much to do. Prior to heading to work, I needed to finish crafting the remaining six centerpieces for Violet's soirée. Last night before going to bed, too wound up by Fiona's possible stranger sighting, I'd planted the centerpiece pots with two-inch lime-green coleus, scratch moss for ground cover—I loved this kind of moss because it was durable and would grow tiny white flowers—and miniature ivy that was trailing slightly over the edges of the pots.

"Rise and shine," I said to Pixie.

She gazed lazily at me from her spot by my feet as if to say *Not a chance.*

Fiona, on the other hand, was rocketing around the house liked she'd overdosed on honey. "Ready and raring to go," she chimed. "Ready, ready, ready." She orbited my head. "Did you sleep well?"

"I did," I said, lying through my teeth. Why make her anxious by telling her about my restless night?

I texted Meaghan to ask how she'd fared.

She responded in seconds: *Safe and sound. Come to Flair after the tea.*

I sent her a thumbs-up emoji and went to the kitchen to make a pot of coffee. When it had brewed, I filled my favorite BELIEVE mug, the one with a playful fairy using a magic wand—I would need a little magic to finish everything I had to do in a timely fashion—and then I dressed in grubbies and hurried to the greenhouse.

In a matter of minutes, I settled on the color schemes for each of the remaining centerpieces. When I finished designing them, I stood in the center of the greenhouse, my hands on my hips, and admired the selection. "Not too shabby," I said with pride.

Fiona agreed. "Violet should be pleased."

"If she's not . . ." I began, and chuckled. How silly of me to think she wouldn't be. So far, she was adoring everything I'd made. And the whimsical nature of these fairy gardens would be hard for her not to like.

To ease the tension in my shoulders, I took a quickie ten-minute run on the beach—I didn't have time for more—before hurtling my-self into the shower. Twenty minutes later, I dressed in a yellow-striped sundress and flats and trotted to work.

"What's on your agenda today?" I asked Fiona as we crossed Lincoln Avenue. Pixie wriggled in my arms. I adjusted her for a smoother ride. "Any seminars with Merryweather of Song?"

"Nope, but I'm coming to the tea."

"Great," I said. "The customers will love having you around."

When I breezed into the shop, Twyla Waterman was there unpacking wind chimes, and Joss was paying Renee Rodriguez. On the counter stood another set of fairy pots.

Joss finished counting out the cash as she delivered it into Renee's palm, then said, "Good morning, boss."

Renee turned and smiled. "How pretty you look, Courtney."

I set Pixie on the floor and twirled, the skirt of my sundress fluting out. "I like to get decked out for the teas. The cool thing? This one has pockets." I demonstrated.

"Très chic. I owe you two more pots."

"No rush," I said. "Will you be attending the book club tea today?"

"If I can find someone to cover me at the shop. I have one employee out with a cold, and another is attending her sister's wedding."

"You can always turn the Open sign to Closed," I suggested.

"I might do that. I read the book and really enjoyed it. Of course, Dylan caught sight of it and made fun of the title." Renee spun in a circle. "Is Fiona here?"

"Yes, she's doing a tap dance on your shoulder."

"C'mon. I'd feel that if she was." Renee flicked a finger at the air above her left shoulder.

"Wrong one," I said.

She reached for her right shoulder, but Fiona darted away, reeling with laughter. Twyla and Joss both stifled a giggle.

Renee puffed out a laugh. "Ha-ha."

"Maybe you'll see her next time," I said.

After she left with her empty container, Joss drew near. "I heard you had after-dinner drinks with Brady's ex-wife and George Pitt."

"Who told you that?"

"Twyla."

Twyla swept her dark hair behind her ears. "My mother was dining at the café last night."

I was pleased to hear she was out and about. Due to a tragic incident in her past, Tish Waterman wasn't very social. The Happy Diggers had tried to enlist her in the garden club, but she'd always demurred, claiming the Peaceful Solution Spa required all her time. It didn't, but Hattie hadn't pressed.

"So . . ." Joss hitched up the sleeves of her aqua-blue plaid shirt, flipped her hands over, and wiggled her fingers. "C'mon. Details."

I recounted the evening, and her eyes went wide.

"What a buffoon," she said.

"He was actually charming. How he puts up with Finley's antics is beyond me. But he does seem enthralled by her. Who's going to be at the tea today?" I skimmed the list of tea attendees. When we'd first started hosting the teas, we'd allowed any and all to come, but they'd become so popular in the past year that we'd been forced to require reservations.

"Eudora, Hattie, the Diggers," Joss recited.

"Who's Ella, no last name?" I asked.

"That's Hunter Hock's daughter."

"Oh. That's odd. He called her Cinders when they came in that one time."

Joss tittered. "She's a devout reader and an ace soccer player."

"How do you know that?"

"I'm a huge fan of Hock's work. There was a write-up about him in the *Pine Cone*."

"I read that," Twyla said.

The Carmel Pine Cone was a weekly newspaper serving Carmel-by-the-Sea as well as the Monterey Peninsula, Carmel Valley, and Big Sur communities.

"Ulani Kamaka wrote it," Twyla said. Ulani was a reporter who had helped rescue Twyla when she'd run away from the cult.

"It was a fluff piece," Joss said, "but it had a lot of tidbits about him and his daughter. Supposedly, Hunter and his ex are amicable again. Family dynamics can be so complicated, can't they?"

"Tell me about it," Twyla said in a wry tone.

"Excuse me." Joss fetched the feather duster and skirted around me. "Gotta get this done. Renee distracted me." She sashayed through the main showroom, dusting shelves and wind chimes.

I lugged Renee's pots to the patio. Over my shoulder, I said, "Joss, is Yoly helping today?"

Yolanda Acebo—she preferred the name Yoly, believing it was hipper—was close to my age and, like her sister Yvanna, had dark hair, caramel brown eyes, and an easy smile. For the past year, she'd often assisted Yvanna at the teas. A few months ago, her hours at the diner where she worked were cut, so we'd hired her to work in the showroom on weekends and occasional Tuesdays and Wednesdays.

"Yep," Joss said, "and she's very excited. She read the book and is totally into mermaids."

"Water witches," Twyla corrected.

I set the pots on the patio by the storage cabinet and returned to the showroom. "What time is she coming?"

"Around noon," Joss said. "Yvanna will bring treats at one, and they'll set up the tea together. If it's okay, seeing as everyone is on board, I'm going to leave at that time to visit my mother. The home is also having a tea, and they'd like me there to chaperone her."

"Absolutely."

For the better part of an hour, I attended to yesterday's receipts and restocked items in the showroom. We'd had a stream of customers yesterday. Next, with Twyla's support, I rearranged furniture on the patio, set out extra chairs, and shifted the lectern into place.

When I was done, I wiped my hands on a cloth and admired my handiwork.

"Looks good." Fiona winged to me. "What can I do?"

"Circle the room and sprinkle it with positive fairy dust."

As she did, Pixie scampered beneath her, allowing herself to receive some of the good vibes. When Fiona finished, Pixie bounded onto a chair and instantly fell asleep.

For the next two hours, I tended to customers, offering suggestions for gardens and giving tips to some of my more seasoned patrons. At twelve-thirty, Hattie arrived with the Happy Diggers and secured a table near the lectern. They all set their books on the table and roamed the shop. Invariably, they bought new items. Their enthusiasm for the craft of fairy gardening couldn't be contained.

At one p.m., Yvanna showed up with goodies for the party. "Scones, Russian tea cakes, Earl Grey shortbread cookies, and dark chocolate chai cookies," she said.

"Yum." It dawned on me I hadn't eaten lunch. I retreated to my office to grab a snack. If I didn't, I'd be tempted to pig out on sugary treats. I skirted the chalked chestnut desk and opened the mini fridge behind it. I took out a lemon-flavored Greek yogurt and kicked the door shut, scored a spoon, and sat in the desk chair. Meditatively, I ate the yogurt in eight bites. As I was finishing, Fiona sailed in.

"Do it," she said.

"Do what?"

She pointed to the whiteboard that stood to my left. Whenever I planned out large fairy gardens, like I had for Violet Vickers's dozen, I often sketched out my ideas on the board. All of my designs were created with dry-erase pens so I could revise or start over, if necessary. Today, the board was blank.

"You're thinking about the murder," she said.

"I am not."

She folded her arms and frowned, her wings working overtime.

Okay, I had been thinking about it, but only because I was concerned about Meaghan and Ziggy and, well, to be honest, Carmel. I hated that another murder had occurred in our gentle town.

"Write down who you suspect." She perched on the rim of the Zen garden that I'd set on the upper right of the desk and kicked her feet back and forth. Sand sprayed daintily from her antics.

"Fiona," I chastened.

"C'mon. Humor me or I'll make a mess." Her mouth curled up on both sides.

I shook my spoon near her nose. "You look *humored* enough."

"Payton Buley," she said. "He's your main suspect."

I dumped the yogurt container in the trash, set the spoon aside to wash in the kitchen, and crossed to the board. I picked up the dry erase marker and wrote Payton's name in the upper left corner of the whiteboard, and added *Debt, brother issues.* I turned to Fiona. "I wonder how much money we're talking about."

"Good question. Who else?" She crossed her legs and smoothed the skirt of her dress. "How about that guitar maker?"

"Sassy Jacobi," I said. "She was in love with him." At least Violet Vickers seemed to think so. Sassy hadn't denied it, saying they were friends with benefits, but then she'd added that she'd had to knock some sense into him. Why had her sister broken it off with Nicolas? Was that when Meaghan had come into the picture?

I wrote Sassy's name down and added *Sister had a relationship with Nicolas; Sassy jealous? Why kill him? Why not kill Meaghan or sister?* I considered Sassy's comment that Payton Buley had been abusive to Nicolas after their parents died. Had Nicolas become abusive as a result? He'd wrenched Meaghan's arm. Had he hit Sassy's sister? Was that what had made her end it?

"Not much to go on," I murmured.

"Courtney," Joss called from the hall. "Yoly's here, so I'm leaving. She'll man the register. Twyla will help after her performance."

"Got it. Say hello to your mother." I set the marker down and smacked my hands together. "Back to work."

Fiona followed me out.

At one-thirty, Twyla passed me on the patio with her flute in hand. "I'm going to warm it up," she said, and strolled toward the lectern I'd put in place yesterday. She stowed her case behind it and played something melodic.

A customer turned, a smile on her lips, and summoned me to join her. "That's pretty. Is she here every weekend?"

"No, ma'am, but often."

The woman pressed a hand to her heart. "My late husband used to play the flute. It was so romantic. You know, I'd love to make a fairy garden honoring true love. Can you help me?"

After making all of Violet's love-themed fairy gardens, I was sure I could.

At that moment, Brady's mother, Eudora Cash, hurried onto the patio, her hair swept into a fashionable chignon, her pale-yellow linen suit classic, like her. I'd known her all my life as Dory and had been surprised to learn she was a famous historical romance author. "Courtney," she said, puffing as if she'd run to the shop, "you won't believe what Lissa told me!"

Chapter 14

A little fairy comes at night,
Her eyes are blue, her hair is brown,
With silver spots upon her wings,
And from the moon she flutters down.
　　—Thomas Hood, "Queen Mab"

Lissa Reade, the seventy-something librarian for Harrison Memorial Library who didn't look a day over fifty-nine, emerged from the showroom. Like her friend, she'd dressed in a stylish pantsuit. Hers was pale blue, the jacket double-breasted.

Eudora said, "Brady said you were upset that Ziggy Foxx has been arrested, Courtney. I thought what Lissa said might help in that regard."

Lissa—whom I used to know as *Miss Reade* until she'd started moderating the book club teas—clasped my elbow and drew me toward the fountain. Sotto voce, she said, "On the afternoon of the murder, I was taking a walk, trying to clear my head. The day at the library had been awash with aggravation. Inclement weather can make patrons testy. Anyway"—she fanned the air—"there I was strolling along in the drizzle, my thoughts muddled, when I saw Adeline Tan—Addie; she prefers Addie—leaving Meaghan Brownie's yard."

I was always amazed how many people in Carmel knew everybody's business, but Lissa Reade knowing where patrons lived didn't surprise me. She was an expert when it came to Carmel-by-the-Sea's history.

"About what time was it?" I asked.

"I'm terrible with time, but I think around four-thirty. Anyway, Addie's a patron of the library," she went on. "She's a nice woman and very involved in the crafts that she teaches. Why, many of the library's patrons send their children to the aquarium to take her classes."

"I'm sorry"—I placed a hand on Eudora's arm, stopping her—"but you said Addie was exiting Meaghan's yard?"

"Yes. Well, no, not exactly. She was closing the gate. She looked upset as she dashed away."

"Upset?"

"Like she'd meant to go in but couldn't find the courage."

"Did you see Nicolas Buley?" I asked, wondering if Addie had followed him there.

Lissa wagged her head. "No, I didn't, but I wasn't paying attention, because I was concerned and turned to watch Addie, trying to decide if I should hurry after her."

"Did you see Ziggy Foxx?"

"No."

"You should share everything you know with the police," I said, "whether you think it's significant or not."

Eudora bobbed her head. "That's what I told her."

"After the tea," Lissa said.

Fiona wafted on the breeze near Lissa. "Don't worry," she said.

"I'm not . . ." Lissa began, and sighed. "Yes, I suppose I am. I've never been a witness in a murder case, and I don't want to think that Addie could possibly . . ."

Fiona kissed Lissa's cheek. "Let Merryweather of Song be your guide."

Eudora regarded Lissa. "Are you talking to us, or to . . ." She, like Brady, couldn't see fairies. Yet.

"The latter." Lissa slung an arm around her friend. "I'm ready for a spot of tea before the book club chat, aren't you?"

"Absolutely."

As the two of them ambled to the far end of the patio and Twyla launched into a beautiful song, Ella Hock dashed through the French doors. "This way, Daddy." She trotted to the baker's racks of figurines, her long dark pigtails bouncing on her back. At nine years old, she was formidable, even though she was teensy in size. She had a pixielike face, bright eyes, and a curious nature. "You said I can get one today if I finished the book, and I did!"

Like a doting father, Hunter followed her, giving me an all-knowing look that one figurine wasn't going to do the trick. He'd dressed nicely for the tea in a cream silk sweater and gray trousers. His red hair was a tinge redder than it had been the other day. A touch-up dye job, I guessed.

Hunter's sister, Janna Hamilton, followed him in. Hunter's niece—the youngest of Janna's three daughters—scampered in behind them. She was a pretty girl about Ella's age, with white-blond curly hair. It was the color of her father's, she'd told me on a previous occasion when she'd come into the store with her dark-haired mother—the father who had left them a month after she was born. With a very serious face, she'd added that it was okay he was gone because her mommy was a brilliant doctor, like the two went hand in hand. Today, her chin was tilted upward, as if she were searching for fairies.

"I'm so happy to see you all here," I said, joining them. "Ella, I have to admit I didn't know your first name. The other time you came in with your father, he called you Cinders."

"Cinders," she said, and wrinkled her nose. "As in Cinder-ella. It's so . . . ugh."

"*Ugh*," Hunter mimicked.

"He thinks it's funny," Ella said. "He's got a weird sense of humor."

Fiona fluttered to Ella and did a little twirl in front of her. Ella smiled. Hunter's niece didn't.

"Ella's a pretty name," I said.

She wrinkled her nose. "It's okay."

I hadn't liked my name at her age, either. People often told me it was a boy's name.

Ella plucked a red-haired mermaid from the shelf. "Oh, look, Daddy. Can I ple-e-ease make a garden about mermaids?"

"Water witches," he corrected.

She sniggered. "They're the same thing. You can't fool me. Hey, did I tell you I've seen a mermaid out in the bay?"

"You haven't," her cousin said.

"Have so. My mom saw her, too."

Hunter heaved a sigh and said, "Fantasy."

Janna elbowed him. "They'll grow out of it."

I hoped they wouldn't.

"I'm getting us a table to sit at," Hunter said. "Ella, you've got five minutes to pick three items."

"Five."

"Four."

Knowing she'd won the battle, Ella shuffled to the next baker's rack and chose a lighthouse.

Her cousin lifted a dolphin figurine. "Look!" She wiggled it in Ella's face. "Kaylene would've loved this!"

Janna noticeably flinched.

"You okay?" Hunter slung a protective arm around her to steady her, but she shrugged him off.

Kaylene had been the eldest of Janna's three daughters. Last month, she had fallen to her death. A week ago Wednesday, Janna, who was decidedly grief-stricken and was taking a sabbatical from work, had come into the shop with her youngest to make fairy gardens. While her daughter crafted a garden, Janna told me how much Kaylene had enjoyed butterflies and life and books set in the future. I didn't press for details about her passing. I recalled Fiona doing her best to comfort Janna.

"Say, Hunter," I said to change the subject and hopefully lighten the mood, "before you and your family sit down, I wanted to ask you where you bought the solar globe that you left on Meaghan's doorstep yesterday."

He gave me the side-eye, like I was way off base with my conjecture.

"Oh, c'mon," I said. "It had to be you. Nobody else leaves her gifts. So where did you get it? I'd like to give one to Violet Vickers. She's been instrumental in expanding my business these last few months, and her garden could use a bit of whimsy."

"Your fairy gardens aren't enough whimsy for her?" He winked.

"She could use more." I winked back.

"I found it on a trip to Savannah."

"Do you remember the name of the store? Maybe I could order one online."

"I'll have to go through my stuff. It was ages ago when I was on a ghosts and gravestones tour."

"O-ooh," I hummed. "I've never been on one of those. Was it fun?"

"If you like ghosts and gravestones."

Fiona perched on my shoulder and shivered. Fairies didn't like ghosts. They didn't like hobgoblins or banshees, either, and considered them malignant creatures, unable to do good.

"Did you find the gazing ball that you gave Meaghan in Savannah, too?" I asked.

"I honestly can't remember. I do a lot of shopping when I travel. I buy gifts for my daughter and nieces and a whole slew of people."

"Too many gifts," his sister gibed.

"If I can remember where, I'll touch base."

Hunter and Janna moved on to find a table.

"Ladies and gentlemen"—Lissa Reade tapped the lectern with a pen—"and children . . . I see many of you in the audience . . . How wonderful to have such eager readers. Let's settle in our seats. Yvanna and Yoly will bring out the tea and treats and we'll start the book club chat after you've all been served. I hope you all brought your books with you. Wasn't this a fun read?" She pulled a copy of *A Spell for Trouble* from her tote and waggled it. "In the meantime, enjoy the enchanting flute music. Thank you, Twyla Waterman."

For an hour and a half, Lissa guided the group in a discussion, asking them what they thought about water witches, apothecaries, and magic. Ella and her cousin were the most vocal with answers. With Lissa's expert supervision, no one gave away any spoilers in case any of the attendees hadn't finished the book. After the book club disbanded—it was a huge success for the shop; we sold lots of mermaid merchandise—Yvanna and I began clearing tables while Yoly and Twyla tended to the sales in the showroom.

"Oh," I murmured when I found a copy of *A Spell for Trouble* on a chair. I opened it. Inside was a bookplate that read THIS BOOK BELONGS TO ELLA. She and her family had been the first at the register and were long gone. I set the book on top of the table, making a mental note to return it to her soon.

"How is Meaghan doing?" Yvanna asked as she bussed china cups and saucers into a tub she'd set on the top shelf of the teacart. "She seemed pretty low when I saw her entering the gallery earlier."

I gathered discarded napkins and sugar packets and dumped them into the tub on the bottom shelf of the teacart. "She's worried about Ziggy." I couldn't believe Miss Judge hadn't sprung him from jail yet. Did Summers truly believe he was guilty?

"Is she pining over Nicolas, too?"

"I don't think so. They'd broken up. But his murder has been a shock."

"He sure didn't get along with people."

"What do you mean?"

"He and his brother were outside Sweet Treats the other day, and his brother grabbed his shoulder and spun him around. Nicolas knocked his brother's hand away and stormed off. And that wasn't the first time I'd seen him argue with someone." Yvanna shook her head. "How did Meaghan cope with his fiery temperament all that time?"

"She deals with lots of artists."

"But to live with someone like that?" Yvanna sniffed. "You will never see me accept that kind of behavior."

"What day was that?" I asked.

"Wednesday afternoon. A little after four."

So Payton had hooked up with his brother after his tirade at Violet's house, right about the time I'd returned to the shop and had seen Nicolas in the courtyard. Did Payton follow his brother to Meaghan's house? I flashed on what Lissa had said about seeing Addie Tan in the neighborhood. Was it possible Addie had witnessed Payton arguing with Nicolas at Meaghan's house, and that was why she'd run off?

"I told the police," Yvanna said.

"Great. Thanks."

After we finished up and Yvanna left, I phoned the aquarium and asked if Addie Tan was working. I was informed that she had a class until five, but then she was off for the night. That gave me about a half hour to get there. I asked Yoly if she was okay handling the store and closing up. She was delighted to be put in charge.

Speedily, I raced home with Pixie and Fiona. I stowed the cat inside the house, promised I'd return soon, and hopped into my MINI Cooper. Fiona whizzed into the car behind me. Together, we drove to Monterey.

The aquarium was located on the famous Cannery Row. Its oceanfront location and the many programs and exhibits were a huge draw for visitors. One of the exhibits involved visitors engaging with the manta rays. That was where I found Addie saying goodbye to her students.

She spied me and frowned. "What do you want?" She adjusted her rimless glasses and smoothed the front of her black floral shirt, which was a little less grim than the black shirt she'd worn to Devendorf Park, but not by much. Her long hair was tied back with a black ribbon. The harsh afternoon sunlight drew attention to her wrinkles.

"Could we chat?" I asked.

"Okay."

She guided me to a nearby bench and sat first. Fiona alit on the back of the bench, spread her wings, and shimmied with joy. She loved visiting the aquarium.

"What's up?" Addie asked.

"On Friday, I saw you teaching children at Devendorf Park. I thought you only taught at parks on weekends."

"That was a special trip for my homeschooled students."

"You looked in your element. I was wondering if you'd like to teach a class of *zhezhi* at Open Your Imagination. I'd pay you, of course. We have many crafters as customers."

"That would be great."

I opened my cell phone and asked for her contact information. I typed it in and pocketed my phone.

"Truthfully, why are you here?" Addie asked.

Fiona clucked her tongue. "'The truth will out,'" she reminded me.

"I saw Lissa Reade today, and she said she spied you at Meaghan Brownie's house on Wednesday, close to the time Nicolas was killed."

"It's a lie. I wasn't there." Addie's gaze was fixed, as if she was working hard not to blink.

"Lissa said you were closing Meaghan's gate but something spooked you, and you ran away."

"No," she protested. "I wasn't there."

"Addie." I started to reach for her and pulled back, sensing she wasn't the kind of person who would appreciate being touched. "It's okay. No one is accusing you of murdering Nicolas."

"I didn't."

"I know." Okay, I didn't know, but I didn't think she was a killer, and I wanted to get answers. "Why were you there? Please tell me."

She pressed her lips together.

"Did you see Nicolas?" I asked.

She remained mute.

"He was there, wasn't he? Was he dead?"

"No!" she blurted. "He was alive. He was sitting. On the steps. Waiting."

"Waiting for what?"

"For Meaghan, I presumed. He looked so tense. No, I mean, intense." The words spilled out of her. "Like he was poised for an argument. I didn't want to talk to him when he was like that, so I ran away."

Lissa Reade said she hadn't seen Nicolas, but if he was sitting, he might have been hidden from view.

"Was it raining?" I asked.

"It was drizzling. The heavy rain didn't start for another fifteen minutes."

That meant she'd seen Nicolas around a quarter to five.

"What did you do after you left?" I asked.

She didn't answer.

"Why were you there in the first place?" I tried again. "Did you follow him?"

"No, I . . ." She studied her fingernails.

Fiona vaulted off the back of the bench and hovered above Addie. She sprinkled her with silver dust, a potion meant to calm her. A fairy's magic couldn't make someone tell the truth.

Addie drew in a deep restorative breath and looked around, as if ensuring no one could hear us before returning her gaze to me. "I wanted to talk to Meaghan."

"What about?"

"I thought Meaghan might give me tips on how to win Nicolas's heart."

It sounded partially true, but I sensed she was keeping something from me. I folded my arms, willing to wait her out. I often had to do the same with customers when they were deliberating on their purchases.

Finally, she said, "When I saw Nicolas sitting on Meaghan's steps, I realized he'd never want me. He wanted her. So I left." She straightened her spine. "I didn't kill him. I loved him."

That explained why she'd been wearing all black since he'd died. She was in mourning.

"He had something of yours," I coaxed. "What was it?"

"I have to go." She bolted to her feet and hustled away.

I shouted to her and begged her to go to the police to tell her story, but she didn't stop.

Chapter 15

Do you seek the road to Fairyland . . .
I'll tell; it's easy, quite.
Wait till a yellow moon gets up
O'er purple seas by night.
—Ernest Thompson Seton, "Do You Seek the Road to Fairyland?"

All through dinner and long into the night, I thought about Addie and her reason to want Nicolas dead. She'd had a dream, a hope, a wish . . . and he'd dashed it by continuing to pursue Meaghan. Was Addie a killer? She admitted that she'd gone to Meaghan's house and had seen Nicolas there. Lissa Reade couldn't testify to anything more than seeing Addie running away. Would Addie go to the police like I'd suggested? Would she tell them her side of the story, that she'd seen Nicolas alive and fled? If only I knew what Nicolas had of hers that she wanted back.

I sat at the desk in my living room and jotted down the timing of events on Wednesday afternoon and evening. I'd add them to the whiteboard in my office in the morning.

4:00 I returned to OYI and saw Nicolas outside Sweet Treats.
4:00 Meaghan went to her mother's house to watch "Bridgerton" and eat bonbons.

*4:00 or thereabouts, Yvanna saw Nicolas argue with Payton.
Afterward, Nicolas went to Meaghan's house to wait for her.*

*4:45 or close to it, Lissa spied Addie outside the gate and running
away. It wasn't raining hard yet, according to both women. Per
Addie, she saw Nicolas alive, sitting on Meaghan's steps.*

*5:00 Zinnia Walker saw Ziggy closing Meaghan's gate when the
downpour hit. She admitted to running off with her dogs tucked
under her raincoat. Ziggy saw a woman in a green raincoat—
Zinnia—then found Nicolas dead and phoned me at five minutes
past five.*

5:10 or close to it, I arrived at Meaghan's.

I added a caret symbol between Lissa's account and Ziggy's arrival. Whoever had killed Nicolas had done so then. A fifteen- or
twenty-minute window of opportunity. Did Payton Buley follow
Nicolas after their argument? Did he see Addie and hide? Who else
might have followed Nicolas? Had Sassy Jacobi left Violet's soon after
me? Had she caught up with Nicolas somewhere along the route? I
couldn't discount Hunter Hock. He'd admitted to hating Nicolas but
said he was in his house all night painting. No witnesses. What if he
had gone to Flair that afternoon and had spotted Nicolas outside
Sweet Treats? I added his name to the list.

Fiona alit on my shoulder and perused the paper. "Perhaps you
should tell Detective Summers what you've learned."

I sniffed. "And get my head chewed off? Not on a dare. He undoubtedly has come up with the same list I have. Lissa and Zinnia
must have spoken to him by now. I'm purely writing this down because it's gnawing at me. Ziggy didn't kill Nicolas. So who did?"

After I arrived at the shop Sunday morning—no church bells
were gonging that early—I set Pixie on the patio to romp, and I went
to the office. Fiona followed me.

I reviewed what I'd previously written on the whiteboard. Payton wanted repayment of a loan. Would he kill for it? How much

had Nicolas owed him, and for what? Meaghan said Nicolas had plenty of money. His art was selling well.

Sassy Jacobi . . . I tapped her name with my fingertip. Had she truly been Nicolas's friend? I hadn't seen her interact with him. Had she been furious with him for breaking her sister's heart? Did she kill him as retribution? Was her story to Violet that she and Nicolas had a *thing* a total fabrication to remove suspicion from herself?

I added the timeline that I'd written last night and underlined Addie's name. She had craved Nicolas's love. Would she have killed him for rejecting her? She swore she didn't, but could I believe her? I flashed on my theory about a rival artist killing Nicolas and added Hunter Hock to the list of suspects. He had been jealous of Nicolas's relationship with Meaghan, plus he considered him his nemesis, but would he risk losing any future with Meaghan if he was charged with murder? I doubted it. He brought her gifts. He held out hope.

Joss poked her head into the office. "Ah, there you are. Nice duds."

Needing a bit of an emotional pick-me-up after my morning run, I'd thrown on a bright pink blouse and floral capris. "I was inspired when I saw my garden in full bloom."

"Me, too," she said, tweaking the sleeves of her daisy-themed T-shirt. "Not *your* garden. *My* garden. I love how azaleas are still blossoming at this time of year."

Fiona settled on Joss's arm. "Top of the morning."

"And the rest of the day to you," Joss said with an Irish lilt. She nodded at the whiteboard. "Are you theorizing, boss?"

"Trying to clear my head." I told her about my visit with Addie Tan.

"It stirred the little gray cells." Fiona tapped her temple.

"I don't see Addie as a killer," Joss said. "True, I've only met her the one time, but she's so docile. On the other hand, I've been surprised in the past."

I explained why I considered Payton Buley the best suspect. "All

I can think of is Cain slaying Abel, except Cain didn't kill his brother for money. He killed him because God loved Abel more."

"Jealousy is a mighty motivator," Joss said. "What was their family dynamic?"

"Their mother died when they were young, and their father died when they were teenagers. Payton raised Nicolas from that point on. Sassy Jacobi told me that Payton was abusive to him."

"Was their father the same?"

"I don't know," I said, although I recalled Nicolas had told Meaghan his father wasn't a nice guy.

"Abuse breeds abuse," Joss said. "Studies indicate about one-third of people who are abused in childhood become abusers themselves."

"Wow. I had no idea you were so knowledgeable."

"Once a student, always a student. The moment I finished reading up on dementia, I started in on other psychology- and genetic-related topics." Joss loved to further her education. "Don't forget, you have another fairy door class today. It's a Girl Scout troop."

"Right. Help me set up."

"Sure."

I abandoned the whiteboard and headed to the stockroom. I indicated the pots Renee had made that I'd set aside so no one would be tempted to buy them.

Joss lifted four of them. "Do we have enough soil?"

"Yoly texted that the guy showed up late yesterday and refreshed our stockpile." We kept soil in a garbage can–style container in the cabinet where I stored the tools. Plus, we sold small bags of it to our customers. If necessary, we could always open a few of those.

I picked up the remaining pots and headed to the showroom, closing the door with my foot. Right as I reached the sales counter, the telephone rang.

"Violet Vickers," Joss said, looking at the readout. "She's all yours."

Fiona flew to the patio to play with Pixie.

I set the pots down and answered. "Good morning."

"Courtney, it's Violet. I'm very pleased with the gardens. They're lovely."

Lovely. I tamped down a giggle.

"But . . ." She paused. I heard her slurp back tears.

"What's wrong, Violet?"

"It's so awful."

Uh-oh. Did something break? Was she going to ask me to make more gardens? That wouldn't be *awful*, but she did see things in the extreme. Or, I gulped, did someone else die? Please, no!

"The caterer that was going to do my event . . . the Happy Caterer. You know her, don't you? Her first name is Happy, as it were."

I'd heard of her but had never met her. She had a stellar reputation.

"Her elderly mother broke her hip."

"I'm sorry to hear that," I said, but breathed a tad easier. No extra work for me. No dead bodies.

"I'm so distraught," Violet went on. "Happy is such a tremendous caterer, but she sadly can't do the soirée. She must help her mother. I was wondering if you could ask that darling Brady Cash to take on the task."

"You could contact him yourself. He doesn't bite."

"Yes, but you'll sweet-talk him and make sure he says yes, won't you? For me?"

I imagined Violet batting her eyelashes and chuckled. "Yes, I'll call him."

"Wonderful! Bless you. Oh, by the way, your father is almost done with the installation. Whatever you said to him yesterday did wonders regarding his attitude. Could you stop by this afternoon and tell him how marvelous everything is?"

Again? My father didn't need hand holding.

"Thank you," she said, anticipating my answer. "You know, if he wasn't dating Wanda Brownie, I'd snatch him up myself. Ciao."

I hung up the phone and laughed out loud. My father and Violet Vickers? Nope. I couldn't see that happening in a million years.

"What's so funny?" Tish Waterman asked as she breezed into the shop.

"Nothing."

I was surprised to see her. She had a fairy—Zephyr—and she could see her, yet she'd never ventured in to Open Your Imagination. We were on good terms, so that wasn't the reason she stayed away.

"Pretty outfit," I said.

The black cigarette pants and form-fitting crop top highlighted how whip-thin she was, by nature, not by choice. I noticed gray roots were showing beneath her jet-black hair, which was unlike her. She was meticulous about her appearance because of the scar that ran the length of her right cheek, an injury incurred from a spill she took when she was going through a very dark time in her life.

"How can I help you?" I asked.

"I need a gift certificate for my niece. Her birthday is coming up. She's about Twyla's age and is very much into crafting, though she's never made a fairy garden. Twyla suggested I buy her a gift certificate so she can pick her own things."

"That's a great idea," I said. "She can also use the certificate to take a class, if she wants."

"Perfect. Make it for one hundred dollars."

As I filled out the certificate—we had pretty white-and-gold ones with images of gold fairies in the corners—I said, "When will you be making a garden?"

"Oh, fluff!" she said. "I'm no good with anything like this. I can't even grow an African violet, and I hear they're hard to kill."

"I could teach you," I said. "Zephyr could help you nurture it. She's taking classes with Fiona. They're learning about plant psychology right now, as a matter of fact."

Tish's mouth opened wide. "I had no idea."

"To be honest, I thought you were avoiding making a fairy garden because you didn't want to spoil your beautiful manicure."

Tish tittered. "Nonsense. I can always get another one. I own a salon! In fact, I'm scheduled to take a pottery class at Seize the Clay next week."

"Excellent. I hear Renee is a terrific teacher. She makes beautiful pots." I motioned to the ones on the counter.

Tish lowered her voice. "You know, the other day, I was on my way into Seize the Clay to sign up—Monday, I think it was—when I saw that young artist who was murdered. He was arguing with a woman with a long, blue-streaked ponytail." She gestured to the top of her head.

She was describing Sassy Jacobi. I wondered if it was the same spat Renee had witnessed.

"There were so many onlookers," Tish added.

"Did you happen to hear what the argument was about?"

"It had something to do with Africa."

"Africa?" That made me think of George Pitt and the movie he was doing about an elephant poacher.

"Yes, Africa. Mentioning the violets a minute ago triggered my memory." Tish lifted one of Renee's pots and turned it right and left to inspect it. "This lavender fairy reminds me of Zephyr."

I nodded. "Did you hear anything else?"

"No. I'm not a snoop like some people I know." She threw me an amused look.

"I'm not—"

"Just kidding. If not for you, I wouldn't have my beautiful Twyla back, and I never would've admitted that I could see fairies." She set the pot down and pulled a credit card from her crossbody purse. "After I leave you, I'm off to Flair Gallery to buy a little something for her. She'll be turning forty next month, and she adores fine art."

"If she likes small works of art, check out the Hock series."

As Tish was leaving, Detective Summers strode into the shop, dressed in tan cargo shorts and a royal blue polo shirt—not his typical attire.

I eyed his outfit. "Day off?"

"I'm going golfing."

"Is my Dad supposed to meet you here? Is that what brings you in?"

"Nope. He had to cancel. He's finalizing things at Violet Vickers's place. I'm here"—Summers folded his muscular arms across his chest—"because you've been sending a steady stream of people to see me."

Aha, he'd come to chastise me. Well, he'd have to think again. I was feeling strong and feisty. I smiled sweetly. "Did you stop in to thank me? You're welcome."

His gaze turned flinty. "Why are you investigating Nicolas Buley's murder?"

"Investigating?" I nearly choked on the word. "I'm not investigating."

"You questioned Adeline Tan."

Okay, I might have gone to Addie and pressed her for answers, and yes, I might have tried to wheedle information out of Sassy Jacobi when I'd inadvertently blocked her VW Rabbit at Violet's house, but that was all. Everything else I'd learned by chance, and I was always in agreement with Miss Marple. Any coincidence was always worth noticing. "People have a tendency to tell me things."

"Because you ask them questions."

"I've always been curious by nature." Not nosey, as Tish had joked.

Fiona rushed into the showroom and soared around Summers's head. She didn't douse him with anything, and she didn't land on his hair as she had in the past. No tap dances. No antics. She was listening. Hard.

"Did you find the murder weapon?" I asked.

Summers's chest heaved.

"No?" I continued. "Not buried in Meaghan's yard? Not discarded in the garbage? *Hmm*." I tapped the counter by the register. "That is a quandary, isn't it? How could Ziggy have gotten rid of it in such a short time? I mean, Mrs. Walker saw him arrive at the property as the heavy rain started. That was about five p.m. Seconds later, he found Nicolas's body and phoned me. I was there in less than five minutes."

"He could have left the vicinity and returned."

"Okay, let's say your hypothesis has merit. Ziggy didn't drive there, so I'd bet you and your team have searched the surrounding properties within a two-and-a-half-minute walk or jog, looking for a globelike object. Am I right?" I held up my palm. "Before you remind me, no, I'm not a forensics expert, but because of my craft, I'm good at evaluating spaces. I know exactly the right plant or figurine or environmental piece that can fit in a certain spot. My father often tells me I have good spatial awareness. It's one of my gifts. So I'm pretty sure that something round, about this big"—I mimed the shape—"like a gazing ball or perhaps a Magic 8 Ball or a seer's crystal ball is what made the dent in Nicolas Buley's skull."

"I agree with you."

I gasped. "You do?"

He nodded.

Taking that as an invitation to tell him more of what I was thinking, I said, "If Addie Tan spoke to you, then you know Nicolas was alive at around a quarter to five. She said it was drizzling, not raining. Lissa Reade said the same. That gives the person you're looking for a fifteen- or twenty-minute window to kill Nicolas. If—"

"Stop." Summers stepped toward me and grasped my shoulders. "Courtney, look, your father is concerned about you. So am I. We know your heart is in the right place, but you have to let me do my job."

"I am. I do." I felt my cheeks blaze with embarrassment mixed with indignation. I didn't stick my oar in the wrong river, which was one of my late nana's favorite expressions. I only pursued the truth when it involved my family and friends.

Summers released me and slipped his hands into his pockets. "If I let Ziggy Foxx out on his own recognizance, will you step away from this?"

"Yes. Oh, yes. That would be—"

"Hello-o!" A Girl Scout troop leader tramped into the shop, arm raised overhead. Like Joss, she sported a pixie cut. Her smile was infectious. "We're here."

A gaggle of uniformed girls pranced into the store behind her, each *ooh*ing appreciatively at our wares. Three of the girls' sashes held at least twenty badges.

"Careful, ladies," the leader said.

"Courtney, think about what I said, okay?" Summers said under his breath. "I promised your father I'd have this talk."

"Good talk," I replied sassily.

He glowered and then headed for the exit.

"We're a little early," the troop leader said as she approached. "I hope it's okay. I wanted to give the girls plenty of time to explore. My neighbor has raved about the store. I'm so sorry I haven't been in before, but I'm excited. We all are."

"We'll convene on the patio," I said, gesturing to the French doors.

"Excellent. This way, girls." As she walked away, she said over her shoulder, "We'll be ready when you are, Courtney. Give a whistle."

Fiona, who had tailed Summers to the door, spun in the air and trilled at the top of her lungs. Twyla couldn't have made a purer sound on her flute. To my surprise, neither the troop leader nor any of the scouts seemed to have heard her. They continued to file through the shop to the patio.

Disgruntled, Fiona fisted her hands on her hips and muttered,

"Harrumph. This group of humans will take some work. I intend to win one new believer by noon." She retreated to the patio, danced across the water in the fountain, and dive-bombed Pixie. None of her clowning drew a glance from our newest visitors.

"Hi, beauty." Brady sauntered into the shop, a big grin across his face. "Did you tick off Detective Summers?" He hooked a thumb toward the door.

"Little old me?" I placed my hand on my chest. "Impossible."

"I could've sworn he was smoldering when he was jogging across the street."

"Oh, you know him. He runs hot and cold. Nice to see you." I kissed him on the cheek. "Why are you here?"

He clasped my hand. "I was hoping you'd have time for lunch."

I frowned. "Not today. I'm slammed. I have a class, and I've committed to returning to Violet's to inspect my father's installation."

"Well, we still have our date tomorrow, right? A hike and a picnic."

"I wouldn't miss it. Speaking of Violet Vickers, she's wondering if the Hideaway could cater her soirée."

"I thought the Happy Caterer was on board."

I explained why she'd had to cancel.

"I'll be, um, *happy* to," he joked.

I knuckled his arm. He winced like I'd hurt him. I kissed my fingertips and tapped them on the spot where I'd nicked him. "Better?"

"Like"—he rubbed his hands together and mimed pulling a tablecloth off a table—"magic."

We both burst into laughter.

"Have you seen your ex since Friday night?" I asked.

"Nope. I'm pretty sure she's too embarrassed for words. A picture memorializing the evening made it into the tabloids."

"Oh, no."

"Oh, yes." He pecked my cheek and said, "I hope you like a good hero."

"I always like a good hero."

"Sandwich. For lunch."

"I knew what you were talking about."

As he passed through the doorway, I caught a glimpse of Payton Buley charging through the courtyard in the direction of Flair Gallery. He looked ticked to the high heavens.

Chapter 16

Her flower couch was perfumed
Leaf curtains drawn with care,
And there she sweetly slumbered,
With a jewel in her hair.
—Laura Ingalls Wilder, "The Fairy Dew Drop"

Worried for Meaghan, I said to Joss, "I'll be right back. Make sure the Girl Scouts find some figurines. Sorry I didn't help you set up. I got sidetracked."

She said, "No worries."

I tore up the stairs of the courtyard, taking them two at a time. Fiona trailed me. We entered Flair Gallery, and I let the door swing shut.

Payton Buley strode to the sales counter, his finger aimed at Meaghan. Her mother Wanda was standing by a statue. Tish Waterman was also present. She was studying the price tag of a petite watercolor.

"I want the money Nicolas owed me," Payton demanded. His fleshy face was beet red, his eyes pinpoints of anger. "You have it. I know you do."

Wanda gasped. Tish spun around, hand to her chest, her face tight with alarm.

"He told me you sold something of his this week," Payton said, continuing his rant. "It should cover the debt. Cash him out and give it to me."

"I . . . I can't do that," Meaghan sputtered. She turned as pale as the cream-colored boho dress she was wearing. "The police said everything—all of his art—will have to go into a trust and be evaluated. Do you know his attorney? You should speak to him about Nicolas's will."

"He didn't have a will, and he sure as heck didn't hire an attorney," Payton said. "I'm his sole heir. He had no children. No wife. No girlfriend anymore," he added nastily for Meaghan's sake. "Our parents are dead."

So he knew he would inherit intestate, I reflected. *Interesting. That certainly gives him motive.*

"What was the amount?" Wanda asked, moving closer.

Payton shot her an ugly look. "Stay out of this."

"How much?" Meaghan asked, raising her chin with indignation.

"Fifty thousand."

"Yipes," Wanda bleated.

Tish hiccupped.

Hurriedly, Fiona doused the women with silver dust.

"Why would he need to borrow money from you?" Meaghan asked. "He had plenty of his own. We sold two of his paintings in March and one in April. I sent him nearly forty thousand dollars to his address in Arizona."

"He blew through it," Payton hissed.

Wow. He sure came up with that answer in a hurry. Was it a lie? If so, what else was he hiding? "Did Nicolas ever travel to Africa?" I asked, hoping to distract Payton.

He swung around and scowled at me, his expression reminding me of a jackal ready to attack its prey. It took all my resolve not to flinch. "He never went out of the US," Payton said. "He hated flying."

"That's true." Meaghan regarded me curiously, trying to make sense of my off-the-cuff question.

I mouthed: *Not important.*

"Back to why he owes you money," Meaghan said to Payton. "How could he blow through what he had in Sedona, of all places? It's much less expensive to live there than in California, and he was renting his apartment. He—"

"He was living high on the hog," Payton cut in.

Meaghan shook her head. "I don't believe you. Nicolas was a minimalist in everything other than his art."

And his flashy car, I mused.

Tish's comment that Nicolas had argued with Sassy about Africa gnawed at me. Had he been illegally trading something? Or into drugs? Did his brother find out and threaten to expose him if Nicolas didn't pay a demand for blackmail? No, if that had been the case, then Nicolas would've had motive to kill Payton, not the other way around.

"Mr. Buley," I said, "where did you go after you stormed into Violet Vickers's house on Wednesday afternoon?"

"None of your danged business."

"I heard you fought with Nicolas in front of Sweet Treats." I jutted a finger in the direction of the shop.

"Okay, sure. I caught up to him there."

"So you admit to having seen him on the day he was murdered."

"I saw him, and I told him to pay up. He refused. I told him he owed me and said I'd get the money somehow."

"By killing him!" Meaghan blurted.

And inheriting his estate, I thought.

"No." Payton raised a hand, as if he wanted to slap Meaghan. She let out an *eek,* and he instantly lowered his arm and ran his fingers through his thinning hair. By the look on his face, he was mortified by his knee-jerk reaction. "I . . . I . . ." He stammered. "I'm sorry. I'm upset. I'm not a violent man."

I said, "Oh, no? Someone told me you abused your brother after your father died."

"Shut up," he snapped.

I stepped closer to Meaghan. "Do you have anger issues, Mr. Buley?"

He didn't reply.

"Where did you go after your altercation outside Sweet Treats?" I pressed.

"Home."

"Not to your office? Don't comptrollers keep regular hours?"

"I work hybrid hours. Two days on, three days off one week; three and two the next."

"Who saw you when you got home?" I asked.

He shifted feet. "Nobody."

"You're not married?"

"I'm divorced."

Big shocker. "What did you do after you got home?"

"I popped open a beer and watched sports on TV. I can recite all the scores," he said huffily.

"You can look at an app to do that," I countered, thinking no witnesses was becoming an epidemic. There were none for Hunter Hock's whereabouts, and now there were none for Payton Buley. Plus, there was no murder weapon. Detective Summers must be having a field day trying to find a clue to unearth the killer. No wonder he'd come to me with a chip on his shoulder.

"He's lying," Tish said, stepping sheepishly toward us. "I saw him that night. I was on my way home and spied him lurking at the corner of Eleventh and Dolores."

The intersection of 11th Avenue and Dolores Street wasn't far from where Meaghan lived.

"It was around five-thirty," Tish added.

"Five-thirty," I repeated, and addressed Payton Buley. "Based on other witness statements, your brother was murdered a little after four forty-five. Did you kill him and hang around, hoping to catch a glimpse of the police investigation?"

"No." He hissed like a cornered snake. "I . . . I . . . When we split up, he went into the gallery. I hung around outside for a minute, and I heard him say to someone that he was going to talk to Meaghan. I . . ." He rubbed the sides of his trousers with his palms. "You were right. I do have anger issues. Nicolas did, too." He jutted his arm at me, palm up. "We were both hotheads, and there was no love lost between us, but I didn't kill him. I went home to cool down. Later, I took a walk. I live on Dolores at Santa Lucia, not far from where she saw me." He pointed at Tish. "I wasn't loitering. I was working through stuff." He inhaled deeply. After a long moment, he expelled the air he was holding. "Look, my brother's dead. What's done is done. I simply want the money he owed me."

So much for ruing his brother's demise.

"I don't have it." Meaghan shook her head. "And I wouldn't give it to you if I did. You'll have to talk to the police or a judge or something. Leave." She gestured to the door.

Payton stepped toward Meaghan.

Wanda and I flanked her. Tish drew near, too. And Fiona hovered over Meaghan's head as if ready to do something the queen fairy would frown upon.

"Don't!" I shouted at her.

Payton pulled up short and splayed his arms. "I wasn't going to do anything. Geez. What do you take me for?" He leveled Meaghan with his gaze. "You're better off without him. That's all I'm saying. The world is better off." He turned on his heel and marched out the door.

I extended my palm for Fiona to light on.

"Sorry," she murmured. "Merryweather taught me a protective spell, but you're right, she hasn't said I could use it yet."

Lowering my voice, I whispered, "You've got to be wise."

Fiona nodded. "And patient."

Hunter Hock entered as Payton was slogging out. He hooked his thumb. "Who was that unhappy customer?"

Meaghan said, "Nicolas's brother."

"What did he want?"

"To clear his conscience," she replied. "But it didn't work. We all think he killed Nicolas. Why are you here?"

He pulled a small frame from the inside of his bomber jacket. "I painted something new. Hope you like it."

She viewed it, and her face lit up. "It's wonderful. I have the perfect buyer."

I returned to Open Your Imagination and started the Girl Scout class by taking a group picture, and then we crafted together for a solid hour. We had a blast creating stories for all their figurines. Their enthusiasm was contagious. For that short while, I forgot about the set-to with Payton Buley and felt my spirit lighten.

After the scouts left, I assisted customers and tidied the patio and shop. At three-thirty, I dropped off Pixie at home and drove to Violet's with Fiona as my companion. There were cars parked every which way in the driveway. So as not to block anyone, as I had the last time, I chose to park on the street, and I sauntered to the entrance, admiring what my father had done with the front gardens. He'd planted more azaleas and plenty of beds of colorful annuals, all in the pink, white, or purple family including majestic stock, Icelandic poppy, snapdragons, peonies, sage, and trellis-supported sweet peas.

I rang the doorbell, but no one answered.

"The door's ajar," Fiona said. "Go in."

I poked my head inside and shouted, "Violet, hello!"

Her housekeeper bustled down the staircase, brushing her hands on the skirt of her double-breasted gray uniform. She wasn't nearly as humorless as the other day when Payton Buley had barged in. She smiled, and her eyes actually crinkled with warmth.

"Miss Courtney, so nice to see you. Mrs. Vickers is in the back with your father. She said tea will be served shortly." The woman motioned to a table dressed with lavender-colored linens.

"Super." I'd skipped lunch, and my stomach was angry with me.

I weaved through the living room, taking note this time of the gorgeous, oversized white furniture and mahogany tables and side tables. Fiona whistled. I was pretty sure my mouth was hanging open, too. The items almost certainly would bring as much as my cottage if I was to sell it. The French doors were ajar. I passed through the opening and strolled across the terrace.

"Isn't the ocean beautiful?" Fiona chirped. "I never tire of seeing it."

I spied my father, once again, on the lower level. I trotted down the stairs, noting each planting he'd installed. Gigantic azaleas, Indian hawthorn, and hydrangeas were clustered at every turn. At the base of each bush were more of the annuals.

When I reached the lower level, I yelled, "Dad, wow! It's fabulous. Everything. All of it."

He rose to a stand and dusted off the knees of his jeans, then he straightened the front of his navy polo shirt and brushed a piece of dirt off one sleeve. He was trying to act nonchalant, but I could tell he was crowing inside.

"Absolutely every aspect is as you'd planned," I said, drawing near.

"Not every aspect," he grumbled.

I knuckled him on the shoulder. "Every aspect," I repeated. "It's colorful and fun, yet timeless."

His gaze met mine, and he smirked. "How much did Violet pay you to lavish me with praise?"

I cocked a hip. "Ten K."

He chuckled. "Are you done for the day?"

"Yep."

"Want to catch a quick bite?"

"Sure."

Fiona flew to the koi pond and landed on a lily pad. She did a pirouette and curtsied. I bit back a laugh.

"What's so funny?" my father asked.

"Nothing." I eyeballed the koi pond. "I see you took my suggestion." I pointed to the two-piece stone mermaid with the center part of her torso buried beneath the soil so only her upper torso and tail were visible.

"Did you mention it to Violet?" He arched an eyebrow.

"I didn't. You mean she came up with the idea herself?"

"She said a fairy told her."

"Ha!" I gazed at Fiona, who shook her head, signaling *Not me*. I peered up at the terrace.

Violet was looking in our direction. Blithely, she waved. Had she had an encounter with a fairy? Did she have one in her garden? I spun right and left but didn't see any. Fiona flitted away, searching the nearby cypress trees. Fairies loved to hide. When she returned, she shook her head. No sightings. It was possible Violet had visited the library and gotten the idea from Merryweather of Song via Lissa Reade, I reasoned. I'd have to ask.

"Wanda contacted me," my father said. "She told me about the set-to at Flair Gallery between Payton Buley and Meaghan. How is she?"

"She's okay. She stood her ground. I think he's . . ." I pressed my lips together.

"You think he's the killer. Go ahead. Say it. So does Wanda."

"He's extremely volatile." I told him how Payton had abused Nicolas as a boy, using him as a punching bag. "And his alibi is iffy at best."

"Very iffy," Fiona echoed.

"I'm sure he's on Dylan's radar," my father said.

"But can Detective Summers prove it? Or will Nicolas's murder ultimately be labeled a cold case, leaving Ziggy and possibly others under suspicion for the rest of their lives?" The thought sickened me.

"Kitten"—my father placed a calming hand on my shoulder— "don't stew over this. It will be solved. I promise."

Fiona landed on the back of his hand. He didn't react. When he lowered his hand, she spiraled upward and then dove at him, intentionally missing his nose.

He swatted the air. "Darned bees," he said.

My cell phone buzzed in my pocket. I pulled it out and scanned the readout. Meaghan was calling. "I have to answer this."

My father nodded for me to go ahead and crouched to touch up something by the koi pond.

I sidled away and pressed Send. "Hey, what's up?"

"Ziggy is free!"

Chapter 17

Children, children, don't forget
There are elves and fairies yet
Where the knotty hawthorn grows
Look for prints of fairy toes.
—Andrew Lang, "Children, Children, Don't Forget"

To say I was relieved didn't quite capture my mood. I was exuberant. "That's wonderful news!"

"Without a smoking gun, Miss Judge said they had nothing to hold him on."

I told her about my encounter with Summers earlier. I'd been hopeful that he'd release Ziggy by end of day, but I hadn't been sure and hadn't wanted to raise Meaghan's hopes when I'd seen her at Flair.

"I'm going to dinner with my father," I said. "Want to join us?"

"No thanks. Ziggy and I are going out to celebrate and talk shop."

I wished her well, told her to give Ziggy my best, and ended the call. My father stared at me expectantly. I filled him in.

"That's cause to celebrate," he said. "I know how much you like Ziggy."

"Without him, I wouldn't be able to do this." I showed him a couple of karate moves.

He mirrored my moves without making contact. "Not difficult with air as your sparring partner."

I placed my fists on my hips. "I'll have you know I've leveled Ziggy a couple of times, and that's saying something."

"Dinner," he said, rising. "At six. The Hideaway Café."

"You're on."

I returned to the terrace to have tea with Violet, who had dressed in a purple-themed floral frock and a chunky silver necklace. She motioned for me to sit. Seconds later, her housekeeper appeared with a plate of lemon scones iced with a lemon drizzle that looked amazing. I picked up a scone and bit into it, and my taste buds did a happy dance.

For the next ten minutes, I sipped tea and drank in the view as I listened to Violet gush over the list of invitees and the amount of donations she'd garnered so far.

"George Pitt and his wife stopped by earlier today," she said. "He's very handsome and ever so charming."

I wondered if George and Finley would be dining at the café tonight but brushed the thought aside. If I saw them, I saw them. I couldn't stew about it. If Finley was condescending to me or Brady, so be it, and if George attempted another flashy display, I'd laugh along with the others.

"Now, later on this week"—Violet took a sip of tea and set her cup on the saucer—"I'd like you to come over and supervise the placement of all your beautiful pots."

"You made a map for where each should go."

"Yes, but heaven forbid something happen to one while it's being positioned. I want them to look exactly as you intended."

"Sure. I'll be glad to."

"Also, what do you think about me auctioning off your services? I was envisioning a shopping spree and private class at Open Your Imagination. Are you game?"

"I'd love to take part. I heard you're commissioning one of Wanda Brownie's works for the event."

"Yes, I'm thrilled. Carmel-by-the-Sea has such a wealth of talent."

The cultural migration after the 1906 earthquake in San Francisco was the reason for the town's diversity. Artists, authors, and actors migrated south to establish a community that was welcoming to creative types.

"I can't wait to see it all displayed," I said.

"Is she here? Your fairy?" Violet swiveled in her chair and searched the area. She didn't have a clue that Fiona was beneath her chin, toying with her chunky necklace.

"She is, and she thinks your backyard is splendid and filled with charm."

"But is it magical?"

"We'll have to see." I winked at her.

Dinner with my father went off without a hitch. We both raised a glass of wine to toast Ziggy's release. Brady celebrated with a glass of sparkling water. Neither Finley nor George made an appearance, which honestly relieved me. I would see them at Violet's soirée, of course, but if I didn't have to encounter Finley in the meantime, I was happy. After dinner, on my way out the door, Brady cornered me and said he'd pick me up at ten a.m. sharp and to bring my camera. I asked where we were going, but all he'd say was Jacks Peak Park.

I woke as I often did, to the sound of birds announcing the new dawn. After a brisk jog on Carmel Beach, I fed Pixie and Fiona, downed a quick bowl of protein-rich almond kashi, and dressed in a pair of overalls and a long-sleeved floral T-shirt. The morning was still cool, and if we were going hiking in Jacks Peak Park, that meant we'd walk in the shadows of the forest and not encounter a lot of sun.

While I waited for Brady to arrive, I sat at the desk in the living room and typed up a blog about fairy doors and how to make them. During the night, I'd come up with the idea because I'd taken so many pictures over the past week at the classes I'd taught. I barely had to work at making the blog entertaining and interactive. Soon, I mused, I had to consider making a few videos of classes. I'd need my students' consents, of course, but I was sure most would get excited about being social media stars.

The doorbell chimed, and Fiona whooshed into the room. "Let's go!"

"I thought you wanted to hang out with your fairy friends today," I said.

"I changed my mind. I want to torment Brady." She snickered.

"Hop on." I tapped my shoulder. When she was nestled against my neck, I slung on the knapsack I'd filled with my camera equipment as well as bottles of water and snacks, told Pixie we'd be back later, and opened the door.

Brady was standing there, thumbs slung into the small pockets of his jeans. "Aren't you a sight for sore eyes," he said.

Fiona yelped. "Don't listen to him. You look good."

I laughed. "He was paying me a compliment."

"He was?"

"Mm-hmm."

Brady inclined his head. "Are you talking to Fiona?"

"I am. She didn't understand the term, 'a sight for sore eyes.'"

He chuckled. "Many people don't understand the saying. My mother explained it to me once. Sore eyes sound painful, but when the phrase is used, it typically means something different, like feelings of fear, worry, or sorrow. Therefore, the person being viewed brings relief to the beholder."

"That makes sense," I said.

"The first recorded use of the term was penned by Jonathan Swift for the book *A Complete Collection of Genteel and Ingenious Conversation*, also known simply as *Polite Conversation*."

I grinned. "Well, aren't you a wealth of information so early in the morning."

"Joss would approve," Fiona chimed.

"My mother loves history and enjoys imparting fun facts when she can," Brady said. "My father hates when she does, but I absorbed them throughout my youth." He pecked my cheek and held out his hand. "Let's go."

I grabbed hold, locked my front door, and ambled with him to his Jeep Wrangler.

"I don't think I've ever been in your car," I said as I buckled my seat belt and stowed my knapsack by my feet.

"You haven't. On all of our adventures, you've driven. I figured it was my turn to show off my driving skills." He pulled onto the street. "Hope you're hungry. I brought lunch."

"I'm always hungry when it comes to your cooking."

"I didn't bring anything for Fiona," he said, searching for her, his eyes glimmering with hope, and, falling short, resignation.

"She'll eat what we find along the way. Are we fairy hunting today?" I asked teasingly.

"Nope. I'd like you to give me pointers about macro photography."

"Oho, I have to work?" I elbowed him across the console.

"I have wine and nutty blond brownies to pay you for your services."

"How well you know me."

Jacks Peak Park, named after a Scottish immigrant David Jack, was a county park in Monterey County and featured Jacks Peak, the highest point on the peninsula. Hiking trails wound through the cathedral-like forests to breathtaking views from ridgetop vistas. I wasn't sure why an apostrophe wasn't included in the name, but it wasn't, which often became a topic of discussion for newbies to Carmel.

Brady decided to take the Iris Trail and Rhus Trail, a beautiful two-mile loop rife with wildflowers. For two straight hours, we talked photography, which lens I used, how close I needed to be to get the proper focus. He had always been a big-picture guy. My mother had taught me how to pay attention to detail.

Around noon, we found a picnic area with tables—there were a number of locations in the park—and we settled into a comfortable silence, listening to birds while we dined on hero sandwiches and sipped prosecco wine.

"Yum, what's in the sauce?" I asked after my second bite of the sandwich.

"It's a secret."

"C'mon, you can tell me."

"Okay. An extra dash of white pepper gives it its kick."

Fiona spiraled into the air and perched on Brady's earlobe. She did a little jig. Like my father had, Brady must have felt her because he swiped the air. She soared away.

"Ready for dessert?" he asked.

"Yes, please." I'd been craving a brownie since he'd mentioned them.

I waited patiently as he unwrapped them. When he handed me one, Fiona coasted in for a sniff. "I wish I could eat chocolate," she said. "It smells so good."

Fairies favored fruits and flowers, but chocolate—even white chocolate—was too rich for their systems.

I took a bite of the brownie and said, "Wow. So good."

"Glad you approve."

He swung around on the picnic bench and leaned his back against the table. "Any portal sightings today?"

"None that I noticed."

"Is Fiona here?"

"She's sitting on your knee."

He squinted in that direction and back at me. "What are you staring at?"

"*Shh.*" I pointed. "There are two fairies in that Monterey pine."

"Two? Why can't I see . . ." He eyed me warily. "This is all stuff and nonsense, isn't it?"

"If you don't believe, you'll never see. And, by the way, I will never pull your leg about fairies. Ever." I polished off my brownie and said, "I could use some coffee. How about you?"

"I didn't bring any."

"Let's go to Sweet Treats. I'm buying."

The bakery was hopping when we arrived, but we found a table in the back and ordered two cappuccinos. I spotted Addie Tan sitting with the blond woman who'd been consoling her Friday. A plate of miniature pink cupcakes sat between them, a teensy candle in one. Addie caught sight of me and gave a curt nod. At the same time, her friend rose to her feet and walked to the restroom beyond the counter. I stood up, with the intent of saying hello to Addie, but thought better of it and proceeded to the restroom.

Addie's friend, who was wearing a Monterey Bay Aquarium polo shirt tucked into jeans, was facing the mirror, applying pink lipstick that matched the paint on the restroom walls. She spied me and said in a neutral tone, "I know you. You're the woman who sees fairies. Addie told me she went to your shop. She said it was captivating."

That was an adjective I hadn't heard. "I'm glad she felt that way. Do you work with her?"

"Not with her. No. I work at the Sandy Shore and Aviary exhibit. I'm a bird person." She returned her lipstick to her purse, slipped the strap of the purse onto her shoulder, and swiveled to face me. "Ivanka Voss," she said, introducing herself.

"Courtney Kelly. Isn't it a workday for you?"

"It's my birthday. Addie insisted she buy me Sweet Treats cupcakes. This is her favorite place." Ivanka attempted a smile, but it was tight. "Look, Courtney, I'm a woman who gets right to the point. You upset Addie the other day when you questioned her about her relationship with Nicolas Buley."

"I'm sorry. My friend was in jail, and I thought Addie might have pertinent information about Nicolas's death. She was in the vicinity near the time of the murder."

"Hmm." Ivanka's gaze was icy and unfriendly. "They worked well together at the aquarium, Addie and Nicolas. I know they were at least a decade apart in years, but I have to say they could have made a good couple. Addie fell madly in love with him."

I wondered whether Brady was growing impatient for me to return. My cappuccino was getting cold, and yet I felt compelled to hear more of what Ivanka might say. "Addie must have been sad when he moved away."

"Very. She wrote him letter after letter. She's broken up about his death."

Again I wondered if Addie's unrequited love had made her lash out at Nicolas. Was there a round object at the aquarium about the size of a gazing ball? A fishbowl, perhaps? "Addie told me Nicolas had something of hers."

Ivanka's gaze narrowed. "Did she tell you what it was?"

"Not exactly, but I sensed it was very personal. What was it?"

Ivanka didn't answer.

"Why did he have it?" I asked.

"She said he took it for safekeeping."

He *took* it, meaning she'd hadn't given it to him.

"And he wouldn't give it back?" I asked.

Ivanka snorted.

Had Nicolas wanted Addie to fork over some cash for whatever it was he'd taken? Had he been blackmailing her so he could pay back his brother?

Ivanka *tsk*ed. "Uh-uh, don't go there."

"Go where?" I asked innocently.

"I've heard about how you and your fairy solve crimes. If I were you, I'd do a hard pass on Addie. She is sweetness to her core. She was love-crazed, not crazy. Got it?" She strode out of the restroom without looking back.

I watched her go and determined she wasn't warning me or threatening me. Her sole purpose was to defend a good friend. I'd have done the same. I washed my hands, fluffed my hair with my fingertips, and exited.

Brady watched me curiously when I resumed my seat. "You okay?"

"I'm hunky dory."

Chapter 18

❧❀❧

I am off down the road
Where the fairy lanterns glowed
And the little pretty flittermice are flying.
—J.R.R. Tolkien, "Goblin Feet"

When we were finishing our cappuccinos, Brady received a call from the café. His head chef had to go home sick, so Brady begged off dinner with me—I was going to cook for him, and we'd dine in the garden—but after a tender kiss, he promised he'd make it up to me.

With all the makings for stir-fried shrimp at the ready, I decided not to waste it. I rustled up one of my mother's favorite recipes, adding lots of spicy mustard to the soy sauce and oil, and plated my dinner on Pacific Splash china. I fixed a dinner of mallow for Fiona, who was dog-tired after her antics with Brady, and with Pixie along for company, went to my backyard. The sound of night critters scrambling and skittering warmed my heart. The twinkling lights added to the ambiance.

"Courtney," Holly said from her backyard, "look who I invited for dinner."

Ulani Kamaka, a reporter for *The Carmel Pine Cone*, raised a glass of wine in greeting. With almond-shaped eyes, raven hair, and mocha-colored skin, she reminded me of the actress in *Crouching Tiger, Hidden Dragon.* Ziggy had ordered me to watch it numerous times to study her fighting technique. And like that actress, Ulani was more powerful than she let on. "Your garden looks amazing," she said.

Holly's cat Phantom leaped onto the fence top and eagle-eyed Pixie.

"Uh-uh, cat," I warned. "Don't get any ideas. Pixie is a lover, not a fighter."

Holly clutched Phantom and stroked his head. "He'd never." Her yappy Pomeranians were with her but out of sight. She shushed them.

"I didn't know you knew Holly," I said to Ulani.

"Holly and I go way back," Ulani said. Like Holly, she was wearing a light sweater over a silk dress.

"Waa-aay back. We met a whole year ago." Holly tittered. "She asked to interview me, and I told her I didn't have time."

"But now she does," Ulani said.

When we met over a year ago, Ulani had grated on me, but after she helped Twyla Waterman find her way back to her mother, she'd grown on me. She was smart and thorough. "I'm going to be doing a number of local color pieces for the *Pine Cone*," she said. "My editor wants to tout the creativity in Carmel. My initial interview is Holly because of her family's ties to Carmel and her vibrant art. Then I've got Zinnia Walker on deck. You know Zinnia, don't you? Her father designed a fabulous resort hotel and spa in Carmel Valley, and she designed one in Santa Barbara."

"It's perfect timing for the article, don't you think, Courtney?" Holly set Phantom down. He scampered away. "Especially with Violet's upcoming soirée."

"Perfect." I took a sip of the sauvignon blanc I'd brought out to accompany my meal. As I did, a notion came to me, one that might help ferret out more information about the women in Nicolas Buley's life and maybe help the police solve his murder. "Ulani, who else will you be interviewing?"

"How about you?" She offered a sly smile. "Your crafts are unique."

"Sure, down the line." Owning one's own business was always about spreading the word. "But first there are a few interesting people in town who could use the publicity. Have you heard of Sassy Jacobi?"

"The guitar maker?"

"Yes, plus there's a teacher at the Monterey Bay Aquarium. It's a low-profile story. She doesn't sell her art, but she does teach kids how to do origami, or as she calls it, *zhezhi*."

Ulani let out an excited *eek*. "That's what I call it, too. Kindred spirits. Yes, yes! Please get her on board."

"I could invite them to tea at the shop and introduce you. I could even field a few questions if you get stuck."

"I never get stuck," she said with mock-smugness.

"Why don't you come to the shop tomorrow afternoon around four?" I said. "I'll hook you up with those two women and a possible third." Eudora Cash came to mind, not because of the murder but to preclude Summers from suspecting that I was, in any way, shape, or form, conducting an investigation. After all, Ulani was writing a legitimate exposé.

"I look forward to it."

Ulani and Holly settled at a table in Holly's yard, and I finished my dinner in silence, savoring each morsel, wishing Brady was there to share it with me.

As I fell into bed remembering his tender kiss goodbye, I took solace knowing, in my heart of hearts, that he and I would share many more dinners together.

The next morning, Fiona hooted, which made me shoot upright in bed. I searched for her. She was at the window, peering out. I scrambled from beneath the duvet and hurried to her, slipping on a light robe as I went.

"What's up?" I asked, my heart pounding.

"Look."

"Is there a stranger lurking?"

"No. C'mere."

It was still dim outside. The sun had barely risen.

"There. In the cypress," she said. "Do you see it?"

I shook my head. The cypress appeared like it always did at dawn—tall, dark, and somewhat foreboding.

"Look harder."

I searched for what I expected to be a fairy, but I couldn't make out anything. "Describe what you see."

"It's a portal."

"In my tree?" I cupped my hands by the sides of my eyes to help me focus but still couldn't make it out.

"Near the base. I think the queen fairy initiated it, as an invitation. I'm going to go through."

"Wait." I pinched her wing. "Are you allowed to go in alone? I think you should get Merryweather's permission."

"But it's there." She shot out a hand. "Right there. In our yard."

"It could be a test," I said, holding her back. "To see if you can be patient."

She shimmied from my grasp. As she fluttered in front of me, I could see she was working through the ups and downs of my argument. Finally, she said, "You're right. I don't know the answer. And so . . . I'm off to the library." In an instant, she was gone.

For another five minutes, I stood at the window and stared at the cypress, searching for the portal. I didn't see it and wondered if Fiona had been toying with me.

After a quick jog on Carmel Beach, running barefoot because I needed my senses stirred and sand always did the trick, I cleaned up, dressed in my daisy-themed overalls and a yellow long-sleeved T-shirt, fed Pixie, ate an English muffin topped with brie and honey, and hurried to work.

When I arrived at the shop, I was surprised to see Glinda with her niece Georgie standing by the sales counter. Both were dressed in gray leggings and soft, cuddly hoodies. Both appeared agitated. I set Pixie on the floor and patted her rump. She darted to the patio.

"Good morning," I said. "Why are you two here so early? Joss didn't schedule a private class without telling me, did she?" Georgie, a tennis phenom, found fairy gardening relaxing and had made over twelve gardens to date. "And shouldn't you be in school? It's Tuesday."

"It's teacher-parent day today," Glinda said on her niece's behalf. "The students have it off."

"Where is Joss, by the way?"

"On the patio," Glinda said.

I glimpsed my associate tweaking the figurines on the bakers' racks. In her shale-green denim jacket and matching trousers, she almost blended in.

"Georgie has something to tell you." Glinda nudged her niece. "About the night of the murder."

I gazed at Georgie expectantly, and my stomach lurched. Had she seen the killer? Had she been too afraid to step forward, thinking he . . . or she . . . might come after her?

"I was in your neighborhood, Courtney," Georgie said. "Near the Congregational church."

Okay. Not near Meaghan's house. That was a relief.

"Go on," Glinda urged.

"I'm going on, Aunt Glinda. Sheesh. Not everyone speaks as fast as you do." Georgie returned her gaze to me. "I saw someone rooting around the church's garden."

"Rooting around?" I echoed.

"You know, bent over, like they were pulling weeds, except I don't think that's what they were doing. I didn't want to tell my parents because . . ." Georgie chewed on her lower lip. "Because I was out with my boyfriend."

"Her *older* boyfriend," Glinda revised.

"They don't approve of him, because he's in college." Georgie was a sophomore in high school and a straight *A* student who needed to stay focused. I understood her parents' angst. "So I lied and said I was going to the library with a girlfriend."

Fiona flew to Georgie and perched on her shoulder. "Lying isn't okay," she whispered.

Two of Georgie's friends could see Fiona, but Georgie hadn't been able to. Yet. She turned her chin ever so slightly. Had she heard Fiona this time?

"I know I shouldn't lie," Georgie said. "And I won't ever again."

Fiona blew her a kiss and wafted to me.

"So why did you think what Georgie saw might pertain to the murder, Glinda?" I asked.

Glinda elbowed Georgie. "Tell her."

"She was sort of furtive, you know, looking over her shoulder. My boyfriend thought she was burying something."

"She?" I said.

"Uh-huh. She had a long, blue-streaked ponytail flowing from the top of her head." Georgie used her hands to explain.

Lots of women wore their ponytails high, and lots had blue ombre hair, but the sole person who came to mind was Sassy Jacobi. Had she killed Nicolas and gone to the church to conceal the murder weapon? It seemed like an odd place for her to choose. On the other hand, perhaps she was a regular parishioner, and after attending frequently, she'd figured out the perfect hiding spot that no one would consider. I thanked Glinda and Georgie for their information and told them I'd convey it to the police. Then I offered Georgie a free fairy figurine if she'd come clean to her parents about the boyfriend. Glinda might be able to cover for the girl's secret, but I didn't want to have to harbor it. Georgie promised she would.

When they left, I dialed the precinct. Detective Summers wasn't in. The female desk officer who answered said he'd been summoned on an emergency. She didn't share what kind of emergency, so I left a message for him to touch base, adding that I had some pertinent information regarding the Nicolas Buley murder.

The more I thought about Georgie's account, the more I knew I had to follow up. What if Georgie told a friend, and the friend told someone else, and via the grapevine, Sassy found out that the police could be on to her? She might go to the church and move whatever she'd hidden.

I went to the patio and told Joss I was going out for a bit. "Could you call Addie Tan, Sassy Jacobi, and Eudora Cash and ask them to tea at four p.m. this afternoon? Ulani Kamaka would like to interview them for the *Pine Cone*."

"I imagine Eudora will be available," Joss said. "She keeps her own hours. But the others might be working."

"I think Addie can wriggle free for this. Here's her number." I pulled up her contact on my cell phone. "And didn't you say Sassy worked mornings at Take Flight? If so, she might have the time."

"Do you have her number?"

"No, but she's a performer. I'd bet her number is listed."

Joss smiled. "I'll do my best, boss."

"I'm coming with you," Fiona said, whizzing into view. "I spoke to Merryweather. She's checking out that thing."

"What *thing*?" Joss asked, tilting her head.

I told her about the portal in my yard that I couldn't see but Fiona could.

"Will wonders never cease," she said.

"You were right, Courtney," Fiona continued. "Merryweather said I shouldn't go through it without permission. So I have to be patient."

"Not your strong suit," I teased.

Fiona pulled a face and jumped onto my shoulder to hitch a ride.

Chapter 19

I have gone out and seen the lands of Faery,
And have found sorrow and peace and beauty there,
And have not known one from the other, but found each
Lovely and gracious alike, delicate and fair.
—Fiona Macleod, "Dreams Within Dreams"

"You look worried," Fiona said as we passed through the Dutch door.

"I'm not," I said matter-of-factly.

"Then why are you in such a hurry?"

"I'm being proactive."

We hustled to the Congregational church, and I paused at the entrance to its garden. It boasted a collection of herbs as well as perennials like yarrow, bee balm, coneflowers, and lavender, all of which attracted butterflies. Fiona, like all fairies, adored butterflies. She winged to one and tried to engage it while I began my hunt for what Sassy might have hidden. I searched under the walkway leading to the chapel. Behind the base of the peppermint gum tree. Between a nesting of rocks.

Not finding anything overt, I weaved along the crushed rock path, peering into each of the flower beds for earth that might have been upturned but found nothing.

The pastor, a sweet woman who owned an adorable sharpei, emerged from the church's office and hailed me. "Courtney, can I help you?"

"Good morning. I was . . ." I swallowed hard. I didn't want to tell her I suspected a murderer might have buried a weapon on church property. "I was curious which herbs were thriving in our climate."

"I have a full list of everything planted," she said. "People are often asking what this is and that is, and I am not a gardener by any stretch of the imagination. That's one of the reasons I've never been into your shop."

"I could teach you."

She chortled melodically. "I created a cheat sheet. Would you like to see it?"

"That's all right. Another time. Thank you."

"Have a blessed day," she said, and returned to the office.

Fiona said, "What next?"

"I think we should talk to Sassy Jacobi."

I headed to Take Flight, hoping Joss had been right about Sassy's work schedule. The place was as charming as any in Carmel-by-the-Sea. It had a European-like exterior featuring traditional ornamental detail. The interior was equally as rich in flavor. Prior to Take Flight assuming ownership, the coffee-wine bar had been an English pub with dartboards and raucous customers. Now customers sat on high stools at tall tables, chatting softly. The aroma of coffee tickled my taste buds. I strolled toward the dark mahogany bar at the far end of the room, where a barista was drawing an espresso. Sassy was sitting beside a stone fireplace, her feet resting on the lower rung of a ladderback chair, her guitar strapped over one shoulder and perched on her right thigh. The song she was singing, a soulful rendition of "Cause We've Ended as Lovers," struck a chord with me. Sassy told me she and Nicolas had been friends with benefits. Had he ended that arrangement, so she'd terminated him?

As I passed her, she acknowledged me with a nod but continued singing.

I asked the barista for a flight of the daily special espressos. Small signs explained each of the tastings. The first was fruity with notes of lemon and blackberry. The second was caramelly, with flavors of maple syrup and roasted almonds. The third was fragrant with hints of cardamom and coriander.

As the woman drew up the order, I turned and watched Sassy. Like the first time I'd met her, she was dressed in jeans tucked into boots and a lacy peasant blouse. Her fringed leather vest was slung over the top rail of the ladderback chair.

She finished her song precisely as the barista set a small wood tray with three white espresso-sized cups on the bar in front of me. The woman described which was which—each cup was a different shape— and asked me for payment. I handed her a twenty-dollar bill, and she provided change. After leaving a tip, I carried my tray of tastings to an empty table. Sassy announced to the crowd she'd resume in fifteen minutes and set her guitar on her chair.

She ambled to me. "I've never seen you in here before."

"I recently heard about the place." I sipped the espresso that had hints of blackberry and hummed my approval. "You have a beautiful voice."

She swept her ponytail over her shoulder and perched on the stool opposite me.

The barista brought Sassy a cup of coffee in a plain white mug, for the staff, I presumed, and moved on to attend to other customers.

Sassy eyed me warily. "I've heard about you. You're curious to a fault. So get to the point. Why are you really here? I'm not fond of anyone who pussyfoots around."

"Me, either," Fiona said, and flew to Sassy's shoulder. She brushed Sassy's ear with a fingertip.

Sassy didn't seem to feel it. She sipped her coffee and regarded me over the rim of the mug.

After debating how to approach this, I went with the truth.

"When we last spoke, I told you someone heard you and Nicolas arguing about a debt. Another person heard you mention Africa."

"Whoever it was misheard."

"Was Nicolas involved in something illegal? Did you threaten to expose him?"

"Ha!" The laugh was harsh. "Don't you think I'd be the victim instead of him if that was the case? Nicolas didn't abide fools or threats."

Which begged the question, what if Nicolas had something on her?

"You were seen rooting around in the Congregational church's yard on the night of the murder," I said.

She pushed her coffee aside and folded her arms on the table. "Like I was gardening? Not on a bet. Plants hate me. I can't even keep a pothos alive, and they're indestructible."

"You aren't denying you were there."

She kept silent.

"The person who saw you said you were bent over. Did you, um, bury something?" I asked.

"Bury something like a pet hamster? Ugh!" She groaned. "That's gruesome."

A few customers gazed in our direction. Fiona flitted off Sassy's shoulder and orbited her head while chanting in her native tongue. I didn't understand a word, but I wasn't worried. Her chants were always for good. Even so, I hated being out of the loop.

After a long moment, Sassy drew in a deep breath and exhaled. "I was praying."

"I didn't make her say it," Fiona said, flying to me.

"Praying," I repeated.

"Yes. I was upset about Payton's outburst at Violet's and worried what he might do to Nicolas, so I left Violet's and went straight to the church. My mother always said when in doubt, pray. I'm not very spiritual. I mean, I am, sort of. My music . . . my art . . ." She shrugged. "I do find peace in that garden, though. Probably because that's the church my mother used to go to. She loved smelling the lavender."

"I see." I sipped the caramelly coffee and detected the flavor of maple syrup, but I didn't taste the toasted almonds. "Sassy, you appreciate directness," I continued. "So let me ask again. Why did you and Nicolas argue about Africa?"

"I'm telling you we didn't. End of discussion." She stood up. "I've got to get back to my gig."

Frustrated, I returned to the shop and found Joss at the sales counter, finalizing sales for a line of three customers. I helped her bag the purchases.

Out of the side of her mouth, she said, "I got hold of Addie but couldn't reach Sassy."

"That's okay. I tracked her down."

"Oh? And . . ."

"In a sec," I said.

When we completed the transactions, she asked what I'd discovered.

I told her about coming up empty at the Congregational church and filled her in about the exchange with Sassy at Take Flight.

"So you can rule her out. She didn't kill Nicolas."

"If she's telling the truth, but that argument still has me guessing. She was so evasive."

"I almost forgot. Renee called," Joss said. "She has those last two pots for you, but she can't break free to deliver them."

"I'll go over now. Be back soon."

Fiona grabbed hold of the collar of my T-shirt and rode behind me as if I were a fairy horse. The sandwich board outside Seize the Clay stated that Renee was giving an intensive two-day class on how to make garden pots next week, and I winked at Fiona. "Sounds like something I should try." I was all thumbs when it came to making pottery, but if I took the class, I might meet new customers.

I entered the shop and drew in a deep breath. Something about the aroma of pottery and wet clay and burning sage—the three main

scents permeating Seize the Clay—calmed me; plus, Renee always
had instrumental music playing through speakers. I went to the sales
counter and asked the freckle-faced saleswoman if Renee was available. Her office and the area where she taught pottery lessons lay beyond the closed drape.

"She's not here," the saleswoman said. "Detective Summers
rang. He needed her to go to Payton Buley's house."

"Why?"

"I don't know if I should say."

"What happened?"

The woman lowered her voice. "I think Mr. Buley killed himself." She juddered, as if saying the words had rattled her to the core.

"Oh, no," Fiona squealed.

I echoed her, understanding why Summers wanted Renee to be
with him. A few months ago, she'd shared that he'd lost his college
roommate to suicide, adding that he would never take that kind of
death lightly. Who could?

I recalled Payton Buley saying he lived on Dolores near Santa
Lucia. I headed over. If he'd killed himself because he couldn't live
with the fact that he'd beaten his brother to death, and he left a note
to that effect, the murder was solved.

Three police cars were parked on the street in front of Payton's
house. No officers were standing guard, and no crime scene tape had
been posted yet. I headed to the front door. The house was simple in
style. Light brown with green trim. The garden was mostly pavers
and sawdust with a few drought-tolerant plants. On the porch was
one ochre-colored pot that held a lone milkweed plant. If Payton
Buley had been hoping to attract monarch butterflies, he should have
planted additional nectar-rich flowers in the container.

"Go inside," Fiona urged.

I stepped into the foyer and noticed movement to my left. I entered the dining room and halted. It had been converted into an office. An officer I didn't recognize was placing numbered A-frame
markers in various positions, to denote evidence, I presumed. I glimpsed

Detective Summers outside, leaning against a tree. His mouth was taut, his skin greenish, his hair tousled, and his white shirt not completely tucked into his chinos. Fiona zoomed to him and nestled against his neck. He didn't acknowledge her, but I knew she was whispering a soothing prayer in his ear.

I returned my gaze to the room. There were a few three-drawer metal file cabinets. A printer sat atop a two-drawer file cabinet. The crystal chandelier that should have been hanging in the center of the room had been swagged over the teacher-style desk. Payton Buley, his lower torso wrapped in a bath towel, was sitting in a mesh office chair, his arms and upper body slumped forward on the desk, a gun by his right hand. Thankfully, from my angle, I couldn't see where the bullet had entered his skull. Even so, I teetered.

Renee emerged from the kitchen, her fashionably oversized sweater swallowing her, her dark hair tied in a knot. She hurried to me and braced me by the shoulders. "What are you doing here?"

"I went to Seize the Clay. For the pots. When I heard . . . I thought I might be able to help. What happened? He killed himself? How? When?"

Renee released me. "It must have been last night or early this morning. The coroner is on his way. Buley's gardener saw him this morning"—she swallowed hard—"through the window."

"Did he leave a note?" I asked.

"A note?"

"Did he admit to murdering his brother?"

"He wrote one saying he embezzled from his employer, adding he wasn't the only one who should be caught, but, no, he didn't cop to murder. He did it, though. He killed Nicolas."

"How can you be certain?"

"One of the officers found the murder weapon in his clothes bin." She pointed toward the kitchen.

More A-frame markers blazed a path to what I supposed was the laundry room.

"What was the weapon?" I asked.

"A gazing ball, like the one in Meaghan Brownie's yard."

"I told—" I bit back my words. No one needed to hear me say, *I told you so.*

Instead, I edged toward Payton Buley's desk.

"Don't," Renee cautioned.

But I didn't heed her warning. The desk was cluttered with an array of papers, a stack of journals, a container of No. 2 pencils, and receipts shoved onto a silver spike memo holder. The suicide note was lying faceup in the printer tray. It had been typed, not hand-written. Like Renee said, Payton hadn't admitted to the murder.

A signature on the topmost impaled receipt drew my attention. "Are you sure he killed himself, Renee?" I said over my shoulder.

"Every indication says yes."

"His handwriting suggests he was left-handed. If so, why would he shoot himself using his right?"

Renee looked where I was pointing. "You must be wrong. His handwriting tilts to the right."

"That's because lefties are often taught by right-handed teachers, who correct them, which can make the handwriting tilt to the right. I remember my mother, who was left-handed, showing me how the cross of a *T* can be an indicator. She pointed it out on the signature for one of her pen-and-inks." My mom had mostly painted oils, but occasionally she'd used other mediums. "A sharp point at the end will show where the writer, or in her case, where the artist left off. See Payton's middle initial, *T*? He crossed to the left."

Renee said, "Wow. Good catch."

"What if whoever murdered Nicolas killed Payton, too?"

Renee patted my shoulder. "Don't, Courtney. Don't theorize. Besides, how would a murderer be able to position him like this?"

I turned to her. "Maybe the killer sedated him."

Renee scoffed.

"Think about it," I said. "Why would Payton Buley own a gazing ball? He doesn't prettify his yard."

"Prettify?" She cocked his head. "Is that a word?"

"Yes, it means to adorn or decorate." I used the word often when speaking to customers. "He doesn't have any kinds of ornaments. No wind chimes. No metal statues. No doodads whatsoever."

Renee glanced out the window. At Summers, I supposed. He hadn't budged from the tree. "Dylan thinks Payton saw the one in Meaghan's yard, and believing Nicolas had given it to her, got the idea to use a similar item."

"A laundry bin seems like a weird place for him to hide it, don't you think? Perhaps the real killer planted the gazing ball in the bin to frame him." My mind jump-shifted to the set-to between Addie Tan and Payton Buley at Devendorf Park. She had been very upset with him. Did she believe Payton had come into possession of whatever Nicolas had taken from her? Did she steal into his house to find it? Did Payton catch her in the act? No, there hadn't been a scuffle. He would have accosted her. I supposed it was possible Addie had appealed to him in a more refined way, by bringing him a peace offering like a gift of a drink laced with GHB, the date rape drug.

I suggested the same to Renee. "Is there anything in the kitchen like a washed glass or an empty bottle or even a gift bag?"

"Stop, Miss Kelly," Summers barked as he entered the room. "Just stop!"

Chapter 20

And scattering o'er its darkened green,
Bands of the fairies may be seen,
Chattering like grasshoppers, their feet
Dancing a thistledown dance round it.
—Walter de la Mare, "The Ruin"

I gulped. Whenever Detective Summers reverted to using formal names, it was not a good sign. "Stop what?" I asked innocently.

Fiona whizzed into the room, looking frustrated. Clearly, she hadn't been able to comfort him.

"I know you're theorizing." Summers's color seemed better. He'd smoothed his hair and fixed his clothes.

Fiona flew to him and settled on his shoulder.

"How about I tell you what else we found?" Summers asked. "Will that stop you from theorizing and get you out of my hair?"

"I'm all ears." I twisted an imaginary key in front of my lips.

"Payton Buley was embezzling from his work. He had a gambling problem and was in huge debt," Summers said.

That had to be why he'd needed his brother to repay the loan.

"The way I figure it," Summers went on, "Payton Buley killed his brother and was so overcome with guilt that he decided to end his life."

"Payton came into Flair Gallery the other day," I said, "and demanded Meaghan give him fifty thousand dollars from the proceeds of any of Nicolas's sales."

"I said stop—"

"Sir, at that time, Payton Buley admitted that he was the sole heir to Nicolas's estate. Why kill himself if he knew he'd inherit a bundle? Wouldn't the inheritance have covered the debt he'd accrued—"

"We don't know any of that yet," Summers cut in. "We're digging deeper to get all the financials. For now, his confession is enough for us to wrap up the Nicolas Buley murder."

"Except he didn't confess." I aimed a finger at the note in the printer tray.

Summers scowled. Renee petted his arm.

"What if Nicolas knew about his brother's addiction and was blackmailing him?" I hesitated, pondering that angle. No, it didn't make sense. Why would Payton say Nicolas owed *him* if it was the other way around? "Do you know if Nicolas traveled to Africa?" I asked.

"Africa?" Summers huffed. "That's out of left field."

"Tish Waterman saw Nicolas and Sassy Jacobi arguing a week ago Monday." I opted not to mention that Renee had told me she'd witnessed the same argument. Why throw her under the bus? "She said they were arguing about Africa. Maybe Nicolas was into some kind of illegal trafficking, and his brother found out—"

"Okay, enough. Payton Buley's motive was simple. He was mad at his brother for not paying a debt. He lashed out. We have the murder weapon. Case closed."

I shared a glance with Renee, who ever so slightly hitched her shoulder, signaling I should give up. There was no way I was going to win this debate. And Summers was, in all probability, correct. His reasoning made sense. Payton Buley realized that even if he did inherit his brother's estate, the amount wouldn't be enough to dig him out of a hole the next time he went into debt, so he gave up and ended his life. Except Nicolas would have kept producing art. With the proper coercion, he could have been Payton's meal ticket. So why would Payton have killed him?

Seeing the man slumped on the desk made my stomach churn. I thought about the receipt with his signature. Would Renee mention the left-handed clue to Summers? I had to hope she would. I was disinclined to open my mouth.

Summers rotated his neck to remove tension.

Just in time, Fiona flitted out of the way and missed getting whacked by his ear. She fluttered to Renee and kissed her cheek. Renee touched her face and smiled. She'd definitely felt Fiona's affection.

Fiona and I returned to Seize the Clay to collect the pots Renee had made and headed back to the shop.

Joss met me in the stockroom as I was unpacking the pots. "You're humming," she noted.

"Am I?"

Fiona hadn't left my side. She said, "Yes, and slightly off-key."

"*Moi?* I'm never off-key," I joked. I liked to sing, but I wouldn't win any awards. Fairies had perfect pitch. "I hum when I'm thinking."

"About?" Joss asked.

I told her about Payton Buley.

She clicked her tongue. "There's no worse way to lose somebody you love. You always feel as if you should've been able to see the signs. To save them. I'm not diminishing serious illnesses and fatal accidents, but suicide . . ."

I agreed. "You know what bothers me most about this?" I set a pink-themed fairy pot to one side. "Payton Buley didn't confess to his brother's murder, yet he came clean about the embezzlement."

"One sin is definitely worse than the other," she said. "He figured that was all his wife could handle."

"He's not married. And another thing. Why would he have used a gazing ball as a weapon?" I unwrapped a yellow pot. "It's not the most lethal thing in the world. Plus, why not use the gazing ball that was in Meaghan's garden? Why come with one in hand?"

"Didn't you tell me it wasn't on its pedestal? They found Meaghan's under her porch?"

"Good point." I carried the pots to the showroom and set them on the sales counter. Joss and Fiona trailed me. "I think we should set these around the shop and put herbs in them. Let's make them look festive." We had plenty of containers of herbs on the patio. I headed there and fetched three of mint and returned to the showroom. "Back to Payton Buley and the gazing ball," I said as I set one container of mint in a pot and pinched off the dead leaves. "Where did he buy it? Hunter Hock purchased his in Savannah. Have you seen any for sale in shops around here?"

"No," Joss said. "Only online."

"I wonder if the police found a receipt for it?" I told her about the impaled receipts on Payton's desk as I handed her one of the pots of mint and motioned for her to set it on a display table. "And why did he hide the ball in the laundry bin? Why not toss it in a public garbage can far away from his home?"

"What if he didn't buy it?" Fiona chirped. "What if someone else did and planted it in his place to frame him?"

I'd wondered the same thing. "Like who?" I asked.

"Addie Tan," Fiona suggested.

"The same person I'd guessed." I explained why.

Joss's eyes went wide. "No. I can't see her breaking and entering."

"If someone is a killer, they're capable of anything," I said. "What about Sassy Jacobi?"

"Why would she frame Payton?" Joss lifted another pot filled with mint and set it by the wind chimes display.

I reiterated the basics of Nicolas and Sassy's argument. "If Sassy knew Nicolas was into something illegal, like ivory poaching, and was blackmailing him to keep quiet, she might've figured she could pin the blackmailing scheme on his brother, who was very vociferous about his brother not repaying his debt. Or . . . wait . . ." I gazed at Joss, remembering my theory earlier. "Switch that around. Let's say

Sassy was the one who was into something illegal, and Nicolas was blackmailing her. She killed him and worried that Payton might figure it out, so she—"

"Time out!" Joss snapped. "Whether or not Nicolas was the blackmailer, or Sassy was and Payton knew, it doesn't matter now. Both of the Buleys are dead. End of story."

Was it?

Midafternoon, I needed to take a walk. My stomach felt like it was tied up in knots. I couldn't get the image of Payton Buley slumped on his desk out of my mind.

"I need some air," I muttered to Joss. I glimpsed Ella Hock's copy of *A Spell for Trouble* on the shelf beneath the cash register and grabbed it. "I'm going to take this over." My father had made me a fan of the old adage: *Touch something; take care of it.* That way, one would never have too long a to-do list. "Are you okay here alone?"

"Sure," she said. "Yoly is due soon."

"I'm coming, too!" Fiona cried.

Hunter Hock lived around the corner from me. I'd seen him parking his BMW on numerous occasions in front of a white storybook house with green shutters. His sister owned the house. Hunter's cottage stood beyond it. The front yard continued the storybook theme, complete with lush grass fitted with stepping-stones, a water wheel, a fountain with a dwarf on top, and numerous dwarfs and oversized enamel toadstools peeking from beneath the azaleas and cypress.

As I was walking up the path, my breathing more regulated and my stomach less tense, I caught sight of Janna Hamilton bent over a flower bed, a flat of white impatiens to her right, but she wasn't planting. She was bracing her forehead with one hand, and her shoulders were quivering.

"Oh, no," Fiona said, keeping pace with me. "She's crying."

"Are you all right?" I asked Janna gently as I approached.

She turned her head. Her face was tearstained and smudged with dirt. "I'm fine," she said. "It's just that . . ." She held out a large rock. "Kaylene made this for me."

I inched closer to inspect the rock. It had been painted with butterflies and the words *I will love you forever, Mommy.* "I'm so sorry for your loss," I murmured.

"I miss her so much. I'm raw. I keep hoping I'll grow numb, but I don't think that will ever happen. Suicide? Why would she commit suicide?"

My insides seized. She'd killed herself? I thought she'd slipped and fallen. I hadn't asked for details. I hadn't wanted to intrude.

"I should have seen the signs. I should have . . ." She sucked back a sob. "Hunter wants me to see a therapist, but I can't. Not yet. Not knowing why eats at me, you know?"

I nodded.

Janna set the rock on the ground. "Kaylene was always a happy girl. Confident. Talented. She loved her job at the newspaper."

"She worked at the *Pine Cone*?"

"No, another one. As an art reviewer. I'd hoped she'd become a doctor, but she always had an eye for art. She got that from Hunter."

I wondered if Ulani had known Kaylene. Most likely not. They were a good ten years apart, and an art reviewer might not cross paths with someone who wrote local color stories.

"She stopped communicating one day. No daily texts, as she normally did. She sent a few postcards, but something seemed off. We—Hunter and I—were worried."

"I'm sure you—"

"Aunt Janna!" Ella yelled as she rounded the corner of the house with a tray of flowers ready for planting. The flounce of her blue top wafted as she ran. "Are these what you wanted?" She skidded to a stop when she saw me. "Oh, it's you."

"It's me. I brought your book back." I extended it to her.

Ella put the tray on the ground and accepted the book. "I wondered where I'd left it. I'm always losing stuff. Do you and your fairy want to see my fairy garden? I finished it. C'mon." She took hold of my hand. "Daddy's painting, but he won't mind. It's my week to live with him. Next week, I'm going back to my mom's house."

Ella led me to the backyard and across a cobblestone path to the cottage in back. It was about the same size as mine and continued with the storybook theme—white porch, green shutters. In the garden were items similar to ones in Meaghan's garden, including a trio of fairies dancing on a metalwork dandelion and a metal cat silhouette that cast a shadow as the sun passed through it.

Fiona, fluttering alongside me, whispered, "Does Ella like going back and forth to her parents' houses?" Her forehead was puckered, as if she were weighing the grim possibility that she might have to travel back and forth from the fairy kingdom to the human world.

"Poor Aunt Janna," Ella said, climbing the steps to the front door. "She cries all the time. It makes Daddy sad because he can't help her."

"Do you miss your cousin?" I asked.

"Uh-huh. My uncle and my other cousins don't cry like Aunt Janna, but they're sad, too. Daddy"—Ella pushed open the front door—"I'm taking Courtney and her fairy to my room." She darted inside and raced down a narrow hall.

I stopped in the entrance and took in the view of Hunter's kitchen to the left. I peeped around the door and caught sight of his studio to the right. Hunter, wearing a painter's apron over a long-sleeved black T-shirt and black jeans, was facing a miniature canvas set on an easel. The burgundy drapes were open, allowing sunlight to spill through the large picture window. Two yellow butterfly palms, good for improving air quality by absorbing harmful gases in the home—perfect for an artist who used potentially noxious paints—stood at the far corners in decorative brown pots. On Ikea-style shelving stood dozens of Hunter's works and dozens of baby rubber plants, emerald ripple peperomia, pothos, and Eden rosso. A massive pinewood table to his right held an artist's essentials—daylight lamp, palettes and scrapers, jars of brushes, myriad paints, turpentine, sketch pads, and more. A smaller table held an array of spiky coral. Some largish canvases were slotted between the tables. I'd never seen any of his bigger works. Had Meaghan or Ziggy?

Hunter swung around, brush and palette in hand. "Hi." His apron was splattered with a pinkish paint, and he was wearing black-rimmed glasses that magnified his bushy eyebrows. "What brings you around?"

"Your daughter left her copy of the book club selection at the shop. I wanted to return it."

Wings flapping hard, Fiona examined his work, one at a time.

"That's very decent of you," he said, unaware of her presence. "You could've left a message. I would've stopped by."

"It's been a tough day. I needed a walk."

"Want some coffee or water?" He set his brush and palette on the table and wiped his hands with a towel.

"Could I get a peek at your work first?" I motioned to the art displayed on the shelving.

"Sure. I'm a terrible host. Come in."

I stepped into the space, inhaling the aroma of the paint. "Do you paint every day?" I asked.

"I try to, but I'm not always inspired to create. I'm sure you understand that. You don't make a fairy garden daily, do you?"

I smiled. "No, but when I have a deadline, I dig deep for inspiration, even in the wee hours of the morning." Like I had for Violet's gardens. "These are great," I said, studying the petite works. Fiona was correct. He liked painting coral. "Why does coral excite you?"

"My father was a scuba diver. He taught me when I was eight. He thought, given my vertically challenged physique"—he gestured to his body—"I might feel more comfortable with the fish. I didn't like fish, it turned out. I didn't like otters, either."

Carmel and Monterey were known for the playful otters that resided in the bay. The aquarium had a terrific exhibit.

"But I was fascinated with the artistry of coral," he went on. "Each piece is unique. Like people, honestly, when you think about it. No two are alike, not even identical twins."

Beyond the shelving, I noticed a set of handprints glazed with white paint. One was much larger than the other. "Are those Ella's and her mother's?"

"No. Ella's and Kaylene's. She adored her older cousin. She was like her little shadow."

Ella swept into the studio and joined us by the handprints. "There you are." She wasn't talking to me. She was looking straight at Fiona. "Are you coming?"

Fiona looked to me for approval. I nodded.

"Daddy, I put the mail on the counter in the kitchen," she said, and dashed out of the room.

"She's got a lot of energy," I said.

He smiled. "And it's not from sugar. She's not allowed to eat that. It's all natural. How about that water?" He headed toward the kitchen.

The kitchen wasn't dirty, but it was comfortably disorganized. Like the studio, things were out and near at hand. A long time ago, Meaghan told me that artists had a different mindset when it came to attending to life's details. *Helter-skelter* was the phrase she'd used. Hunter's counter was a case in point. Clean plates were set on the counter, not in cupboards. Glasses, too. Mail was stacking up in a rattan basket near the refrigerator. Receipts that had been tossed into a second rattan container were spilling onto the counter. Those made me think of Payton Buley's left-handed signature on the receipt on his desk, but I put the thought from my mind. I had to believe Renee had told Summers my theory.

"Ice?" Hunter asked as he filled a glass with water.

"Room temp is fine."

He handed me the glass. "So why is today tough?"

I took a sip and held the glass between both hands. "I learned that Nicolas Buley's brother, Payton—the man you saw storming out of Flair—committed suicide."

Hunter gasped. "Man, that's rough. Did he have a family?"

"Divorced. No children."

"Well, at least that's something," he said, rubbing a hand down his neck. Was he thinking about the many people his niece had left behind? "Why'd he do it?"

"The police think he couldn't live with himself after killing Nicolas." I didn't add anything about the embezzlement. Summers would frown on me revealing particular aspects of the crime scene.

"He killed Nicolas? They're sure?"

"They found the murder weapon . . ." I hesitated and decided that much I could share. "They found it at his house."

"Did he leave a note?" Hunter slinked past the refrigerator and peeked down the hall, undoubtedly to make sure his daughter wasn't heading our way and might overhear our conversation. "I'm sorry. It's none of my business. You don't need to answer."

"Not a note about killing Nicolas, no. He—" I stopped again, this time choosing brevity as the proper approach. "He was troubled."

Fiona flitted into the kitchen and settled on my shoulder. "You need to see Ella's bedroom."

"Hunter," I said, "I promised Ella I'd look at her fairy garden."

"Sure thing. Follow me." He took my water glass, set it in the sink, and headed down the dark hall. "I need to get that light fixed," he said, pointing overhead. "I'm always letting things go."

I bit back a chuckle. Like Meaghan said, it was the artist's mindset.

Ella's room was fit for a princess. White and pink were the dominant colors. The four-poster bed had a beautiful fairy-light canopy. The sheer curtains were fairy-lit, as well. To the right of the bed was a desk with a lamp and a pink fairy-themed blotter and desk set. Beyond that stood three shelves. On each was a fairy garden.

Ella beamed as we entered. She clasped my hand. "This is my latest one. Don't you love it?"

"It's spectacular," I said. She'd filled a large tray with sand. On top, she'd set the lighthouse and the mermaid fairy figurines. But she'd also added a red-striped, shipwrecked toy boat. "Did you paint the boat?"

She nodded.

"You have your father's talent."

"Do not." She snorted. "I suck."

"Ella, language," Hunter cautioned.

"Sorry." She signaled to an array of other items. "Don't you love the lobster and the buried treasure and the pelican, Courtney?"

"I do. Where did you get all of these items?" I certainly didn't sell them at the shop.

"The toy store in Monterey. It's near the aquarium, and they have loads of ocean stuff. Daddy spoiled me."

"He sure did." I glanced over my shoulder at Hunter.

He shrugged. "I only get to see her every other week. It's what fathers do."

My father had spoiled me after my mother died, too. He rarely said no.

"I want to make another one, Daddy. Or . . . or . . . Courtney could make me one. Wouldn't that be cool?"

"We'll see." He winked at me.

"What're these doing in your arrangement, Ella?" I asked, pointing to bell-shaped flowers on staffs.

"I know." She swept her braids over her shoulder. "They don't go with the theme, but so what? They're pretty, and they glow in the dark."

"Not unless they get sunlight throughout the day," I said. The fairy gardens were in the darkest part of her room. The sunlight was spilling through a far window.

"Ha!" She shot a look at her father. "That's why they're so dim, Daddy. Oh, I almost forgot"—she swiped a piece of paper off her desk—"here's the receipt from the aquarium store. You said you needed it back. I checked off my things so you can tell the difference between your stuff and mine."

"Thanks." He tucked it into the pocket of his apron.

"Hey, you should show Courtney what you bought there," Ella said. "Ask her opinion."

"No."

"Show her. See if she thinks Miss Brownie will like it." She clapped him on the arm.

"Ella, stop."

Ella said to me, "Daddy bought her an ornament for her garden because he likes her."

Hunter's cheeks blazed red.

"What did you buy this time?" I asked, keeping my voice neutral. "Meaghan has loved all the other things you've bought her."

Okay, *loved* was a stretch, but she had been enjoying how all the trinkets dressed up her garden.

"It's a piece of coral," Ella said. "Not a big piece. A teensy one. It's so beautiful. It's white with spikes, but it's lacy and . . ." She used her hands to express herself.

Hunter sighed. "I'm going to wait awhile to give it to her. When the time's right."

I wasn't sure the time would ever be right, but I kept mum.

Chapter 21

The same that oftimes hath
Charm'd magic casements, opening on the foam
Of perilous seas, in faery lands forlorn.
—John Keats, "Ode to a Nightingale"

When I returned to the shop, Joss was setting a tray for tea.

I extended a hand. "Let me help you set up. Where's Yoly?"

"On the patio dealing with customers."

In jeans and paisley V-neck with batwing sleeves, Yoly looked chic and hip. I waved. She caught sight of me and waved back. I fetched some maple-pecan madeleines as well as shortbread cookies that I kept in the freezer and unwrapped them and placed them on a pretty Royal Albert Rose Confetti-patterned plate.

Close to four p.m., as Joss and I were arranging teacups and saucers on the patio, Ulani strolled out.

Fiona swirled around Ulani's head, checking her up and down. "I like her dress."

Ulani had donned a fall-toned, floral wraparound that hugged her curves and went well with her coloring. Big hoop earrings adorned her ears. She wore no other jewelry, following the less-is-more rule. "This looks terrific," she said.

"Adeline Tan will be here shortly," Joss said, "but I'm afraid Eudora Cash can't make it."

"Too bad," I said. "Ulani, Eudora is very colorful. You should definitely reach out for an interview. I can have Lissa Reade set it up at the library. You know Lissa."

"Sure do."

"Also, Sassy Jacobi won't be able to make it." Given the testy nature of our encounter, I hadn't invited her.

Ulani smiled. "Well, then it'll simply be me and Miss Tan."

"When you're through, I said, I'd like to pick your brain about something." Janna Hamilton's grief about her daughter was gnawing at me.

"You're on."

"I'm here," Addie Tan said. "Sorry I'm late." She tripped down the stairs to the patio, preventing herself from falling by grabbing the back of a chair. "Oops. Darned espadrilles." She was clad in a long-sleeved black sheath and strands of black beads. The severe look didn't suit her. She came across stern, not sad.

"You're not late," I said. "Slow down."

She smoothed her hair and extended a hand to Ulani. They shook. "Hello. I'm Adeline Tan. People call me Addie. You look like your profile picture in the *Pine Cone*, Miss Kamaka."

"Call me Ulani. It's nice to meet you." Ulani released Addie's hand. "Sit. Please."

"Will you join us, Courtney?" Addie asked. "It looks like we have a setup for one more."

I smiled. That was exactly what I was hoping she'd say. "One other person canceled."

"More time for me." Addie set her handbag on a side chair and folded her arms on the table. Her eyes weren't puffy. She didn't have a tissue jutting from beneath the sleeve of her dress. Was her grieving complete? "My friend Ivanka is happy you're doing this. She said it's about time the arts and crafts program at the aquarium gets recognition."

"I couldn't agree more. Tea?" I asked, holding up the pot. "It's chamomile."

"Sure."

Ulani said, "I'd love some."

I filled the three teacups. Fiona whizzed from Addie to Ulani and back again before alighting on the teapot handle to observe. Ulani was meticulously setting up her work items: notepad, pen, and side notes. I noticed a couple of customers staring surreptitiously in our direction. Joss must have noticed, too, because she strode through the French doors, gave me a thumbs-up, and made a beeline to them.

"So, Adeline—" Ulani began.

"Addie, please."

"Addie, where do you hail from?"

"Here. Born and raised. Well, here meaning Monterey. I'm, like, a California girl," she said with an exaggerated Valley Girl accent. "I've always loved the ocean. I've been drawn to it as if it's where I belong. Not in it, but around it. I enjoy working with others who love it." She took of a sip of tea and set a madeleine on a plate but didn't eat it.

"I heard you teach *zhezhi*," Ulani continued. "My grandmother taught me. I'm Hawaiian, but she was Chinese."

Addie *eek*ed as Ulani had the other day. "You know what *zhezhi* is?"

Ulani nodded. "I find it soothing to do."

"Me, too."

Ulani jotted a note. "So you're in your thirties, right?"

Addie flicked the air. "Hardly. I'm well into my forties now."

"You don't look it."

I marveled at Ulani's expert way of conducting an interview.

Connecting, flattering. I supposed I did the same with my customers to find out exactly what their needs were.

"Married?" Ulani asked.

"No. Never. No children, either." Her mouth turned down in a frown. "I was always hopeful, but I never met the right man."

Until Nicolas, I reflected.

Addie squinted at me, as if I'd said the thought out loud.

Ulani said, "Where did you work before the aquarium?"

"I've always worked there. During college, I served as an intern on weekends. When I graduated college with a degree in education, they hired me full-time. I'm fortunate enough to make my own hours."

"Are you an artist outside of work?" Ulani asked.

"Oh, no. *Pfft*." She waved a hand. "Me? Art? Uh-uh."

Ulani wagged her pen at Addie. "*Zhezhi* is an art. Don't dismiss it."

Addie tittered.

"From what I understand," Ulani continued, "it traditionally focuses on boats and hats rather than on animals and flowers. Is that what you teach the children to make?"

"I teach them to make fish because the aquarium is all about fish, of course. I figured boats . . . fish . . . they go together." She made a swishing gesture with her hands. "But I also teach them to make geodesic balls."

Like I'd seen them crafting at the park.

"Those are very educational," she went on. "And we make hats. Kids love hats." She offered a full-throated laugh that sounded forced.

Fiona mimicked it and delightedly clutched her torso, pleased with her imitation.

Ignoring her, I said, "Addie." I set a shortbread cookie on my plate. "Did you teach Nicolas how to do *zhezhi*?"

"Yes." Her eyes filled with sadness. "He enjoyed it. He said it made him feel like a kid. He didn't have a great childhood."

"No?" I tilted my head.

"He lost his mother as a boy, and then his father died, and his brother . . ." She didn't finish.

I said, "I heard his brother was cruel to him. Is that so?"

Addie blanched. Ulani glanced between us but held her tongue.

"Addie?" I prompted.

"Yes." Her gaze filled with what could only be disgust. "Nicolas said his brother beat him up with regularity. Family can be so heartless."

Fiona flitted to Addie and perched atop her head. Gently, she petted Addie's hair, whispering, "There, there."

Yoly swung by the table carrying a white tray set with fairy figurines. "Forgive me for intruding, but would either of you like to purchase a figurine? For one hour, these are half off. Joss gave the go-ahead, Courtney," she added quickly.

"I think it's a great idea," I said. "Have at it."

Addie took a fairy with an orange bodice, green skirt, and purple wings who was chatting with a large blue butterfly.

"That's one of my favorites," I said.

"I adore butterflies," Addie murmured.

I flashed on the rock that Kaylene Hamilton had painted for her mother and shuddered. What a sad story hers was, gone too soon from this world.

"Addie, I have a very specific question to ask you," I said. "It's not about your work."

She set the figurine aside and lifted her teacup. She took a sip. "I spoke to the police. I told them what I told you."

"Yes, I heard you did, and thank you. That was the right thing to do. But I've got to know. I saw Payton Buley give you guff at Devendorf Park. You said Nicolas took something of yours that you wanted back. What was it?"

Her hand shook. She replaced her teacup on the saucer with a *clack*.

"It sounded like it was personal," I continued. "You told him you didn't want anyone to see it. Was it something illegal? Something you stole?"

"It was my license," she blurted, and peeked toward the French doors as if she wanted to escape.

Ulani exchanged a glance with me and took up the gauntlet. "C'mon, Addie, tell us more. Had you had too much to drink? Is that why he took it?"

"He . . . I . . ." Addie could barely find her voice. Her shoulders slumped. "I suppose you'll find out, Ulani, if you dig. I'm . . . I'm not actually from here. I lied about that. My license was proof. I was born in Chicago. I ran away from my family years ago."

"Why did you run?" I asked.

"My father was a very mean man. When Nicolas and I worked at the aquarium and we took coffee breaks, he got me to open up. He didn't judge me. He said his father was vile, too, and he was proud that I'd found the courage to run away from mine."

I thought of what Joss had said, *Abuse breeds abuse.* Had Nicolas's father beaten Payton, too? Was that why Payton had become an abuser?

"But one day," Addie went on, "when I invited Nicolas over for dinner, he was rummaging through my things—"

"No!" Ulani exclaimed.

"Yes. He could be intrusive, believing he had every right. Anyway"—Addie folded her hands on the table, fingers laced as if to anchor herself—"he found my license. The one I got when I was sixteen. It had my real name on it."

"You've changed your name?" I asked. That meant the tale about her being named after a famous physician and author was baloney. It was part of her new origin story.

"Yes. Legally," she said. "Nicolas waved it overhead and claimed he wanted to hold onto it for me. To protect it for me. I thought he was joking, but he took it with him that night, and then he turned mean to me. Every time I saw him, he brought up the past and lorded it over me, like I was *less than*. He said if I was stronger, I'd call my father and tell him off, or at the very least I would contact the authorities and sic them on my father. Of course"—Addie bit her lower lip—"that's actually what Nicolas wished he could have done to his father, but he was dead."

I said, "Changing one's identity and keeping it a secret is a pretty powerful motivator—"

"I didn't kill him!" Addie cried. "I simply didn't want him telling my parents where I was."

Ulani leaned forward. "I'm the same. I don't want my parents to find me."

Addie stiffened. "Did they abuse you, too?"

"No, but my parents want control over me. They don't trust me to think for myself."

Addie nodded in understanding. "I was young and vulnerable when I made the decision to run away. I'm older now. I could handle my father if the situation arose."

"Did Nicolas blackmail you, Addie?" I asked. Did he threaten to contact your father if you didn't pay up?" As I'd theorized earlier, getting out from under a blackmailer's thumb was a good motive for murder.

"He never asked for money, but he . . ." She rubbed her arm in a way that reminded me of Meaghan whenever she thought of Nicolas.

I swallowed hard. "He hurt you."

She lowered her chin. "Yes. Once. He punched my arm. He told me to wise up. He was ashamed, of course, and swore he'd never hurt me again."

That was what he'd said to Meaghan.

"After he relocated to Arizona, he wrote and said he was seeing a therapist and learning to curb his anger."

What a line. *A zebra never changes its stripes*, my nana had told me often. How I missed her level-headed wisdom.

Addie removed a spiral hair tie from her purse, slipped it over her hair, and pulled her hair into a messy bun. "Nicolas often said he would've confronted his father, but . . ." Her shoulders sagged.

"How did he die?" I asked.

"He fell down a flight of stairs."

I gagged. "No way. That's how his mother died, too." I flashed on Payton Buley, using his brother as a punching bag. Was it possible he'd killed both his mother and father and lorded his dominance over his younger brother? The thought made me want to retch. "Addie, I believe you when you say you didn't kill Nicolas."

Her shoulders relaxed.

I said, "Please tell us where you went after you ran away from Meaghan's house the night Nicolas was killed."

She lowered her head. "To the mission on Del Rio Road. Whenever I have dark moments, I go there to find my center."

The mission, one of the most authentically restored missions in California, was a national historic landmark. It was the only Spanish mission that still had its original bell and bell tower.

"Did anyone see you?" *Please don't say there were no witnesses.*

"Three people. They know me. They see me there often." Addie recited their names. "If you don't mind, I'd like to finish my interview with Miss Kamaka now and leave."

"Sure. Thank you for being open with us." I rose to my feet.

Ulani flipped a page of her notebook and pressed on, asking Addie about her experiences at the aquarium, her favorite students, and her most memorable moments as a teacher.

Half an hour later, when they ended the interview, I wrapped the fairy figurine for Addie, giving it to her gratis for her honesty.

After she left, Ulani cornered me at the sales counter. "You said when I arrived that you wanted to talk to me about something. Please tell me you don't want to dredge up my family history."

"No, I won't intrude."

She smiled. "Does it have to do with Nicolas Buley's murder?"

"No." I told her about Janna Hamilton's daughter, Kaylene. "Her family is heartbroken. Her mother is, suffice it to say, struggling. She wishes she could learn *why* Kaylene ended her life. I was thinking, you, being a journalist, could sniff around and find out what happened and help the family find closure."

"Where did she work?"

I'd forgotten to ask and didn't feel I could at this juncture. I explained that to Ulani.

"I'll do my best," she said.

Chapter 22

'*Twas while I watched them dancing,*
The sunshine told me true
That my sparkling little fairy
Was lovely Drop O'Dew.
—Laura Ingalls Wilder, "The Fairy Dew Drop"

At the end of the day, I stood in my office, feeling a crushing sense of gloom. Images of Payton's and Nicolas's bodies scudded through my mind. I studied the whiteboard. Pixie, lying on the chair to my right, lifted her head and tracked me with her gaze. I stared at Payton's name. Despite his brutal history with Nicolas, why would he kill him? If he'd been patient, he would have inherited whatever wealth Nicolas had amassed and been able to pay his debts. His life wasn't hopeless. On the other hand, anger could have gotten the best of him, and he'd lashed out. But if that were so, why would he have been upset enough to have taken his own life? I shook my head. I was missing something.

I studied Sassy Jacobi's name. She'd been elusive earlier. I jotted the word *Africa* on the whiteboard and tapped on it with the pen. Africa. Why had Sassy and Nicolas argued about Africa?

Joss opened the door. Fiona glided past her and balanced on the rim of the Zen garden on my desk.

"I'm off to see my mother," Joss said. "Are you ready to pack it in?"

"Yes. It's time to go home. I could use the time to update the website or write a blog."

"Or chill." She winked.

"Or *chill*." An unlikely prospect, but in order to fall asleep, I'd have to occupy my mind with something other than murder. "Give your mom my best. I hope she's lucid tonight."

"Me, too." Joss offered a weak smile. "Hey, I'm sorry about what happened today. You . . . seeing another body."

I shivered. "I shouldn't have gone to Payton Buley's house. It was my fault. Wrong place, wrong time."

"Except you were able to get fresh eyes on the crime scene. The police should be thankful."

"Ha!" I perched on the edge of the desk and folded my arms. "I'm glad we were able to clear Addie Tan."

She agreed and waved goodbye.

Fiona stood up on tippy-toe. "I'm off, too, if that's okay. I have a seminar tonight."

Rats. I was hoping she'd hang out with me. "More plant psychology?"

"Yes." She didn't sound enthused.

"What's wrong? You loved the first class."

"Sure, because it was spectacular. But now we have to take a step backward and study the chemistry of plants." She yawned dramatically. "Boring."

"I loved chemistry."

"I mean, it's okay, but it's so blah. See, when fairies are born, we're all given a complete knowledge of the basics. Every one of us." She tapped her fingertips. "Photosynthesis, seasonality, dormancy, how plants reproduce."

"I had no idea."

"We even know pretty much everything about biology and chemistry. It's sort of in our DNA. But psychology? That's unique. Unknown." She spun in a circle. "Learning what makes a plant cry?

Wow!" She mimed an explosion next to her head. "That's what we all thought we'd be learning."

"Plants cry?"

"Yes, they release fluid to protect themselves from harmful stuff, like fungi and bacteria."

I whistled, impressed.

"But Merryweather said we had to review first. Gotta go, or I'll be late." She bussed my cheek, her wings tickling my skin. "And for the record, I'm glad, too, about Addie."

As she zipped out the door, I turned back to the whiteboard, thinking about Joss's and now Fiona's parting words. Had we, in fact, cleared Addie? Was she off the hook because of the alibi that she'd provided? She'd given the names of three people who saw her. Would they lie on her behalf? She'd wanted her license back from Nicolas. Had he promised to bring it to her and reneged? Had she killed him in a fit of anger? And when Payton wouldn't hand it over, did she go to his house and demand he return it? How would she have been able to wheedle her way inside and sedate him like I'd suggested to Renee? I couldn't wrap my head around that scenario—Payton being stubborn; Addie pleading. Not to mention, I couldn't see her shooting him point-blank.

I spotted Hunter Hock's name on the whiteboard. As much as I liked him, I *could* see him killing Nicolas. Jealousy was a powerful motivator. But why would he frame and kill Nicolas's brother? And how on earth would he have cajoled his way into Payton's place and sedated him? I supposed he could have shown up with some kind of tranquilizer in hand. Though smaller in size, Hunter was muscular. He might've charged in and injected Payton with something. I shuddered, remembering how a famous actress had come to town for a birthday party and was knocked out with ether before being poisoned.

My stomach grumbled. Pixie rose to her feet and did a downward dog pose followed by a cat-cow stretch. If I didn't know better, I'd swear she'd been watching the yoga class I occasionally streamed.

My cell phone jangled with Meaghan's *crystals* ringtone. My father's ringtone was *motorcycle*. Brady's, *cosmic*. I answered.

"Could you come to Flair and help me and Ziggy out?" she asked. "I have snacks."

"I'll be there in five."

After promising Pixie I'd return shortly, I ran up the courtyard steps to Flair and entered. Only Ziggy and Meaghan were there. He was wearing one of his classically flamboyant shirts and black jeans. She looked beautiful in a flowing, white clip-dot dress with puff sleeves. How she pulled off such ethereal outfits astounded me. It would have swallowed me whole. Ziggy and she were addressing works of art that had been stacked upright against a wall. There were no customers. Their part-timer was nowhere to be seen.

"There's cheese, and I've opened wine." Meaghan pointed to the counter, where a red lacquered plate of sliced cheese sat beside a bottle of pink wine and three long-stemmed glasses. "It's rosé, if you're interested."

A glass actually sounded good. I poured myself some and took a sip and downed a bite of cheese. Sharp cheddar, my favorite. "So what are you up to, and why do you need my help?"

Ziggy said, "These are all Nicolas's works. Two will be going to Violet's for exhibition. We have to choose which two."

"Are these the ones you took home with you?" I asked.

"I tried to explain to the police why they were in my closet, but they thought I was hiding them."

"It wasn't like that," Meaghan said in his defense. "Hanging a painting on display for an extended period of time can be detrimental for a piece. It can cause fading."

"And cracking," Ziggy added.

"One of the main reasons why paintings deteriorate is from being exposed to too much light." Meaghan gestured to the gallery. "That's due to the chemical reaction of certain mediums and ultraviolet light. We need to let in sunlight so buyers can see the true beauty of the work. But—"

"But"—Ziggy cut in—"if we hang them for too long and they decline, we depreciate their value."

"The ideal place to store art is in a cool, dry, dark place with minimal temperature fluctuations," Meaghan said. "You've seen me constantly checking the humidity level in the gallery."

I had.

"Ziggy thought that because our storage room was jam-packed"—she motioned to the back of the gallery—"he would take a few of Nicolas's works home and protect them until Violet's event."

"I didn't note everything on the log." Ziggy groaned. "Big mistake."

"And you didn't write up receipts," I said.

"Nope. I'd taken art before and housed it with no problem, but when the police found them this time, they thought it gave me motive to kill Nicolas." He heaved a sigh of relief. "I'm glad we got that resolved."

Meaghan said, "They still haven't determined who did it, though, have they?"

I said, "They think his brother did. You heard about Payton, right?"

They both nodded glumly.

"I still can't believe it," Meaghan said. "Both brothers . . . dead."

"I don't think Payton killed himself," I said, and explained why.

"You told the police your theory?" Meaghan asked.

"I said as much to Renee. She has Summers's ear." Wine in hand, I moseyed to the framed art and tipped the front piece forward so I could see the next. "Nicolas's work was always so turbulent."

"*Passionate* is the word we use," Meaghan said. "He had a lot of angst to work out. Now he'll never . . ." She pulled a tissue from her dress pocket and dabbed her eyes.

I crossed to her and clasped her shoulder.

She rallied, stuffed the tissue back in her pocket, and said, "Help us hang them. Ziggy will advise from a distance so we get them level."

I set my wineglass aside and brushed my hands on my jeans. "Ready."

An hour later, after they'd selected two paintings, I retrieved Pixie from Open Your Imagination and walked home. As I approached the cottage and spied the drift of milkweed that I'd planted a couple of months ago, I thought again of Payton Buley—the lone milkweed plant on his porch—and wondered if Summers had come to any further conclusion about the man's death. If I reached out to Renee, would she tell me if I was correct about him having been drugged? No. Doubtful. She may not even know.

I slogged inside and headed for the kitchen. I took solace whenever I dined in my kitchen, knowing my mother would have loved what I'd done with the décor. Tiered glass shelves over the sink held rows of herbs in a variety of white mug planters. I'd painted the hutch and buffet faux-antique white to match the kitchen cabinets.

Pixie mewed.

I said, "Yes, little girl, you're first."

I fed her her favorite tuna cat food and prepared a small shredded chicken salad with a sriracha-based dressing for myself. Then I poured a glass of iced tea and sat at the white table in the nook. I ate listlessly, preoccupied with my thoughts. How I wished another murder hadn't occurred in Carmel. We had such a beautiful, serene community populated by people who wanted to enhance the living experience for everyone. I supposed other communities where murder occurred felt the same. Did their residents agonize over it as much as I did? Did I worry more because I'd tapped into the universal goodness of the fairy world?

The doorbell rang. I startled and dropped my fork. It clattered on my plate. Pixie raised her head as I peeked at my watch. Well past seven. Brady was at work. Dad was probably with Wanda.

"It's okay," I murmured to her, and nabbed my cell phone. Hesitantly, I tiptoed to the door, peeked out the peephole, and bit back a gasp.

Sassy Jacobi was standing on my doorstep, dressed in a leather bomber-style jacket, V-neck sweater, and jeans, a crossbody crocheted purse slung across her chest. Her arms were clutching her torso as if she needed to steady herself. She didn't look threatening. In fact, she appeared to be on the verge of tears.

I shook out the tension in my shoulders, pocketed my cell phone, made sure that the shovel I kept in the foyer for protection was at the ready, and opened the door. A chill gripped me. The fog had rolled in. "Hi."

"May I come in?"

I peered beyond her. I couldn't see far, due to the murkiness, but no one seemed to have accompanied her. Even so, I said, "Let's sit on the porch." I'd added a second weather-resistant, mission slat rocking chair recently. Pixie slipped past my ankles and jumped onto one of the chairs.

"You don't trust me," Sassy said.

"I don't *not* trust you," I said, "but—"

"Payton Buley is dead!" she exclaimed, hugging herself harder. "Dead!"

"I know."

"You know? I just found out. I can't believe it. He and Nicolas . . ." She started to blubber.

Quickly, I plucked a shawl from the coat rack, slung it over my shoulders, and stepped outside. The aroma of rosemary and basil from the plants on the verdigris stand filled the air. A gentle breeze made the wind chimes tinkle.

"Sit." I nudged Sassy.

She slumped into the leftmost rocking chair. Pixie sprang from the chair she'd been occupying and into Sassy's lap.

"She's hypoallergenic," I said.

"It's okay. I love cats," Sassy said, stroking her.

I sat down and waited for her to continue. Why had she come to my house? She'd dismissed me earlier. She must have friends who could console her in her grief.

"What the heck is going on?" Sassy asked as she wiped her nose with the sleeve of her jacket. "The police say Payton killed himself. How horrible is that? Don't get me wrong. I'm not sorry he's dead. He was a despicable man."

I didn't respond.

She scowled at me. "You don't think he offed himself, do you? Why not?"

"I was at the crime scene."

"You saw him?" She shuddered. "Ick." For a long time, she stroked Pixie with fervor. When she stopped, she said, "I came to see you because the police respect you."

I frowned.

"It's true. I heard Detective Summers talking about you to his partner. The other day. At Violet Vickers's house."

"I didn't see Officer Reddick there."

"He'd left by the time you arrived, but the detective told him you have a good mind."

I recalled Renee's account of Summers grousing that he didn't need two Courtney Kellys offering their two cents. She'd taken it as a compliment. I wasn't so sure.

"I'm not lying," she said. "I don't have any reason to." Using her toes, she pushed the porch to start the rocker in motion. Pixie leaped off and hid behind my ankles.

As Sassy swung back and forth, her face softened, making her look about half her age. After a few more minutes passed, she stopped swinging and twisted in the chair. She propped her elbows on the armrest and gazed at me intently. "If I tell you something, will you help me smooth it over with the police?"

Chapter 23

And when Spring comes back, with its
Mild soft ray,
And the ripple of gentle rain,
The fairies bring what they've taken away,
And give it us all again.
—Jean Ingelow, "About the Fairies"

I swallowed hard. If I didn't say I'd help her, would she kill me? I didn't see anger in her eyes. I saw fear. Hoping against hope that she wasn't a murderess, I said, "I can't promise anything." That was what my father had said when I was in high school and I'd asked him to intervene with the principal on my behalf. I hadn't really done anything wrong. A friend had. She'd cheated off my trigonometry test. She hadn't told me until the tests were turned in. My friend—who wasn't a friend anymore—had stunk at math, but she'd needed an *A* grade in order to get into calculus, a course required by her college of choice. Before weighing in with a response, my father had listened, and then he'd led me by the elbow to the principal's office. I could still remember the embarrassment I'd felt.

"Does it have to do with something illegal in Africa, Sassy?" I asked.

She worked her tongue inside her mouth. After a long moment, she said, "Yes."

"I knew it. Nicolas was into something. Was it drug trafficking?"

"No. He wasn't . . . He didn't . . . It was me. I made a guitar using illegal Madagascar rosewood."

"Whoa," I murmured.

"Only one!" She held up a finger. "But Nicolas found out and got mad."

I'd heard about the rosewood trade. Rosewood was the most bartered, wild product in the world, prized for its use in furniture. "Did you kill him to silence him?"

"What? No!"

Pixie yowled in fear.

"Sorry, cat." Sassy lowered her voice. "One of my clients—and no, before you ask, Courtney, I won't reveal his name—smuggled in the wood. Because of his status, he was able to bypass a whole bunch of legal hoops."

That suggested her client had political muscle. Could it be the Saudi prince Violet had hinted about?

"Nicolas said he was going to turn me in." Sassy picked at the cuffs of her jacket. "He hated anybody who cut corners."

"He did?"

"Yeah, because his father, who was an architect, bilked clients by doing that exact same thing."

The word *huh* escaped my lips.

"Man, he hated his father with a passion"—Sassy pressed her palms together, not in prayer, but as a way to stop fussing—"not because he was a thief, but because he was mean and rotten to the core."

I thought of what Addie Tan had said and revised my earlier thought. Had Mr. Buley beaten both of his sons? Had Nicolas become an abuser like Payton because of it? Would an abuser be upset that his father was a thief? Would he worry that his friend had used illegal wood? The ethical issues weren't matching up.

"Sassy, did Nicolas hit you?"

"Never." She pinned her lower lip between her teeth.

"Did he hurt your sister?" I asked gently. "Is that why she left town?"

"Yes . . . he shoved her. She stumbled into a door. She came to me for help. I urged her to pack up and go." Sassy sniffed. "But back to the rosewood thing."

The rapid change of subjects, from Africa, to abuse, to therapy, and back to Africa was making me feel like a ping-pong ball in a world-champion competition.

"I pleaded with Nicolas not to tell the police what I'd done." Tears leaked from her eyes. "I promised I'd go to the proper authorities and report what happened. I vowed I would pay my debt."

That was why Renee had heard the word *debt* when Sassy and Nicolas had argued. "And did you? Pay it?"

"That's the real reason I went to the church last Wednesday. To pray. After Payton's outburst at Violet's house, I realized I had to do what Nicolas wanted me to do if I was ever going to get him to love me."

"Hold on. You knew he hit your sister, you knew he was an abuser, and yet you wanted to be in a relationship with him?"

"He was going to change. He was seeing a therapist."

I thought how Addie had believed he would change, too, and how she'd dreamed of winning his love. What was it about the guy that had made women crazy for him?

"After I left the church, I went home and contacted a lawyer in San Francisco who might be able to help me out of my problem," Sassy went on. "I left a message for her to call me back. There should be a record of that, right? Like a phone log? That will prove I couldn't have killed him."

"Maybe, but you could have made that call from Meaghan's house."

She screwed up her mouth.

"You haven't followed through with the lawyer, though, have you?" I tilted my head. "You realized with Nicolas dead, you didn't have to."

"No, but after talking to you earlier today"—her tone was a piteous whine—"I realized I do want to tell the truth. For Nicolas. To honor his memory." She placed a hand over her heart. "He was so special. So talented."

She truly did have a warped image of him, but I wouldn't debate her.

"What's the lawyer's name?" I asked, deciding to give it to Detective Summers.

Sassy pulled her cell phone from her purse, swiped through contacts, and flashed the display at me. "This is her info."

"Send it to me." I told her my phone number, and she texted the contact. I immediately sent it to Summers with a note that Sassy Jacobi had something pertinent to tell him that might clear her from being a suspect in Nicolas Buley's murder. I showed her what I'd written. "Detective Summers will be expecting your call."

Sassy slid her cell phone into her purse. "Yeah, okay."

As I watched her slog down the path, ponytail swishing, a theory came to me that made me queasy. Had Payton taken up where Nicolas had left off? Had he blackmailed Sassy and threatened to expose her if she didn't pay him a hefty sum? Was she the one who might have wheedled her way into his house and killed him?

She climbed into the ragtop Jeep she'd parked behind my MINI Cooper. As she was driving away, I spotted the glow of a cigarette. Across the street. Because of the fog, I couldn't tell who it was. A shiver ran down my spine. Was it the same person Fiona had seen watching me? I raced inside and slammed and bolted the door, my heart chugging so fast I could barely breathe. I bent over, braced my hands on my thighs, and inhaled and exhaled slowly until I felt calmer.

Fiona appeared. She must have entered through the kitchen vent. She hovered midair. "What's wrong?"

I told her.

"I'll be right back." She sped away. Seconds later, she returned. "There's no one there."

I pondered the possible scenarios. Maybe the observer had been a policeman who considered Sassy a suspect and was tracking her movements, which would explain why he had gone. Or it could have been the pastor of the church, out with her dog, although I'd never once seen her smoke.

My appetite quashed, I returned to the kitchen and washed my dinner plate. Fiona followed, chattering on about her class and what she'd learned. As I was setting the dish in the rack to dry, another thought occurred to me. About Sassy. I spun around. Pixie had settled into her bed. Fiona was perched on the point of Pixie's ear.

"You," I said accusatorily.

"Me, what?"

"Did you, you know, mess with Sassy Jacobi?"

Fiona spiraled into the air and stopped, her wings flapping to keep her in place. "I didn't make her say anything at the coffee shop. Fairy's honor." She crossed her heart.

"Not then," I said. "But a few minutes ago?"

Fiona looked totally confused.

"She was here," I went on. "She came to talk to me. Did you take a side trip after class and track her down and coerce her to come here? Because she spilled everything to me like she'd been doused with a truth potion."

"I didn't do it." Fiona's voice squeaked with despair. "I can't, remember? I'm not allowed. If I did, I couldn't go back to the fairy kingdom ever. And I won't jeopardize that."

She flew into the crook of my neck and sobbed.

I plucked her away and set her on my palm. Staring into her sorrowful eyes, I said, "Okay. I believe you."

Licking tears off her lips, she said, "I want to look at the portal in the cypress. I won't go in, but I want to see it up close. Is that okay?"

"Sure." I lifted my hand, and she flew away.

As she did, I kept wondering about the person I'd seen across the street. I wished I could have made out features or size or gender. I wasn't cowardly by nature, but something about today's events was setting me off. Going to the church searching for a murder weapon. Seeing Payton Buley dead. Learning Addie's true story. Sassy showing up on my doorstep. I wanted—no, I *craved*—company. I dialed Meaghan. She didn't answer. I tried Brady at the café. His hostess said he was slammed. Reluctantly, I dialed my father. He answered after one ring.

"What's up, sweetie?" he asked.

"Could you come over?"

"Is something wrong?"

"Nothing. Okay, yes. I'm not sure." I filled him in.

"I'll be there in five, and I'm bringing Gus with me."

"I don't need Gus." Gus worked for my father's landscaping firm. He guarded projects that required expensive onsite equipment. He was enormously tall and intimidating with a pussycat's demeanor, unless riled.

"Like you didn't need him the last time?" my father quipped.

I moaned. "I didn't. Remember? Nothing untoward happened."

"Because he was sitting guard on your porch."

Knowing my father wouldn't be deterred, I didn't argue. "I'll make you coffee."

"Water will be fine."

He arrived at my house in a matter of minutes. I was pretty sure he'd broken speed limits. All limits within the city's confines were less than twenty-five miles per hour, and some were as low as fifteen. Gus, looking grim, took up his position on the front porch, throwing a mylar blanket over himself for warmth.

Swell.

After my father left, I didn't write a blog. I didn't tend to anything business-related. Instead, I climbed into bed and fell fast asleep. Unfortunately, my dreams—nightmares—were plagued with impaled receipts, lacy coral, and gazing balls flying through the air like asteroids on a collision course.

Wednesday morning, I awoke in a sweat and gazed out my bedroom window. I didn't see Fiona. I didn't see the portal. I panicked.

She hadn't gone through, had she, after Merryweather had warned her not to?

I opened the window and called out, "Fiona?" I heard her teeny voice. She was crying. I threw on a robe and ventured outside to find her. She was sitting cross-legged at the base of the cypress, her wings at rest by her sides.

"It's gone," she wailed. "Gone."

Chapter 24

'I believe in Fairies,' say it loud and
Say it clear.
For every time you say it, another fairy
will survive.
—Felicia Dorothea Browne-Hemans, "I Believe"

"There, there." I sat beside her and brushed the crest of her shoulder. "Don't fret. Another portal will appear when it's time."

"But this one was special. It was here. In our yard." She began to weep again.

For a good thirty minutes, we sat staring at the base of the tree before she roused and found her footing.

"I'm off," she said resolutely. "I must speak to Merryweather." With that pronouncement, she zipped away.

I returned inside, skipped my morning run, and fed the cat. Then I woke Gus and handed him a muffin and thanked him for his service. Once he left, I showered, threw on a pair of khaki capris, my favorite clogs, and an olive-toned shirt with the words: GARDEN FAIRIES DO EXIST. THEY TURN FLOWERS INTO FOOD. Then I grabbed a to-go breakfast of yogurt and a banana and sped to work with Pixie.

When I arrived, I learned I had to add one more to-do item to my list. Plus I needed to prepare for an afternoon fairy door class as well as touch base with all our suppliers—we were low on plants as well as fertilizer. As if that wasn't enough, Hunter Hock had left a message asking me to make a companion mermaid garden for his daughter. Could I have it for him by noon?

Why not? In record time, I landed on a theme, and I had all the items. When I phoned him back to say yes, Pixie mewed at me like I was nuts. I scrubbed her under the chin, which seemed to appease her.

The learning-the-craft area was as neat as a pin when I sat down to make the garden, first focusing on the kingdom—a very small kingdom—where a wee mermaid finds the use of her legs. I created a lagoon and fashioned the path to the kingdom by hot-gluing crushed red rock and pebbles to a windy piece of water-resistant foam. As I was placing the path in the garden, the red rock stirred a memory. A month ago, Meaghan had shown me a note she'd received from Nicolas. He said he was doing well in Sedona, and his artwork was receiving high praise. He'd included a copy of one of the reviews published in the *Sedona Red Rock*. I recalled the attribution for the article went to K.L. Hamm. Remembering the name jarred me. Was it possible K.L. Hamm was Kaylene Hamilton? Had she moved to Arizona to be an art reviewer? Was it conceivable that Nicolas, with his wandering eye, had hooked up with her? Had he sent the piece to Meaghan, hoping she'd put two and two together and be jealous?

I pulled my cell phone from my pocket. I didn't have Janna Hamilton's number. So, I dialed Hunter's. I told him I was almost done with the fairy garden and asked if he had a sec. He did, and I launched ahead with my query.

His voice was husky with emotion when he said, "Yes, K.L. Hamm was Kaylene. How did you know?"

I told him about Nicolas sending Meaghan a copy of Kaylene's review. "Did you realize she'd critiqued Nicolas's work?"

"I imagine she met a lot of artists. I introduced her to a few."

"Do you know if she and Nicolas—"

"Look, I'm sorry. I've gotta go. Time crunch. If you don't m-mind"—his voice snagged—"would you ask Meaghan if my sister could have that article, that is, if she still has it and didn't toss it? Kaylene didn't send any of her reviews to her mother."

"Sure." When I hung up, before I reached out to Meaghan, I texted Ulani about K.L. Hamm and the *Sedona Red Rock*. This was a lead she could follow.

Joss arrived as I was carrying Hunter's daughter's garden to the counter. "Cute," she said. "We have another mermaid believer?"

"No, this is for Ella Hock. Hunter's spoiling her."

"It's adorable. I love the way you set half of the mermaid above the water."

I'd had to modify one of the mermaid figurines, but I couldn't resist using the idea I'd given my father for Violet's koi pond. I set it aside, wrote up a sales slip, and tended to the coffee machine. I desperately needed a cup of coffee; I'd skipped it at home. "How's your mom doing?" I asked.

"Same old. I took Buddy with me last night. Mom thought he was my father. It was a tad embarrassing. She nearly kissed him on the lips." Joss chuckled while hanging her sweater on a hook beyond the coffee setup. "Buddy took it in stride." Her eyes brightened whenever she talked about him. I was happy for her.

As I was pouring myself a cup of coffee, a woman warbled, "Hello-o-o!" at the entrance to the shop. "Hope you don't mind us barging in."

I spun around and saw Violet Vickers cutting her way around the display tables. Finley and George Pitt entered on her heels—Finley, chic in a floral sheath and ballet slippers, and George, camera-ready in blue suit and striped shirt, sans tie. His wavy hair was expertly combed, and if I were to guess, he'd applied a gel bronzer to his face. He seemed tanner than he had the other night.

"We aren't quite ready for customers," I said.

Joss was on the patio, wiping down the tables and chairs. Pixie was snoozing by the fountain. I'd already tweaked the racks filled with figurines. Fiona hadn't returned from her meeting with Merry-weather.

"We don't mind." Violet waved to me. Over her white slacks, she was wearing a billowy lavender top that did nothing for her figure but looked comfortable and, as always, expensive. "George and Finley came by the house yesterday. George wanted to see the gardens before the soirée."

"They're beautiful," George said.

Finley, who'd swept her banged bob into a pearl-and-gold claw clip, was fingering everything she passed. Wind chimes. Teacups. Macramé holders. She *ooh*ed when she spied the Sara Biddle mystic crystal spirits fairy I'd housed in a Plexiglas box. A limited first-edition, it was handcrafted with layered wings, glitter, and gold trim. "I want this," she said, lifting the box.

George took it from her and brought it to the counter. "We were very impressed with the fairy gardens you made for Violet. She convinced us we should take a class and learn how to make them." He scanned the area, as if searching for a fairy. Leaning toward me, he whispered, "Is it true you can see them?"

I smiled indulgently.

Finley swatted his arm. "Oh, George, cut it out. Of course she can't."

Violet said, "But she can, dear. It's true."

"Can you, Violet?" Finley asked, a hint of snideness in her tone.

"Well, no, but that doesn't mean they aren't real."

"I've felt their presence," George said.

"You have not." Finley snorted, which gave her a porcine look that didn't go along with her pretty features.

"I might've even seen one at Violet's," George added.

Finley choked out a laugh. "Oh, George, stop. My leg hurts you're pulling it so hard."

"It was green and fluttery." He wiggled his fingers.

Had he seen Calliope? She liked to roam about town.

"Stop." Finley flicked George's arm again.

"So can we take a class, Courtney?" Violet asked.

"All three of you?"

"Yes. I'll pay you handsomely for a private one right now. I know we should have made reservations, but George and Finley showed so much interest last night, and they can only spare the morning. Otherwise, George is booked with PR events. Our very own Ulani Kamaka is interviewing him at noon."

I hoped Ulani would have enough time to follow my lead. By now, she must have lined up lots of appointments with celebrities.

"Sure," I said. "I don't have anything scheduled until the afternoon." Calls to the suppliers could wait.

Violet clapped her hands together. "Excellent."

"Would you like some coffee or tea?" I motioned to the beverage station behind the sales counter.

"We ate a huge breakfast around the corner," George said, patting his firm belly. "I don't think there's room for even a drop of water." He continued to gaze upward.

"Follow me." I handed them each a small shopping basket and led them to the patio. Quickly, I explained to Joss what we were doing. She nodded and went to the showroom as I guided my threesome through the process of coming up with a story for their fairy gardens, then picking a pot and choosing some figurines as well as environmental pieces. "I'll make sure you have the right plants, if that's okay."

"Phew," George said dramatically. "After hearing Violet talk, I was afraid I was going to have to get a diploma in agriculture before I could make one of these."

Finley tittered. She was a perfect foil—I meant *audience*—for all his antics.

Violet said, "Courtney, do you have gloves? I'm worried about my manicure."

"Me, too," Finley said.

I didn't have a lot of customers who cared about getting their hands dirty, but there were a few, so I kept plenty of clean garden gloves on hand. I fetched two pairs from the storage closet and placed them on the workstation table.

"I'm going to create my lovely new yard," Violet said while selecting a fairy figurine in a purple dress, a landscaping fairy carrying a shovel, a floral arch, and a pond. "Your father . . ." Her voice sounded dreamy. "Oh, my, what he can do with his hands."

"Well, do tell, Violet." George chuckled. "What can he do with his hands?"

"Oh, George," Finley said. "Don't tease."

"Hey." He threw his arms wide. "When given an opportunity like that, I gotta dive in."

Violet's cheeks burnished red. "I meant . . . All I wanted to say . . ." She set her items on the table and sat. "Courtney, George told me all about his film project."

"The one he's shooting in Africa?" I asked, flashing on Sassy and her dilemma. Had she reached out to Detective Summers and come to any resolution? Would she be going to jail for dealing in illegal wood? More importantly, did her alibi for the night of Nicolas's murder hold up?

"No, the next movie," Violet continued. "It's hush-hush, but he'll be shooting in Iceland."

"*Brr.*" Finley wrinkled her nose. "He's going without me. I hate the cold."

"It's not that cold." George set two figurines on the table and returned to the racks. "And we'll be dressed appropriately."

She shook her head and tapped his nose affectionately. "No, sweetie. I'm all for taking safaris and battling mosquitoes, but this one you get to do solo."

George adjusted the collar of his shirt and rotated his neck ever so slightly to work out a kink. Had her refusal miffed him? Did he expect her to go everywhere he went? Was there trouble in paradise?

For the next half hour, I guided them through the steps: filling the pots they'd selected with dirt; tamping it down so there were no air pockets; inserting most of the plants—some could be installed after figurines were in place—and finally dressing up the pot with stones or gravel and other colorful items.

Halfway through, Fiona soared to the patio, upbeat and bubbly. When she saw us, she zoomed to George and perched on his earlobe. He reached for her. She bustled to the other side. He shook his head.

Giggling, she flew directly in front of Finley and hovered. Finley wasn't the least interested. Not one to give up, my sweet fairy folded her arms and waited. She tapped her foot. She checked her nonexistent watch, as she'd seen me do when I was impatient. Finally, she huffed and said, "Well, she has no imagination."

Violet craned an ear. Had she heard Fiona?

"Courtney!" Brady called as he crossed the threshold to the patio. "Joss said you were—" He drew to a halt. "Oh, sorry. I didn't realize you were giving a—" His eyes went wide. "Well, look who's here."

Finley swung around on the bench. "Brady, darling, join us. We're summoning fairies."

He exchanged a look with me.

I crossed to him. "C'mon. We're making gardens and opening our hearts and minds to the possibility."

"Make gardens with my ex?" He pulled a face. "I'll pass."

"Why are you here?"

"You phoned the restaurant last night. Everything okay?"

I told him about my conversation with Sassy.

"Well, aren't you the go-to person when it comes to confessions," he teased.

I shrugged. "She thought I could smooth it over with Summers."

"And did you?"

"I texted him. I suppose I should follow up and see if she went in to talk to him. He didn't send me flowers or balloons or a thank-you note." I laughed. "When she left, I saw someone with a cigarette looking in my direction. I couldn't make out features because of the fog. I reached out to you and then my dad. He came over and brought Gus." Brady knew all about Gus.

"So you slept like a baby."

I hadn't. Not with the nightmares.

"Brady, c'mon, sit," Finley ordered. "There's space. George, make room."

"Sorry." Brady hooked a thumb over his shoulder. "I've got to get back to the café."

George chuckled. "I envy your skills, man. I burn toast."

"But you can act, and I can't," Brady said judiciously. He hadn't liked one movie George had been in, but then, he was a film snob. He preferred foreign films and documentaries and the occasional spaghetti western. He bussed me on the cheek. "See you. Ring me." He made a telephone gesture with his thumb and pinky.

At the same time, my cell phone jangled in my pocket. I pulled it out and read the screen. Hunter Hock was calling.

"Brady, wait," I said, and addressed my impromptu class. "I'll be right back, everyone. Discuss your creations amongst yourselves." I pressed Send on the phone and said, "Hey, Hunter. You can come in and pick up the garden at any time."

"That's not what I'm calling about," he said.

I headed to the office to keep the conversation semi-private. Brady trailed me and closed the door behind us.

"I found the receipt for the solar globe," Hunter added.

"You mean I found it, Daddy," Ella yelled in the background. "It was on top of the pile in the kitchen."

If it had been on top of the pile, he should have been able to locate it the other day, but I let that slide. Meaghan's comment about the disarray of artists' lives came back to me.

"The store is The Greenhouse," Hunter went on. "And I came across the one for the gazing ball, too. Ow!" He wailed. "Okay, Ella found that one, too." I presumed she'd playfully poked him. "It was a little place in Florida called Garden Beauty. If you want, I can take a picture of them and text them to you."

"I'd appreciate it. Thanks!"

"I saw other gazing balls yesterday," Ella chimed, her voice reedy in the distance.

"Where?" Hunter asked her.

"At the nursery outside of town on Carmel Valley Road. I went there with Aunt Janna. She needed more plants for the garden."

Clearly, Janna's sabbatical was providing more time to garden. I hoped she was finding it healing.

"Well, there you have it," Hunter said. "They can be purchased anywhere."

"I'll let the police know," I said, and ended the call.

Good to his word, the images came through immediately. Viewing them, I thought again of the receipts on Payton's desk and pictured his left-handed signature. Convinced I was right about that aspect and uncertain whether Renee had shared that tidbit with Detective Summers, I dialed the precinct and asked for him. The desk officer said he wasn't in and offered to take a message.

"Is Officer Reddick available?" I asked. "Tell him it's Courtney Kelly with pertinent information about the Payton Buley matter."

Brady was straining to see the images on my cell phone. I flashed them at him. He shrugged a shoulder, not understanding why I was calling the police.

"I'll explain in a sec," I whispered, and kept holding for Reddick. He would know as much as Summers about the status of Payton Buley's death and might be more willing to reveal something to me. *Might.* I pressed my cell phone speaker and placed the phone faceup on my desk. That way, Brady could listen in.

"Good morning, Miss Kelly. How might I assist you?" Reddick asked.

"First of all, are you interested in Meaghan Brownie? Because if you are, I think she would be amenable to a date. Just saying."

Brady knuckled me on the arm. I giggled.

Reddick hummed for a moment. "Thank you for that invaluable information," he said in a stiffly professional tone. "I was told you reached out about the Payton Buley case."

"Did you run a toxicology report?"

Reddick remained mute.

"Officer Reddick, I was at the crime scene and pointed out to Renee Rodriguez, who was also at the scene, that Payton Buley might be left-handed, and if that was the case, why would he kill himself using his right hand? I proposed that a killer might have incapacitated him with a sedative to immobilize him. So . . ." I let the word hang. "Have you run a toxicology report, and was I right? Did someone knock him out?"

He kept silent.

"Did you nail down the time of death?" I asked. "You can tell me that much."

"The coroner says the window was early Monday morning."

"Was anyone seen in the vicinity?"

"C'mon, Miss Kelly."

"It's a simple question, Officer. Let me be more specific. Did anyone see Sassy Jacobi in the area?" Ever since her surprise appearance at my house, I'd had doubts about her.

"Miss Jacobi? No. Why?"

"Payton Buley might have been blackmailing her." It was a long shot, but I wasn't convinced I was wrong.

"Blackmailing her for what?"

"An illegal business transaction she was involved in."

Reddick hummed. "Noted. I'll follow up. However, to your question, yes, someone fitting Adeline Tan's description was spotted in the neighborhood around four a.m. Detective Summers will be bringing her in for questioning."

Oh, my. She was seen in the area? That wasn't good.

"Hold on," I said. "Payton Buley's house isn't far from the mission on Del Rio Road. That was where Addie—Adeline—was when Nicolas Buley was murdered. I suppose she could have been headed there Monday morning, too."

Although four a.m. seemed mighty early to be out and about, I reflected.

Brady stepped toward my desk. "Red, hi, it's Brady Cash. May I say something?"

Reddick cleared his throat. "Wish I knew you'd been listening in, Brady."

"That's my fault, Officer," I said sheepishly.

"Go on, Brady," Reddick replied, a little more warmly. He and Brady had known each other for years because they both coached basketball at the Y in Monterey.

"If you're looking for someone to establish Adeline Tan's alibi," Brady said, "I can vouch for her. She was at the gym Monday morning. From five a.m. to seven a.m. Does that cover the window of opportunity?"

Chapter 25

Oh! Where do fairies hide their heads,
When snow lies on the hills,
When frost has spoiled their mossy beds,
And crystallized their rills?
—Thomas Haynes Bayly,
"Oh! Where Do Fairies Hide Their Heads?"

"As a matter of fact, it does," Reddick said. "Could you come to the precinct and fill out an affidavit?"

"Will do," Brady replied.

"Officer," I cut in. "There's one more thing." I told him about the nursery on Carmel Valley Road selling gazing balls. "Ella Hock and her aunt saw them there. They might have a list of customers they've sold them to."

"Now, that *is* pertinent information. Thank you." He ended the call.

Brady drew near and clasped my upper arms. "May I see you tonight?"

"Don't you have to work?"

"I'll get someone to cover my shift. I miss you."

"We had a date two days ago."

"It wasn't nearly long enough."

As he stroked my shoulders, his gaze melted me into a pool of desire. I agreed to a date, and he kissed me goodbye.

When I returned to the craft area to instruct Violet and friends, I was feeling more confident. I'd given the police the information I had. Plus, I'd steered them toward Sassy Jacobi. And, most likely, Brady had cleared Addie Tan of murder.

"Hey, everyone, I'm back. How are you doing?" I asked.

"Great," George said.

I noticed he'd added a blue fairy to his garden. Had he seen Fiona? Had the others? I checked out George's dreamy eyes that had won over the hearts of myriad fans . . . and saw they were aglow with newfound energy. Violet's and Finley's eyes appeared the same as before; they were interested in their projects, but neither woman had been enlightened.

Fiona fluttered to me and landed on my shoulder. "Yes, he can see me, but *shh.*" She held a finger to her lips. "He doesn't want anyone to know. He's afraid Finley will think he's crazy."

"Got it."

"He adores her," she added.

"I can tell." Because, honestly, he would have to in order to tolerate her flightiness.

When I found the opportunity, I winked at George. He winked back. It would be our secret.

After they left, the remainder of the morning sped by with phone calls to suppliers, multiple sales of items in the shop, and sign-ups for future group and one-on-one classes. When I found an hour to myself, I went to the patio and created a new fairy door for a garden that I knew was lacking. I often tweaked gardens I'd made when they didn't continue to speak to me. I would swap out arches for doors or switch new plants for old ones and so on—anything that might make the gardens more interesting. I did the same to the gardens in my yard.

I was standing on the patio, taking in my latest handiwork, making myself available if any of the dozen customers browsing the figurines and plant selections needed my assistance, when Joss said, "You have a phone call, boss. Line one."

"Who is it?"

"Ulani Kamaka. She tried your cell, but you didn't answer."

I scanned my cell phone. Indeed, I'd missed a call. "I'll take it in the office," I said, and asked her to tend to the customers.

"Will do. Yoly arrived. I've got her dusting and tweaking the showroom."

"Perfect."

Fiona winged behind me and settled atop the whiteboard as I closed the office door.

I picked up the phone and punched the button to connect me. "Hi, Ulani, what's up?"

"Are you sitting down?"

Automatically, I sat in the chair. Fiona sailed to the rim of the Zen garden, her curiosity piqued.

"I've got the scoop on Kaylene Hamilton, aka K.L. Hamm. She did reviews for the *Sedona Red Rock*."

As I'd deduced and Hunter had confirmed.

"I touched base with a colleague, a food columnist, and to hear her tell it, Kaylene—K.L.—was an up-and-comer in the art world. Every artist for miles around wanted her to review their work. The food columnist, who happened to be a good friend, said suddenly Kaylene disappeared. She called and left messages, but Kaylene didn't touch base."

I recalled Janna saying daily texts from Kaylene had stopped.

"Soon after, her uncle showed up," Ulani said. "He talked to local police."

Neither Hunter nor Janna had mentioned that to me, but why would they have? I wasn't a close personal friend.

"The cops wouldn't file a missing person's report," Ulani went on, "because Kaylene hadn't been out of the picture long enough. But her uncle was worried. He told the police Kaylene had called her mother the week before saying she was afraid of her boyfriend. Her mother offered to buy her a plane ticket home, but Kaylene turned her down. She said she would work things out."

Fiona let out a soft moan.

"Still the police wouldn't do anything?" I asked.

"Nope. It was hearsay. No domestic dispute calls had been received." Ulani clicked her tongue.

"Did Hunter tell the police the name of the boyfriend?" I asked, my fingertips itching with curiosity.

"He said he didn't know who it was."

"Had the food columnist met the boyfriend?" I asked.

"Uh-uh. Apparently, the relationship was very hush-hush."

"Something's off," Fiona said.

I felt the same. Had Nicolas been the boyfriend? Had he worried that if they'd made their relationship public, her reviews wouldn't hold as much weight?

Fiona hopped to her feet and started pacing the Zen garden, though her tiny feet barely left tracks.

"Using rock climbing pictures that his niece sent her mother," Ulani continued, "Hunter Hock searched for her. Kaylene was an avid climber. Later the next day, he spotted her body at the bottom of a steep cliff."

"No way!" I exclaimed. Poor Hunter. I couldn't imagine the shock.

"He led the police to her, and they determined it was a suicide."

"Did her friend have a clue why Kaylene would kill herself?" The sadness I felt surprised me. I hadn't known the girl.

"No. She's beside herself with grief. She said Kaylene was an upbeat, positive kind of person. It didn't make sense."

That was exactly what Janna had said about her daughter.

I flashed on what had happened to Nicolas and Payton Buley's parents, both meeting their respective deaths by falling down stairs, and a horrid thought flooded my mind. Had my theory about Payton killing his parents been faulty? Had Nicolas killed them? If Addie, Meaghan, and Sassy could be believed, he had a history of abuse, too.

Had he befriended Kaylene? After they'd grown close, did something set him off? Did he push her to her death?

"Was there any sign of foul play?" I asked.

"The police didn't determine any," Ulani replied. "One set of footprints. No sign of a scuffle."

"Did she write a note?"

"No."

That struck me as odd for someone who documented other people's work.

"Hunter Hock pressed and pressed, but the police wouldn't change their findings," Ulani added.

"Did the police pin down who the boyfriend was?"

"They wouldn't tell me."

I thanked her for the information and ended the call, sad that Hunter Hock had tried valiantly to find closure for his family, and sadder that Janna Hamilton wouldn't get any. Ulani's account said so much about Hunter and his big heart and his readiness to go the extra mile to help his sister. Even with Meaghan, he'd been willing to put his heart on the line, despite the fact she didn't share his affections.

Thinking of him and his gifts to Meaghan made me remember the images of receipts he'd sent me. I pulled up the one from The Greenhouse for the solar orb.

"What's that?" Fiona asked, looking at the picture.

"A receipt Hunter sent me. I want to buy one of these for Violet Vickers as a thank-you gift for all of her business. It'll look nice in her yard, don't you think?"

"Yes, but why does it look like he bought two? See the total?"

I examined the receipt. "Maybe he bought one for his sister." I paused. Or perhaps he'd bought a matching one for himself so his garden would look similar to Meaghan's. He'd given her a cat silhouette and had placed one in his yard. He'd also gifted her a trio of dancing fairies that corresponded to the one in front of his cottage.

An idea niggled the edges of my mind. I swiped the phone's screen to view the receipt for the gazing balls. The number two had been erased to the left of the words *gazing balls* and replaced with the number one, but like on the Greenhouse receipt, the total purchase price was for two items.

My stomach wrenched as another notion surfaced. Had Hunter lied to the police? Had he figured out Kaylene's boyfriend was Nicolas? Had he blamed him for his niece's death and bought the second gazing ball to use as a murder weapon when Nicolas returned to town? No, that didn't make sense. Why wait until he moved back? Why not kill him in Arizona?

I dialed the phone number listed at the top of the receipt.

A genial woman answered. "Good afternoon. Garden Beauty. How may I assist you?"

I asked if she could answer a question about a purchase that had occurred two months ago.

She said she could, proudly adding that she was living in the twenty-first century; she digitalized everything. "Do you have an order number and date?"

I recited the information from the receipt.

"One moment." I heard her tapping what I presumed were computer keys. "Here we go. Yes, we sell a lot of gazing balls. What's your question?"

"Was the order for one or two gazing balls?"

"Two. The purchase price reflects that. One is seventy-nine ninety-five. This order totaled approximately one hundred and sixty dollars, plus tax."

"The receipt I'm looking at has the number one to the left of the words *gazing balls*."

"Oh, no, that's incorrect. Our receipt clearly states that two were purchased."

I thanked her, ended the call, and stared harder at the receipt.

"What are you thinking?" Fiona asked.

"Hunter Hock was jealous of Nicolas, but if his hatred ran deeper . . ."

"That reminds me of a line in *Othello*." She stopped pacing and spread her wings. "'He hath a daily beauty in his life that makes me ugly; and besides, the Moor may unfold me to him—there stand I in much peril. No, he must die.'"

"Your expanding knowledge of literature continues to amaze me," I said, tapping her nose fondly. "I'm going to have to knuckle down and read along with you."

She beamed at the compliment.

"What if he believed Nicolas Buley was responsible for Hunter's niece's death?" I went on. "Except I can't figure out why he would have sent me the altered receipt. Did he think, with this receipt as evidence, I might corroborate his innocence by vouching that he'd only bought one?" I wiggled my cell phone.

"You should let Detective Summers know."

"Exactly what I was planning to do." I texted the picture to him with a note explaining why Hunter had sent it to me, adding that, out of curiosity, I'd contacted Garden Beauty and confirmed that Hunter had purchased two, not one, gazing balls.

I thought of Meaghan. After a reasonable amount of time, would Hunter swoop in and try again to win her heart? If she denied him, would he hurt her? No. Nonsense. He loved her. Even so, I texted her. *Got a moment?*

She answered: *On my way to Janna Hamilton's house with a piece of art.*

I responded: *Why?*

Meaghan: *Hunter bought it for her as a surprise. Duh.* [silly face emoji]

I flinched. Had Hunter bought a piece of art for his sister as a ploy to get Meaghan alone?

I typed: *Stop. Don't go there.*

Meaghan: *Too late. Pulling up now.*

I wrote: *Don't go in.*

But she didn't reply.

Heart chugging, I raced to the main showroom and told Joss where I was headed and why. Fiona grabbed hold of my shirt collar and rode with me as I sprinted to Janna's house. It was hard to gain purchase in my clogs, but I hunkered down. At the same time, I tried calling the precinct, but my bumpy movements prevented me from hitting the right numbers on my cell phone.

Nearing the white storybook house with its enchanting garden, I saw Janna, her two daughters, and Ella driving by in a Chevy Tahoe. The girls were in the back seat, gesturing like they were dancing to whatever song they were singing.

I spotted Meaghan's car parked in front of the house. Hunter's BMW was in the driveway. I stole to Janna's house first and peeked in the front windows but didn't see any sign of Meaghan. I skirted the house and headed toward Hunter's cottage. On my way, I spied a wrought-iron, four-legged pedestal exactly like the one in Meaghan's yard, the kind of stand that would hold a gazing ball, except this one was empty. How had I missed it before?

Cursing under my breath, I hurried up the steps to Hunter's porch. I tried the front doorknob. It twisted. I eased the door open.

"Hunter, stop!" Meaghan screamed.

Chapter 26

Ah! There's a tiny fairy!
She's in the garden bed!
It's little Ray O'Sunshine
Who makes the roses red.
—Laura Ingalls Wilder, "The Fairies in the Sunshine"

I cut around the door to the right. Hunter was in his art studio, wrestling with Meaghan over a large painting. Both had a grip on the gilded frame. It was one of Nicolas's works—a turbulent coastal storm with lots of frothing waves.

"Please, Hunter, you'll hurt it," Meaghan pleaded.

"I don't care. I bought it. I can do what I want with it."

"I thought you'd put your anger with him behind you. When he died, he was no longer your competition. He—"

Hunter tugged. Meaghan yelped.

"Hunter!" I charged forward. "It's over. I know what happened."

He glowered at me. "What are you talking about?"

Fiona dashed to him and doused him with a green potion. He didn't stop wrestling with Meaghan. She tried a purple potion. Nothing. Flummoxed, she peeked under her flapping wings as if wondering whether any magic was drifting from them.

"I know why you killed Nicolas," I said.

Meaghan squealed. "What? You killed him?"

"No!" he protested.

"Yes," I stated. "It's not simply because you were jealous of him for winning Meaghan's heart. You were furious because he romanced your niece, Kaylene."

"What is she talking about?" Meaghan cried.

Like a trapped animal, Hunter released the painting and staggered backward. His lower back collided with the table that held the spiky coral, and in true domino effect, the impact made the larger paintings stored between the tables propel the massive pine table backward, which caused many of the items on it, including the lamp, paints, and art tools, to topple to the floor. Hunter whirled to steady everything but failed. He spun back and roared at Meaghan. "Look what you've done!"

"I didn't," Meaghan said, clapping a hand to her chest.

Fiona raced to Meaghan and chanted, "*By dee prood, den feole agus anam.*"

Out of nowhere, a glistening silver cloud enshrouded my pal.

"What the—" Hunter spluttered. He must've been able to see it.

Meaghan raised her hands. She touched the bubbly cloud and drew back in fear.

"Don't worry, she's okay," Fiona said to me. "You're all right, Meaghan. It's a protection spell. Loosely translated, it means 'May God protect her flesh and soul.' I'm allowed to use it now. He can't touch you in there."

"You!" Hunter whirled on me. "Did your fairy do that?" He grasped a piece of coral. It was sharp and lethal.

Fiona *eek*ed. "I can't do a second spell, Courtney."

I took a defensive stance Ziggy had taught me, one leg braced behind me, both hands raised at angles, prepared to do a roundhouse kick if necessary. Hunter couldn't fling the coral like a dart. He'd have to run at me to hurt me. But he didn't charge me. Why was he holding back? Did he worry that he'd lose Meaghan's love if he killed me? That was a pretty good bet.

"I knew you were getting closer," Hunter said. "Asking so many questions."

I spied a pack of cigarettes and ashtray sitting on one of the shelves beyond him. I'd missed seeing them on my previous visit. Was he the one who'd stood outside my house last night when Sassy was leaving? Was he ruing his decision not to have dealt with me then?

"Hunter, tell me about Kaylene," I said, hoping to mollify him. "You loved her very much."

His face softened. His eyes flooded with tears. I lowered my guard, ever so slightly.

"Like a daughter," he said. "When the girls' father walked out, I became like one to them."

"When Kaylene left California, you were concerned."

He nodded. "She wouldn't tell us why she wanted to go. She said it was for her career, but that didn't make sense. She had a fine offer at the *San Francisco Chronicle* for the same job. So why go to a smaller market like Sedona? We told her it would be a major setback."

"Sedona," Meaghan whispered from within her bubble. "Did she and Nicolas . . ." She didn't finish and instead moaned, grasping the gravity of her question.

"He was a cad. A user." Hunter snarled at her.

"You went to Sedona when Kaylene went missing," I said.

"What's your point?"

"Was that the first time you learned she and Nicolas were involved?"

"I went once before, right after she moved. I didn't figure out what was going on at that time. Sure, I saw Nicolas's work, front and center in all the galleries, paired with reviews by my niece, and thought what a joke. Who paints seascapes in Arizona? Except it was a brilliant move. He was a novelty act." He studied the coral in his hand. Was he wondering how to use it to get rid of me?

I glanced at the front door. Had Joss thought to call Detective Summers? Had she told him where I'd gone and why? I said,

"Hunter, after Kaylene phoned Janna to tell her she was scared of her boyfriend, she stopped communicating with you and her mother. You went to Sedona and asked the police for help, but they refused, claiming your niece hadn't been missing long enough."

"They were slackers."

"You told them you didn't know who her boyfriend was, but by then, you'd done the math. Why did you keep Nicolas's name out of it?"

His lip curled up on one side.

"Aha," I murmured. "Because you believed Nicolas had pushed her to her death, and you thought if the police went after him, he'd convince them he was innocent. You didn't want to give him the chance. You wanted to exact your own punishment."

He didn't rebut me.

"Tell me about Kaylene," I prompted. "Janna said she loved butterflies."

"And books. And chocolate chip cookies. And museums." His tone was wistful. "She was pretty and tall, like you, Meaghan." Hunter shot a look at her. "But she was also delicate and impressionable. She loved writing about artists. She worshipped their ability. She didn't have an ounce of talent, but she appreciated art like nobody's business."

"Thanks to you," I said.

"Thanks to me."

"When did you realize she'd relocated to be with Nicolas?" I asked. "She must have met him here."

"She must have, but she never let on. That girl . . ." His shoulders rose and fell. "She was so adamant about going. I didn't realize that's where he'd wound up. She sent postcards about her work and her outdoor adventures. Every one she wrote made her sound so happy. What could her mother do? Wrangle her? She was an adult. She had every right to live her life." He switched the spiky coral to his other hand.

Fiona circled his head. Landed on his ear. On his nose. He didn't flinch. Nothing distracted him.

"But then a month after Kaylene left town," he continued, "Janna reached out to me, hysterical. Kaylene was in the hospital with a busted eardrum. She claimed she hadn't been abused. She'd fallen. Before I got down there, the danged hospital had released her."

Tears pressed at the corners of Meaghan's eyes.

"So I went to her place of business. I didn't have a home address. Kaylene told me to go back to Carmel. She'd handle it. What could I do? I hung around until quitting time. I spied Nicolas picking her up, and that was when I knew for sure she'd hooked up with him." The jaws in his neck flexed with tension. He ran a finger over one of the spikes of the coral. "A month later, Kaylene was in the hospital again. I hopped a plane right away. Her eye was black and blue. Man, I wanted to kill him right then and there, but she begged me not to. She loved him. She told me to leave."

Meaghan whimpered. It was clear by her pained expression that she was realizing she'd dodged a bullet with Nicolas.

"What happened next?" I asked.

"After that visit, Kaylene continued to send postcards, but she stopped texting and wouldn't answer her phone. Her mother got worried. Not having any direct means of communication felt off to her. So I went to Sedona the first week in April, and I tracked down Nicolas. I threatened him. He swore she'd left him and moved back here. Then three weeks ago, we couldn't even ping her cell phone. It was out of juice. So I went back to talk to the police." He scrubbed his hair with his free hand. "They pretty much laughed in my face. When I flashed the postcards she'd been sending, they noted the postcards had real-time postmarks. They figured she had ditched the family, and it was time to move on."

"The postcards," I said. "Where did she send them from?"

"From all over. San Diego. Albuquerque. Palm Springs. At first glance, it looked like she was on the move, but she sure as heck wasn't in Carmel."

Meaghan groaned.

"Yep, Meaghan." Hunter held up a hand. "You figured it out. Nicolas had showings in all of those places."

And had affairs with other women, to boot, I thought.

"Think about it. Nicolas was an artist," Hunter went on. "He could have faked Kaylene's handwriting on the postcards. When I tracked him down at his apartment in Sedona, I'd noticed a dozen or more paintings of hiking areas on his walls. Bad ones. He couldn't figure out how to paint something that wasn't wet. But I recognized them. They were places Kaylene had hiked. Devil's Bridge. Cathedral Rock. She'd sent selfies to her mother. She was happy in those photos. Nicolas probably figured the best way to get rid of her was to take her hiking. Somewhere she loved. Someplace dangerous.

"So that's where I searched for her. I hiked trail after trail. I was the one who found her. At the bottom of a ravine. I alerted the police. They ruled it a suicide. There was one set of boot tracks. Not Nicolas's. Of course, he could have erased his using a broken branch. And there were no witnesses. When I found out Nicolas was moving back here and going to be part of Violet Vickers's event, well . . ." He splayed his hands. "I couldn't let him get away with it. You understand." His voice quavered. "We fought at Flair, but that was purely a precursor. I followed him to Meaghan's, and when I saw him there, waiting to talk to her"—he focused on Meaghan—"to *you,* I lost it. I bashed in his head."

"You went with a gazing ball in hand," I said. "That's premeditated murder."

He sniggered. "Okay, sure, it was premeditated. I couldn't wait to kill him, and I'm glad I did. If I'm completely honest, the only thing I'm sorry about is my daughter will have a murderer as a father." He eyed the piece of coral in his hands. His lips turned up at the corners. Viciously, he broke a spike and placed it against his throat. "If I kill myself, Ella won't have to live with the shame."

"Hunter, don't!" I shouted.

"Meaghan, you will always be my muse," he rasped.

Meaghan choked back a sob. "Please don't, Hunter."

Fiona swirled around him while dousing him with a golden potion. Nothing happened to him. He didn't relent.

"Hunter!" I hollered to shake him up. "Your daughter will rally, one way or another. And she'll forgive you when she learns how you avenged your niece, but without you, she'll falter. She doesn't deserve that. C'mon." I held out my hand. "Give me the piece of coral."

He recoiled.

Fiona flitted to the plants on Hunter's shelves and sang softly to the pothos. The long tendrils of the plant wiggled. I didn't have a clue what she was doing, but I didn't have time to question her.

"It's all his idiot brother's fault," Hunter grumbled.

"Because he abused Nicolas?" I asked.

"Because he encouraged him."

"No, Payton hated Nicolas's art. He—" I halted as Hunter's accusation spurred a realization. "Hunter, did you have anything to do with Payton Buley's death?"

He met my gaze.

"Did you kill him," I continued, "because he knew what Nicolas had done to Kaylene and was blackmailing him to keep the secret?"

"Is that true?" Meaghan asked, her voice thin and childlike.

He glared at her. His nostrils flared. "Yes, it's true. I found emails on Payton Buley's computer to his brother, saying, 'I know what you did.' And there were emails demanding money. 'Pay up or pay the price.' The first one was for forty K."

Was that the forty thousand Meaghan had remitted to Nicolas that Payton said his brother had blown through? Had Payton planned on dunning his brother for eternity?

"When did you see the emails?" I asked.

"When I broke in to plant the gazing ball in his laundry bin. I mean, let's face it, he was the obvious suspect. He was a blowhard. The computer was open. He was probably getting ready to purge the emails." Hunter coughed out a bitter laugh. "He should have turned his brother in, but he didn't, because he wanted to make money off my niece's death." Hunter jabbed the air with the coral spike. "That made him an accomplice. He deserved to die."

"You said you stole into his house?"

"Yeah. He was taking a shower and came out and found me. I vamped and told him I'd heard about his outburst at Violet's demanding Nicolas repay him and said I'd also heard through the grapevine that he was in need of cash. I told him I wanted to buy the whole lot of Nicolas's paintings. You should have seen him. He couldn't offer me something to drink fast enough. Coffee. Tea. Something stronger. I asked for water. As he was pouring me a glass, I came up behind him and dosed him with midazolam."

That was a heavy sedative. My father had received it when he'd had his knee repaired. "Where did you get it?"

Hunter's lips retracted from his teeth. "My dear sister is a doctor. But not just any kind of doctor. She's an anesthesiologist."

I'd never thought to ask and berated myself for not being more curious. "You came prepared to inject him."

"Yeah, well . . ." His mouth quirked up on one side.

"You should turn yourself in to the police," I said evenly, not wishing to upset him further. Though I didn't think he'd hurt Meaghan, a person on the edge was unpredictable. "They'll understand why you did it."

"You know that's not true." He switched the coral spike to his other hand.

Did he intend to hurl it at me? I wasn't going to wait to find out. I kicked out one leg in a roundhouse, the way Ziggy had taught me. My clog flew off my foot and slammed into Hunter's torso. It didn't hurt, I was sure, but it had shocked him. He reeled. The spike fell from his hand.

At the same time, the yellow butterfly palms pitched forward, knocking Hunter to the ground. Then the pothos tendrils, which had quadrupled in length, snaked around his body. He writhed to get free, but the plants were relentless.

"What's happening?" Meagan squawked.

Fiona said, "Don't worry. He won't die."

"How did you do that?" I asked.

"Plant psychology at its finest." Fiona polished her fingertips on her bodice. "We finally got a full crash course."

"I'm glad you're a quick study, "I said. "How did you do it?"

"I coaxed the pothos to subdue and restrict him. I told them they were strong and necessary to the universe to balance light and darkness, good and evil."

Wow!

"Merryweather is going to be so proud of me," she added.

I sure hoped so.

"Courtney Kelly!" a man yelled from outside.

The door sprang back. Detective Summers bolted inside. Officer Reddick followed him. Both were armed and ready to shoot.

When Summers saw Hunter bound by the plant, he holstered his gun. "Holy heck," he said. "What the—"

"You wouldn't believe it if I told you." I smiled with relief. "How did you know where to find me?"

"Miss Timberlake phoned, but I was already on my way. The image of the receipt you sent helped solve the case."

"Hunter Hock killed Payton Buley, too," I said.

Summers pursed his lips. "About that. Tell me more about the slant of a *T*?"

Chapter 27

If you see a fairy ring
In a field of grass,
Very lightly step around,
Tip-Toe as you pass.
—Anonymous

"Courtney, isn't this fabulous?" Violet Vickers waved to me from across the terrace of her backyard. She was standing with Brady's mother, Eudora Cash.

Easel after easel of artwork graced the area. Despite the tragic end to his life, Violet had included Nicolas Buley's large-sized works. Smaller pieces, like Hunter Hock's—yes, despite his notoriety in the news, Violet had wanted to include his art, too—stood on pedestals. My fairy gardens were placed exactly as she'd designed. My father hadn't quibbled about that.

Violet drew nearer with Eudora. Clad in a lavender trumpet-sleeved handkerchief dress, her hair bejeweled with rhinestones, Violet resembled a human-sized fairy. "And isn't the weather lovely?"

"It's *lovely*," I said with a wink.

She tittered. Eudora had recently made Violet aware of how often she said the word. Now she was doing it on purpose.

"Having the event in the middle of the day was a brilliant idea," I said. The temperature was moderate. There was a slight breeze but not gusty enough to mess anyone's hair.

"When else would you serve high tea?" she asked.

Good point. "I noticed Sassy Jacobi is playing earlier than planned."

"Yes. Guests were yawning during the string quartet. The music was so serene. We can't have yawning right off the bat," she said. "I asked the foursome to take a two-hour break. I'll bring them back at the end and pay them double. They were happy to oblige."

Sassy was seated on a tall stool by the railing, a microphone positioned in front of her. She'd come into the store the other day to tell me her news. Her attorney had worked out a deal with the source of her illegal rosewood, still unnamed, to pay a fine of over three hundred thousand dollars—Sassy wasn't the sole person to whom he'd provided Madagascar rosewood—and he would also make a handsome community service payment to the U.S. National Fish and Wildlife Foundation to promote conservation. Sassy would have to donate two hundred service hours to cleaning up wildlife areas, but she would be free to continue singing and making guitars.

"Yes, doesn't she sound . . ." Victoria caught herself. "Fabulous. I adore her voice. I'm so pleased you were able to help her out."

"She helped herself," I said.

"She said your fairy had something to do with it."

Fiona, who had accompanied me to the party, applauded and whispered that she was off to see who else was around—meaning which other fairies. Merryweather had cleared her to socialize, within limits.

"You look splendid, Courtney," Violet said.

"Thanks." I'd splurged and purchased a cap-sleeved dress that the salesperson said was sunrise in color. It was red-orange and had a gentle movement to it. I particularly liked the inch-below-the-kneecap length. I was teetering on my espadrilles, unused to wearing heels, but I managed not to fall. I scanned the partygoers.

"Brady's on the lower terrace, tending to the dining, if you're wondering," Violet said, as if reading my mind. "Thank you for making that happen, by the way. His food is out of this world. I'm thinking I should invest in another restaurant for him. Spread the word."

"If you do, he won't have any time for me," I joked.

"True. True. One can only have so much success without it ruining one's personal life."

"Will he have enough food to feed this many people?" I flourished a hand. Violet had planned on one hundred guests. There were more than two hundred in attendance.

"Absolutely. I always double the amount. Word of mouth draws donors out of the woodwork. If there are leftovers, the staff is always happy to take some home. Brady had his pastry chef make an absolutely gorgeous Mother's Day cake in honor of all the mothers in attendance."

"That was sweet of him," I said. "Are all the guests donors?"

"Other than the artists and celebrities, yes. The theater foundation will be reaping the benefits." She lowered her voice. "See that woman in pink with the long willowy neck over there? She is the prima ballerina for the San Francisco ballet. And see the handsome, broad-shouldered man with the distinctive beard?"

I nodded.

"He's the basso for the opera. You should hear him sing *Othello*. He has lower registers that remind me of a cello or bass viol. Ex-quisite."

Eudora leaned in. "I've been encouraging Violet to introduce herself and ask him out."

Violet scoffed. "Don't be ridiculous."

"If I was single, I would," she teased.

A waiter in a white suit slowed and asked if we'd like a salmon and dill appetizer. I took one and downed it in one bite. I was already feeling the effects of the half a glass of wine I'd imbibed and would soon switch to iced tea.

Eudora said, all joking aside, "Courtney, I haven't seen you since, you know . . ."

Since Hunter Hock had been arrested. Since Meaghan had started therapy. Since Dylan Summers had read me the riot act, even though he had acknowledged my help had been invaluable.

"How are you?" She tapped my forearm fondly.

"I'm fine and glad the murder . . ." I paused and revised. "The *murders* have been resolved."

"I heard your fairy did quite a magical act," Eudora said. "I do hope to make her acquaintance, sooner rather than later."

"She did," I admitted. Summers hadn't seen the bubble. It vanished the moment Hunter had been tamed. The army of plants, on the other hand, had kept Summers guessing. "She has a deft touch with plants."

I couldn't say more, but after the fact, Fiona had revealed a secret. She hadn't solely used plant psychology to make Hunter's plants do what she'd wanted. The queen fairy had complete command over nature. Being a queen fairy-in-training, Fiona had been imbued with extra talents.

"Daughter," said my father as he approached with Wanda on his arm. He looked handsome in his navy blue suit. She had dressed to match in a navy blue jacquard sheath. I loved how happy they always seemed together. They were a good fit. "Your fairy gardens are the hit of the party."

"Ha!" I said. "You hate them."

"Do not. I think they add a whimsical touch. Why, I think I even spied a fairy. Sort of troll-like features, big ears." He gestured with hands flapping.

Wanda flicked his arm. "Don't be sassy, Kip."

"Honestly, Kipling," Violet clucked her tongue. "I do hope you'll grow up soon."

"Don't count on it." He chuckled. "Let's see how many guests are bidding on your work, hon." He drew Wanda toward the railing. Violet had asked Wanda to offer her largest work, very Georgia O'Keeffe in feeling.

"Yes," Violet said. "Mingle. Inspire."

"Courtney! Violet!" Holly Hopewell said as she weaved through guests to greet us. Her sisters, Hattie and Hedda, were with her, as was Zinnia Walker. Each was carrying a high-end brochure of the art that was up for auction. "What a bash!"

"I love your outfit, Holly," I said.

"This old thing?" Her ruffled floral dress reminded me of Monet's flower garden in Giverny.

Hedda said, "Don't believe her. It's not old. It's brand new."

Hattie frowned. "Holly never wears the same thing twice."

"Not true," Holly protested.

Zinnia giggled. "It is so. Why, I've seen lots of your clothes at the gently used clothing store."

"That's because I like to donate to good causes." Holly batted Zinnia with her brochure. "And, do tell, why were you at Finding Treasures?"

"I, too, was donating." Zinnia shimmied her shoulders. "You're not the only one in town who lives to give, give, give." A laugh burbled out of her. "Listen to me. I'm starting to sound like Violet."

"Soon you'll be saying everything's *lovely*," Holly teased.

The group laughed heartily and ambled on.

I bid Violet and Eudora goodbye and trotted down the stairs to the lower tier, where I spotted Brady across the way, handsome but harried. He waved, but I could see he didn't have time to chat. I signed *See you later,* and he gave me a thumbs-up. I'd invited him for a light dinner after the event. I figured he could use the rest.

Meaghan was standing with Ziggy beside the table that had been assigned to them as well as to my father, Wanda, and me. She glanced up as I advanced. In her simple ecru sheath, she paled in comparison to Ziggy's lime-green ensemble—a print-patterned camp shirt over lime green pants. Whew! Not many men would be bold enough to wear it. I stifled a grin.

"Hey." Meaghan raised her glass of white wine. "What a shindig. All of the pieces we loaned have been getting huge bids." Flair Gallery had offered a number of pieces on consignment. They would split their commission with the foundation. "I'm so impressed with the quality of donors. We're talking very deep pockets."

As if on cue, Finley and George Pitt appeared. Okay, Ziggy had worn a wild outfit, but George's ensemble would win an Oscar for worst ever. Was he color blind? A striped-blue summer sweater over salmon-colored golf pants? Hadn't Finley had a say in the matter? She'd dressed to the nines as if prepared to walk the red carpet— white sheath, white strappy four-inch heels, and bling that made my eyes ache.

"Will you look at that," Finley said as she swept her bangs off her face. "We're sitting right next to you, Courtney." She pointed to the neighboring table.

"How about that?" I smiled.

"Did you hear? George got an offer to do another movie after he wraps up this one and the next one."

I said, "Congratulations."

"It's the role of a lifetime," Finley added. "He thinks he got it because he can see fairies now."

"You told her?" I eyed him.

She chortled. "Oh, c'mon, he's fooling."

George winked at me.

As if summoned, Fiona whizzed to him and did a curtsey mid-air.

George put his finger out and said, "Climb on." Fiona rested on it.

"Oh, George, stop!" Finley clutched her stomach, laughing. "You'll make me bust the seams of my dress." She stopped her fake laugh, latched onto his arm, and said, "I hear the koi pond is something to see. Shall we?"

"We shall," he said graciously.

"My father redid all the gardens here," I said before they departed.

"So that's where you get your green thumb from," George said. "Can he see fairies, too?"

"No, and he doesn't want to." I let out a frustrated puff of air.

Finley leaned in. "By the way, Courtney, how are you doing after facing off with a murderer?"

Her question took me aback. I didn't think she cared for anyone other than herself and her husband. "I'm fine. Thanks for asking."

"You know, I'm thinking of writing a screenplay," Finley said.

"That's nice." I took a sip of wine.

"It's about a hostage situation. You could be my consultant."

I almost spewed my wine. "Uh, thanks, but no thanks. I've got plenty to keep myself busy."

"Well, if you change your mind, I think we'd make a great team."

Brady's ex and me a team? Uh, no! I smiled. "Go enjoy the koi pond."

When they were out of earshot, Meaghan said, "She has chutzpah. You've got to grant her that."

"Or she lacks all sense of awareness." I giggled. "Hey, did I hear that Officer Reddick asked you on a date?"

"Yep."

"And will you go?"

"I already did. We went on a hike at Jacks Peaks Park. We're going to the zoo next week."

"In San Francisco?"

"Yep. We'll take a long drive up the coast."

Ziggy made smooching sounds. "Sounds romantic."

Meaghan knuckled his arm. "It's a date. Don't read anything into it."

"Me, read?" Ziggy fanned the air. "I never read."

As they moved away, Ulani Kamaka approached, her eyes outlined dramatically and her cheeks brushed with a pink blush that matched her wraparound dress. "Nice gig," she said.

"Did you get all the interviews you wanted?"

"I still have a few to go, but let's just say my editor is extremely pleased. By the way, I heard Adeline Tan is back at the aquarium and doing fine."

After Hunter's arrest, Addie had retreated to a Buddhist temple for a week of silence and contemplation.

"Meditation can be good for the soul," I said.

"Indeed."

The rest of Violet's soirée went off without a hitch. All of the works of art sold at top dollar. Finley was over the moon to get one of Hunter Hock's pieces. She said it would be the talk of the town.

Around four-thirty, Fiona flew to me, and we drove home.

After changing out of my party garb and throwing on jeans and a scallop-necked sweater, I puttered around the kitchen preparing dinner for Brady. I doubted he'd eaten a thing at the event. I hadn't tasted more than a few appetizers, as good as I knew the food was. Since finding out Hunter Hock had killed not one but two men, I hadn't had much of an appetite.

Pixie roused in her bed and meowed for a treat. I fed her tuna and then fetched napkins and silverware and a pair of shears and headed to the rear yard. I set the wicker table and tramped to my vegetable garden, a small plot to the left near the greenhouse. The plants were loving the location. I snipped basil, chives, and parsley and returned inside with them.

Fiona floated alongside me. It was clear she had something she wanted to talk to me about but couldn't bring herself to do so. "What are you making for dinner?"

"Poached salmon and a green salad with fresh herb dressing."

In the kitchen, I pulled a small, glass cruet from the cupboard and poured one part oil and two parts champagne vinegar into it. Then I diced the herbs and added them and a dash of salt and pepper. I shook the mixture so it would emulsify and tasted it with the tip of a spoon. Perfect. Then I wrapped the salmon in parchment and set it in the oven.

On time as always, Brady arrived at six with a bottle of my favorite chardonnay. He pecked me on the cheek and ran a finger along the back of my neck, which sent a delicious swirl of desire down my spine. He did a quick search for Fiona, but didn't see her and settled for some love from Pixie. Then he opened the wine and poured two glasses.

"There was supposed to be a moon tonight, but the fog has drifted in," he said.

"Violet has to be happy the fog didn't come in earlier and ruin her party. Still want to eat outside?"

"I'm warm. You'll need to throw on another layer."

Dinner was ready, so I plated it, grabbed a peacoat, and headed outside. Brady lit the candle at the center of the table with a long match, settled into a chair, and let out a contented sigh.

"Long day?" I asked, putting a plate in front of each of us.

"Yes, but a huge success. I'll have more business than I know what to do with for the next year. You?"

"Over twenty orders for fairy gardens, and I booked five group classes and gave away at least two dozen business cards."

We raised our wineglasses in a toast and dug into our dinners.

"Mmm," he murmured. "Love the lemon and salt on the salmon. Perfection."

"From a premier restaurateur, that's a hefty compliment."

"Courtney!" Fiona zoomed into view, impatience oozing out of her.

I set my glass down and said to Brady, "I have to address something."

"Sure."

I rose to my feet and signaled my sweet fairy. Near the greenhouse, I held out my hand and asked her to sit. "What's wrong?"

"The portal. It's there again."

I gazed at the cypress but didn't see it. "You can't go through it," I warned.

"That's the thing. Merryweather was at Violet Vickers's house, and she said after my successful feat at Hunter Hock's house, I may."

My mouth opened. "You're serious?"

"Yes." She chewed on her lower lip and wrapped her wings around her torso protectively. "I'm scared."

"What could happen? Your mother gives you a tongue lashing?"

"No. She doesn't raise her voice, ever." Her laughter sounded like the tinkle of wind chimes. "But what if . . ." She spread her wings wide. "I've got to do it."

"Then do it," I said, giving her a nudge.

She kissed my cheek, her lips as soft as the brush of a feather, and said, "I'll be back before you know it."

"You'd better be."

She soared to the cypress and stood on the tufted grass nearby. Suddenly, the tree, which still resembled a tree, lit up at the base, as if a door to a golden cave had been opened.

I shivered. Fiona peeked over her shoulder at me. She waved . . . and then she tiptoed into the light . . . and disappeared.

RECIPES

From Yvanna:

These are one of my abuela's favorite cookies. They're so easy to make, and they look so elegant. Dust well with powdered sugar. And make sure you have plenty on hand. Your guests will gobble them up.

Cashew Tea Cookies

(Yield: 30–36 cookies)

1 cup unsalted butter, at room temperature
½ cup confectioners' sugar, plus more for coating baked cookies
1½ teaspoons vanilla extract
1¾ cups all-purpose flour (you may also use gluten-free flour)
¼ teaspoon cinnamon
1 cup cashews, chopped into very small pieces
Add water if necessary

Preheat the oven to 350 degrees F.

Line cookies sheets with parchment paper.

Using an electric mixer, cream the butter and sugar at low speed until it is smooth. Beat in the vanilla extract. Gradually add in the flour and cinnamon.

To chop the nuts, I like to use a food processor or a manual food chopper. You can also put them in a cellophane bag and smash them with a meat tenderizer. Mix the nuts into the flour mixture with a spatula.

For each cookie, use 1 tablespoon of dough and shape it into a ball the size of a walnut. Dust your hands with flour, if necessary, as you make more cookies. They can be sticky.

Place cookies onto prepared cookie sheets. Bake for 12–14 minutes.

When the cookies are cool enough to handle but still warm, roll the cookies in more powdered sugar to coat.

Cool entirely before eating. They can be surprisingly hot at the center! Store in an airtight container.

From Yvanna:

This is one of my family's favorite coffee cakes, and it's gluten-free! We love the cake's firm texture and abundant cinnamon flavor. Yes, it does require a number of cooking bowls, so the clean-up is a bit daunting, but it's so worth it. My abuela tells me that cinnamon is very rich in antibacterial properties. My abuela is never wrong.

Cinnamon Coffee Cake

Gluten-free Version

(Serves 12–24)

For the cake:
4 large eggs
1½ cups sour cream, divided
3½ teaspoons vanilla extract, divided
2⅔ cup gluten-free flour blend (see gluten-free flour blend below)
1¼ cups sugar
1 tablespoon baking powder
1 teaspoon salt
¾ teaspoon baking soda
¼ teaspoon xanthan gum
8 tablespoons unsalted butter, cut into 1/4-inch pieces, softened
1 tablespoon cinnamon

For the topping:
1 cup confectioners' sugar
5 teaspoons milk
Cinnamon for dusting

To make the cake:

Preheat oven to 350 degrees F. Grease an angel food-like tube pan.

In a medium bowl, whisk together the eggs, 1 cup of the sour cream, and 3 tablespoons of the vanilla extract.

In a stand mixer fitted with a paddle or in a food processor, mix the gluten-free flour blend, sugar, baking powder, salt, baking soda, and xanthan gum until combined. Add the remaining ½ cup sour cream and softened butter, and mix until the dry ingredients are moistened and the butter is the size of peas. Gradually add the egg mixture in small portions to the dry mixture, beating after each addition. When it's all added, scrape down the bowl, and then beat on medium-high until the batter is fluffy, about 1 minute. This will be a thick batter.

Put 1 cup of the batter into a small bowl and add in the remaining ½ teaspoon vanilla extract and cinnamon.

Pour the regular batter into the tube pan. Drop dollops of the cinnamon batter on top. Using a knife, work the cinnamon batter into the regular batter, swirling so the cinnamon batter will be inside the cake. Don't overmix.

Bake the cake for 45–55 minutes. Remove from oven and let the cake stand for 30 minutes. Remove the cake from the pan and let cool on a wire rack for an hour.

For the topping:

In a small bowl, whisk together the powdered sugar and milk. Pour the glaze evenly over the top of the cooled cake. Dust with cinnamon, if desired.

Tip: Coffee cake is best eaten right after it's been baked, but you can save this by cutting slices and wrapping them individually in a good plastic wrap. It should last at least 3 days, and if frozen, up to 3 months.

Gluten-free Flour Blend: I like to combine 2 cups (less 2 tablespoons) of sweet rice flour and ⅔ cup tapioca starch, plus 2 tablespoons of whey powder. The total will measure 2⅔ cups of blended flour.

From Yvanna:

I love the flavor of coconut. It's a delicious breakfast flavor. These muffins conjure up wonderful times with my abuela, who gave me the recipe. For this recipe, I use sweetened coconut. If you want a muffin that isn't sweet and more on the bread side of flavors, then use unsweetened coconut. I've experimented with both. I'm sharing the gluten-free version with you, as well.

Chocolate Coconut Muffins

(Yield: 12–14 muffins)

2 eggs
1 cup granulated sugar
½ cup milk
8 ounces (½ cup) melted butter
1 tablespoon vinegar
1 teaspoon coconut extract
1 teaspoon vanilla extract
⅔ cup sweetened coconut
2 cups flour
3 teaspoons baking powder
½ teaspoon salt
1 teaspoon cinnamon
⅓ cup semi-sweet chocolate chips
4–5 tablespoons Sugar in the Raw or crystallized sugar

Preheat oven to 425 degrees F. Insert liners into 12–14 muffin cups and spray with non-stick cooking spray.

In the bowl of a stand mixer, whisk the eggs and sugar. Add the milk, butter, vinegar, coconut and vanilla extracts, and mix on low. Add in the sweetened coconut and mix again on low.

In a small bowl, whisk together the flour, baking powder, salt, and cinnamon. Add to the sugar mixture and mix on low. Add in the chocolate chips and mix only until incorporated. Scrape down the sides.

Using an ice cream scoop, cookie scoop, or soup ladle, scoop batter into the muffin tins until filled to the top. Sprinkle with Sugar in the Raw. Bake for 5 minutes and reduce oven temperature to 375 degrees F. Bake for 13 minutes more. Cool for about 5 minutes in the pan, and then remove and cool on racks. May be served warm.

To preserve muffins, store in airtight container and refrigerate.

Chocolate Coconut Muffins

Gluten-free Version

(Yield: 12–14 muffins)

2 eggs
1 cup granulated sugar
½ cup milk
8 ounces (½ cup) melted butter
1 tablespoon vinegar
1 teaspoon coconut extract
1 teaspoon vanilla extract
⅔ cup sweetened coconut
2 cups gluten-free flour
½ teaspoon xanthan gum
1 tablespoon whey powder
3 teaspoons baking powder
½ teaspoon salt
1 teaspoon cinnamon
⅓ cup semi-sweet chocolate chips
4–5 tablespoons Sugar in the Raw or crystallized sugar

Preheat oven to 425 degrees F. Insert liners into 12–14 muffin cups and spray with non-stick cooking spray.

In the bowl of a stand mixer, whisk the eggs and sugar. Add the milk, butter, vinegar, coconut and vanilla extracts, and mix on low. Add in the sweetened coconut and mix again on low.

In a small bowl, whisk together the gluten-free flour, xanthan gum, whey powder, baking powder, salt, and cinnamon. Add to the sugar mixture and mix on low. Add in the chocolate chips and mix only until incorporated. Scrape down the sides.

Using an ice cream scoop, cookie scoop, or soup ladle, scoop batter into the muffin tins until filled to the top. Sprinkle with Sugar in the Raw. Bake for 5 minutes and reduce oven temperature to 375 degrees F. Bake for 13 minutes more. Cool for about 5 minutes in the pan, and then remove and cool on racks. May be served warm.

To preserve gluten-free muffins, wrap each individually in plastic wrap and store in airtight container.

From Yvanna:

Now there are a couple of ways to drizzle chocolate. This can be tricky! You can pour the ganache into a sandwich-size plastic bag and snip off a TEENSY bit of the corner with scissors and press the chocolate out in a zig-zag pattern over the cookies. Or you can use a pastry bag with a very teensy tip. Or you can use the prongs of a fork or tip of a knife dipped into the chocolate. This decorating technique took me a lot of experimenting before I was ready to make cookies for a tea. Whatever you do, try to enjoy the experience. Just so you know, the cookies are delicious even without the chocolate drizzle.

Dark Chocolate Chai Cookies

(Yield: 18–24 cookies)

4 chai tea bags
1½ cups sugar
2½ cups all-purpose flour
1 teaspoon ground cinnamon
1 teaspoon ground ginger
½ teaspoon ground allspice
½ teaspoon ground cardamom
¼ teaspoon ground cloves
¼ teaspoon finely ground black pepper
¼ teaspoon salt
¾ teaspoon baking powder
2 sticks unsalted butter, softened
1 large egg
1 teaspoon pure vanilla extract
1 cup dark chocolate chips

In a small saucepan, bring 2 cups of water to a simmer and add the tea bags. Add 1 cup sugar. Simmer 3 minutes, then remove and discard the tea bags. Now, boil the syrup for about 10 minutes until it reduces by half. You will have about 1 cup of syrup. Pour ¼ cup into a small container and cool completely. You may use the remaining tea syrup to add to your regular tea. It's delicious. It keeps in the refrigerator.

Meanwhile, in a small bowl, whisk together the flour, cinnamon, ginger, allspice, cardamom, cloves, pepper, salt, and baking powder.

In the bowl of a stand mixer, beat the softened butter and remaining ½ cup sugar on medium until fluffy. Add in the cooled tea syrup, egg, and vanilla extract. Mix until smooth.

Reduce the mixer speed to low and add in flour mixture until combined, scraping down the sides as necessary. Divide the dough in half—it might be sticky—and form into 7-inch round logs. Wrap in plastic wrap and refrigerate until firm, about 4 hours.

Preheat the oven to 325 degrees F. Line 2 baking sheets with parchment paper. Slice the logs into rounds about ⅓-inch thick. Arrange the rounds on the baking sheets about ½-inch apart. They spread, but not a lot. Bake for 14–16 minutes. Let cookies cool completely on racks.

Meanwhile, make the chocolate icing. Melt the chocolate chips in a small bowl in the microwave at about 50 percent power, stirring every 20–30 seconds, until completely melted. Do not over zap! When ready, drizzle onto the cookies.

From Meaghan:

When I was a little girl, I landed on a recipe that was cinchy. I think my grandmother taught it to me. I can't remember. It's for cooks who don't want to work too hard but still want deliciousness in every bite. I remember needing to unwrap dozens of caramels, you know, the little square ones, to make this. Half of those went into my mouth. Now, there are caramel "bits" in bags ready to go. One less hassle.

Double-Chocolate Caramel Brownies

(Yield: 12–16)

1 devil's food cake mix (you may also use a gluten-free mix)
2 eggs
⅓ cup evaporated milk
¾ cup melted butter, (1½ sticks)
1 (11-ounce) package caramel bits
¾ cup semi-sweet chocolate chips
⅓ cup evaporated milk, additional

Preheat oven to 350 degrees. Spray a 9 x 13 baking dish with non-stick cooking spray and line with parchment paper. Set aside.

In a large mixing bowl, whisk together cake mix, eggs, ⅓ cup evaporated milk, and ¾ cup melted butter until smooth. Spread half of the batter into the prepared 9 x 13 pan.

Bake for 8 minutes.

Meanwhile, in a saucepan over medium-low heat, melt the contents of a package of caramel bits in ⅓ cup evaporated milk. Stir until smooth, about 5–6 minutes.

When you take the brownies out of the oven, drizzle the melted caramel over the top. Pouring straight from the saucepan is the best way to do this. If needed, spread with a spatula. It will be slightly messy because the bottom layer isn't completely cooked. That's okay. Sprinkle chocolate chips on the caramel.

Top with remaining batter. Again, because it's all warm, this might be messy as you spread it with a spatula. Don't worry. It turns out great.

Bake for 20–25 minutes more until the top layer is set. Remove from oven and cool completely, at least 20 minutes. Brownies are easier to cut when cooled.

From Joss:

These are my mother's favorite cookies. She loves her tea. She might not remember me right now, but she remembers these cookies. I bring her a fresh batch every couple of weeks. When I was growing up, she loved taking tea with me and my dolls. It is one of my fondest memories. Courtney tells me she has similar memories with her mom.

Earl Grey Shortbread Cookies

(Yield: 12 cookies)

1 cup flour
1 tablespoon loose Earl Grey (or tea of your choosing) tea leaves
    (two tea bags, cut open)
¼ teaspoon salt
6 tablespoons confectioners' sugar
½ teaspoon vanilla extract
1 stick butter, softened to room temperature

In a food processor, pulse the flour, loose tea, and salt. Add the confectioners' sugar, vanilla extract, and butter. Pulse until a dough is formed, about 10–20 pulses. Remove dough from container and place on a sheet of plastic wrap. Roll the dough into a log about 6–7 inches long and 2 inches around. Refrigerate for one hour.

Preheat oven to 375 degrees F.

Slice the log into ⅓-inch-thick rounds. Place on parchment-lined baking sheets about 2 inches apart. Bake until the edges are just brown, about 11–12 minutes.

Let the cookies cool on sheets for 5 minutes, then transfer to wire racks and cool to room temperature.

Earl Grey Shortbread Cookies

Gluten-free Version

(Yield: 12 cookies)

1 cup gluten-free flour
1 tablespoon loose Earl Grey tea leaves (two tea bags, cut open) (or
    tea of your choosing)
¼ teaspoon salt
6 tablespoons confectioners' sugar
½ teaspoon vanilla extract
1 stick butter, softened to room temperature

In a food processor, pulse the gluten-free flour, loose tea, and salt. Add the confectioners' sugar, vanilla, and butter. Pulse until a dough is formed, about 10–20 pulses. Remove dough from container and place on a sheet of plastic wrap. Roll the dough into a log about 6–7 inches long and 2 inches around. Refrigerate for one hour.

Preheat oven to 375 degrees F.

Slice the log into ⅓-inch-thick rounds. Place on parchment-lined baking sheets about 2 inches apart. Bake until the edges are just brown, about 11–12 minutes.

Let the cookies cool on sheets for 5 minutes, then transfer to wire racks and cool to room temperature.

From Joss:

My aunt Bibi was a wonderful baker. I remember spending lots of delicious hours in the kitchen at her side, learning how to bake. She had a particular fondness for citrus things. Lemon pie. Lemon cake. Lemonade. These butter cookies are so easy to make, and they hold up well. They even freeze well. They're my all-time favorite cookie. Enjoy.

Lemon Butter Cookies

(Yield: 12–16 cookies)

For the cookie:
1 stick unsalted butter, softened
½ cup confectioners' sugar
½ tablespoon lemon zest
¾ tablespoon lemon juice, freshly squeezed
1 cup flour (you may use gluten-free flour)
¼ teaspoon salt

For the glaze:
¼ cup confectioners' sugar
½ tablespoon lemon juice
½ tablespoon unsalted butter, softened
Finely grated lemon zest for garnish

Preheat the oven to 350 degrees F.

In a large bowl using a mixer, beat the butter with the confectioners' sugar until smooth. Add in the lemon zest (finely grated) and the juice. Then mix in the flour and salt.

Refrigerate the dough for 30 minutes.

Roll the dough into 1-inch balls. Arrange the balls on a baking sheet lined with parchment paper. Using your fingers, flatten each cookie to about ¼-inch thickness. These will SPREAD.

Bake for 12–14 minutes, until the cookies are lightly browned and firm.

Let the cookies cool on the baking sheet for 2 minutes. Transfer to a rack to cool.

Meanwhile, make the glaze. In a small bowl, whisk the confectioners' sugar with the lemon juice and softened butter until smooth.

Spread the glaze on the cooled cookies and dust with lemon zest. Let stand until the glaze is set.

These can be stored in an airtight container for 2–3 days. The dough can also be frozen, if desired, and thawed before baking.

From Courtney:

These are delicious cookies, but be forewarned that the maple syrup in the mixture makes it just a little harder to tap these out of the mold. It's sticky stuff. I love how these remind me of brunch, one of my favorite meals. And here are some bragging rights. Yvanna taught me how to make them, and now I'm a pro. By the way, she tells me that the gluten-free version is just as good as the regular. Gluten-free flours do well when making cookies.

Maple Madeleines

(Yield: 32–36 cookies)

¾ cup butter, melted (1½ cubes), plus more for greasing molds
⅔ cup sugar
3 eggs
3 tablespoons maple syrup
½ teaspoon vanilla extract
½ teaspoon baking powder
¼ cup finely minced cashews or almonds
1 cup cake flour, plus more for dusting the molds
¼ teaspoon salt
1 tablespoon powdered sugar, sifted, for decorating when cookies
    are cooled

In a large bowl, combine butter and sugar. Add the eggs and beat until creamy. Add maple syrup and vanilla extract and mix well.

Add in the baking powder and finely minced nuts. You can use a food processor to mince the nuts or put them in a plastic bag and crush them with a mallet.

Add in the flour and salt. Sift if necessary. Mix until just combined. Batter can be used immediately or refrigerated overnight.

Preheat oven to 400 degrees F.

Grease madeleine molds with the extra butter, and lightly dust with extra flour. You will want to tap out any excess flour. Put a tablespoon of batter into each mold. Don't overfill. Like for a cupcake, the mold should only be two-thirds to three-quarters full.

Bake for 9–10 minutes, until the edges of the madeleines are browned and the domed tops spring back when pressed lightly. If you're using chilled dough, bake one minute longer. Do not overbake.

Remove pan from oven and immediately turn the madeleines out onto a baking rack. Let cool completely.

If you need to make in batches, wash and cool the pan in between and prepare as before with grease and dusting with flour.

Cookies can be made ahead and stored at room temperature for 1 day in an airtight container or frozen for 1 month if you wrap them in airtight plastic wrap.

To serve, lightly sprinkle "shell" side of madeleines with powdered sugar.

Maple Madeleines

Gluten-free Version

(Yield: 32–36 cookies)

¾ cup butter, melted (1½ cubes), plus more for greasing molds
⅔ cup sugar
3 eggs
3 tablespoons maple syrup
½ teaspoon vanilla extract
½ teaspoon baking powder
¼ cup finely minced cashews or almonds
1 cup gluten-free flour, plus more for dusting the molds
¼ teaspoon xanthan gum
¼ teaspoon salt
1 tablespoon powdered sugar, sifted, for decorating when cookies
    are cooled

In a large bowl, combine butter and sugar. Add the eggs and beat until creamy. Add maple syrup and vanilla extract and mix well.

Add in the baking powder and finely minced nuts. You can use a food processor to mince the nuts or put them in a plastic bag and crush them with a mallet.

Add in the gluten-free flour, xanthan gum, and salt. Sift if necessary. Mix until just combined. Batter can be used immediately or refrigerated overnight.

Preheat oven to 400 degrees F.

Grease madeleine molds with the extra butter, and lightly dust with extra gluten-free flour. You will want to tap out any excess flour. Put a tablespoon of batter into each mold. Don't overfill. Like for a cupcake, the mold should only be two-thirds to three-quarters full.

Bake for 9–10 minutes, until the edges of the madeleines are browned and the domed tops spring back when pressed lightly. If you're using chilled dough, bake one minute longer. Do not over-bake.

Remove pan from oven and immediately turn the madeleines out onto a baking rack. Let cool completely.

If you need to make in batches, wash and cool the pan in between and prepare as before with grease and dusting of flour.

Cookies can be made ahead and stored at room temperature for 1 day in an airtight container or frozen for 1 month if you wrap them in airtight plastic wrap. Gluten-free baked goods do better when wrapped individually.

To serve, lightly sprinkle "shell" side of madeleines with powdered sugar.

From Brady:

This is one my mother's favorite dishes. My father came up with the recipe, and I keep it on hand at the Hideaway Café so Mom can always order a slice if she wants. Yep, I'm that kind of son. Making the potatoes creamy is key. If you want, you can swap out the cheese for any other of your favorite cheeses that melt well. Enjoy.

Meat Loaf Pie

(Yield: 8 portions)

2 eggs
½ cup milk
1 cup panko (use gluten-free panko if necessary)
¼ cup finely chopped onion
1 teaspoon salt
½ teaspoon oregano powder
¼ teaspoon white pepper
3 tablespoons chopped fresh parsley
1 pound ground beef
2 russet potatoes, peeled and chopped into quarters
½ cup milk
2–4 tablespoons butter
1 teaspoon spicy mustard
1 teaspoon salt
½ cup shredded sharp cheddar cheese, or other meltable cheese
Dash of paprika

In a large bowl, combine the eggs, milk, panko, onion, salt, oregano powder, white pepper, and parsley. Add in the beef and mix well. Press into a 9-inch pie plate.

Bake the meat loaf for 35-40 minutes until the meat is cooked through.

Meanwhile, bring a large pot of water to boil. Add the potatoes and cook for 15 minutes until a fork comes out easily. Remove from heat, pour off the water, and mash the potatoes with a masher. Add the milk, butter, mustard, and salt. Stir until the potatoes are creamy and smooth.

Remove the meat loaf from the oven. Drain the meat loaf and then spread mashed potatoes on top. Sprinkle with shredded cheese and a dash of paprika. Bake the pie for about 5–10 minutes until the cheese is melted. Let stand for 5 minutes before cutting into wedges.

Recipes   293

From Brady:

This is the most popular brownie dessert on the menu at the café. Fair warning: because of the nuts, they can be crumbly. But one of the most fun things about eating any brownie is snacking on all the crumbs left on the plate. Tip: I place the nuts in a plastic bag and use a mallet to crush them, but if you want a finer texture, pulse them in a countertop food processor. Also, you may make these in two different-sized pans. For a thicker brownie, choose the smaller pan. I've noted the baking times.

Nutty Blond Brownies

(Yield: 12–24)

½ cup butter, softened
¾ cup sugar
¾ cup packed brown sugar
2 large eggs, room temperature
2 teaspoons vanilla extract
1½ cups all-purpose flour
1 teaspoon baking powder
½ teaspoon salt
1 cup white chocolate baking chips
1 cup semisweet chocolate chips
¾ cup macadamia nuts, chopped and divided

Preheat oven to 350 degrees F. Grease either a 7 x 11 pan or a 9 x 13 pan.

In a large bowl, cream butter and sugars until light and fluffy. Beat in eggs and vanilla extract.

In a small bowl, combine the flour, baking powder, and salt. Add it to the egg mixture and mix well. Mix in the white chocolate baking chips, semisweet chocolate chips, and half of the chopped nuts.

Spoon the mixture into either a greased 7 x 11 pan or a 9 x 13 pan. Spread evenly. Sprinkle with the remaining chopped nuts.

Bake until the top begins to crack and is golden brown, 25–30 minutes for the smaller pan; 22–26 minutes for the larger pan. Cool on a wire rack for at least 20–30 minutes. Cut into squares.

Nutty Blond Brownies

Gluten-free Version

(Yield: 12–24)

½ cup butter, softened
¾ cup sugar
¾ cup packed brown sugar
2 large eggs, room temperature
2 teaspoons vanilla extract
1½ cups gluten-free flour
1 tablespoon whey powder
¼ teaspoon xanthan gum
1 teaspoon baking powder
½ teaspoon salt
1 cup white chocolate baking chips
1 cup semisweet chocolate chips
¾ cup macadamia nuts, chopped and divided

Preheat oven to 350 degrees F. Grease either a 7 x 11 pan or a 9 x 13 pan.

In a large bowl, cream butter and sugars until light and fluffy. Beat in eggs and vanilla extract.

In a small bowl, combine the gluten-free flour, whey powder, xanthan gum, baking powder, and salt. Add it to the egg mixture and mix well. Mix in the white chocolate baking chips, semisweet chocolate chips, and half of the chopped nuts.

Spoon the mixture into either a greased 7 x 11 pan or a 9 x 13 pan. Spread evenly. Sprinkle with the remaining chopped nuts.

Bake until the top begins to crack and is golden brown, 25–30 minutes for the smaller pan; 22–26 minutes for the larger pan. Cool on a wire rack for at least 20–30 minutes. Cut into squares.

Don't miss the previous enchanting Fairy Garden mystery
from Daryl Wood Gerber . . .

A HINT OF MISCHIEF

**From Agatha Award-winning author Daryl Wood Gerber,
the third in an enchantingly whimsical series featuring
Courtney Kelly, the owner of a fairy-gardening and tea shop
in Carmel, California. It's a special place brimming with
good vibes and the kind of magical assistance its proprietor
will need to prepare for an old sorority sister's birthday bash
while solving a puzzling murder!**

Courtney has thrown a few fairy garden parties—for kids. But if a
local socialite is willing to dip into her trust fund for an old sorority
sister's fortieth birthday bash, Courtney will be there with bells on.
To make the job even more appealing, a famous actress, Farrah
Lawson, is flying in for the occasion, and there's nothing like a
celebrity cameo to raise a business's profile.

Now Courtney has less than two weeks to paint a mural, hang up
tinkling wind chimes, plan party games, and conjure up all the details. While she works her magic, the hostess and her girlfriends head
off for an indulgent spa day—which leads to a fateful facial for Farrah, followed by her mysterious death. Could the kindhearted eyebrow waxer who Farrah berated in public really be the killer, as the
police suspect? Courtney thinks otherwise, and with the help of her
imaginative sleuth fairy, sets out to dig up the truth behind this puzzling murder . . .

Available from Kensington Publishing Corp. wherever books are sold.

Chapter 1

'Tis merry, 'tis merry in Fairy-land,
When fairy birds are singing,
When the court doth ride by their monarch's side,
With bit and bridle ringing.
—Sir Walter Scott, "Alice Brand"

"Thief!" a woman cried outside of Open Your Imagination, my fairy garden and tea shop. I recognized the voice. Yvanna Acebo.

I hurried from the covered patio through our main showroom, grabbed an umbrella from the stand by the Dutch door, and headed outside, quickly opening the umbrella so it protected me from the rain. "Yvanna, what's going on?"

Yvanna, a baker at Sweet Treats, a neighboring shop in the courtyard, was dressed in her pink uniform and standing at the top of the stairs that led through the courtyard, hands on hips—no umbrella. She was getting drenched.

"Yvanna!" I shouted again. "Were you robbed? Are you okay?"

She pivoted. Rain streamed down her pretty face. She swiped a hair off her cheek that had come loose from her scrunchie. "I'm fine," she said with a sigh. "A customer set her bag down on one of the tables so she could fish in her purse for loose change. Before we knew it, someone in a brown hoodie slipped in, grabbed the bag, and darted out."

"Man? Woman? Teen?"

"I'm not sure." Her chest heaved. "That's the second theft in this area in the past twenty-four hours, Courtney."

"Second?" I gasped. Carmel-by-the-Sea was not known as a high-crime town. Well, that wasn't entirely true. We had suffered two murders in the past year. Flukes, the police had dubbed them. "Where did the other theft occur?"

"There." She pointed to the Village Shops, the courtyard across the street from ours. Carmel-by-the-Sea was known for its unique courtyards. "At Say Cheese."

"The thief must be hungry," I said. Say Cheese had a vast array of cheeses, crackers, and condiments. "Were you scared?"

"No. I'm miffed." A striking Latina, Yvanna was one of the most resilient women I knew. She rarely took a day off because she had a family of six to feed—two cousins, her grandparents, her sister, and herself.

"Call the police," I suggested.

"You can bet on it."

We didn't have CCTV in Cypress and Ivy's courtyard yet. Maybe I should mention it to our landlord. I returned to Open Your Imagination, stopped outside to flick the water off the umbrella, and then moved inside, slotted the umbrella into the stand, and weaved through the shop's display tables while saying hello to the handful of customers. Before heading to the patio, I signaled my stalwart assistant Joss Timberlake that all was under control.

"Do not argue with me!" Misty Dawn exclaimed. "Do you hear me? I want tea. Not coffee. Tea!" Misty, a customer, was standing by the verdigris baker's racks on the patio, wiggling two female fairy figurines. When she spotted me, she uttered a full-throated laugh. "You're back, Courtney. Is everything okay outside? Did I hear the word 'thief'?"

"You did."

"Hopefully nothing too dear was stolen."

In addition to my business, the courtyard boasted a high-end jewelry store, a collectibles shop, an art gallery, and a pet-grooming enterprise.

"Bakery goods," I said.

"And no one got hurt?"

"No one."

"Phew." Misty gazed at the figurines she was holding. "I swear, I can't get over how young I feel whenever I visit your shop. It takes me back to my childhood, when I used to play with dolls. I'd make up stories and put on plays. At one point, maybe seventh grade, I thought I was so clever and gifted with dialogue that I'd become a playwright, but that didn't come to pass."

Misty, a trust fund baby who had never worked a day in her life, even though she had graduated Phi Beta Kappa and had whizzed through business school, had blazed into the shop twenty minutes ago, hoping to hire me to throw a fairy garden birthday party for her sorority sister. In the less than two years that the shop had been open, I'd only thrown three such parties, each for children.

"Let's get serious." Misty returned the figurines to the verdigris baker's rack, strode across the covered slate patio to the wrought-iron table closest to the gnome-adorned fountain, and patted the tabletop. "Sit with me. Let's chat. I have lists upon lists of ideas." She opened her Prada tote and removed a floral notepad and pen.

Fiona, a fairy-in-training who, when not staying at my house, resided in the ficus trees fitted with twinkling lights that surrounded the patio, flew to my shoulder and whispered in my ear. "She sure is bossy."

I bit back a smile and said, "The customer's always right."

"How true," Misty said, oblivious to Fiona's presence.

To be fair, Misty was a force. She was tall and buxom with dark auburn hair, sturdy shoulders, a broad face, and bold features; I doubted she had ever been a wallflower. Every time I'd seen her at this or that event, always dressed in stunning jewel tones as she was now, her red silk blouse looking tailor-made, I'd been drawn to her like a moth to a flame.

Pixie, my adorable Ragdoll cat, abandoned the mother and child customers she'd been following for the past three minutes and leaped into Misty's lap. Misty instantly started stroking the cat's luscious fur. Pixie didn't hold back with her contented purring.

"Sweet kitty," Misty cooed.

"Pixie doesn't like just anyone," I said.

"Of course not. She knows a cat lover when she sees one, don't you, Pixie?" Misty tipped up the cat's chin. "Yes, you do. You know you do. I have three handsome friends for you to play with, Pixie. A calico, a tuxedo, and a domestic shorthair that I rescued. I love them all." She returned her gaze to me. "Now, Courtney, where were we?"

"You want to throw a party."

"For my good friend Odine." She stressed the O in her friend's name. I'd met Odine Oates a few times and was pretty certain she pronounced her name with the accent on the second syllable. "She's a descendant of one of the first families of Texas. She moved here when she was fourteen, and we became fast friends."

"Nice."

"And she's the first of us to turn forty," Misty continued. "I'm the last." That fact seemed to tickle her. "She has always loved fairies. She displays fairy art everywhere in Fantasy Awaits." Odine owned a jewelry and exotica art shop. "Have you visited it in the Doud Arcade?"

"I have."

Much of the shop's jewelry featured fairies, sorcerers, or mythical creatures. The art included distinctive pieces that she'd found around the world, including kimonos, vases, swords, statues, and so much more. For her wall décor, she had commissioned a local artist to re-create well-known fantasy artwork, including dragons and gnomes and the famous Cicely Mary Barker fairies, all depicted on four-by-six-foot canvases.

"I remember that place," Fiona whispered. "You bought that necklace for Joss."

A dragon pendant with an emerald eye. Joss adored dragon paraphernalia.

"It was scary there," Fiona added.

To a fairy Fiona's size, I imagined seeing giant-sized fairies, gnomes, and dragons would be frightening. She wasn't more than a few inches tall with two sets of beautiful green adult wings, one set of smaller junior wings, and shimmering blue hair. Her silver tutu and silver shoes sparkled in any light. By now, she should have grown three full sets of adult wings and lost her junior wings, but she'd messed up in fairy school, so the queen fairy had booted her from the fairy realm and subjected her to probation.

"I want to have the party in my backyard," Misty went on.

At one time Misty's family had owned a grand Spanish estate on the iconic 17-Mile Drive, the road popular because it led to Pebble Beach golf course, beaches, viewpoints, and more, but she had downsized recently, wishing to live in Carmel proper so she could walk to restaurants and art galleries at a moment's notice. She had purchased a two-story gray-and-white home on 4th Avenue with the charming name of Gardener's Delight—many homes in Carmel had names—and had hired my father's landscaping company to revamp both the front and rear yards. Her gardens were the envy of all her neighbors.

"Here we go." Joss placed a tray set with two Lenox Butterfly Meadow–pattern teacups, a plate of lemon bars, and the fixings for chamomile tea on the table. "May I pour?"

"Please," I said.

"Boss, we have a ton of things to do," she said, filling Misty's cup first. "A shipment is coming in and a busload of tourists is about to disembark. They'll be swarming the courtyard in less than an hour."

"She won't be long," Misty said on my behalf. "I'm very organized. This will only take a few minutes." She held up her notepad.

Joss pursed her lips, trying not to smile, which made her look even more elfin than normal.

"I like your shirt, by the way," Misty said to Joss.

"This old thing?" Joss plucked at the buttons of the parrot-themed shirt she'd bought in Tijuana. "It's fun. I like color."

"So do I." Misty opened her notepad, silently dismissing Joss.

Over fifty and seasoned in the picking-up-clues department, Joss winked at me and returned to the main showroom. Through the windows, I watched as she moved from display to display, straightening teacup handles, garden knickknacks, and strings of bells—fairies enjoyed the sound of bells.

Misty took a lemon bar, bit into it, set it on her saucer, and started reading the bullet-pointed list she'd created. "I want to have wind chimes everywhere."

Something breakable inside the shop went *clack . . . shatter.* Joss *eek*ed, and then Fiona shrieked, and my stomach lurched. Fairies hated breakage of any kind. Joss waved to me that she was all right and held up a multicolored wind chime. Was the accident a freak moment of timing, or was it fate?

Fiona zipped off to check on Joss. She couldn't help pick up the broken pieces, of course, but she could offer Joss a whisper of encouragement. Joss, like me, could see Fiona.

Misty hadn't seemed to notice the fracas, too intent on her list. "I want the guests to make fairy gardens. You'll instruct them, of course."

In addition to selling fairy gardens and items for fairy gardens, I taught a weekly class and gave private lessons about how to construct them. I experienced a childlike joy whenever I completed a project. So did my customers.

"I want party games and favors," Misty went on, "like you would for a children's fairy party, but more adult."

That would take a bit of thinking on my part. Children relished games like the lily pad relay and a fairy tale obstacle course. What would adults enjoy?

"And I'll want you to paint a mural on the wall facing the backyard."

"Me? Paint?" I snorted. My talent was purely in the gardening department. My mother had been the painter. A painting that she'd titled *Starry Night*, like the van Gogh painting, hung on the bedroom wall in my cottage. My father hadn't been able to part with any of the others.

"Hire someone." Misty flourished the pen. "I want the mural to feature lots of flowers and vines with fairies frolicking throughout. I saw one on the DIY Garden Channel and it was stunning. I'll download some pictures and email them to you."

Fiona circled Misty's head, waving an imaginary wand, I'd thought, until I realized she was mimicking Misty's gestures with the pen. I couldn't very well say *Cut it out,* so I frowned. Fiona stopped and soared to a ficus branch so she could hold her belly while laughing.

Later, I would have to have a chat with my sassy fairy. Because she was classified as a righteous fairy, which meant she needed to bring resolution to embattled souls, she could earn her way into the queen fairy's good graces by helping humans such as myself. But she had to toe the line. She couldn't act like an imp all the time.

Only last year did I learn that there were classifications of fairies. Four, to be exact. Intuitive, guardian, nurturer, and righteous. Up until then, I'd always thought fairies were merely types, like air fairies, water fairies, and woodland fairies—Fiona being the latter. Also, up until then, I'd forgotten about fairies. As a girl, I'd seen one, but I'd lost the ability when my mother passed away. That is, until Fiona came into my life.

"Alrighty then," Misty said, standing. "Come up with a plan."

"Would you mind leaving me your list?"

"I'll text it to you." She took a picture of her list, requested my cell phone number, and sent me a copy of it. "There you go. Oh, and I'd like to have the party Saturday."

"In three days?" I gulped.

"No, silly, next Saturday. Ample time. Eons before you get hit with Valentine's Day traffic."

Ten days! Ha! The last fairy party I'd thrown had taken me a month to prepare. On the other hand, because it had taken a month, the birthday girl's mother had thought she could make numerous changes to the menu, favors, and events. A tighter timeline might make this party, for adults, easier to manage.

"Can do?" Misty asked in shorthand. "There will be twelve of us."

"Can do," I chimed.

As Misty left the store, Fiona followed me to the modest kitchen behind my office. I set the tray fitted with tea goodies on the counter, filled the sink with soapy water, and started by washing the teacups.

"Something feels off to me," Fiona said, perching on the teapot's handle. "That's the right word, isn't it? *Off?*"

"Yes, that's the correct word. What feels off?"

"She's in too much of a hurry."

"Or she's not as organized as she claims," I countered. "I'm sure everything will go as steady as—"

A teacup slipped from my hand and plunged into the water. When I lifted it, I realized it had cracked in two.

"Oh my." Fiona clutched her head with her hands. "This is not good. Not good at all."

"What isn't good?"

"Misty. Her excitement for this party."

Suddenly, my insides felt jittery, probably because I'd recently grasped that I should trust my fairy's instincts. According to Fiona's mentor, Merryweather Rose of Song, the more mature Fiona became, the more her intuitive instincts would kick in. In addition, Merryweather had been teaching Fiona how to cast spells—good spells, not evil ones—making certain that whatever new ability she learned wouldn't go haywire.

"Go on," I urged.

"She's too eager." Fiona fluffed her wings.

"She seemed fine to me."

"What about the way she said her friend's name?"

"I'm not following."

"She said, 'O-dine.'" Fiona stressed the O as Misty had. "But that's not how you say her name. When we were at her shop, Odine told us how to pronounce it," Fiona went on. "She chanted, 'Odine. Odine. Odine.'"

My fairy was right. Odine had repeated her name, sounding much like a witch preparing for an incantation.

Fiona swatted my hair. "I'm telling you. Something's off."

And then lightning lit the sky, thunder rumbled overhead, and Fiona nearly swooned.

Visit our website at
KensingtonBooks.com
to sign up for our newsletters, read
more from your favorite authors, see
books by series, view reading group
guides, and more!

BOOK CLUB
BETWEEN THE CHAPTERS

Become a Part of Our
Between the Chapters Book Club
Community and Join the Conversation

Betweenthechapters.net

Submit your book review for a chance to win exclusive
Between the Chapters swag you can't get anywhere else!
https://www.kensingtonbooks.com/pages/review/